Faith And Unfaith
A Novel

By

Duchess

Double9 BOOKS

Faith And Unfaith
A Novel
by Duchess

Copyright © 2024

ISBN: 978-93-61421-53-2

Published by

DOUBLE 9 BOOKS
2/13-B, Ansari Road
Daryaganj, New Delhi – 110002
info@double9books.com
www.double9books.com
Tel. 011-40042856

ABOUT THE AUTHOR

The author known as Duchess, a pseudonym for Margaret Wolfe Hungerford, was a prolific Irish novelist whose writings were extremely popular in the late 1800s. Among her many works, "Faith and Unfaith" stands out as a masterpiece, capturing the essence of Victorian society via a detailed investigation of love, treachery, and moral quandaries. Hungerford had a rare knack for diving into the subtleties of the human heart, and "Faith and Unfaith" exemplifies her profound understanding of interpersonal interactions and cultural expectations. "Faith and Unfaith" provides readers with a fascinating tale that connects the lives of its protagonists in an entertaining and thought-provoking way. Duchess' writing is distinguished by its wit, rich characterizations, and sympathetic handling of emotional issues. Her narrative explores issues such as fidelity, the restrictions of society conventions, and the quest of pleasure, all of which strike a deep chord with the reader. Her ability to create diverse characters who face moral quandaries and psychological growth makes "Faith and Unfaith" a great and lasting piece of fiction.

CONTENTS

CHAPTER I 7

CHAPTER II 18

CHAPTER III 21

CHAPTER IV 25

CHAPTER V 31

CHAPTER VI 40

CHAPTER VII 45

CHAPTER VIII 51

CHAPTER IX 58

CHAPTER X 67

CHAPTER XI 75

CHAPTER XII 85

CHAPTER XIII 94

CHAPTER XIV 103

CHAPTER XV 108

CHAPTER XVI 118

CHAPTER XVII 127

CHAPTER XVIII 133

CHAPTER XIX 138

CHAPTER XX 145

CHAPTER XXI 156

CHAPTER XXII 163

CHAPTER XXIII 174

CHAPTER XXIV 183

CHAPTER XXV 191

CHAPTER XXVI 199

CHAPTER XXVII 208

CHAPTER XXVIII 222

CHAPTER XXIX 232

CHAPTER XXX 239

CHAPTER XXXI 247

CHAPTER XXXII 258

CHAPTER XXXIII 261

CHAPTER XXXIV 269

CHAPTER XXXV 276

CHAPTER XXXVI 281

CHAPTER XXXVII 287

CHAPTER XXXVIII 291

CHAPTER I

"A heap of dust alone remains of thee:
'Tis all thou art, and all the proud shall be!" — Pope.

In an upper chamber, through the closed blinds of which the sun is vainly striving to enter, Reginald Branscombe, fifth Earl of Sartoris, lies dead. The sheet is reverently drawn across the motionless limbs; the once restless, now quiet, face is hidden; all around is wrapt in solemn unutterable silence, — the silence that belongs to death alone!

A sense of oppressive calm is upon everything, — a feeling of loneliness, vague and shadowy. The clock has ticked its last an hour ago, and now stands useless in its place. The world without moves on unheeding; the world within knows time no more! Death reigns triumphant! Life sinks into insignificance!

Once, a little flickering golden ray, born of the hot sun outside, flashes in through some unknown chink, and casts itself gleefully upon the fair white linen of the bed. It trembles vivaciously now here, now there, in uncontrollable joyousness, as though seeking in its gayety to mock the grandeur of the King of Terrors! At least so it seems to the sole watcher in the lonely chamber, as with an impatient sigh he raises his head, and, going over to the window, draws the curtains still closer to shut out the obnoxious light; after which he comes back to where he has been standing, gazing down upon, and thinking of, the dead.

He is an old man, tall and gaunt, with kind but passionate eyes, and a mouth expressive of impatience. His hands — withered but still sinewy — are clasped behind his back; every feature in his face is full of sad and anxious thought.

What changes the passing of a few short hours have wrought — so he muses. Yesterday the man now chilled and silent for evermore was as full of animation as he — his brother — who to-day stands so sorrowfully beside his corpse. His blood had run as freely in his veins, his pulses throbbed as evenly, his very voice had been sounding strong and clear and hearty, when Death, remorseless, claimed him for his own.

Poor Reginald! Had he known of the fell disease that had nestled so long within his heart? — or had no symptoms ever shown themselves to give him kindly warning? Certainly no hint of it had ever passed his lips, even to those most near and dear to him. He had lived apparently free from care or painful forebodings of any kind,—a good and useful life too, leaving nothing for those behind (who loved him) to regret. Indeed, of late he had appeared even gayer, happier, than before; and now—

It seems such a little time ago since they both were lads together. A tiny space taken from the great eternity, when all is told. How well the living man remembers at this moment many a boyish freak and light-hearted jest, many a kindness shown and gift bestowed by the dead, that until now had wellnigh been forgotten!

He thinks of the good old college days, when they worked little, and fought hard, and trained their fresh young limbs to mighty deeds, and walked, and rode, and held their own with the best, and showed open defiance of dons and deans and proctors; he lingers, too, on the day still farther on, when Reginald, having attained to his kingdom, lavished with no meagre hand upon his more extravagant brother the money so sorely needed.

Now Reginald is gone, and he, Arthur, reigns in his stead, and——Alas! alas! poor Reggy!—Poor, dear old fellow!

He rouses himself with an effort, and, going very softly to a small door that opens from the apartment, beckons gently to somebody beyond.

An old woman, dressed in deepest mourning, and of the housekeeper type, answers his summons, her eyes red with excessive weeping.

"I am going now," Lord Sartoris whispers to her in a low tone. "I have finished everything. You will remain here until my return."

"Yes, Mr. Arthur,—yes, my Lord," she answers, nervously; and then, as she gives the old title for the first time to the man before her, she bursts out crying afresh, yet silently, in a subdued fashion, as though ashamed of her emotion.

Sartoris pats her shoulder kindly, and then with a sigh turns away, and passes from the room with bent head and hands still clasped behind him, as has become a habit with him of late years.

Down the stairs and along the hall he goes, until, reaching a door at the lower end, he pauses before it, and, opening it, enters a room, half library, half boudoir, furnished in a somewhat rococo style.

It is a room curiously built, being a complete oval, with two French windows opening to the ground, and a glass door between them—partly stained—that leads to the parterre outside. It is filled with mediæval furniture, uncompromising and as strictly uncomfortable as should be, and has its walls (above the wooden dado) covered with a high-art paper, on which impossible storks, and unearthly birds of all descriptions, are depicted as rising out of blue-green rushes.

This room is known as "my lady's chamber,"—having ever been the exclusive property of the mistress of the house, until Mrs. Dorian Branscombe, in default of any other mistress, had made her own of it during her frequent visits to Hythe, and had refurnished it to suit her own tastes, which were slightly Æsthetic.

Now, she too is dead and gone, and the room, though never entirely closed or suffered to sink into disrepair, is seldom used by any of the household.

As Lord Sartoris goes in, a young man, who has been standing at one of the windows, turns and comes quickly to meet him. He is of good height, and is finely formed, with brown hair cut closely to his head, a brown moustache, and deep-blue eyes. His whole appearance is perhaps more pleasing and aristocratic than strictly handsome, his mouth being too large and his nose too pronounced for any particular style of beauty.

Yet it is his eyes—perfect as they are in shape and color—that betray the chief faults of his disposition. He is too easy-going, too thoughtless of consequences, too much given to letting things go,—without consideration or fear of what the end may bring; too full of life and spirits to-day, to dream of a sadder morrow;—so happy in the present that the future troubles him not at all.

"How ill you look!" he says, anxiously, addressing his uncle. "My dear Arthur, you have been overdoing it. You should not have remained so long in that room alone."

"Well, it is all over now," Sartoris says, wearily, sinking into a chair near him. "I was glad to finish it once for all. Those private papers he kept in his own room should be examined sooner or later; and now my task is at an end I feel more contented."

"Was there anything beyond?——"

"Very little. Just one letter sealed and directed to me. It contained a desire that poor Maud's letters should be buried with him. I found them in a drawer by themselves neatly tied with pale-blue ribbon,—her favorite color,—and with them an old likeness of her, faded almost white."

"For how long he remembered her!" says the young man, in a tone of slow astonishment.

"Too long for our present day," returns his uncle, absently. Then there is silence for a moment or two, broken only by the chatter of the birds in the sunlit garden outside. Presently Sartoris speaks again. "Where is Horace?" he asks, indifferently.

"He was here, half an hour ago, with Clarissa. She came over when she heard of——our sad news. They went out together,—to the stables, I think. Shall I find him for you?"

"No, I do not want him," says Sartoris, a little impatiently. "How strange no one told me of Clarissa's coming! And why did you not go with her to the stables, Dorian? Surely you know more about horses than he does."

About twenty years before my story opens, Dorian, fourth Lord Sartoris, died, leaving behind him three sons,—Reginald (who now, too, has passed into the land of shadows), Arthur, the present earl, and Dorian, the younger.

This Dorian alone, of all the brothers, had married. But his wife (who was notable for nothing beyond her deceitful temper and beautiful face, being as false as she was fair) having died too, in giving birth to her second child Horace, and her husband having followed her to the grave about three years later, the care of the children developed upon their uncle Reginald, who had been appointed guardian.

But Reginald—being a somewhat careless man in many respects, and little given to children—took small heed of them, and, beyond providing masters for them at first, and later on sending them to school and college, and giving them choice of professions, had left them very much to their own devices.

True, when college debts accumulated, and pressing bills from long-suffering tradespeople came pouring in, he would rouse himself sufficiently to remonstrate with them in a feeble fashion, and, having received promises of amendment from both boys, he would pay their bills, make each a handsome present (as atonement for the mild scolding), and, having thus dropped a sop to Cerberus,—or conscience,—would dismiss money matters, nephews, and all from his thoughts.

So the children grew, from youth to boyhood, from boyhood to early manhood, with no one to whom to appeal for sympathy, with no woman's voice to teach them right from wrong,—with few hardships, fewer troubles, and no affections.

Arthur Branscombe, indeed, who had come back from India six months after his father's death, and had stayed at Hythe for two interminable years (as they seemed to him), had during that time so worked himself into the heart of the eldest boy Dorian, and had so far taken him into his own in return, that long years had failed to efface the fondness of either. Indeed, now that he has returned from abroad (only, as fate has willed it, to take his brother's place), he finds the love he had grafted in the child still warm in the heart of the man.

Horace, the younger, had chosen his profession, and gone in heavily for law. But Dorian, who inherited two thousand a year from his father, and a charming residence,—situated about three miles from Hythe, and two from the pretty village of Pullingham,—had elected to try his hand at farming, and was at first honestly believed in by confiding tenants, who discussed him as a being up to his eyes in agricultural lore and literally steeped in new and improved projects for the cultivation of land.

But time undeceived these good souls. And now, though they love him better, they believe in him not at all. To adore one's horses, and to be a perfect slave to one's dogs, is one thing; to find a tender interest in the price of guano, and a growing admiration for prize pigs, is quite another. When Dorian had tried it for six months, he acknowledged, reluctantly, that to him mangels were an abomination, and over-fed cattle a wearying of the flesh!

Every now and then, indeed, he tells himself that he must "look about him," as he calls it, and, smothering a sigh, starts for a quick walk across his land, and looks at a field or two, or into the nearest paddock, and asks his steward how things are going on, and if all is as satisfactory now as in the old days when his father held the reins of government, and, having listened absently to comfortable answers and cheerful predictions for the future, strolls away again, thoroughly content, not caring to investigate matters further.

He is fond of London life, and spends a good deal of his time there; is courted and petted and made much of by enterprising dowagers with marriageable daughters, as a young man charming, well bred, altogether *chic*, and undoubted heir to an earldom; for of Arthur Sartoris's ever marrying, now he has so long passed the prime of life, no one ever dreams.

He knows all the best people in town, and puts in a good time when there; is a fair hand at whist, and can beat most men at billiards; will now and then put money on a favorite for the Oaks or the Grand National, but cannot be said to regard gambling as an amusement. He is extravagant in many ways, but thoroughly unselfish and kind-hearted, and generous to a fault. He is much affected by women, and adored by children, who instinctively accept him as a true friend.

Horace, both in face and in figure, is strangely like his brother,—in character very different. He is tall and well built, with eyes large, dark, and liquid, but rather too closely set to be pleasing. His mouth is firm and somewhat hard, his smile soft, but uncertain. He is always charming to women, being outwardly blind to their caprices and an admirer of their follies, and is therefore an immense favorite with a certain class of them, whose minds are subservient to their bodies. Yet to every rule there is an exception. And by women good and true, and loyal, Horace has been, and is, well beloved.

As Lord Sartoris and Dorian cross the hall, they meet Horace, and a pretty girl—tall, slender, and graceful—coming towards them. She appears sad, and slightly distressed, but scarcely unnerved: there is a suspicion of tears about her large gray eyes. Her gown, of violet velvet (for, though they are in the merry month of May, the days are still cold and fretful), sits closely to her perfect figure; a Langtry bonnet, to match her dress, covers her head and suits admirably her oval face and Grecian nose and soft peach-like complexion.

Going up, with impulsive grace, to Lord Sartoris, she lays both her ungloved hands upon his shoulders, and presses her lips with tender sympathy to his cheek.

"How sad it all is!" she says, with a little break in her voice. "How can I tell you all I feel for you? If you had only had the faintest warning! But it was all so sudden, so dreadful."

"What a kind child you are, Cissy!" says Sartoris, gently; "and to come to us *so soon*, that was so good of you."

"Was it?" says Clarissa, quickly. "That is what has been troubling me. We only heard the terrible news this morning, and papa said it would be intrusive to call so early; but I—I could not keep away."

"Your presence in this gloomy house is an undeniable comfort," says Sartoris, sadly. "I am glad you understood us well enough to know that. It is my greatest wish that you should regard us all with affection."

He glances from her to Dorian, as he speaks, with anxious meaning. But Dorian's gaze is fixed thoughtfully upon the stained-glass window that is flinging its crimson and purple rays upon the opposite wall, and has obviously been deaf to all that has been passing. As for Clarissa, she has turned, and is looking into Horace's dark eyes.

Sartoris, catching the glance, drops Miss Peyton's hand with a sigh. She notices the half-petulant action, and compresses her lips slightly.

"Now I have seen you, I shall feel better," she says, sweetly. "And—I think I must be going."

"Will you desert us so soon?" says Sartoris, reproachfully. "At least stay to luncheon— —." He pauses, and sighs profoundly. Just now the idea that the routine of daily life must be carried on whether our beloved lie dead upon their couches or stand living in our path, is hateful to him.

"I hardly like," says Clarissa, nervously; "I fear— —"

Dorian, rousing himself from his thoughts, comes back to the present moment.

"Oh, stay, Clarissa," he says, hurriedly. "You really must, you know. You cannot imagine what a relief you are to us: you help us to bear our gloomy memories. Besides, Arthur has tasted nothing for hours, and your being here may tempt him, perhaps, to eat."

"If I can be of any use— —," says Clarissa, kindly. Whereupon Sartoris gives her his arm, and they all adjourn to the dining-room.

It is a large, old-fashioned, stately apartment, oak-panelled, with large mullioned windows, and a massive marble chimney-piece that reaches high as a man's head. A pleasant, sociable room at ordinary times, but now impregnated with the vague gloom that hangs over all the house and seeks even here to check the gaudy brightness of the sun that, rushing in, tries to illuminate it.

At the sideboard stands Simon Gale, the butler and oldest domestic of Hythe, who has lived with the dead lord as man and boy, and now regrets him with a grief more strongly resembling the sorrowing of one for a friend than for a master.

With downcast eyes and bowed head he stands, thinking sadly how much too old he is for new cares and fresh faces. Reginald had been all the world to him: the new man is as nothing. Counting friendships as of little worth unless years have gone to prove their depth and sincerity, he feels no leaning towards the present possessor,—knows him too short a time to like or dislike, to praise or blame.

Now, as his eyes wander down the long table, to where he can see the empty chair of him who rests with such unearthly tranquillity in the silent chamber above, the thought of how soon a comparative stranger will fill it causes him a bitter pang. And, as he so muses, the door opens, and they all come in,—Sartoris first, with Clarissa, pale, and quiet; the brothers—so like, yet so unlike—following.

Old Simon, rousing himself, watches with jealous eyes to see the place so long occupied by Reginald usurped by another. But he watches in vain. Sartoris, without so much as a glance in its direction, takes the chair at the lower end of the table; and the others, following his lead, seat themselves at the sides without comment of any kind; whereupon Gale draws a long breath, and vows fidelity to his new lord upon the spot.

It is a dismal meal, dull, and dispiriting. The ghastly Egyptian mummy seems present in full force, if not in the letter at least in the spirit. Sartoris, having taken a glass of sherry, trifles with the meat upon his plate, but literally eats nothing. No one appears possessed with a desire to speak, and indeed there is little to be said. When luncheon is nearly over, a small dark object, hitherto unseen, creeps out from some forgotten corner, and stretches itself forlornly; it is poor Reginald's favorite dog, that ever since his death has lain crouching out of sight, but now, driven by the pain of hunger, comes creeping forward, whining piteously.

He goes up to the accustomed chair, but, finding it for the first time empty and deaf to his complainings, turns disconsolately away, and passes from seat to seat, without accepting food at any of their hands, until he comes to Clarissa. She, stooping, raises him to her knee (her lashes wet with tears), and feeds him tenderly with the dainty scraps upon her plate.

The whole scene, though simple, is suggestive of loss and loneliness. Sartoris, leaving the table with some haste, goes to the window to hide his emotion. Dorian follows him. Whereupon Horace, rising too, crosses to where Clarissa sits, and, bending over her, says something in a low tone.

The moments fly. A clock upon the mantel-piece chimes half-past four. Some bird, in the exuberance of its mad joy, scurries wildly past the windows. Sartoris, with a sigh, turns from the light, and, seeing Miss Peyton and Horace still deep in conversation, frowns slightly.

"Horace, will you tell Durkin I want to see him at once, in the library," he says, very quietly, yet with some latent irritability.

"In one moment," replies Horace, unmoved, going back to the low-toned dialogue he has been carrying on with Clarissa.

"I am afraid I must lay myself open to the charge of rudeness," says Sartoris, still very quietly, but with a peculiar smile. "But it is important, and I must see Durkin at once. My dear Horace, oblige me in this matter."

"Shall I not see Clarissa to her carriage first?" says Horace, raising his dark eyes for one moment to his uncle's face.

"Dorian will see to that," says the old man, slowly, but so decisively that Horace, bidding the girl a silent but warm farewell, with a bad grace departs.

"How late it grows," says Miss Peyton, glancing at the clock; and, drawing from a side-pocket her own watch, she examines it attentively, as though to assure herself the huge timepiece on the mantel-shelf has not told a deliberate lie. "I must go home! Papa will wonder where I have been all this long time. Good-by, Mr. Branscombe" (she is still, naturally, forgetful of the new title). "I hope," very sweetly, "you will come to see us as soon as ever you can."

"Thank you, yes, I shall come very soon," says Sartoris; and then she bids him good-by, and Dorian follows her from the room into the great dark hall outside.

"How changed he is!" she says, turning suddenly to him, and indicating, by a little backward motion of her head towards the room she had just left, the person of whom she speaks. "How altered!—Arthur, I mean. Not now, not by this grief; it isn't that: his manner, to me especially, has been altogether different for a fortnight past. Ever since that last picnic at Anadale—you remember it—he has not been quite the same to me."

"Let me see; that, I think, was the evening you and Horace drove home alone together, with that rather uncertain brown mare, was it not?" says Dorian, with no apparent meaning in his tone. "My dear child, I dare say you are mistaken about Arthur. Your imagination is leading you astray."

"No, it is not. I am the least imaginative person alive," says Miss Peyton, with an emphatic shake of her pretty head. "I can't bear that sort of people myself; they are always seeing something that isn't there, and are generally very tiresome all around. I'm rather vexed about Arthur, do you know?"

"Don't mind him," says Branscombe, easily. "He'll come all right in time. He is a peculiar fellow in many ways, and when he sets his heart on any hobby, rides it to the death."

"Has he a hobby now?"

"Yes. He has just formed, and is now trying to work out, a gigantic scheme, and cuts up a little rough every now and then because all the world won't see it in the light that he does."

"Poor man!" says Clarissa, sympathetically, "No wonder he seems strange at times: it is so depressing to be baffled. Why don't you help him, Dorian?"

"It would take two to help him," says Mr. Branscombe, looking faintly amused.

"Could I be of any use?"—eagerly. "I would do anything I could for him."

"No, would you?" says Branscombe, his amusement growing more perceptible. "I'm sure that's very good of you. I dare say, if Arthur could hear you say that, he would go wild with joy. 'Anything' is such a comprehensive word. You're sure you won't go back of it?"

"Quite sure," —with some surprise.

"My dear Clarissa, is it possible you have not yet seen through Arthur's latest and greatest design?"

"If you intend to tell me anything, do so: beating about the bush always fatigues me to death," says Miss Peyton, in a tone of dignified rebuke. "What does Arthur want?"

"A little thing, —a mere trifle. He simply wants you to marry me."

"Really, Dorian," says Clarissa, coloring slowly, but warmly, "I think you might find some other subject to jest on."

"I never made a joke in my life; I hope I never shall," returns Branscombe, reproachfully. "What have I done, that you should accuse me of such a crime? I have only spoken the plain, unvarnished truth. To see you my wife is the dream of Arthur's life, his sole ambition. And just now, you know, you said you were quite prepared to do anything for him. You can't, with any sense of honor, back out of your given word."

"I never heard anything so absurd, so foolish, so nonsensical!" says Miss Peyton, resentfully.

"Nonsensical! My dear Clarissa! pray consider my——"

"It is more! it is right down stupid of him," says Clarissa, who plainly declines to consider any one's feelings.

"You needn't pile up my agony any higher," interposes Branscombe, meekly. "To my everlasting regret I acknowledge myself utterly unworthy of you. But why tell me so in such round terms? I assure you I feel excessively hurt and offended. Am I to understand, then, that you have refused me?"

"You shall understand something worse, if you say another word," says Clarissa, holding, up before him a little clinched hand in a would-be threatening manner. And then they both laugh in a subdued fashion; and she moves on towards the open hall-door, he following.

"Well, I forgive you," he says, as she steps into her low phaeton, and he arranges the rug carefully around her. "Though you don't deserve it. (What ridiculous little hands to guide such refractory ponies!) Sure you are quite comfortable? Well, good-by; and look here," —teasingly,—"I should think it over if I were you. You may not get so excellent a chance again; and Arthur will never forgive you."

"Your uncle, though charming, and a very dear, is also a goose," says Miss Peyton, somewhat irreverently. "Marry you, indeed! Why, I should quite as soon dream of marrying my brother!"

"Well, as I can't be your husband, it would be rather nice to be your brother," says Mr. Branscombe, cheerfully. "Your words give me hope that you regard me in that light. I shall always think of you for the future as my sister, and so I am sure" — with an eloquent and rather mischievous pause — "will Horace!"

Miss Peyton blushes again, — much more vividly this time, — and, gathering up the reins hastily, says "good-by" for the second time, without turning her flushed face to his, and drives rapidly up the avenue.

Branscombe stands on the steps watching her until she is quite lost to sight behind the rhododendrons, and then strokes his moustache thoughtfully.

"That has quite arranged itself, I should fancy," he says, slowly. "Well, I hope he will be very good to her, dear little thing!"

CHAPTER II

"Her form was fresher than the morning rose
When the dew wets its leaves." — Thomson.

Pullingham-on-the-Moors is a small, untidy, picturesque little village, situated on the side of a hill. It boasts a railway-station, a police-barrack, a solitary hotel, and two or three well-sized shops. It is old-fashioned, stationary, and, as a rule, hopelessly harmless, though now and then, dissensions, based principally on religious grounds, will arise.

These can scarcely be avoided, as one-half of the parish trips lightly after Mr. Redmond, the vicar (who has a subdued passion for wax candles, and a craving for floral decorations), and looks with scorn upon the other half, as, with solemn step and slow, it descends the high hill that leads, each Sabbath, to the "Methody" Chapel beneath.

It never grows older, this village, and never younger; is seldom cast down or elated, surprised or demonstrative, about anything. In a quaint, sleepy fashion, it has its dissipations, and acknowledges its festive seasons, — such as Christmas-tide when all the shops burst into a general bloom of colored cards, and February, when valentines adorn every pane. It has also its fair days, when fat cattle and lean sugar-sticks seem to be everywhere.

A marriage is reckoned an event, and causes some gossip: a birth does not, — possibly because of the fact that it is a weekly occurrence. Indeed, the babies in Pullingham are a "joy forever." They have their season all the year round, and never by any chance "go out;" though I have heard people very foolishly liken them to flowers. They grow, and thrive, and blossom all over the place, which no doubt is greatly to the credit of the inhabitants. Occasionally, too, some one is good enough to cause a little pleasurable excitement by dying, but very seldom, as the place is fatally healthy, and people live here until they become a social nuisance, and almost wish themselves dead. There is, I believe, some legend belonging to the country, about an old woman who had to be shot, so aggressively old did she become; but this is obscure.

About two miles from the town, one comes to Sartoris, the residence of Dorian Branscombe, which runs in a line with the lands of Scrope Royal, the property of Sir James Scrope.

Sir James is a tall, rather old-young man of thirty-two with a calm, expressive face, kindly eyes, and a somewhat lanky figure. He has a heart of gold, a fine estate, and — —a step-sister.

Miss Jemima Scrope is not as nice as she might be. She has a face as hard as her manners, and, though considerably over forty, is neither fat nor fair. She has a perfect talent for making herself obnoxious to all unhappy enough to come within her reach, a temper like "Kate the Curst," and a nose like the Duke of Wellington.

Somewhere to the left, on a hill as high and pompous as itself, stands the castle, where three months out of the twelve the Duke and Duchess of Spendleton, and some of their family, put in a dreary time. They give two balls, one fancy bazaar, a private concert, and three garden-parties—neither more nor less—every year. Nobody likes them very much, because nobody knows them. Nobody dislikes them very much, for just the same reason.

The castle is beautifully situated, and is correct in every detail. There are Queen Anne rooms, and Gothic apartments, and Elizabethan anterooms, and staircases of the most vague. There are secret passages, and panels, and sliding doors, and trap-doors, and, in fact, every sort of door you could mention, and all other abominations. Artists revel in it, and grow frenzied with joy over its impossibilities, and almost every year some room is painted from it and sent to the Academy, But outside lies its chief beauty, for there are the swelling woods, and the glimpse of the far-off ocean as it gleams, now green, now steel-blue, beneath the rays of the setting sun. And beyond it is Gowran, where Clarissa lives with her father, George Peyton.

Clarissa is all that is charming. She is tall, slight, *svelte*: indeed, earth has not anything to show more fair. She is tender, too, and true, and very earnest,—perhaps a degree too earnest, too intense, for every-day life. Her eyes, "twin stars of beauty," are deep and gray; her hair is dark; her mouth, though somewhat large, is perfect; and her smile is indescribable, so sweet it is, so soft and lingering.

Her mother died when she was nine years old, and from that time until she was twelve she spent most of her life with the Branscombe boys,— riding, fishing, sometimes even shooting, with them. The effect of such training began to make itself felt. She was fast degenerating into a tomboy of the first water (indeed, one of the purest gems of its kind), when James Scrope, who even then was a serious young man, came to the rescue, and induced her father to send her from Gowran to a school at Brussels.

"Virtue is its own reward," they tell us: let us hope Scrope felt rewarded! Whether he did or not, I know he was considerably frightened when Clarissa (having discovered who had been the instigator of this "plot" to drive her from her beloved Gowran) came down to Scrope Hall, and, dashing into his presence like a small whirlwind, abused him for his well-meant interference in good round terms, and, having refused even to say good-by to him, had slammed the door in his face, and, starting from home next morning, had seen no more of him for six long years.

At seventeen, her aunt, the Hon. Mrs. Greville, had brought her back from Brussels to her own house in town, where she kept her for twelve months, and where she once more renewed acquaintance with her old friends, Dorian and Horace Branscombe. Mrs. Greville took her to all the most desirable balls of her season, to concerts and "small and earlies," to high-art entertainments of the most "too, too," and, having given her free scope to break the hearts of half the men in town, had sent her at last to her father, hopelessly in love with a detrimental.

The detrimental was Horace Branscombe. Mrs. Greville was intensely annoyed and disgusted. After all her care, all her trouble, to have this happen! She had married her own girls with the greatest *éclat*, had not made one false move with regard to any of them, and now to see Clarissa (who, with her beauty and fortune, might have married any one) throw herself away upon a penniless barrister seemed to her to savor of positive crime.

Horace, certainly, so far, had not proposed in form, but Mrs. Greville was not to be hoodwinked. He meant it. He was not always at her niece's side for nothing; and, sooner or later, Clarissa, with all her money, would go over to him. When she thought of this shocking waste of money, she groaned aloud; and then she washed her hands of the whole affair, and sent Clarissa back to Gowran, where her father received her with open arms, and made much of her.

CHAPTER III

"O Helen, fair beyond compare!
I'll make a garland of thy hair,
Shall bind my heart for evermair,
Until the day I die!"

Across the lawn the shadows move slowly, and with a vague grace that adds to their charm. The birds are drowsy from the heat, and, sitting half hidden in the green branches, chant their songs in somewhat lazy fashion. All nature has succumbed to the fierce power of Phœbus Apollo.

"The morn is merry June, I trow:
The rose is budding fain."

Each flower in the sunlit garden is holding up its head, and breathing fragrant sighs as the hours slip by, unheeded, yet full of a vague delight.

Miss Peyton, in her white gown, and with some soft rich roses lying on her lap, is leaning back in a low chair in the deep embrasure of the window, making a poor attempt at working.

Her father, with a pencil in his hand, and some huge volumes spread out before him, is making a few desultory notes. Into the library—the coseyest, if not the handsomest, room at Gowran—the hot sun is rushing, dancing lightly over statuettes and pictures, and lingering with pardonable delay upon Clarissa's bowed head.

"Who is this coming up the avenue?" she says, presently, in slow, sleepy tones, that suit the day. "It is—no, it isn't—and yet it is—it must be James Scrope!"

"I dare say. He was to have returned yesterday. He would come here as soon as possible, of course." Rising, he joins her at the window, and watches the coming visitor as he walks his horse leisurely down the drive.

"What a dear little modest speech!" says Miss Peyton, maliciously. "Now, if I had been the author of it, I know some one who would have called me vain! But I will generously let that pass. How brown Jim has grown! Has he not?"

"Has he? I can scarcely see so far. What clear eyes you must have, child, and what a faithful memory to recollect him without hesitation, after all these years!"

"I never forget," says Clarissa, simply, which is quite the truth. "And he has altered hardly anything. He was always so old, you know, he really couldn't grow much older. What is his age now, papa? Ninety?"

"Something over thirty, I fancy," says papa, uncertainly.

"Oh, nonsense!" says Miss Peyton. "Surely you romance, or else you are an invaluable friend. When I grow brown and withered, I hope you will prove equally good to me. I shall expect you to say all sorts of impossible things, and not to blush when saying them. Ah!—here is Sir James" as the door opens, and Scrope—healthy and bronzed from foreign travel—enters quietly, staid and calm as ever.

When he has shaken hands with, and been warmly welcomed by, Mr. Peyton, he turns with some diffidence towards the girl in the clinging white gown, who is smiling at him from the window, with warm red lips, half parted and some faint amusement in her friendly eyes.

"Why, you have forgotten me," she says, presently, in a low tone of would-be reproach. "While I—I knew you at once."

"I have not forgotten," says Scrope, taking her hand and holding it, as though unconsciously. "I was only surprised, puzzled. You are so changed. All seems so different. A little child when last I saw you, and now a lady grown."

"Oh, yes, I am quite grown up," says Miss Peyton, demurely. "I can't do any more of that sort of thing, to oblige anybody,—even though papa—who adores a Juno, and thinks all women should be divinely tall—has often asked me to try. But," maliciously, "are you not going to ask me how I have progressed (isn't that the right word?) with my studies? You ought, you know, as it was you who sent me to school."

"I?" says Sir James, rather taken aback at this unexpected onslaught.

"Yes, you," repeats she, with a little nod. "Papa would never have had the cruelty even to think of such a thing. I am glad you have still sufficient grace left to blush for your evil conduct. Do you remember," with a gay laugh, "what a terrible scolding I gave you before leaving home?"

"I shall remember it to my dying day," says Sir James. "I was never so thoroughly frightened before, or since. Then and there, I registered a vow never again to interfere with any one's daughter."

"I hope you will keep that vow," says Miss Peyton, with innocent malice, and a smile only half suppressed, that torments him in memory for many a day. And then George Peyton asks some question, and presently Sir James is telling him certain facts about the Holy Land, and Asia generally, that rather upset his preconceived ideas.

"Yet I still believe it must be the most interesting spot on earth," he says, still clinging to old thoughts and settled convictions.

"Well, it's novel, you know, and the fashion, and that," says Sir James, rather vaguely. "In fact, you are nowhere nowadays if you haven't done the East; but it's fatiguing, there isn't a doubt. The people aren't as nice as they might be, and honesty is not considered the best policy out there, and dirt is the prevailing color, and there's a horrid lot of sand."

"What a dismal ending!" says Clarissa, in a tone suggestive of disappointment. "But how lovely it looks in pictures! — I don't mean the sand, exactly, but the East."

"Most things do. There is an old grandaunt of mine hung in the gallery at Scrope——"

"How shocking!" interrupted Miss Peyton, with an affected start. "And in the house, too! So unpleasant! Did she do it herself, or who hanged her?"

"Her picture, you know," says Scrope, with a laugh. "To hear that she had made away with herself would be too good to be true. She looks absolutely lovely in this picture I speak of, almost too fine for this work-a-day world; yet my father always told me she was ugly as a nightmare. Never believe in paint."

"Talking of Scrope," says Clarissa, "do you know, though I have been home now for some months, I have never been through it since I was a child? I have rather a passion for revisiting old haunts, and I want to see it again. That round room in the tower used to be my special joy. Will you show it to me? — some day? — any day?"

"What day will you come?" asks Scrope, thinking it unnecessary to express the gladness it will be to him to point put the beauties of his home to this new-old friend, — this friend so full of fresh and perfect beauty, yet so replete with all the old graces and witcheries of the child he once so fondly loved.

"I am just the least little bit in the world afraid of Miss Scrope," says Clarissa, with an irrepressible smile. "So I shall prefer to come some time when you are in. On Thursday, if that will suit you. Or Friday; or, if not then, why, Saturday."

"Make it Thursday. That day comes first," said Scrope.

"Now, that is a very pretty speech," declares Miss Peyton, vast encouragement in her tone. "Eastern air, in spite of its drawbacks, has developed your intellect, Jim. Hasn't it?"

The old familiar appellation, and the saucy smile that has always in it something of tenderness, smites some half-forgotten chord in Scrope's heart. He makes no reply, but gazes with an earnestness that almost amounts to scrutiny at Clarissa, as she stands in the open window leaning against a background of ivy, through which pale rose-buds are struggling into view. Within her slender fingers the knitting-needles move slowly, glinting and glistening in the sun's hot rays, until they seem to emit tiny flashes as they cross and recross each other. Her eyes are downcast, the smile still lingers on her lips, her whole attitude, and her pretty graceful figure, clad in its white gown, is

"Like a picture rich and rare."

"On Thursday, then, I shall see you," he says, not because he has tired of looking at her, but because she has raised her eyes and is evidently wondering at his silence. "Good-by."

"Good-by," says Clarissa, genially. Then she lays down the neglected knitting (that, indeed, is more a pretence than a reality), and comes out into the middle of the room. "For the sake of old days I shall see you to the hall door," she says, brightly. "No, papa, do not ring: I myself shall do the honors to Jim."

CHAPTER IV

"All thoughts, all passions, all delights,
Whatever stirs this mortal frame,
All are but ministers of Love
,And feed his sacred flame." —Coleridge.

All round the drawing-room windows at Scrope a wide balcony has been built up, over which the creepers climb and trail. Stone steps leads to it from the scented garden beneath, and up these runs Clarissa, gayly, when Thursday morning had dawned, and deepened, and given place to noon.

Within the drawing-room, before a low table, sits Miss Scrope, tatting industriously. Tatting is Miss Scrope's forte. She never does anything else. Multitudinous antimacassars, of all shapes, patterns, and dimensions, grow beneath her untiring touch with the most alarming rapidity. When finished, nobody knows what becomes of them, as they instantly disappear from view and are never heard of afterwards. They are as good as a ghost in Pullingham, and obstinately refuse to be laid. It was charitably, if weakly, suggested at one time, by a member of the stronger sex, that probably she sent them out in bales as coverings for the benighted heathen; but when it was explained to this misguided being that tatted antimacassars, as a rule, run to holes, and can be seen through, even he desisted from further attempts to solve the mystery.

Miss Peyton, throwing up one of the window-sashes, steps boldly into the drawing-room and confronts this eminent tatter.

"Good-morning," she says, sweetly, advancing with smiling lips.

Miss Scrope, who has not heard her enter, turns slowly round: to say she started would be a gross calumny. Miss Scrope never starts. She merely raises her head with a sudden accession of dignity. Her dignity, as a rule, is not fascinating, and might go by another name.

"Good-afternoon, Clarissa," she says, austerely. "I am sorry you should have been forced to make an entrance like a burglar. Has the hall door been removed? It used to stand in the front of the house."

"I think it is there still," Miss Peyton ventures, meekly. "But" —prettily— "coming in through the window enabled me to see you at least one moment sooner. Shall I close it again?"

"I beg you will not distress yourself about it," says Miss Scrope, rising to ring the bell. "When Collins comes in he will see to it."

It is a wild day, though warm and sweet, and the wind outside is tearing madly over lawn and shrubberies into the wood beyond.

"But in the mean time you will perhaps catch cold, of rheumatism, or something," says Clarissa, hesitating.

"Rheumatism! pugh! nonsense!" says Miss Scrope, disdainfully. "I simply don't believe in rheumatism. It is nothing but nerves. I don't have those ridiculous pains and aches people hug nowadays, and I don't believe they have either; it employs their idle time trying to invent them."

"Is Jim in?" asks Clarissa, presently, having seated herself in a horribly comfortless but probably artistic chair.

"*James is* in," says Miss Scrope, severely. "Do you mean my brother? It is really almost impossible to understand young people of the present age."

"Don't you like the name Jim?" asks Clarissa, innocently, leaning slightly forward, and taking up the edge of Miss Scrope's last antimacassar to examine it with tender interest. "I think it such a dear little name, and so happily wanting in formality. I have never called him anything else since I can remember, so it comes most naturally to me."

"I think it a most unmaidenly way of addressing any gentleman whose priest christened him James," says Miss Scrope, unflinchingly. "What would you think of him werehe to call you by some hideous pet name, or, more properly speaking, nickname?"

"I shouldn't mind it in the least; indeed, I think I should rather like it," returns Clarissa, mildly.

"I believe that to be highly probable," retorts Miss Jemima, with considerable scorn.

Clarissa laughs,—not an irritating laugh, by any means, but a little soft, low, girlish laugh, very good to hear.

"If you scold me any more I shall cry," she says, lightly. "I always give way to tears when driven into a corner. It saves time and trouble. Besides," returning with some slight perversity to the charge, "shall I tell you a secret? Your brother likes that little name. He does, indeed. He has told me so a thousand times in the days gone by. Very frivolous of him, isn't it? But—ah! here he is," as the door opens, and Sir James comes in. "You are a little late, are you not?" leaning back in her chair with a certain amount of languid, but pleasing, grace, and holding out to him a slender ungloved hand, on which some rings sparkle brilliantly.

"Have I kept you waiting?" asks he, eagerly, foolishly, glad because of her last words, that seem to imply so much and really mean so little. Has she been anxious for his coming? Have the minutes appeared tedious because of his absence? "I hurried all I knew," he says; "but stewards will be stewards."

"I have been quite happy with Miss Scrope; you need not look so penitent," says Clarissa. "And who am I, that I should compete with a steward? We have been having quite a good time, and an excellent argument. Come here, and tell your sister that you think Jim the prettiest name in the world."

"Did any one throw a doubt on the subject? Lives there a soul so dead to euphony as not to recognize the music in those three letters?—Jim! Why, it is poetry itself," says Sir James, who is not so absent that he cannot scent battle on the breeze. As he speaks, he smiles: and when James Scrope smiles he is almost handsome.

"Some day you will regret encouraging that child in her folly," remarks Miss Scrope, severely. At which the child makes a saucy little grimace unseen, and rises to her feet.

"What a solemn warning!" says Scrope, with a shrug. "I hope," turning to Clarissa, "you have taken it to heart, and that it will keep you out of imaginary mischief. It ought, you know. It would be a shabby thing to bring down public censure on the head of one who has so nobly espoused your cause."

"My conduct from this day forth shall be above suspicion," says Clarissa. "Good-by, Miss Scrope," stooping to press her fresh warm lips to the withered cross old cheek beneath her: "I am going to tread old ground with—James."

She follows him across hall and corridor, through two modern rooms, and past a *portière*, into another and larger hall beyond. Here, standing before a heavy oaken doer, he turns the handle of it, and, as it swings back slowly and sleepily, they pass into another room, so unexpectedly and so strangely different from any they have yet entered, as almost to make one start.

It is a huge old-fashioned apartment, stone-floored and oak panelled, that once, in olden days, must have been a refectory. Chairs carved in oak, and built like bishops' thrones, line the walls, looking as though no man for many a hundred years has drawn them from their present position. Massive cabinets and cupboards, cunningly devised by crafty hands in by-gone days, look out from dusky corners, the hideous faces carved upon them wreathed in their eternal ghastly smiles. From narrow, painted windows great gleams of sunset from the gay world without pour in, only to look sadly out of place in the solemn gloomy room. But one small door divides it from the halls outside; yet centuries seem to roll between it and them.

In one corner a door lies half open, and behind it a narrow flight of stairs runs upward to a turret chamber above,—a tiny stairway, heavily balustraded and uncarpeted, that creates in one a mad desire to ascend and learn the secrets that may lie at its top.

Miss Peyton, scarce noticing the monkish refectory, runs to the stairs and mounts them eagerly, Sir James following her in a more leisurely fashion.

"Now for my own room," she says, with some degree of quickness in her tone. She reaches the turret chamber as she speaks, and looks around her. It is quite a circle, and apparently of the same date as the one they have just quitted. Even the furniture, though of lighter make and size, is of a similar age and pattern. Ugly little chairs and unpleasantly solid tables are dotted here and there, a perfect wealth of Old-World work cut into them. Everything is carved, and to an unsympathetic observer it might occur that the carver must have been a person subject to fiendish visions and unholy nightmares. But no doubt the beauty of his designs lies in their ugliness, and his heads are a marvel of art, and his winged creatures priceless!

The high chimney-piece is *en rapport* with all the rest, and scowls unceasingly; and the very windows—long and deep—have little faces carved on either side of them, of the most diabolical.

Miss Peyton is plainly entranced with the whole scene, and for a full minute says nothing.

"I feel as though I were a child again," she says, presently, as though half regretful. "Everything comes back to me with such a strange yet tender vividness. This, I remember, was my favorite table, this my favorite chair. And that little winged monster over there, he used to whisper in my ears more thrilling tales than either Grimm or Andersen. Have you never moved anything in all these years?"

"Never. It is your own room by adoption, and no one shall meddle with it. When I went abroad I locked it, and carried the key of it with me wherever I went; I hardly know why myself." He glances at her curiously, but her face is averted, and she is plainly thinking less of him than of the many odd trifles scattered around. "When I returned, dust reigned, and spiders; but it has been made spick and span to day for its mistress. Does it still please you? or will you care to alter anything?"

"No, nothing. I shall pay a compliment to my childish taste by letting everything stay just as it is. I must have been rather a nice child, Jim, don't you think? if one passes over the torn frocks and the shrewish tongue."

"I don't think I ever saw a tear in your frocks," says Sir James, simply, "and if your tongue was shrewish I never found it out."

Miss Peyton gives way to mirth. She sits down on a wretchedly uncomfortable, if delightfully mediæval, chair and laughs a good deal.

"Oh, wad some power the giftie gie us
To see oursels as others see us!"

she quotes, gayly. "Those lines, meant by poor Burns as a censure on frail humanity, rather fall short at this moment. Were I to see myself as you see me, Jim, I should be a dreadfully conceited person, and utterly unbearable What a good friend you make!"

"A bad one, you mean. A real friend, according to my lights, is a fellow who says unpleasant things all round and expects you to respect his candor. By and by, when I tell you a few home truths, perhaps you will not like me as you do now."

"Yes, I shall always like you," says Clarissa. "Long ago, when you used to scold me, I never bore malice. I suppose you are one of those rare people who can say the ungracious thing in such a manner that it doesn't grate. But then you are old, you know, Jim, very old,—though, in appearance, wonderfully young for your years. I do hope papa, at your age, will look as fresh."

She has risen, and has slipped her hand through his arm, and is smiling up at him gayly and with a sweetness irresistible. Sir James looks as pleased as though he had received a florid compliment.

"What a baby you are!" he says, after a pause, looking down at her admiringly. Judging by his tone, babies, in his eyes, must possess very superior attractions. "There are a good many babies in the world, don't you think?" he goes on, presently. "You are one, and Geoffrey Branscombe is another. I don't suppose he will ever quite grow up."

"And Horace," says Clarissa, idly, "is he another?"

But Sir James, though unconsciously, resents the question.

"Oh, no!" he says, hastily. "He does not come within the category at all. Why," with a faint smile, "he is even older than I am! There is no tender baby-nonsense about him."

"No, he is so clever,—so far above us all, where intellect is concerned," she says, absently. A slight smile plays about her lips, and a light, that was not there a moment since, comes to life within her eyes. With an effort, she arouses herself from what were plainly happy daydreams, and comes back to the present, which, just now, is happy too.

"I think nature meant me to be a nun," she says, smiling. "This place subdues and touches me so. The sombre lights and shadows are so impressive! If it were indeed mine (in reality), I should live a great part of my time in it. Here, I should write my pleasantest letters, and read my choicest books, take my afternoon tea, and make welcome my dearest friends, — you among them. In fact, if it were practicable," nodding her pretty head emphatically, "I should steal this room. There is hardly anything I would not do to make it my own."

Scrope regards her earnestly, with a certain amount of calm inquiry. Is she a coquette, or merely unthinking? If, indeed, the face be the index of the mind, one must account her free of all unworthy thought or frivolous design. Here is

"A countenance in which do meet
Sweet records, promises as sweet."

Her eyes are still smiling up at him; her whole expression is full of a gentle friendliness; and in his heart, at this moment, arises a sensation that is not hope, or gladness, or despair, but yet is a faint wild mingling of all three.

As for Clarissa, she stands a little apart, unconscious of all that is passing in his heart, and gazes lovingly upon the objects that surround her, as one will gaze now and then on things that have been fondly remembered through the haze of many years. She is happy, wrapped in memories of a past all sunshine and no shade, and is ignorant of the meaning he would gladly attach to her last words.

"While I stay here I sin, — that is, I covet," she says, at length, surprised by his silence, "and it grows late. Come, walk with me a little way through the park: I have not yet seen the old path we used to call the 'short cut' to Gowran, long ago."

So, down the dark stairs he follows her, across the stone flooring, and into the hall outside, that seems so brilliant by contrast, and so like another world, all is so changed, so different. Behind, lie silence, unbroken, perfect, a sad and dreamy light, Old-World grandeur; here, all is restless life, full of uncertain sounds, and distant footsteps, and voices faint but positive.

"Is it not like a dream?" says Clarissa, stopping to point backwards to the turret they have just quitted.

"The past is always full of dreams," replies he, thoughtfully.

CHAPTER V

"A violet by a mossy stone
Half hidden from the eye!
Fair as a star, when only one
Is shining in the sky." — Wordsworth.

The baby morn has flung aside its robes, and grown to perfect strength. The day is well advanced. Already it is making rapid strides towards rest and evening; yet still no cooling breeze has come to refresh the heart of man.

Below, in the quiet fields, the cattle are standing, knee-deep in water, beneath the spreading branches of the kindly alder. They have no energy to eat, but munch, sleepily, the all-satisfying cud, and, with gentle if expressionless eyes, look out afar for evening and the milkmaid.

"'Tis raging noon; and, vertical, the sun
Darts on the head direct his forceful rays.
O'er heaven and earth, far as the ranging eye
Can sweep, a dazzling deluge reigns; and all,
From pole to pole, is undistinguished blaze.
Distressful Nature pants!
The very streams look languid from afar,
Or, through th' unsheltered glade, impatient, seem
To hurl into the covert of the grove."

A tender stillness reigns over everything. The very birds are mute. Even the busy mill-wheel has ceased to move.

Bright flashes of light, that come and go ere one can catch them, dart across the gray walls of the old mill, — that holds its gaunt and stately head erect, as though defying age, — and, slanting to the right, fall on the cottage, quaint and ivy-clad, that seems to nestle at its feet. The roses that climb its walls are drooping; the casements all stand wide. No faintest breath of air comes to flutter Ruth's white gown, as she leans against the rustic gate.

All millers' daughters should be pretty. It is a duty imposed upon them by tradition. Romance, of the most floral description, at once attaches itself to a miller's daughter. I am not at all sure it does not even cast a halo round the miller himself. Ruth Annersley at least acknowledges this fact, and does her duty nobly; she gives the lie to no old legends or treasured nursery superstitions; she is as pretty as heart can desire, —

"Fresh as the month, and as the morning fair."

She is small, piquant, timid, with large almond-shaped eyes and light-brown hair, a rounded supple figure, and hands delicately white. Perhaps there is a lack of force in her face, an indefinable want, that hardly detracts from her beauty, yet sets one wondering, vaguely, where it lies, and what it can be. The mouth, mobile and slightly parted, betrays it most.

Her lashes, covering her brown eyes, are very long, and lie a good deal on her cheeks. Her manner, without a suspicion of *gaucherie*, is nervous, almost appealing; and her smile, because so rare, is very charming, and apt to linger in the memory.

She is an only child, and all through her young life has been petted and caressed rather more than is good for any one. Her father had married, somewhat late in life, a woman in every way his superior, and, she dying two years after her marriage, he had fallen back for consolation upon the little one left to his sole care. To him, she was a pride, a delight, a creature precious beyond words, on whom the sun must shine gently and the rain fall not at all.

A shy child from the first, Ruth had declined acquaintance with the villagers, who would, one and all, have been glad to succor the motherless girl. Perhaps the little drop of gentle blood inherited from her mother had thriven in her veins, and thus rendered her distant and somewhat repellent in her manners to those in her own rank of life.

She had been sent early to a private school, had been carefully educated far above her position, and had come home again to her father, with all the pretty airs and unconscious softness of manner that, as a rule, belong to good birth.

She is warm-hearted, passionate, impulsive, and singularly reserved, — so much so that few guess at the terrible power to love, or hate, or suffer, in silence, that lies within her. She is a special favorite with Miss Peyton and the vicarage people (Mr. and Mrs Redmond and their five children), with those at Hythe, and indeed with most of the country people, Miss Scrope excepted, who gives it freely as her opinion that she will come to no good "with her books and her high society and general fiddle-faddling." Nobody knows what this last means, and every one is afraid to ask.

Just now, with her pretty head bare, and her hand shading her eyes, she is gazing down the dusty road. Her whole attitude denotes expectancy. Every feature (she is off her guard) expresses intense and hopeful longing, —

"Fiery Titan, who
— —with his peccant heat
Has dried up the lusty liquor new
Upon the herbis in the greene mead,"

has plainly fallen in love with her to-day, as he has clothed her in all his glory, and seems reluctant to pass her by on his homeward journey.

The heat has made her pale and languid; but just at this moment a faint delicate color springs into her face; and as the figure of a young man, tall and broad-shouldered, turns the corner of the road, she raises her hand to her cheek with a swift involuntary gesture. A moment later, as the figure comes closer, so near that the face is discernible, she pales again, and grows white as an early snow drop.

"Good-morning, Ruth," says Dorian Branscombe, with a smile, apparently oblivious of the fact that morning has given place to noon many hours agone.

Ruth returns his salutation gently, and lets her hand lie for an instant in his.

"This is a summer's day, with a vengeance," says Dorian, genially, proceeding to make himself comfortable on the top of the low wall near which she is standing. He is plainly making up his mind to a long and exhaustive conversation. "Talk of India!" he says disparagingly; "this beats it to fits!"

Ruth acquiesces amiably.

"It is warm,—very," she says, calmly, but indifferently.

"'Ot I call it,—werry 'ot," returns he, making his quotation as genially as though she understands it, and, plucking a little rose-bud from a tree near him, proceeds to adorn his coat with it.

"It seems a long time since I have seen you," he goes on, presently; and, as he speaks, his eyes again seek hers. Something in her face touches some chord in his careless kindly nature.

"How pale you are!" he says, abruptly.

"Am I? The heat, no doubt,"—with a faint smile.

"But thin, too, are you not? And—and—" he pauses. "Anything wrong with you, Ruth?"

"Wrong? No! How should there be?" retorts she, in a curious tone, in which fear and annoyance fight for mastery. Then the storm dies away, and the startled look fades from her pretty face.

"Why should you think me unhappy because I am a little pale?" she asks, sullenly.

Branscombe looks surprised.

"You altogether mistake me," he says, gently. "I never associated you in my mind with unhappiness. I merely meant, had you a headache, or any other of those small ills that female flesh is heir to? I beg your pardon, I'm sure, if I have offended you."

He has jumped off the wall, and is now standing before her, with only the little gate between them. Her face is still colorless, and she is gazing up at him with parted lips, as though she would fain say something difficult to form into satisfactory speech. At this moment, Lord Sartoris, coming suddenly round the angle of the road, sees them.

Ruth lowers her eyes, and some slight transient color creeps into her cheeks. Sartoris, coming quickly up to them, makes some conventional speech to her, and then turns to his nephew.

"Where are you going?" he asks, coldly.

"I was going to Hythe," returned the young man, easily. "Just as well I didn't, eh? Should have found you out."

"Found me out,—yes," repeats his uncle, looking at him strangely. How long—how long it takes to find out some people, on whom our very hearts are set. "I am going to the village."

"Then so am I," says Branscombe. "Though I should think it would run the original 'deserted' one close on such a day as this. Good-by, Ruth."

He holds out his hand; and the girl, silently returning his warm pressure, makes a faint courtesy to Lord Sartoris. There is no servility, but some nervousness, in the slight salutation.

"How is your father, Ruth?" asks he, detaining her by a quick movement of the hand.

"Quite well, thank you, my lord." Some timidity is discernible in her tone, caused by the unmistakable reproof and sternness in his.

"I am glad to hear it. There is no worthier man in all the parish than John Annersley. I hope nothing will ever occur to grieve or sadden that good old man."

"I hope not, my lord," returns she, steadily, although his voice has meaning in it. In another moment she is gone.

"How does your farming go on, Dorian?" asks Lord Sartoris, presently, rousing himself from a puzzling revery.

"Quite in the model line," says Dorian, cheerful. "That Sawyer is an invaluable fellow. Does all the work, you know, — which is most satisfactory. Looks after the men, pays their wages, and takes all trouble off my shoulders. Never could understand what a perfect treasure is till I got him. Every one says I am most fortunate in my choice of a steward."

"I dare say. It is amazing the amount of information people possess about other people's servants. But you look after things yourself, of course? However faithful and trustworthy one's hirelings may be, one's own eyes should also be in the matter."

"Oh, of course," acquiesces Dorian, still cheerfully. "Nothing like personal supervision, and so on. Every now and then, you know, I do look over the accounts, and ask a few questions, and show myself very learned in drainages, and so forth. But I don't see that I gain much by it. Horrid stupid work, too," — with a yawn. "Luckily, Sawyer is one of the most knowing fellows in the world, or I suppose I should go to smash. He is up to everything, and talks like a book. Quite a pleasure, I give you my word, — almost a privilege, — to hear him converse on short-horns and some eccentric root they call mangels."

"It is possible to be too knowing," says his uncle, depreciatingly.

"Eh? oh, no; Sawyer is not that sort of person. He is quite straight all through. And he never worries me more than he can help. He looks after everything, and whatever he touches (metaphorically speaking) turns to gold. I'm sure anything like those pheasants — — "

"Yes, yes, I dare say. But pheasants are not everything."

"Well, no; there are a few other things," says Dorian, amicably, — "notably, grouse. Why this undying hatred to Sawyer, my dear Arthur? In what has he been found wanting?"

"I think him a low, under-hand, sneaking sort of fellow," says Sartoris, unhesitatingly. "I should not keep him in my employ half an hour. However," relentingly, and somewhat sadly, "one cannot always judge by appearances."

They have reached the village by this time, and are walking leisurely through it. Almost as they reach the hotel that adorns the centre of the main street, they meet Mr. Redmond, the rector, looking as hearty and kindly as usual. Lord Sartoris, who has come down on purpose to meet him, having asked his question and received his answer, turns again and walks slowly homeward, Dorian still beside him.

As they again catch sight of the old mill, Sartoris says, quietly, with a laudable attempt at unconcern that would not have deceived the veriest infant, but is quite successful with Dorian, whose thoughts are far away,—

"What a nice girl that little Ruth has grown!"

"Awfully pretty girl," returns Dorian, carelessly.

"Yes,"—gravely,—"very pretty; and I think—I hope—upright, as she is beautiful. Poor child, hers seems to me a very desolate lot. Far too well educated to associate with those of her own class, she is still cut off by the laws of caste from mixing with those above her. She has no friends, no mother, no sister, to love and sympathize with her."

"My dear Arthur, how you do agonize yourself!" says Dorian. "She has her father, and about as comfortable a time altogether as I know of."

"She reminds me of some lowly wayside flower," goes on the old man, musingly, heedless of the brilliant interlude, "raising its little head sadly among gay garden-plants that care not for her, whilst beyond the hedge that bounds her garden she can watch her own species grow and flourish in wild luxuriance. Her life can scarcely be called happy. There must always be a want, a craving for what can never be obtained. Surely the one that could bring sorrow to that pure heart, or tears to those gentle eyes, should be— —"

"Asphyxiated," puts in Dorian, idly. He yawns languidly and pulls the head off a tall dandelion, that adorns the wayside, in a somewhat desultory fashion. The color in the older man's cheeks grows a shade deeper, and a gesture, as full of impatience as of displeasure, escapes him.

"There are some subjects," he says, with calm severity, "that it would be well to place beyond the reach of ridicule."

"Am I one of them?" says Dorian, lightly. Then, glancing at his uncle's face, he checks himself, and goes on quickly. "I beg your pardon, I'm sure. I have been saying something unlucky, as usual. Of course I agree with you on all points, Arthur, and think the man who could wilfully bring a blush to Ruth Annersley's cheek neither more nor less than a blackguard *pur et simple*. By the by, that last little homely phrase comes in badly there, doesn't it? Rather out of keeping with the vituperative noun, eh!"

"Rather," returns Sartoris, shortly. He drops his nephew's arm, and walks on in silence. As a rule, Dorian's careless humor suits him; it amuses and adds a piquancy to a life that without it (now that Dorian's society has become indispensable to him) would prove "flat, stale, and unprofitable." But to-day, he hardly knows why,—or, perhaps, hardly dares to know why,—his nephew's easy light-heartedness jars upon him, vexing him sorely.

As they turn the corner of the road and go down the hill, they meet Horace, coming towards them at a rapid pace. As he sees them, he slackens his speed and approaches more slowly.

"Just as well I met you," he says, with an airy laugh, "as my thoughts were running away with me, and Phœbus Apollo is in the ascendant: veritably he 'rules the roast.' This uphill work is trying on the lungs."

"Where have you been?" asks Dorian, just because he has nothing else to say, and it is such a bore to think.

"At Gowran."

"Ah! I'm going there now. You saw Clarissa, then?" says Sartoris, quickly. "When do you return to town, Horace?"

"To-morrow, I think,—I hope," says Horace; and, with a little nod on both sides, they part. But when the bend in the road again hides him from view, it would occur to a casual on-looker that Horace Branscombe's thoughts must once more have taken his physical powers into captivity, as his pace quickens, until it grows even swifter than it was before.

Sartoris goes leisurely down the hill, with Dorian beside him, whistling "Nancy Lee," in a manner highly satisfactory to himself, no doubt, but slightly out of tune. When Sartoris can bear this musical treat no longer, he breaks hurriedly into speech of a description that requires an answer.

"What a pretty girl Clarissa Peyton is! don't you think so?"

When Dorian has brought Miss Lee to a triumphant finish, with a flourish that would have raised murderous longings in the breast of Stephen Adams, he says, without undue enthusiasm,—

"Yes, she is about the best-looking woman I know."

"And as unaffected as she is beautiful. That is her principal charm. So thoroughly bred, too, in every thought and action. I never met so lovable a creature!"

"What a pity she can't hear you!" says Branscombe. "Though perhaps it is as well she can't. Adulation has a bad effect on some people."

"She is too earnest, too thorough, to be upset by flattery. I sometimes wonder if there are any like her in the world."

"Very few, I think," says Dorian, genially.

Another pause, somewhat longer than the last, and then Sartoris says, with some hesitation, "Do you never think of marrying, Dorian?"

"Often," says Branscombe, with an amused smile.

"Yet how seldom you touch on the matter! Why, when I was your age, I had seen at least twenty women I should have married, had they shown an answering regard for me."

"What a blessing they didn't!" says Branscombe. "Fancy, twenty of them! You'd have found it awkward in the long run, wouldn't you? And I don't think they'd have liked it, you know, in this illiberal country. So glad you thought better of it."

"I wish I could once see you as honestly"—with a slight, almost unconscious, stress on the word—"in love as I have been scores of times."

"What a melancholy time you must have put in! When a fellow is in love he goes to skin and bone, doesn't he? slights his dinner, and refuses to find solace in the best cigar. It must be trying,—very; especially to one's friends. I doubt you were a susceptible youth, Arthur. I'm not."

"Then you ought to be," says Sartoris, with some anger. "All young men should feel their hearts beat, and their pulses quicken, at the sight of a pretty woman."

"My dear fellow," says Branscombe, severely, removing his glass from his right to his left eye, as though to scan more carefully his uncle's countenance, "there is something the matter with you this morning, isn't there? You're not well, you know. You have taken something very badly, and it has gone to your morals; they are all wrong,—very unsound indeed. Have you carefully considered the nature of the advice you are giving me? Why, if I were to let my heart beat every time I meet all the pretty women I know, I should be in a lunatic asylum in a month."

"Seriously, though, I wish you would give the matter some thought," says Lord Sartoris, earnestly: "you are twenty-eight,—old enough to make a sensible choice."

Branscombe sighs.

"And I see nothing to prevent your doing so. You want a wife to look after you,—a woman you could respect as well as love,—a thoughtful beautiful woman, to make your home dearer to you than all the amusements town life can afford. She would make you happy, and induce you to look more carefully to your own interests, and——and——"

"You mean you would like me to marry Clarissa Peyton," says Dorian, good-humoredly. "Well, it is a charming scheme, you know; but I don't think it will come off. In the first place, Clarissa would not have me, and in the next, I don't want to marry at all. A wife would bore me to death; couldn't fancy a greater nuisance. I like women very much, in fact, I may say, I am decidedly fond of a good many of them, but to have one always looking after me (as you style it) and showing up my pet delinquencies would drive me out of my mind. Don't look so disgusted! I feel I'm a miserable sinner; but I really can't help it. I expect there is something radically wrong with me."

"Do you mean to tell me" —with some natural indignation—"that up to this you have never, during all your wanderings, both at home and abroad, seen any woman you could sincerely admire?"

"Numbers, my dear Arthur,—any amount,—but not one I should care to marry. You see, that makes such a difference. I remember once before— last season—you spoke to me in this strain, and, simply to oblige you, I thought I would make up my mind to try matrimony. So I went in heavily, heart and soul, for Lady Fanny Hazlett. You have seen Lady Fanny?"

"Yes, a good deal of her."

"Then you know how really pretty she is. Well, I spent three weeks at it; regular hard work the entire time, you know, no breathing-space allowed, as she never refuses an invitation, thinks nothing of three balls in one night, and insisted on my dancing attendance on her everywhere. I never suffered so much in my life; and when at last I gave in from sheer exhaustion, I found my clothes no longer fitted me. I was worn to a skeleton from loss of sleep, the heavy strain on my mental powers, and the meek endurance of her ladyship's ill tempers."

"Lady Fanny is one woman, Clarissa Peyton is quite another. How could you fail to be happy with Clarissa? Her sweetness, her grace of mind and body, her beauty, would keep you captive even against your will."

Dorian pauses for a moment or two, and then says, very gently, as though sorry to spoil the old man's cherished plan,—

"It is altogether impossible. Clarissa has no heart to give me."

Sartoris is silent. A vague suspicion of what now appears a certainty has for some time oppressed and haunted him. At this moment he is sadly realizing the emptiness of all his dreaming. Presently he says, slowly,—

"Are you quite sure of this?"

"As certain as I can be without exactly hearing it from her own lips."

"Is it Horace?"

"Yes; it is Horace," says Branscombe, quietly.

CHAPTER VI

"Tread softly; bow the head, —
In reverent silence bow,
Yet an immortal soul
Is passing now." —Caroline Southey.

A little room, scantily but neatly furnished. A low bed. A dying man. A kneeling girl, —half child, half woman, —with a lovely, miserable face, and pretty yellow hair.

It was almost dusk, and the sound of the moaning sea without, rising higher and hoarser as the tide rushes in, comes like a wail of passionate agony into the silent room.

The rain patters dismally against the window-panes. The wind—that all day long has been sullen and subdued—is breaking forth into a fury long suppressed, and, dashing through the little town, on its way to the angry sea, makes the casements rattle noisily and the tall trees sway and bend beneath its touch. Above, in the darkening heavens, gray clouds are scurrying madly to and fro.

"Georgie," whispers a faint voice from out the gathering gloom, "are you still there?"

"Yes, dear, I am here, quite near to you. What is it?"

"Sit where I can see you, child, —where I can watch your face. I have something to say to you. I cannot die with this weight upon my heart."

"What weight, papa?"

"The uncertainty about your future," says the dying man, with some excitement. "How can I leave you, my little one, to fight this cruel world alone?"

"Do not think of me," says the girl, in a voice so unnaturally calm as to betray the fact that she is making a supreme effort to steel herself against the betrayal of emotion of any kind. By and by, will there not be long years in which to make her moan, and weep, and lament, and give herself wholly up to that grim giant, Despair? "Put me out of your thoughts altogether. I shall do very, very well. I shall manage to live as others have lived before me."

"Your Aunt Elizabeth will take you in for a little while, and then— — then— —"

"I shall go out as a governess. I shall get into some kind, pleasant family, and every one will be very good to me," says the girl, still in a resolutely cheerful tone. "It will just suit me. I shall like it. Do you understand me, papa? I shall like it better than anything, because children are always fond of me."

The father's face grows sadder, even grayer, as she speaks. He sighs in a troubled fashion, and strokes feebly the little fragile hand that clings so desperately to his, while the damps of death lie thick upon his brow.

"A governess," he murmurs, with some difficulty. "While you are only a child yourself? What a hard, hard fate! Is there no friend to help and comfort you?"

"I have a friend," replies she, steadily. "You have often heard me mention her. You remember the name, now,—Clarissa Peyton? She was my best friend at school, and I know she will do what she can for me. She will be able to find me some nice children, and— —"

"Friendship,"—interrupts he, bitterly,—"it is a breath,—a name. It will fail you when you most need it."

"Clarissa will not fail me," replies she, slowly, though with a feeling of deadly sickness at her heart. "And, besides, you must not think of me as a governess always, papa. I shall, perhaps, marry somebody, some day."

The dying man's eyes grow a shade brighter; it is a mere flicker, but it lasts for a moment, long enough to convince her she has indeed given some poor hope to cheer his last hours.

"Yes; to marry somebody," he repeats, wistfully, "that will be best,—to get some good man, some kindly, loving heart to protect you and make a safe shelter for you. There is comfort in the thought. But I hope it will be soon, my darling, before your spirit is broken and your youth dulled."

"I shall marry as soon as ever I can," says Georgie, making a last terrible effort to appear hopeful and resigned. "I shall meet some one very soon, no doubt,—very soon: so do not fret about me any more. Why should I not, indeed? I am very pretty, am I not, papa?" In spite of the lightness of her words, a heavy choking sob escapes her as she finishes her little set speech. She buries her face in the bed-clothes, to stifle her rising grief, but her father is almost too far gone to notice it.

"Yes,—so like your mother," he mutters, somewhat thickly, clutching aimlessly at the quilt. "Poor Alice!—poor girl! It was that day on the beach, when the waves were dancing, and the sun— —or was it?— —Did the old man ever forgive— —?"

He is wandering, dreaming his death-dream of happier days, going back, even as he sinks into everlasting sleep, to the gilded hours of youth.

The girl presses his hand to rouse him.

"Think of *me* now," she entreats, despairingly; "it will only be for a little while,—such a little while,—and then you will be with *her* forever. Oh, papa! my dear, my dear; smile at me once again. Think of me happily; let me feel when you are gone that your last hours with me were peaceful."

His eyes meet hers, and he smiles tenderly. Gently she slips her arms round him, and, laying her golden head upon the pillow, close to him, presses her lips to his,—the soft warm lips, that contrast so painfully with those pale cold other ones they touch. So she remains for a long time, kissing him softly every now and again, and thinking hopelessly of the end.

She neither sighs, nor weeps, nor makes any outward sign of anguish. Unlike most people, she has realized to its fullest the awfulness of this thing that is about to befall her. And the knowledge has paralyzed her senses, rendering her dull with misery, and tearless.

Presently the white lids, weary with nights of watching, droop. Her breath comes more evenly. Her head sinks more heavily against the pillow, and, like a child worn out with grief and pain, she sleeps.

When next she wakes, gray dawn is everywhere. The wind still moans unceasingly. Still the rain-drops patter against the panes. She raises her head affrightedly, and, springing to his feet, bends with bated breath above the quiet form lying on the bed.

Alas! alas! what change is here? He has not moved; no faintest alteration can be traced in the calm pose of the figure that lies just as she last saw it, when sleep o'er came her. The eyes are closed; the tender smile—the last fond smile—still lingers on his lips; yet, he is dead!

The poor child stands gazing down upon him with parted lips and clasped hands, and a face almost as ashen as that marble one to which her eyes grow with a horror unspeakable. He looks so peaceful—so much as though he merely sleeps—that for one mad moment she tries not to believe the truth. Yet she knows it is death, unmistakable and relentless, upon which for the first time she looks.

He is gone, forever! without another kiss, or smile, or farewell word beyond those last uttered. He had set out upon his journey alone, had passed into the other happier land, in the cold silence of the night, even while she slept,—had been torn from her, whilst yet her fond arms encircled him.

Impelled by some indefinable desire, she lays her fingers softly on the hand that lies outside the coverlet. The awful chill that meets her touch seems to reach even to her heart. Throwing her arms above her head, with a wild passionate cry, she falls forward, and lies senseless across the lifeless body.

Misery hurts, but it rarely kills; and broken hearts are out of fashion. All this unhappiness came to Georgie Broughton about a year ago, and though brain-fever followed upon it, attacking her with vicious force, and almost handing her over as a victim to the greedy grave, yet she had survived, and overcome death, and returned from the land of shadows, weakened, indeed, but with life before her.

Months passed before she could summon up sufficient energy to plan or think about a possible future. All this time her aunt Elizabeth had clothed and fed and sheltered her, but unwillingly. Indeed, so grudgingly had she dealt out her measure of "brotherly love" that the girl writhed beneath it, and pined, with a passionate longing, for the day that should see her freed from a dependence that had become unspeakably bitter to her.

To-day, sitting in her little room,—an apartment high up in Aunt Elizabeth's house,—she tells herself she will hesitate no longer, that she is strong now, quite strong, and able to face the world. She holds up her delicate little hand between her eyes and the window, as a test of her returning strength, only to find she can almost see the light through it,—so thin, so fragile, has it grown. But she will not be disheartened; and, drawing pen and paper towards her, she tries to write.

But it is a difficult task, and her head is strangely heavy, and her words will not come to her. A vague feeling, too, that her letter will be unsuccessful, that her friend will fail her, distresses and damps her power to explain her position clearly.

Who can say if Clarissa Peyton will be the same at heart as when last they parted, with many words of good will and affection, and eyes dark with tears?

Grief and misery, and too much of Aunt Elizabeth, have already embittered and generated distrust in her young bosom. She is tired, too. All day she has toiled, has worked religiously, and gone through wearying household labor, trying to repay in some faint wise the reluctant hospitality extended to her. At this moment a sense of utter desolation overpowers her, and with a brain on fire, and a heart half broken, she pushes from her the partly-written letter, and, burying her face in her arms, breaks into low but heavy weeping.

"Papa! papa!" she sobs, miserably. It is the common refrain of all her sorrowful dirges, — the sadder that no response ever comes to the lonely cry. Of our dead, if we would believe them happy we must also believe that they have forgotten us; else how (when we think on our bleeding hearts) could they keep their bliss so perfect?

Mournfully as Mariana in her moated grange, the poor child laments, while sobs shake her slender frame. And the day dies, and the sun goes down, and happily some noise in the house—a step, a voice—arouses her, and, starting as though from some ugly dream, she takes up her pen again, and writes eagerly, and without premeditation, to the one friend in whom she still puts faith.

CHAPTER VII

"Life has rising ills." —Dyer.

"Papa, papa," says Miss Peyton, impatiently, without eliciting any response.

It is half-past ten, and breakfast is on the table! So are two little white pigeons, who have flown in through the open window, and are sitting, one on Clarissa's shoulder, the other on the edge of the table, picking crumbs out of her plate. The sun is streaming hotly in, the breath of flowers floating faintly in his train. A bowl of roses, half opened and filled with the dew of early morning, lies near Clarissa's plate. Upon the window-sill, outside, another little pigeon, brown-tinged and timid, stands peeping shyly in, envying his bolder brothers, and longing for the pretty coaxing voice of his mistress that shall make him brave to enter.

But to-day the welcome summons does not come. Miss Peyton has an open letter in her hand, the contents of which have plainly disturbed and interested her to an unusual degree; so that the little bird, whose pretty brown plumage is being transformed by the sun into richest bronze, grows each moment more dejected. Not for him the crumbs and the "flesh pots of Egypt."

"One——two——If you don't answer me before I say three, papa, I shall do something desperate," she says, again, raising her voice a little.

But still papa takes no heed. At this moment, poor man, he is deep in Mr. Forster's Irish Distress Bill, and is deaf to all surroundings.

Clarissa loses patience. Taking up a teaspoon, she makes a sharp "assault and battery" upon an unoffending teacup, thereby creating a din compared to which the noise of tomtoms would be sweetest music.

George Peyton is not proof against this tattoo. He looks up irritably, and for a moment withdraws his mind from Mr. Forster's Bill.

"My dear Clarissa," he says, very justly incensed, "what is it? What on earth is the matter with you? My dear, whatever it is, do stop that unpleasant noise: it plays the very mischief with one's nerves."

"It is only a teaspoon," begins Miss Peyton, delighted with her success.

"And a cup, I think," says Mr. Peyton. "Separately they are unoffending, together they can annoy. If you will put that spoon out of your hand, my dear, you will make me much happier."

"It was only when I was actually hoarse, from trying to attract your attention, that I resorted to violent measures," says Clarissa, severely.

"I beg your pardon," returns he, submissively.

"Now listen to my letter," says Clarissa. "I want your advice. It is such a dear letter, and such a sad one; and — and something must be done at once."

"I quite agree with you," murmurs her father, dreamily. Once again his mind is losing itself in the folds of the fragrant "Times."

"Mannerton, Tuesday, September 24.

"My dear Clarissa, —

"So long a time has elapsed since last I saw or heard of you that I half fear, as you read this, it will puzzle you to remember the writer. Am I quite forgotten? I hope not; as I want you to do me a great service. This reason for wishing myself still in your memory sounds selfish, — almost rude; but what can I do? Must I not speak the truth? And indeed I am in sore trouble. I am friendless, all but homeless, and utterly alone in the world. But, as I am quite determined to fight my own way, I have decided on going out as a governess, and I want you, dear, dear Cissy, to get somebody to try me, — somebody who would not be too hard upon me, just at first, until I had accustomed myself to the life and to the children's ways. You may say I can paint very well, and, though not a brilliant pianist, I have a good voice. (Do you recollect how, at school, you used to say you liked to hear me sing when the day was dying?) I can speak French and German, but I know nothing of Italian or Latin, and I was never very much at arithmetic, or that. I think I could get on, after a little training; and at all events I know I must try, as life here is not endurable.

"Oh, Cissy, if time has changed you, if you have grown cold and careless, as all the rest of this cruel world, what shall I do? But I will not believe that even a hundred years could make you unkind or unfeeling. Do you think you will be very long in answering this? Every hour I shall be listening for the post: write to me, then, as soon as you can. I am very unhappy here with Aunt Elizabeth, who does not care for me.

"I am, dear Clarissa,

> "Your affectionate friend,

> "Georgie Broughton.

"P.S.—If you could get me pretty children, I should be so glad; but of course it must not make any difference, and I dare say ugly ones are just as nice, when one gets used to them. I am dreadfully afraid of boys; but perhaps there may be a few found somewhere amenable to reason, and at least one or two who do not object to knees in their knickerbockers. Do you remember the gardener's babies at Brussels, and how fond they were of me? Dear Cissy, write soon."

This is the letter, with all its pathetic little confidences, its "do you remembers?" and "have you forgottens?" and its tone,—half proud and half beseeching,—that has touched Miss Peyton so deeply.

Her mouth trembles, there are tears in her voice and eyes, as she finishes the last word and turns her face to her father. Something she sees in that vague but kindly man checks her enthusiasm for the moment; a thought but half defined, a suspicion, disgraceful if true, crosses her brain and fills her with indignation.

"Papa! Have you been listening?" she asks, in her sternest tones.

"Listening, my dear? Of course I have. Yes, certainly, with all my might," returns he, with unusual and therefore doubtful alacrity. As a matter of fact, I don't think much would be said about his "distinguished answering" were he to be examined in the letter just read; but all the more for this reason does he assume an air of surprise at Clarissa's question, and covers himself with an expression of injured innocence. Unfortunately for him, however, Miss Peyton is a person not to be done.

"No, you have not," she says, severe but calm. "You have not heard a single syllable. Your mind was full of that miserable paper all the time, and I am positive you were putting together some silly speech that you imagine would electrify those absurd men in the House of Commons."

"I don't think it was a very silly speech, my dear Clarissa," remonstrates Mr. Peyton, feebly.

"Oh, then you do acknowledge you were miles away in thought," says Clarissa, triumphant, if disgusted.

"My dear girl, how you do misjudge me!" protests poor Mr. Peyton, at his wits' end. "I assure you, I was all attention to that very excellent letter from beginning to end."

"Were you?" returns she, sweetly. "Then, of course, you can tell me what was the last word."

She has placed her elbows on the table, and has let her pretty face sink into the palms of her hands, and is now regarding her father with a smile, half mocking, half malicious.

"The last word! Oh, nonsense, my dear Cis! who ever remembered the last word of anything, unless it happened to be 'The Burial of Sir John Moore,' or 'Beautiful Star,' or something that way? But I know your letter was all about a young woman who has got herself into a mess and wants to come to you now as maid or laundress. But there is always danger in that sort of thing, you know, and you mightn't like it afterwards: and— —"

"Oh, what an engrossing speech that imaginary one of yours must have been!" says Clarissa, with a little distracted shake of her head. "I knew you were in the room, didn't I? No, no, no, you are altogether wrong: this is no letter from maid or laundress, but from Georgie Broughton. (You must remember her name, I have so often mentioned it to you.) She is the dearest little thing in the world,—quite that, and more. And she writes, to tell me she is miserably poor, and wants to go out as a governess."

"Poor girl! Of all unhappy resources, the last."

"Yes; isn't it wretched? But, you see, she is bound to do something, and wearing out one's heart in a dingy school-room seems to be the only course left open to a pretty girl like Georgie."

"Try Mrs. Redmond, then. She is looking out for a governess for the children; and your friend might drop in there without further trouble."

"Oh, papa, but all those children! and Mrs. Redmond herself, too, so fretful and so irritable,—so utterly impossible in every way. Her very 'How d'ye do?' would frighten Georgie to death."

"People don't die of chills of that description; and your poor little friend can scarcely expect to find everything *couleur de rose*. Besides, 'all those children' you speak of just resolve themselves into two, as the boys are at school, and Cissy calls herself grown up. I should think Cissy would be, in fact, a great comfort to her, and would be amenable to her, and gentle—and that."

At this, Miss Peyton laughs a little, and bites her lip.

"Amenable," she says, slowly. "Do you know, I am afraid my Georgie is even younger than Cissy?"

"Younger!"

"Well, she will certainly look younger; she has such a little, fresh, babyish rose-bud of a face. Do you think"—anxiously—"that would matter much?"

"It doesn't sound promising; but, if she is a good girl, one might forgive the great crime of being fresh and young. Dear me, it is very awkward. If she had been a nice, sensible, ugly, middle-aged person, now, all would have gone well; but, after all, poor child, of course she can't help her appearance."

"No, she certainly cannot," says Clarissa, with a sigh, heart-felt pity in her tone. "And her eyes are the very color of forget-me-nots,—quite the prettiest I ever saw. It is really too bad."

"Redmond, himself, would make no difficulty about it. He prefers to have young people about him, and was always, you know, rather——rather melancholy when in Miss Prood's society, who was really a most estimable woman, and one whose moral character one could not fail to admire, when one forgot her nose, and her——"

"Temper?"

"Well, yes, she was rather excitable. But, as I was saying, Redmond and your friend would probably pull very well; and then there's the curate. Why,"—brilliantly,—"she might marry the curate!"

"Mr. Hastings?" says Clarissa, with animation, brightening visibly. "Why, really, so she might. Such a good-looking man, too, and clever. It is only a day or two ago since somebody said to me, 'He has the very sort of face they make bishops of nowadays.'"

"What a very disinterested girl you are!" says her father, with a smile, faint but amused: "without a moment's hesitation you surrender every hope of making this embryo bishop your own. Can devotion farther go? Well, take my advice; and, as your heart is set upon this thing, go down to the vicarage to-day; tell Mrs. Redmond you have secured a governess for her; do not discuss the subject,—simply state the fact; and I think you will find her deeply grateful, in that you have put an end to her difficulties, without compelling her brain to bear upon the matter."

"Machiavelli was a poor creature, when compared with you," says Miss Peyton, saucily. "What plots and plans swell out your busy brain! I shall go to the vicarage to-day, as you advise, and be as sweet as honey to Mrs. Redmond, and win my cause against all obstacles. But first"—turning with a soft movement to caress the snowy pigeon that rests upon her shoulder—"little home friends must be fed."

The bird, as though comprehending her words, flies through the open window to the balcony outside, to nestle among its more timid companions; whilst Clarissa, a creature scarcely less fair than they, follows him, to fling breadcrumbs for their morning meal.

A little later, having dressed herself, she starts upon her errand, ready to take the vicarage by storm.

CHAPTER VIII

"'Tis love, love, love, that makes the world go round."

The hot September sun beats fiercely on her as she walks along; the day is full of languor and sweet peace. The summer is almost done, and is dying, rich in beauty, and warm with the ripeness of strength perfected. From out the thickets, little birds, that three months agone scarce knew the power of breath, now warble soft melodies, that thrill the air with joy. Clarissa, glad, and full of purpose, feels her heart at one with these tiny, heaven-taught musicians, as she follows the path beneath the leafy trees that leads to the vicarage.

As she deserts the tinted wood, and gains the road that runs by the old mill, she finds herself face to face with Horace Branscombe, coming towards her in a somewhat laggard fashion. His brow is darkened by a frown: his whole expression is moody and oppressed with discontent.

As he sees Clarissa, his features—as though compelled by a powerful will—undergo a complete change, and he smiles, and comes forward with outstretched hand to greet her.

"Horace! you here again, and so soon?" she says, quickly. Surprise lends haste to her tongue. She has believed him in London; and now to see him thus unexpectedly, and without the usual friendly warning conveyed by letter, causes her not only pleasure, but a vague uneasiness.

"Does it seem 'so soon' to you?" replies he, in a carefully inspired tone. "To me the last two months have appeared almost a year, so heavily have dragged the days spent away from Pullingham."

It is a very stereotyped little sentence, old and world-worn, and smacking faintly of insincerity; but when a woman loves a man she rarely measures his words.

"I seem rude," says Clarissa, with a soft smile. "But you will understand me. And you know you told me you did not intend to return before Christmas."

"Yes, I know." He is silent for a little while, and then, rousing himself, as though by an effort, says, slowly,—

"Did you miss me?"

"I always miss you," returns she, simply: "you know that." She flushes warmly, and lets her long lashes fall leisurely, until at length they hide from view the sweet confession of her eyes. There is a pause that embraces a full minute, and then she speaks again. "You have not yet told me the reason of your return," she says, gently.

"I wearied of town," replies he. "A strange acknowledgment for one like me, but true. For once, I honestly pined for the country—insipid as I have always deemed it—and craved unceasingly for something fresh, new, innocent, something unused to gas, and the glare and unholy glitter of a city."

He speaks bitterly—almost passionately—and as though for the moment he has altogether forgotten the existence of his companion. An instant later, however, he recovers himself.

"I felt I should be happier, more fitted to cope with my work, if I could get even one glimpse of you!"

"Are you not happy, then?" asks she, gently, her heart beating fast, her color growing and lessening rapidly.

"Happy? no. Can a man be happy while a perpetual doubt distracts him? Can he know even the meaning of the word Peace, whilst devoured with a fear that he shall never possess the one great good he desires?"

Again, his thoughts appear to wander; and some passion, not born of the present moment, but borrowed from some other hour, fills his tone.

"Yes," says Clarissa, nervously, questioningly, feeling poor in words, now that the great crisis of her life has come.

"So I am here," he goes on, softly, "to solve my doubt, to gain at least a rest from the gnawing suspense that for so long I have endured. Need I tell you that I love you?—that" (he pauses, and a faint contraction of the features, that dies almost as it is born, disfigures his face for a second)—
—"that you are the one woman in all the world upon whom I have set my heart?"

There is silence. For Clarissa, an intense joy holds her mute; the very intensity of her happiness checks the flow of speech. He, too, seems lost in thought. Presently, however, he breaks the silence, and this time a faint anxiety may be discernible in his voice, though his face is calm and composed, as usual.

"You do not speak, Clarissa. I have told you of my love, and you are silent. I now ask if you can love me? At least, give me an answer. Dearest,"—

glancing at her averted face, and seeing the shy blush that adds another charm to its beauty, — "tell me the truth."

"I can; I do love you!" says Clarissa, sweetly, and with perfect trust. She slips her hand into his. Raising his hat, he lifts the slender fingers to his lips, and kisses them; and, then, together—still hand in hand—they walk along, speechless, yet seemingly content.

The road is dusty; and a few drops of rain fall, like mild blessings, into its parched furrows. The roadside flowers, drooping and languid, fling their rich perfume, with lavish generosity, upon the motionless air. Some sheep, in a far-off meadow, bleat mournfully, and answer back the echo that mocks their lament.

"You have made me happier than I ever hoped to be; but you have not yet said you will marry me." The words come from Horace, but sound curiously far away, the very stillness and sadness of the evening rendering them more distant. Clarissa, glancing at him, can see he is white as Death.

"How pale he is!" she thinks, and then makes herself happy in the belief that he is terribly in earnest about this matter, and that his love for her is infinite.

"Yes, I shall marry you," she says, with tender seriousness. To her, this promise is a solemn bond, that nothing but death or falsehood can cancel.

"When?"

"Oh, Horace, I cannot answer that question so readily. There are so many things. Papa must be told; and James Scrope; and you must tell Dorian and your uncle."

"All that would hardly take half an hour."

"Perhaps; but there are other reasons for delay, more than I can tell you just now. And, besides, it is all so new, so strange." She smiles, as though she would willingly have added the words, "so sweet;" and a little happy far-away look creeps into and illumines her eyes. "Why are you so impatient?"

"Impatient!" returns he, a touch of vehemence in his tone. "Of course I am impatient. The sooner it is all got over the better." He checks himself, draws his breath somewhat quickly, and goes on in a calmer fashion: "What sort of a lover should I be, if I showed no anxiety to claim you as soon as possible? *You* should be the last to blame me for undue haste in this matter. When shall it be, then?—In one month? two? three?" He speaks again, almost excitedly.

"Oh, no, no," gently, but shrinking from him a little. "That would be impossible. Why, think!—it is only this moment you have told me you love me, and now you would have me name our wedding-day!"

"Not exactly that. But tell me some definite time, near at hand, to which I can be looking forward. Everything rests with you now, remember that." His last words convey an unconscious warning, but Clarissa neither heeds or understands it.

"Papa will miss me so terribly," she says, dreamily; "it seems selfish, almost as though I were wilfully deserting him. I should, at least, like another Christmas at home with him. And see,"—turning to him, with gentle earnestness,—"are we not quite happy as we now are, loving and trusting in each other? Why, then, should we not continue this present happiness for another year? You are silent, Horace! You do not answer! Are you angry with me?" She lays her hand lightly on his arm.

"No; not angry." His eyes are on the ground; and he takes no notice of the tender pressure on his arm. "But a year is a long time to wait! So many things may happen in twelve months; and deeds once done, forever leave their mark."

"Do not speak like that, it is as though you would foretell evil," says Clarissa, a faint feeling of superstitious horror making her nervous.

Branscombe, raising his head, regards her curiously.

"Why should there be evil to foretell?" he says, slowly. "And yet, Clarissa, I would ask you always to remember this hour, and the fact that it was you, not I, who wished the postponement of our marriage. If it must be as you say, it will be better to keep our engagement as quiet as possible; perfectly secret will indeed be best."

"Yes; if you wish it. That will please me, too. Only papa need know of it, and——James Scrope."

"And why Sir James?" with a scrutinizing gaze.

"Why?"—with some surprise. "Well, I suppose because papa and I never do anything important without telling him of it. He is quite our oldest friend. We should hardly get on now without Jim."

"Not so old, either. I hope, by and by, you will be able to manage without Sir James as a father-confessor."

"By and by I shall have you," says Clarissa, sweetly, with a smile and a soft blush.

"True! I wonder if you will find that sufficient? I doubt I'm half such a good fellow, Clarissa, as you believe me."

In which he comes nearer the truth than he ever came before.

"You are good enough for me," says Clarissa, with fond conviction. "Will you come with me as far as the vicarage? I must go there to-day, and the walk is such a pretty one, and," —with a little happy laugh, —"now you are quite my own property, I think I should like to make use of you. Look! there is Ruth Annersley standing at her gate. Good-morning, Ruth! What a charming day, is it not? after all yesterday's rain!"

Ruth—who, the moment before, had made a faint movement as though she would willingly have stepped behind the huge rose-bush nearest to her and so have escaped observation—comes slowly forward. She is pale; but the intense heat of the day makes itself felt by all, and has deprived even Miss Peyton's cheeks of some of their usual warmth. She accepts Clarissa's proffered hand, and smiles a faint welcome. But when Horace would, too, have shaken hands with her, she declines to see his meaning, and, bowing slightly, turns aside to listen to his companion's words.

"Were you raking your walks?" asks Clarissa, idly, leaning on the gate, and gazing down the trim-gravelled path that leads to the ivy-clad cottage beyond. "Nobody's walks are ever as clean as yours, I think. And your roses are something too delicious, far better than our out-door flowers at Gowran. And so late in the season, too!"

"May I give you one?" says Ruth, dimpling prettily at her praise.

"Thank you. How sweet they are! No, no, Horace, that is altogether too large for your coat. Ruth, will you give Mr. Branscombe a tiny bud? That one over there, for instance."

"I don't think I see it," says Ruth, quietly. She has grown pale again, and her lips have lost a little of the childish petulant pout that characterizes them.

"Just over there. Don't you see? Why, you are almost looking at it, you stupid child."

"I am stupid, I am afraid," —with a faint smile. "Come in, Miss Peyton, and gather it yourself." She opens the gate, with a sort of determination in her manner, and Clarissa, going up to the rose-tree, plucks the delicate blossom in dispute. Horace has followed her inside the gate, but, turning rather to the left, falls apparently in love with an artless white rose-bud that waves gently to and fro upon its stem, as though eager to attract and rivet admiration.

"I think I prefer this flower, after all," he says, lightly. "May I ask you to give it to me, Ruth?" His manner is quite easy, very nearly indifferent, and his back is turned to Clarissa. But his eyes are on Ruth; and the girl, though with open reluctance and ill-repressed defiance, is compelled to pick the white rose and give it to him.

"Well, I really don't think you have shown very good taste," says Clarissa, examining the two flowers. "Mine is the most perfect. Nevertheless, I suppose wilful man must have his way. Let me settle it in your coat for you."

Almost as she speaks, the flower drops accidentally from her fingers; and, both she and Horace making a step forward to recover it, by some awkward chance they tread on it, and crush the poor, frail little thing out of all shape. It lies upon the gravel, broken and disfigured, yet very sweet in death.

"You trod on it," says Horace, rather quickly, to Clarissa.

"No, dear; I really think—indeed I am sure—it was you," returns she, calmly, but with conviction.

"It doesn't matter: it was hardly worth a discussion," says Ruth, with an odd laugh. "See how poor a thing it looks now; and, yet, a moment since it was happy on its tree."

"Never mind, Horace: this is really a charming little bud," says Clarissa, gayly, holding out the rose of her own choosing: "at least you must try to be content with it. Good-by, Ruth; come up to Gowran some day soon, and take those books you asked for the other day."

"Thank you, Miss Peyton. I shall come soon."

"Good-by," says Horace.

"Good-by," returns she. But it is to Clarissa, not to him, she addresses the word of farewell.

When the mill has been left some distance behind them, and Ruth's slight figure, clad in its white gown, has ceased to be a fleck of coloring in the landscape, Clarissa says, thoughtfully,—

"What a pretty girl that is, and how refined! Quite a little lady in manner; so calm, and so collected,—cold, almost. I know many girls, irreproachably born, not to be compared with her, in my opinion. You agree with me?"

"Birth is not always to be depended upon nowadays."

"She is so quiet, too, and so retiring. She would not even shake hands with you, when we met her, though you wanted her to. Did you remark that?"

"Sometimes I am dull about trifles, such as that."

"Yes. By the by, she did not seem surprised at seeing you here to-day, although she thought you safe in town, as we all did,—you deceitful boy."

"Did she not?"

"No. But then, of course, it was a matter of indifference to her."

"Of course."

They have reached the entrance to the vicarage by this time, and are pausing to say farewell for a few hours.

"I shall come up to Gowran to-morrow morning first thing, and speak to your father: is that what you will wish me to do?" asks Horace, her hand in his.

"Yes. But, Horace," looking at him earnestly, "I think I should like to tell it all to papa myself first, this evening."

"Very well, dearest. Do whatever makes you happiest," returns he, secretly pleased that the ice will be broken for him before his prepares for his *mauvais quart-d'heure* in the library. "And if he should refuse his consent, Clarissa, what then? You know you might make so much a better marriage."

"Might I?"—tenderly. "I don't think so; and papa would not make me unhappy."

CHAPTER IX

"A generous friendship no cold medium knows." —Pope.

Mrs. Redmond is sitting on a centre ottoman, darning stockings. This is her favorite pastime, and never fails her. When she isn't darning stockings, she is always scolding the cook, and as her voice, when raised, is not mellifluous, her family, in a body, regard the work-basket with reverential affection, and present it to her notice when there comes the crash of broken china from the lower regions, or when the cold meat has been unfairly dealt with.

She is of the lean cadaverous order of womankind, and is bony to the last degree. Her nose is aquiline, and, as a rule, pale blue. As this last color might also describe her eyes, there is a depressing want of contrast about her face. Her lips are thin and querulous, and her hair—well, she hasn't any hair, but her wig is flaxen.

As Clarissa enters, she hastily draws the stocking from her hand, and rises to greet her. A faint blush mantles in her cheek, making one at once understand that in by-gone days she had probably been considered pretty.

"So unexpected, my dear Clarissa," she says, with as pleased a smile as the poor thing ever conjures up, and a little weakness at the knees, meant for a courtesy. "So very glad to see you," —as, indeed, she is.

In her earlier days she had been called a belle, —by her own people, — and had been expected, accordingly, to draw a prize in the marriage-market. But Penelope Proude had failed them, and, by so doing, had brought down eternal condemnation on her head. In her second season she had fallen foolishly but honestly in love with a well-born but impecunious curate, and had married him in spite of threats and withering sneers. With one consent her family cast her off and consigned her to her fate, declaring themselves incapable of dealing with a woman who could wilfully marry a man possessed of nothing. They always put a capital N to this word, and perhaps they were right, as at that time all Charlie Redmond could call his own was seven younger brothers and a tenor voice of the very purest.

As years rolled on, though Mrs. Redmond never, perhaps, regretted her marriage, she nevertheless secretly acknowledged to herself a hankering after the old life, a longing for the grandeur and riches that accrued to it (the Proudes for generations had been born and bred and had thriven in the soft goods line), and hugged the demoralizing thought to her bosom that a little more trade and a little less blue blood would have made her husband a degree more perfect.

It pleased her when the county families invited the youthful Cissy to their balls; and it warmed her heart and caused her to forget the daily shifts and worries of life when the duchess sent her fruit and game, accompanied by kind little notes. It above all things reconciled her to her lot, when the heiress of Gowran Grange pulled up her pretty ponies at her door, and running in, made much of her and her children, and listened attentively to her grievances, as only a sympathetic nature can.

To-day, Clarissa's visit, being early, and therefore unconventional, and for that reason the more friendly, sweetens all her surroundings. Miss Peyton might have put in an appearance thrice in the day later on, yet her visits would not have been viewed with such favor as is this matutinal call.

"Cissy is out: she has gone to the village," says Mrs. Redmond, scarcely thinking Clarissa has come all the way from Gowran to spend an hour alone with her.

"I am sorry: but it is you I most particularly wanted to see. What a delicious day it is! I walked all the way from Gowran, and the sun was rather too much for me; but how cool it always is here! This room never seems stuffy or over-heated, as other rooms do."

"It is a wretched place, quite wretched," says Mrs. Redmond, with a depreciating glance directed at a distant sofa that might indeed be termed patriarchal.

"What are you doing?" asks Clarissa, promptly, feeling she cannot with any dignity defend the sofa. "Darning? Why can't I help you?—I am sure I could darn. Oh, what a quantity of socks! Are they all broken?" looking with awe upon the overflowing basket that lies close to Mrs. Redmond's feet.

"Every one of them," replies that matron, with unction. "I can't think how they do it, but I assure you they never come out of the wash without innumerable tears." Whether she is alluding, in her graceful fashion, to her children or their socks, seems at present doubtful. "I sometimes fancy they must take their boots off and dance on the sharp pebbles to bring them to such a pass; but they say they don't. Yet how to account for this?" She holds up one bony hand, decorated with a faded sock, in a somewhat triumphant fashion, and lets three emaciated fingers start to life through the toe of it.

"Do let me help you," says Clarissa, with entreaty, and, stooping to the basket, she rummages there until she produces a needle, a thimble, and some thread. "I dare say I shall get on splendidly, if you will just give me a hint now and then and tell me when I am stitching them up too tightly."

This hardly sounds promising, but Mrs. Redmond heeds her not.

"My dear, pray do not trouble yourself with such uninteresting work," she says, hastily. "It really makes me unhappy to see you so employed; and that sock of all others, — it is Bobby's, and I'm sure there must be something wrong with his heels. If you insist on helping me, do try another."

"No, I shall stitch up Bobby, or die in the attempt," says Miss Peyton, valiantly. "It is quite nice work, I should think, and so easy. I dare say after a time I should love it."

"Should you?" says Mrs. Redmond. "Well, perhaps; but for myself, I assure you, though no one will believe it, I abhor the occupation. There are moments when it almost overcomes me, — the perpetual in and out of the needle, you will understand, — it seems so endless. Dear, dear, there was a time when I was never obliged to do such menial services, when I had numerous dependants to wait on me to do my bidding But then" — with a deep sigh, that sounds like a blast from Boreas — "I married the vicar."

"And quite right, too," says Clarissa, with a cheerful little nod, seeing Mrs. Redmond has mounted her high horse and intends riding him to the death. "I myself shouldn't hesitate about it, if I only got the chance. And indeed where could any one get a more charming husband than the dear vicar."

"Well, well, it was a foolish match notwithstanding," says Mrs. Redmond, with a smile and a wan sort of blush; "though certainly at that time I don't deny he was very fascinating. Such a voice, my dear! and then his eyes were remarkably fine."

"'Were' — *are*, you mean," says the crafty Clarissa, knowing that praise of her husband is sweet to the soul of the faded Penelope, and that the surest means of reducing her to a pliant mood is to permit her to maunder on uninterruptedly about past glories, and dead hours rendered bright by age. To have her in her kindest humor, before mentioning the real object of her visit, must be managed, at all risks. "Yours was a love-match, wasn't it?" she says, coaxingly. "Do tell me all about it." (She has listened patiently to every word of it about a hundred times before.) "I do so like a real love-affair."

"There isn't much to tell," says Mrs. Redmond, who is quite delighted, and actually foregoes the charm of darning, that she may the more correctly remember each interesting detail in her own "old story;" "but it was all very sudden,—very; like a tornado, or a whirlwind, or those things in the desert that cover one up in a moment. First we met at two croquet-parties,—yes, two,—and then at a dinner at the Ramseys, and it was at the dinner at the Ramseys' that he first pressed my hand. I thought, my dear, I should have dropped, it was such a downright, not-to-be-got-over sort of squeeze. Dear me, I can almost feel it now," says Mrs. Redmond, who is blushing like a girl.

"Yes. Do go on," says Clarissa, who, in reality, is enjoying herself, intensely.

"Well, then, two days afterwards, to my surprise, he called with some tickets for a concert, to which my mamma, who suspected nothing, took me. There we met again, and it was there, right, as one might say, under mamma's nose, he proposed to me. He was very eloquent, though he was obliged to speak rather disconnectedly, owing to the music stopping now and then and my mamma being of a suspicious turn: but he was young in those days, my dear, and well favored, no doubt. So we got married."

"That is the proper ending to all pretty stories. But is it true," says Clarissa, with a wiliness really horrible in one so young, "that just at that time you refused a splendid offer, all for the vicar's sake?"

"Splendid is a long word," says Mrs. Redmond, trying to speak carelessly, but unmistakably elated, "yet I must confess there is some truth in the report to which you allude. Sir Hubert Fitz-Hubert was a baronet of very ancient lineage, came over with the Conqueror, or King Alfred, I quite forget which, but it was whichever was the oldest: that I know. He was, in fact, a trifle old for me, perhaps, and not so rich as others I have known, but still a baronet. He proposed to me, but I rejected him upon the spot with scorn, though he went on his knees to me, and swore in an anguished frenzy, that he would cut his throat with his razor if I refused to listen to his suit! I did refuse, but I heard nothing more about the razor. I am willing to believe he put some restraint upon his maddened feelings, and refrained from inflicting any injury upon himself."

"Poor fellow!" says Clarissa, in a suspiciously choky tone.

"Then I espoused the vicar," says Mrs. Redmond, with a sentimental sigh. "One does foolish things sometimes."

"That, now, was a wise one. I would not marry a king if I loved a beggar. Altogether, you behaved beautifully, and just like a novel."

Feeling that the moment for action has arrived, as Mrs. Redmond is now in a glow of pride and vanity well mixed, Clarissa goes on sweetly:

"I have some news for you."

"For me?"

"Yes, for you. I know how delicate you are, and how unable to manage those two strong children you have at home. And I know, too, you have been looking out for a suitable governess for some time, but you have found a difficulty in choosing one, have you not?"

"Indeed I have."

"Well, I think I know some who will just suit you. She was at school with me, and, though poor now, having lost both father and mother, is of very good family, and well connected."

"But the salary?" says Mrs. Redmond, with some hesitation. "The salary is the thing. I hear of no one now who will come for less than sixty or seventy pounds a year at the lowest; and with Henry at school, and Rupert's college expenses, forty pounds is as much as we can afford to give."

"Miss Broughton will, I think, be quite content with that: she only wants to be happy, and at rest, and she will be all that with you and Cissy and Mr. Redmond. She is young, and it is her first trial, but she is very clever: she has a really lovely voice, and paints excessively well. Ethel has rather a taste for painting, has she not?"

"A decided talent for it. All my family were remarkable for their artistic tendencies, so she, doubtless, inherits it; and—yes, of course, it would be a great thing for her to have some one on the spot to develop this talent, and train it. Your friend, you say, is well connected?"

"Very highly connected, on her mother's side. Her father was a lieutenant in the navy, and very respectable too, I believe; though I know nothing of him."

"That she should be a lady is, of course, indispensable," says Mrs. Redmond, with all the pride that ought to belong to softgoods people. "I need hardly say *that*, I think. But why does she not appeal for help to her mother's relations?"

"Because she prefers honest work to begging from those who up to this have taken no notice of her."

"I admire her," says Mrs. Redmond, warmly. "If you think she will be satisfied with forty pounds, I should like to try what she could do with the children."

"I am very glad you have so decided. I know no place in which I would rather see a friend of mine than here."

"Thank you, my dear. Then will you write to her, or shall I?"

"Let me write to her first, if you don't mind: I think I can settle everything."

"Mind?—no, indeed: it is only too good of you to take so much trouble about me."

To which Clarissa says, prettily,—

"Do not put it in that light: there is no pleasure so keen as that of being able to help one's friends."

Then she rises, and, having left behind her three socks that no earthly power can ever again draw upon a child's foot, so hopelessly has she brought heel and sole together, she says good-by to Mrs. Redmond, and leaves the room.

Outside on the avenue she encounters the vicar, hurrying home.

"Turn with me," she says, putting her hand through his arm. "I have something to say to you."

"Going to be married?" asks he, gayly.

"Nonsense!"—blushing, in that he has so closely hit the mark. "It is not of anything so paltry I would unburden my mind."

"Then you have nothing of importance to tell me," says the vicar; "and I must go. Your story will keep: my work will not. I am in a great hurry: old Betty Martin——"

"Must wait. I insist on it. Dying! nonsense! she has been dying every week for three years, and you believe her every time. Come as far as the gate with me."

"You command, I obey," says the vicar, with a sigh of resignation, walking on beside his pet parishioner. "But if you could only understand the trouble I am in with those Batesons you would know some pity for me."

"What! again?" says Clarissa, showing, and feeling, deep compassion.

"Even so. This time about the bread. You know what unpleasant bread they bake, and how Mrs. Redmond objects to it; and really it *is* bad for the children."

"It is poison," says Clarissa, who never does anything by halves, and who is nothing if not sympathetic.

"Well so I said; and when I had expostulated with them, mildly but firmly, and suggested that better flour might make better dough, and they had declined to take any notice of my protest,—why, I just ordered my bread from the Burtons opposite, and——"

The vicar pauses.

"And you have been happy ever since?"

"Well, yes, my dear. I suppose in a way I have; that is, I have ceased to miss the inevitable breakfast-lecture on the darkness and coarseness of the bread; but I have hardly gained on other points, and the Batesons are a perpetual scourge. They have decided on never again 'darkening the church door' (their own words, my dear Clarissa), because I have taken the vicarage custom from them. They prefer imperilling their souls to giving up the chance of punishing me. And now the question is, whether I should not consent to the slow poisoning of my children, rather than drive my parishioners into the arms of the Methodists, who keep open house for all comers below the hill."

"I don't think I should poison the children," says Clarissa.

"But what is to become of my choir? Charlotte Bateson has the sweetest voice in it, and now she will not come to church. I am at my wits' end when I think of it all."

"I am going to supply Charlotte's place for you," says Clarissa, slyly.

"Thank you, my dear. But, you see, you would never be in time. And, unfortunately, the services must begin always at a regular hour. Punctuality was the one thing I never could teach you,—that, and the Catechism."

"What a libel!" says Clarissa. "I shouldn't malign my own teaching if I were you. I am perfectly certain I could say it all now, this very moment, from start to finish, questions and all, without a mistake. Shall I?"

"No, no. I'll take your word for it," says the vicar, hastily. "The fact is, I have just been listening to it at the morning school in the village, and when one has heard a thing repeated fourteen times with variations, one naturally is not ambitious of hearing it again, no matter how profitable it may be."

"When I spoke of filling Charlotte's place," says Clarissa, "I did not allude in any way to myself, but to——And now I am coming to my news."

"So glad!" says the vicar; "I may overtake old Betty yet."

"I have secured a governess for Mrs. Redmond. Such a dear little governess! And I want you to promise me to be more than usually kind to her, because she is young and friendless and it is her first effort at teaching."

"So that question is settled at last," says the vicar, with a deep—if carefully suppressed—sigh of relief. "I am rejoiced, if only for my wife's sake, who has been worrying herself for weeks past, trying to replace the inestimable—if somewhat depressing—Miss Prood."

"Has she?" says Clarissa, kindly. "Worry is a bad thing. But to-day Mrs. Redmond seems much better than she has been for a long time. Indeed, she said so."

"Did she?" says the vicar, with a comical, transient smile, Mrs. Redmond's maladies being of the purely imaginary order.

"What are you laughing at now?" asks Clarissa, who has marked this passing gleam of amusement.

"At you, my dear, you are so quaintly humorous," replies he. "But go on: tell me of this new acquisition to our household. Is she a friend of yours?"

"Yes, a great friend."

"Then of course we shall like her."

"Thank you," says Clarissa. "She is very pretty, and very charming. Perhaps, after all, I am doing a foolish thing for myself. How shall I feel when she has cut me out at the vicarage?"

"Not much fear of that, were she Aphrodite herself. You are much too good a child to be liked lightly or by halves. Well, good-by: you won't forget about the flannel for the Batley twins?"

"I have it ready,—at least, half of it. How could I tell she was going to have twins," says Clarissa, apologetically.

"It certainly was very inconsiderate of her," says the vicar, with a sigh, as he thinks of the poverty that clings to the Batley *ménage* from year's end to year's end.

"Well, never mind; she shall have it all next week," promises Clarissa, soothingly, marking his regretful tone; and then she bids him farewell, and goes up the road again in the direction of her home.

She is glad to be alone at last. Her mission successfully accomplished, she has now time to let her heart rest contentedly upon her own happiness. All the events of the morning—the smallest word, the lightest intonation, the most passing smile, that claimed Horace as their father—are remembered by her. She dwells fondly on each separate remembrance, and repeats to herself how he looked and spoke at such-and-such moments.

She is happy, quite happy. A sort of wonder, too, mixes with her delight. Only a few short hours ago she had left her home, free, unbetrothed, with only hope to sustain her, and now she is returning to it with her hope a certainty,—bound, heart and soul, to the dearest, truest man on earth, as she believes.

How well he loves her! She had noticed his sudden paling when she had begged for some delay before actually naming her "brydale day." She had hardly believed his love for her was so strong, so earnest: even she (how *could* she? with tender self-reproach) had misjudged him, had deemed him somewhat cold, indifferent; unknowing of the deep stratum of feeling that lay beneath the outward calm of his demeanor.

Dear, dearest Horace! She will never disbelieve in him again; he is her own now, her very own, and she loves him with all her heart, and he loves just the same, and— —Oh, if every woman in the world could only be as happy as she is to-day, what a glorious place it would be!

Not that it is such a bad place, by any means, as some people would lead one to imagine. Surely these are disagreeable people, misanthropists, misogamists, and such like heretics; or else, poor souls! they are in a bad strait, without present hope and without any one to love them! This last seems, indeed, a misfortune.

Yet why abuse a lovely world? How bright the day is, how sweet and fresh the air, though evening is nigh at hand! She hardly ever remembers a September so fine, So free from damp; the very birds— —

Had he thought her unloving or capricious when she pleaded for a longer engagement? (Here the tears rise unbidden in her eyes.) Oh, surely not; he understood her thoroughly; for had he not smiled upon her afterwards?

So he will always smile. There shall never be any cross words or angry frowns to chill their perfect love! Their lives will be a summer dream, a golden legend, a pure, fond idyl.

Thus beguiling time with beliefs too sweet for earthly power to grant, she hastens home, with each step building up another story in her airy house, until at length she carries a castle, tall and stately, into her father's house.

CHAPTER X

"I have no other but a woman's reason:
I think him so, because I think him so." —Shakespeare.

"Where is papa?" she asks, meeting one of the servants in the hall. Hearing he is out, and will not be back for some time, she, too, turns again to the open door, and, as though the house is too small to contain all the thoughts that throng her breast, she walks out into the air again, and passes into the garden, where autumn, though kindly and slow in its advances, is touching everything with the hand of death.

"Heavily hangs the broad sunflower
Over its grave i' the earth so chilly;
Heavily hangs the hollyhock,
Heavily hangs the tiger lily."

With a sigh she quits her beloved garden, and wanders still! farther abroad into the deep woods that "have put their glory on," and are dressed in tender russets, and sad greens, and fading tints, that meet and melt into each other.

The dry leaves are falling, and lie crackling under foot. The daylight is fading, softly, imperceptibly, but surely. There is yet a glow from the departing sunlight, that, sinking lazily beyond the distant hills, tinges with gold the browning earth that in her shroud of leaves is lying.

But death, or pain, or sorrow, has no part with Clarissa to-day. She is quite happy,—utterly content. She marks not the dying of the year, but rather the beauty of the sunset. She heeds not the sullen roar of the ever-increasing streamlets, that winter will swell into small but angry rivers; hearing only the songs of the sleepy birds as they croon their night-songs in the boughs above her.

When an hour has passed, and twilight has come up and darkened all the land, she goes back again to her home, and, reaching the library, looks in, to find her father sitting there, engrossed as usual with some book, which he is carefully annotating as he reads.

"Are you very busy?" asks she, coming slowly up to him. "I want to be with you for a little while."

"That is right. I am never too busy to talk to you. Why, it is quite an age since last I saw you!—not since breakfast; where have you been all day?"

"You are a pet," says Miss Peyton, in a loving whisper, rubbing her cheek tenderly against his, as a reward for his pretty speech. "I have been at the vicarage, and have pleaded Georgie's cause so successfully that I have won it; and have made them half in love with her already."

"A special pleader indeed. Diplomacy is your forte: you should keep to it."

"I mean to. I shouldn't plead in vain with you, should I?" She has grown somewhat earnest.

"Oh! with me!" says her father, with much self-contempt; "I have given up all that sort of thing, long ago. I know how much too much you are for me, and I am too wise to swim against the tide. Only I would entreat you to be merciful as you are strong."

"What a lot of nonsense you do talk, you silly boy!" says Clarissa, who is still leaning over his chair in such a position that he cannot see her face. Perhaps, could he have seen it, he might have noticed how pale it is beyond its wont. "Well, the Redmonds seemed quite pleased, and I shall write to Georgie to-morrow. It will be nice for her to be here, near me. It may keep her from being lonely and unhappy."

"Well, it ought," says George Peyton. "What did the vicar say?"

"The vicar always says just what I say," replies she, a trifle saucily, and with a quick smile.

"Poor man! his is the common lot," says her father; and then, believing she has said all she wants to say, and being filled with a desire to return to his book and his notes, he goes on: "So that was the weighty matter you wanted to discuss, eh? Is that all your news?"

"Not quite," returns she, in a low tone.

"No? You are rich in conversation this evening. Who is it we are now to criticise?"

"The person you love best,—I hope."

"Why, that will be you," says George Peyton.

"You are sure?" says Clarissa, a little tremulously; and then her father turns in his chair and tries to read her face.

"No; stay just as you are; I can tell you better if you do not look at me," she whispers, entreatingly, moving him with her hands back to his former position.

"What is it, Clarissa?" he asks, hastily, though he is far from suspecting the truth. Some faint thought of James Scrope (why he knows not) comes to him at this moment, and not unpleasingly. "Tell me, darling. Anything that concerns you must, of necessity, concern me also."

"Yes, I am glad I know that," she says, speaking with some difficulty, but very earnestly. "To-day I met Horace Branscombe."

"Yes?" His face changes a little, from vague expectancy to distinct disappointment; but then she cannot see his face.

"And he asked me to be his wife—and—I said, Yes—if—if it pleases you, papa."

It is over. The dreaded announcement is made. The words that have cost her so much to utter have gone out into the air; and yet there is no answer!

For a full minute silence reigns, and then Clarissa lays her hand imploringly upon her father's shoulder. He is looking straight before him, his expression troubled and grave, his mouth compressed.

"Speak to me," says Clarissa, entreatingly.

After this he does speak.

"I wish it had been Dorian," he says, impulsively.

Then she takes her hand from his shoulder, as though it can no longer rest there in comfort, and her eyes fill with disappointed tears.

"Why do you say that?" she asks, with some vehemence. "It sounds as if—as if you undervalued Horace! Yet what reason have you for doing so? What do you know against him?"

"Nothing, literally nothing," answers Mr. Peyton, soothingly, yet with a plaintive ring in his voice that might suggest the idea of his being sorry that such answer must be made. "I am sure Horace is very much to be liked."

"How you say that!"—reproachfully. "It sounds untrue! Yet it can't be. What could any one say against Horace?"

"My dear, I said nothing."

"No, but you insinuated it. You said Dorian was his superior."

"Well, I think he is the better man of the two," said Mr. Peyton, desperately, hardly knowing what to say, and feeling sorely aggrieved in that he is compelled to say what must hurt her.

"I cannot understand you; you said you know nothing prejudicial to Horace (it is impossible you should), and yet you think Dorian the better man. If he has done no wrong, why should any one be a better man? Why draw the comparison at all? For the first time in all your life, you are unjust."

"No, Clarissa, I am not. At least, I think not. Injustice is a vile thing. But, somehow, Sartoris and I had both made up our minds that you would marry Dorian, and——"

He pauses.

"Then your only objection to poor Horace is that he is not Dorian?" asks she, anxiously, letting her hand once more rest upon his shoulder.

"Well, no doubt there is a great deal in that," returns he, evasively, hard put to it to answer his inquisitor with discretion.

"And if Dorian had never been, Horace would be the one person in all the world you would desire for me?" pursues she, earnestly.

George Peyton makes no reply to this,—perhaps because he has not one ready. Clarissa, stepping back, draws her breath a little quickly, and a dark fire kindles in her eyes. In her eyes, too, large tears rise and shine.

"It is because he is poor," she says, in a low tone, that has some contempt in it, and some passionate disappointment.

"Do not mistake me," says her father, speaking hastily, but with dignity. Rising, he pushes back his chair, and turning, faces her in the gathering twilight. "Were he the poorest man alive, and you loved him, and he was worthy of you, I would give you to him without a murmur. Not that"—hurriedly—"I consider Horace unworthy of you, but the idea is new, strange, and——the other day, Clarissa, you were a child."

"I am your child still,—always." She is sitting on his knee now, with her arms round his neck, and her cheek against his; and he is holding her *svelte* lissome figure very closely to him. She is the one thing he has to love on earth; and just now she seems unspeakably—almost painfully—dear to him.

"Always, my dear," he reiterates, somewhat unsteadily.

"You have seen so little of Horace lately," she goes on, presently, trying to find some comfortable reason for what seems to her her father's extraordinary blindness to her lover's virtues. "When you see a great deal of him, you will love him! As it is, darling, do—*do* say you like him very much, or you will break my heart!"

"I like him very much," replies he, obediently, repeating his lesson methodically, while feeling all the time that he is being compelled to say something against his will, without exactly knowing why he should feel so.

"And you are quite pleased that I am going to marry him?" reading his face with her clear eyes; she is very pale, and strangely nervous.

"My darling, my one thought is for your happiness." There is evasion mixed with the affection in this speech; and Clarissa notices it.

"No: say you are glad I am going to marry him," she says, remorselessly.

"How can you expect me to say that," exclaims he, mournfully, "when you know your wedding-day must part us?"

"Indeed it never shall!" cries she, vehemently; and then, overcome by the emotion of the past hour, and indeed of the whole day, she gives way and bursts into tears. "Papa, how can you say that? To be parted from you! We must be the same to each other always: my wedding-day would be a miserable one indeed if it separated me from you."

Then he comforts her, fondly caressing the pretty brown head that lies upon his heart, as it had lain in past years, when the slender girl of to-day was a little lisping motherless child. He calls her by all the endearing names he had used to her then, until her sobs cease, and only a sigh, now and again, tells of the storm just past.

"When is it to be?" he asks her, after a little while. "Not too soon, my pet, I hope?"

"Not for a whole year. He said something about November, but I could not leave you in such a hurry. We must have one more Christmas all to ourselves."

"You thought of that," he says, tenderly. "Oh, Clarissa, I hope this thing is for your good. Think of it seriously, earnestly, while you have time. Do not rush blindly into a compact that must be binding on you all your life."

"I hope it *will be* for all my life," returns she, gravely. "To be parted from Horace would be the worst thing that could befall me. Always remember that, papa. I am bound to him with all my heart and soul."

"So be it!" says George Peyton, solemnly. A sigh escapes him.

For some time neither speaks. The twilight is giving place to deeper gloom, the night is fast approaching, yet they do not stir. What the girl's thoughts may be at this moment, who can say? As for her father, he is motionless, except that his lips move, though no sound comes from them. He is secretly praying, perhaps, for the welfare of his only child, to her mother in heaven, who at this time must surely be looking down upon her with tenderest solicitude. Clarissa puts her lips softly to his cheek.

"Our engagement will be such a long one, that we think—"

"Yes?"

"We should like it keep it secret. You will say nothing about it to any one?"

"Not until you give me leave. You have acted wisely, I think, in putting off your marriage for a while." Almost unconsciously he is telling himself how time changes all things, and how many plans and affections can be altered in twelve months.

"But surely you will tell James Scrope," he goes on, after a while: "that will not be making it public. He has known you and been fond of you ever since you were a baby; and it seems uncivil and unfriendly to keep him in the dark."

"Then tell him; but no one else now, papa. I quite arranged for James, he is such an old friend, and so nice in every way."

Here she smiles involuntarily, and, after a little bit, laughs outright, in spite of herself, as though at some ridiculous recollection.

"Do you know," she says, "when I told Horace I thought I should like Sir James to know of our engagement, I really think he felt a little jealous! At least, he didn't half like it. How absurd!—wasn't it? Fancy being jealous of dear old Jim?"

"Old!—old! He is a long way off that. Why, all you silly little girls think a man past twenty-nine to be hovering on the brink of the grave. He can not be more than thirty-three, or so."

"He is very dreadfully old, for all that," says Miss Peyton, wilfully. "He is positively ancient; I never knew any one so old. He is so profound, and earnest, and serious, and——"

"What on earth has he done to you, that you should call him all these terrible names?" says Mr. Peyton, laughing.

"He scolds me," says Clarissa, "he lectures me, and tells me I should have an aim in life. You have been my aim, darling, and I have been very devoted to it, haven't I?"

"You have, indeed. But now I shall be out in the cold, of course." His tone is somewhat wistful. "That is all one gains by lavishing one's affection upon a pretty child and centring one's every thought and hope upon her."

"No, you are wrong there; it must be something to gain love that will last for ever." She tightens her arm around his neck. "What a horrid little speech! I could almost fancy James dictated it to you. He is a sceptic, an unbeliever, and you have imbibed his notions. Cynical people are a bore. You wouldn't, for example, have me fall in love with James, would you?"

"Indeed I would," says George Peyton, boldly. "He is just the one man I would choose for you,—'not Launcelot, nor another.' He is so genuine, so thorough in every way. And then the estates join, and that. I really wish you had fallen in love with Scrope."

"I love you dearly,—dearly," says Miss Peyton; "but you are a dreadful goose! James is the very last man to grow sentimental about any one,— least of all, me. He thinks me of no account at all, and tells me so in very polite language occasionally. So you see what a fatal thing it would have been if I had given my heart to him. He would have broken it, and I should have died, and you would have put up a touching, and elaborate tablet to my memory, and somebody would have planted snowdrops on my grave. There would have been a tragedy in Pullingham, with Jim for its hero."

"You take a different view of the case from mine. I believe there would have been no broken heart, and no early grave, and you would have been happy ever after."

"That is a more comfortable theory, certainly for *me*. But think what a miserable life *he* would have had with me forever by his side."

"A very perfect life, I think," says Mr. Peyton, looking with pardonable pride upon the half-earnest, half-laughing, and wholly lovely face so near him. "I don't know what more a fellow could expect."

"You see I was right. I said you were a goose," says Miss Peyton, irreverently. But she pats his hand, in the very sweetest manner possible, as she says it. Then she goes on:

"Horace said he would come up to-morrow to speak to you."

"Very well, dear. That is the usual thing, I suppose. I hope he won't be long-winded, or lachrymose, or anything that way. When a thing is done it is done, and discussion is so unnecessary."

"Promise me to be very, very kind to him."

"I shan't eat him, if you mean that," says Mr. Peyton, half irritably. "What do you think I am going to say to him? 'Is thy father an ogre, that he should do this thing?' But have you quite made up your mind to this step? Remember there will be no undoing it."

"I know that; but I feel no fear." She has grown pale again. "I love him. How should I know regret when with him? I believe in him, and trust him; and I know he is worthy of all my trust."

Mr. Peyton sighs. Some words come to his memory, and he repeats them, — slowly, beneath his breath, —

"There are no tricks in plain and simple faith!"

Truly, her faith is pure and simple, and free from thought of guile.

"I wonder what James Scrope will say to it all?" he says, presently.

"He never says very much on any subject, does he? If you are going over to the Hall, will you tell him about it?"

"No; tell him yourself," says her father, in a curious tone.

"There is the dressing bell," says Clarissa getting up lazily. "I don't feel a bit like eating my dinner, do you know?"

"Nonsense! The love-sick *rôle* won't suit you. And people who don't eat dinner get pale, and lose all their pretty looks. Run away, now, and don't be long. I feel it would be injudicious to put cook into a tantrum again to-night, after last night's explosion. So go and make yourself lovely."

"I'll do my best," says Clarissa, modestly.

CHAPTER XI

"I cannot but remember such things were,
That were most precious to me.

Oh! I could play the woman with mine eyes." —*Macbeth*.

"To tell him herself" has some strange attraction for Clarissa. To hear face to face, what this her oldest friend will say to her engagement with Horace is a matter of great anxiety to her. She will know at once by his eyes and smile whether he approves or disapproves her choice.

Driving along the road to Scrope, behind her pretty ponies, "Cakes" and "Ale," with her little rough Irish terrier, "Secretary Bill," sitting bolt upright beside her, as solemn as half a dozen judges, she wonders anxiously how she shall begin to tell James about it.

She hopes to goodness he won't be in his ultra-grave mood, that, as a rule, leads up to his finding fault with everything, and picking things to pieces, and generally condemning the sound judgment of others. (As a rule, Clarissa is a little unfair in her secret comments on James Scrope's character.) It will be so much better if she can only come upon him out of doors, in his homeliest mood, with a cigar between his lips, or his pipe. Yes, his pipe will be even better. Men are even more genial with a pipe than with the goodliest habana.

Well, of course, if he is the great friend he *professes* to be,—heavy emphasis on the verb, and a little flick on the whip on "Cakes's" quarters, which the spirited but docile creature resents bitterly,—he must be glad at the thought that she is not going to leave the country,—is, in fact, very likely to spend most of her time still in Pullingham.

Not all of it, of course. Horace has duties, and though in her secret soul she detests town life, still there is a joy In the thought that she will be with him, helping him, encouraging him in his work, rejoicing in his successes, sympathyzing with his fai— —, but no, of course there will be no failures! How stupid of her to think of that, when he is so clever, so learned, so— —

Yet it would be sweet, too, to have him fail once or twice (just a little, insignificant, not-worth-speaking-about sort of a defeat), if only to let him see how she could love him even the more for it.

She blushes, and smiles to herself, and, turning suddenly, bestows a most unexpected caress upon "Secretary Bill," who wags his short tail in return—that is, what they left him of it—lovingly, if somewhat anxiously, and glances at her sideways out of his wonderful eyes, as though desirous of assuring himself of her sanity.

Oh, yes, of course James will be delighted. And he will tell her so with the gentle smile that so lights up his face, and he will take her hand, and say he is so glad, so pleased, and——

With a sharp pang she remembers how her father was neither pleased nor glad when she confided her secret to him. He had been, indeed, distressed and confounded. He had certainly tried his hardest to conceal from her these facts, but she had seen them all the same. She could not be deceived where her father was concerned. He had felt unmistakable regret——"Be quiet, Bill! You sha'n't come out driving again if you can't sit still! What a bore a dog is sometimes!"

Well, after all, he is her father. It is only natural he should dislike the thought of parting from her. She thinks, with an instant softening of her heart, of how necessary she has become to him, ever since her final return home. Before that he had been dull and *distrait*; now he is bright and cheerful, if still rather too devoted to his books to be quite good for him.

He might, indeed, be forgiven for regarding the man who should take her from him as an enemy. But Jim is different; he is a mere friend,—a dear and valued one, it is true, but still only a friend,—a being utterly independent of her, who can be perfectly happy without her, and therefore, of course, unprejudiced.

He will, she feels sure, say everything kind and sweet to her, and wish her joy sincerely.

James, too, is very sensible, and will see the good points in Horace. He evidently likes him; at least, they have always appeared excellent friends when together. Dorian, of course, is the general favorite,—she acknowledges that,—just because he is a little more open, more outspoken perhaps,—easier to understand; whereas, she firmly believes, she alone of all the world is capable of fully appreciating the innate goodness of Horace!

Here she turns in the huge gateway of Scrope; and the terrier, growing excited, gives way to a sharp bark, and the ponies swing merrily down the avenue; and just before she comes to the hall door her heart fails her, and something within her—that something that never errs—tells her that James Scrope will not betray any pleasure at her tidings.

Before she quite reaches the hall door, a groom comes from a side-walk, and, seeing him, Clarissa pulls up the ponies sharply, and asks the man,—

"Is Sir James at home?"

"Yes, miss; he is in the stables, I think; leastways, he was half an hour agone. Shall I tell him you are here?"

"No, thank you. I shall go and find him myself."

See flings her reins to her own groom, and, with Bill trotting at her heels, goes round to the yard, glad, at least, that her first hope is fulfilled,— that he is out of doors.

As she goes through the big portals into the ivied yard, she sees before her one of the stablemen on his knees, supporting in his arms an injured puppy: with all a woman's tenderness he is examining the whining little brute's soft, yellow paw, as it hangs mournfully downwards.

Sir James, with a pipe in his mouth,—this latter fact Clarissa hails with rapture,—is also bending anxiously over the dog, and is so absorbed in his contemplation of it as not to notice Clarissa's approach until she is close beside him.

"What is the matter with the poor little thing?" she asks, earnestly, gazing with deep pity at the poor puppy, that whines dismally and glances up at her with the peculiarly tearful appealing expression that belongs to setters.

"A knock of a stone, miss, nayther more nor less," exclaims the man, angrily. "That's the honest truth, Sir James, you take my word for't. Some o' them rascally boys as is ever and allus about this 'ere yard, and spends their lives shyin' stones at every blessed sign they sets their two eyes on, has done this. 'Ere's one o' the best pups o' the season a'most ruined, and no satisfaction for it. It's a meracle if he comes round (quiet there, my beauty, and easy there now, I tell ye), and nobody does anything."

The old man stops, and regards his master reprovingly, nay, almost contemptuously.

"I really don't see why you should think it was the boys, Joe?" says Sir James, meekly.

"'Twarn't anythin' else, anyway," persists Joe, doggedly.

"Poor little fellow!—dear fellow!" murmurs Miss Peyton, caressingly, to the great soft setter pup, patting its head lovingly, as it barks madly, and makes frantic efforts to get from Joe's arms to hers, while Bill shrieks in concert, being filled with an overwhelming amount of sympathy.

"Better leave him to me, miss," says Joe, regarding the injured innocent with a parent's eye. "He knows me. I'll treat him proper," raising his old honest weather-beaten face to Clarissa, in a solemn reassuring manner, "you be bound. Yet them pups" (disgustedly) "is like children, allus ungrateful. For the sake o' your handsome face, now, he'd go to you if he could, forgetful of all my kindness to him. Well, 'tis the way o' the world, I believe," winds up old Joe, rising from his knees,—cheered, perhaps, by the thought that his favorite pup, if only following the common dictates of animals, is no worse than all others.

He grumbles something else in an undertone, and finally carries off the puppy to his kennel.

"I am too amazed for speech," says Sir James, rising also to his feet, and contemplating Clarissa with admiration. "That man," pointing to Joe's retiring figure, "has been in my father's service, and in mine, for fifty years, and never before did I hear a civil word from his lips. I think he said your face was handsome, just now?—or was I deceived?"

"I like Joe," says Miss Peyton, elevating her rounded chin: "I downright esteem him. He knows where beauty lies."

"How he differs from the rest of the world!" says Scrope, not looking at her.

"Does he? That is unkind, I think. Why," says Clarissa, with a soft laugh, full of mischief, "should any one be blind to the claims of beauty?"

"Why, indeed? It is, as I have been told, 'a joy forever.' No one nowadays disputes anything they are told, do they?"

"Don't be cynical, Jim," says Miss Peyton, softly. What an awful thing it will be if, now when her story is absolutely upon her lips, he relapses into his unsympathetic mood!

"Well, I won't, then," says Scrope, amiably, which much relieves her. And then he looks lovingly at his pipe, which he has held (as in duty bound) behind his back ever since her arrival, and sighs heavily, and proceeds to knock the ashes out of it.

"Oh, don't do that," says Clarissa, entreatingly. "I really wish you wouldn't!" (This is the strict truth.) "You know you are dying for a smoke, and I—I perfectly love the smell of tobacco. There is, therefore, no reason why you should deny yourself."

"Are you really quite sure?" says Scrope, politely and hopefully.

"Quite,—utterly. Put it in your mouth again. And—do you mind?"— with a swift glance upwards, from under her soft plush hat,—"I want you to come for a little walk with me."

"To the end of the world, with *you*, would be a short walk," says Scrope, with a half laugh, but a ring in his tone that, to a woman heart-whole and unoccupied with thoughts of another man, must have meant much. "Command me, madam."

"I have something very—very—*very* important to tell you," says Miss Peyton, earnestly. This time she looks at her long black gloves, not at him, and makes a desperate effort to button an already obedient little bit of ivory.

They have turned into the orchard, now bereft of blossom, and are strolling carelessly along one of its side-paths. The earth is looking brown, the trees bare; for Autumn—greedy season—has stretched its hand "to reap the ripened fruits the which the earth had yold."

"Are you listening to me?" asks she, presently, seeing he makes no response to her first move.

"Intently." He has not the very faintest idea of her meaning, so speaks in a tone light and half amused, that leads her to betray her secret sooner than otherwise she might have done. "Is it an honest mystery," he says, carelessly, "or a common ghost story, or a state secret? Break it to me gently."

"There is nothing to break," says Clarissa, softly. Then she looks down at the strawberry borders at her side,—now brown and aged,—and then says, in a very low tone, "I am going to be married!"

There is a dead silence. Sir James says nothing. He walks on beside her with an unfaltering footstep, his head erect as ever, his hands clasped in their old attitude behind his back. The sun is shining; some birds are warbling faintly (as though under protest) in some neighboring thicket; yet, I think Scrope neither sees the sun, nor heeds the birds, nor knows for the moment that life flows within him, after that little, low-toned speech of hers.

Then he awakes from his stupor, and, rousing himself, says, huskily, yet with a certain amount of self-possession that deceives her,—

"You were saying——?"

"Only that I am going to be married," repeats Clarissa, in a somewhat changed tone. The nervousness had gone out of it, and the natural hesitation; she is speaking now quite composedly and clearly, as if some surprise betrays itself in her voice.

Scrope is aware that his heart is beating madly. He has stopped, and is leaning against the trunk of an apple-tree, facing Clarissa, who is standing in the middle of the path. His face is ashen gray, but his manner is quite calm.

"Who is it?" he asks, presently, very slowly.

"Mr. Branscombe," —coldly.

"Dorian?"

"No. Horace."

"I wish it had been Dorian," he says, impulsively.

It is the last straw.

"And why?" demands she, angrily. She is feeling wounded, disappointed at his reception of her news; and now the climax has come. Like her father, he, too, prefers Dorian, —nay, by his tone, casts a slur upon Horace. The implied dislike cuts her bitterly to the heart.

"What evil thing have you to say of Horace," she goes on, vehemently, "that you so emphatically declare in favor of Dorian? When you are with him you profess great friendship for him, and now behind his back you seek to malign him to the woman he loves."

"You are unjust," says Scrope, wearily. "I know nothing bad of Horace. I merely said I wished it had been Dorian. No, I have nothing to say against Horace."

"Then why do you look as if you had?" says Miss Peyton, pettishly, frowning a little, and letting her eyes rest on him for a moment only, to withdraw them again with a deeper frown. "Your manner suggests many things. You are like papa—" She pauses, feeling she has made a false move, and wishes vainly her last words unsaid.

"Does your father disapprove, then?" asks he, more through idleness than a desire to know.

Instinctively he feels that, no matter what obstacles may be thrown in this girl's way, still she will carry her point and marry the man she has elected to love. Nay, will not difficulties but increase her steadfastness, and make strong the devotion that is growing in her heart?

Not until now, this moment, when hope has died and despair sprung into life, does he know how freely, how altogether, he has lavished the entire affection of his soul upon her. During all these past few months he has lived and thought and hoped but for her; and now—all this is at an end.

Like a heavy blow from some unseen hand this terrible news has fallen upon him, leaving him spent and broken, and filled with something that is agonized surprise at the depth of the misfortune that has overtaken him.

It is as a revelation, the awakening to a sense of the longing that has been his,—to the knowledge of the cruel strength of the tenderness that binds his heart to hers.

With a slow wonder he lifts his eyes and gazes at her. There is a petulant expression round her mobile lips, a faint bending of her brows that bespeaks discontent, bordering upon anger, yet, withal, she is quite lovely,—so sweet, yet so unsympathetic; so gentle, yet so ignorant of all he is at present feeling.

With a sickening dread he looks forward to the future that still may lie before him. It seems to him that he can view, lying stretched out in the far distance, a lonely cheerless road, over which he must travel whether he will or not,—a road bare and dusty and companionless, devoid of shade, or rest, or joy, or that love that could transform the barrenness into a "flowery mead."

"He that loses hope"—says Congreve—"may part with anything." To Scrope, just now, it seems as though hope and he have parted company forever. The past has been so dear, with all its vague beliefs and uncertain dreamings,—all too sweet for realization,—that the present appears unbearable.

The very air seems dark, the sky leaden, the clouds sad and lowering. Vainly he tries to understand how he has come to love, with such a boundless passion, this girl, who loves him not at all, but has surrendered herself wholly to one unworthy of her,—one utterly incapable of comprehending the nobility and truthfulness of her nature.

The world, that only yesterday seemed so desirable a place, to-day has lost its charm.

"What is life, when stripped of its disguise? A thing to be desired it cannot be." With him it seems almost at an end. An unsatisfactory thing, too, at its best,—a mere "glimpse into the world of might have been."

Some words read a week ago come to him now, and ring their changes on his brain. "Rien ne va plus,"—the hateful words return to him with a pertinacity not to be subdued. It is with difficulty he refrains from uttering them aloud.

"No; he does not disapprove," says Clarissa, interrupting his reflections at this moment: "he has given his full consent to my engagement." She speaks somewhat slowly, as if remembrance weighs upon her. "And, even if he had not, there is still something that must give me happiness: it is the certainty that Horace loves me, and that I love him."

Though unmeant, this is a cruel blow. Sir James turns away, and, paling visibly,—had she cared to see it,—plucks a tiny piece of bark from the old tree against which he is leaning.

There is something in his face that, though she understands it not, moves Clarissa to pity.

"You will wish me some good wish, after all, Jim, won't you?" she says, very sweetly, almost pathetically.

"No, I cannot," returns he with a brusquerie foreign to him. "To do so would be actual hypocrisy."

There is silence for a moment: Clarissa grows a little pale, in her turn. In *his* turn, he takes no notice of her emotion, having his face averted. Then, in a low, faint, choked voice, she breaks the silence.

"If I had been wise," she says, "I should have stayed at home this morning, and kept my confidences to myself. Yet I wanted to tell you. So I came, thinking, believing, I should receive sympathy from you; and now what have I got? Only harsh and cruel words! If I had known—"

"Clarissa!"

"Yes! If any one had told me you would so treat me, I should—should—"

It is this supreme moment she chooses to burst out crying; and she cries heartily (by which I mean that she gives way to grief of the most vehement and agonized description) for at least five minutes, without a cessation, making her lament openly, and in a carefully unreserved fashion, intended to reduce his heart to water. And not in vain is *her* "weak endeavor."

Sir James, when the first sob falls upon his ear, turns from her, and, as though unable to endure the sound, deliberately walks away from her down the garden path.

When he gets quite to the end of it, however, and knows the next turn will hide him from sight of her tears or sound of her woe, he hesitates, then is lost, and finally coming back again to where she is standing, hidden by a cambric handkerchief, lays his hand upon her arm. At his touch her sobs increase.

"Don't do that!" he says, so roughly that she knows his heart is bleeding. "Do you hear me, Clarissa? Stop crying. It isn't doing you any good, and it is driving me mad. What has happened?—what is making you so unhappy?"

"*You* are," says Miss Peyton, with a final sob, and a whole octave of reproach in her voice. "Anything so unkind I never knew. And just when I had come all the way over here to tell you what I would tell nobody else except papa! There was a time, Jim" (with a soft but upbraiding glance), "when you would have been sweet and kind and good to me on an occasion like this."

She moves a step nearer to him, and lays her hand—the little, warm, pulsing hand he loves so passionately—upon his arm. Her glance is half offended, half beseeching: Scrope's strength of will gives way, and, metaphorically speaking, he lays himself at her feet.

"If I have been uncivil to you, forgive me," he says, taking her hand from his arm, and holding it closely in his own. "You do not know; you cannot understand; and I am glad you do not. Be happy! There is no substantial reason why you should not extract from life every sweet it can afford: you are young, the world is before you, and the love you desire is yours. Dry your eyes, Clarissa: your tears pierce my heart."

He has quite regained his self-control by this time, and having conquered emotion, speaks dispassionately. Clarissa, as he has said, does not understand the terrible struggle it costs him to utter these words in an ordinary tone, and with a face which, if still pale, betrays no mental excitement.

She smiles. Her tears vanish. She sighs contentedly, and moves the hand that rests in his.

"I am so glad we are friends again," she says. "And now tell me why you were so horrid at first: you might just as well have begun as you have ended: it would have saved trouble and time, and" (reproachfully) "all my tears."

"Perhaps I value you so highly that I hate the thought of losing you," says Scrope, palliating the ugliness of his conduct as best he may. His voice is very earnest.

"How fond you are of me!" says Miss Peyton, with some wonder and much pleasure.

To this he finds it impossible to make any answer.

"Whenever I wish I had had a brother, I always think of you," goes on she, pleasantly, "you are so—so—quiet, and your scoldings so half-hearted. Now, even though rather late, wish me joy."

"My dear, dear girl," says Scrope, "if I were to speak forever, I could not tell you how I long for and desire your happiness. If your life proves as calm and peaceful as I wish it, it will be a desirable life indeed! You have thought of me as your brother: let me be your brother indeed,—one in whom you can confide and trust should trouble overtake you."

He says this very solemnly, and again Clarissa's eyes fill with tears. She does now what she has not done since she was a little, impulsive, loving girl: she lifts her head and presses her lips to his cheek.

For one brief moment he holds her in his arms, returning her caress, warmly, it is true, but with ineffable sadness. To her, this embrace is but the sealing of a fresh bond between them. To him it is a silent farewell, a final wrenching of the old sweet ties that have endured so long.

Up to this she has been everything to him,—far more than he ever dreamed until the rude awakening came,—the one bright spot in his existence; but now all is changed, and she belongs to another.

He puts her gently from him, and, with a kindly word and smile, leads her to the garden gate, and so round to where her ponies are impatiently awaiting her coming: after which he bids her good-by, and, turning, goes indoors, and locks himself into his own private den.

CHAPTER XII

"The snow is on the mountain,
The frost is on the vale,
The ice hangs o'er the fountain,
The storm rides on the gale." —Ouseley.

Clarissa's letter to Georgie Broughton receives a most tender response, — tender as it is grateful. The girl writes thankfully, heartily, and expresses almost passionate delight at Clarissa's instantaneous and ready sympathy.

The letter is short, but full of feeling. It conveys to Clarissa the sad impression that the poor child's heart is dry and barren for lack of that gracious dew called love, without which not one of us can taste the blessedness of life.

"Nothing is true but love, nor aught of worth;
Love is the incense which doth sweeten earth."

So sings Trench. To Clarissa, just now, his words convey nothing less than the very embodiment of truth. That Georgie should be unhappy for want of this vital essence cuts her to the heart, — the more so that Georgie persistently refuses to come to Gowran.

"Dearest Clarissa, — Do not think me cold or ungrateful," — so she writes, — "but, were I to go to you and feel again the warmth and tenderness of a home, it might unfit me for the life of trouble and work that must lie before me. 'Summer is when we love and are beloved,' and, of course, such summer is over for me. I know my task will be no light or easy one; but I have made up my mind to it, and indeed am thankful for it, as any change from this must of necessity be pleasant. And, besides, I may not be a governess forever. I have yet another plan in my head, — something papa and I agreed upon, before he left me, — that may put an end to my difficulties sooner than I think. I will tell you of it some time, when we meet."

"Poor darling," says Clarissa, "what a wretched little letter!" She sighs, and folds it up, and wonders vaguely what this other plan of Georgie's can be. Then she writes to her again, and describes Mrs. Redmond as well as is possible.

"Accept her offer by return of post," she advises, earnestly. "Even if, after a trial, you do not like her, still this will be an opening for you; and I am glad in the thought that I shall always have you near me,—at least until that mysterious plan of yours meets the light. Mrs. Redmond is not, of course, everything of the most desirable, but she is passable, and very kind at heart. She is tall and angular, and talks all day long—and all night, I am sure, if one would listen—about her ailments and the servants' delinquencies. She is never without a cold in her head, and a half-darned stocking! She calls the children's pinafores 'pinbefores,'—which is quite correct, but very unpleasant; and she always calls terrible 'turrible;' but beyond these small failings she is quite bearable."

And so on. When Miss Broughton receives this letter in her distant home, she is again solemistress of a sickroom. Her aunt—the hard taskmaster assigned to her by fate—lies on her bed stricken to the earth by fever. To come to Pullingham now will be impossible. "Will Mrs. Redmond wait for a month, or perhaps two?" She entreats Clarissa to do what she can for her; and Clarissa does it; and the worried wife of the vicar, softened by Miss Peyton's earnest explanations, consents to expound Pinnock and "Little Arthur" to the small Redmonds until such time as Miss Broughton's aunt shall be convalescent.

"The inaudible and noiseless foot of Time" creeps on apace, and Christmas at last reaches Pullingham. Such a Christmas, too!—a glorious sunny Christmas morning, full of light and life, snow-crowned on every side. The glinting sunbeams lie upon the frozen hills, kissing them with tender rapture, as though eager to impart some heat and comfort to their chilly hearts.

> "Now trees their leafy hats do bare
> To reverence Winter's silver hair."

The woods are all bereft of green; the winds sigh wearily through them; "no grass the fields, no leaves the forests wear;" a shivering shroud envelops all the land.

But far above, in the clear sky, Sol shines triumphant. Nor ice, nor snow, nor chilling blast has power to deaden him to-day. No "veil of clouds involves his radiant head." He smiles upon the earth, and ushers in the blessed morn with unexpected brilliancy. Innumerable sounds swell through the frosty air; sweet bells ring joyously. All the world is astir.

Except Clarissa. She lies, still sleeping,—dreaming, it may be, that first glad dream of youth in which all seems perfect, changeless, passion-sweet!

Upon her parted lips a faint soft smile is lingering, as though loath to depart. Her face is lightly tinged with color, as it were a "ripened rose." Upon one arm her cheek is pillowed; the other is thrown, with negligent grace, above her head.

"Half-past eight, Miss Peyton, and Christmas morning; too," says a voice more distinct than musical, and rather reproachful. It rushes into Clarissa's happy dream like a night-mare, and sends all the dear shades she has been conjuring to her side back into their uncertain home.

The maid pokes the fire energetically, and arranges something upon the dressing-table with much unnecessary vigor.

Clarissa, slowly bringing herself back from the world in which Hester, however admirable in every respect, bears no part, sighs drowsily, and sits up in her bed.

"Really that hour?" she says. "Quite too disgracefully late! A happy Christmas, Hester!"

"Thank you, miss. The same to you, and very many of them!"

"Is it a cold morning?" asks Clarissa, with a little shiver. She pushes back the soft waving masses of her brown hair from her forehead, and gazes at Hester entreatingly, as though to implore her to say it is warm as a day in June.

But Hester is adamant.

"Terrible cold, miss," she says, with a sort of gusto. "*That* frosty it would petrify you where you stand."

"Then I won't stand," declares Clarissa, promptly sinking back once more into her downy couch. "I decline to be petrified, Hester,"—tucking the clothes well round her. "Call me again next week."

"The master is up this hour, miss," says the maid, reprovingly; "and see how beautifully your fire is burning."

"I can't see anything but the water over there. *Is* that ice in my bath?"

"Yes, miss. Will you let me throw a little hot water into it to melt it for you? Do, miss. I'm sure them miserable cold oblations is bitter bad for you." Perhaps she means ablutions. Nobody knows. And Clarissa, though consumed with a desire to know, dares not ask. Hester is standing a few yards from her, looking the very personfication of all pathos, and is plainly an-angered of the frozen bath.

"Well, then, Hester, yes; a little—a *very* little—hot water, just for once," says Clarissa, unable to resist the woman's pleading, and her own fear of the "bitter chill" that awaits her on the other side of the blankets. "My courage has flown; indeed, I don't see how I can get up at all,"—willfully, snuggling down even more closely into the warm sheets.

"Oh, now get up, miss, do," implores her maid. "It is getting real late, and the master has been up asking for you twice already."

"Is papa dressed, then?"

"An hour ago, miss. He was standing on the doorsteps, feeding the sparrows and robins, when I came up."

"Dear papa!" says Clarissa, tenderly, beneath her breath; and then she springs out of bed, and gets into her clothes by degrees, and presently runs down-stairs to the great old hall, where she finds her father awaiting her.

He is standing at the upper end, with his back to the huge central window, through which

> "Gleams the red sun athwart the misty haze
> Which veils the cold earth from its loving gaze."

A calm, clear light illumes the hall, born of the "wide and glittering cloak of snow" which last night flung upon the land. At its other end stand all the servants,—silent, expectant,—to hear what the master shall say to them on this Christmas morning.

That George Peyton should refuse to address them on this particular day is out of all hearing. His father, grandfather, and great-grandfather had done it before him to the then servants; therefore (according to the primitive notions of the county) he must do the same. Yet it is undeniable that to the present proprietor this task is a terrible one, and not to be performed at any price, could escape from it be shown.

Eloquence is not Mr. Peyton's *forte*. To find himself standing before an expectant audience, and to know they are prepared to hang upon his accents, is not sweet to him,—in fact, fills him with terrors vast and deep. Yet here they are awaiting his speech, in a goodly row, with all their eyes fixed on his, and their minds prepared to receive anything he may say.

He breathes a small sigh of relief as he sees Clarissa approaching, and gives her his customary morning kiss in a rather warmer fashion than usual, which has only the effect of raising mirth in Clarissa's mind. She smiles in an unfilial fashion, and, slipping her hand through his arm, awaits what fate may have in store.

Her father, when he has cast upon her one reproachful glance, turns to the servants, and, with a heightened color and somewhat lame delivery, says as follows:

"I am very glad to see you all again— —" here he checks himself, and grows a degree redder and more embarrassed. It occurs to him that, after all, he saw them yesterday and the day before, and that it is on the cards he will see them again to-morrow. Therefore why express exuberant joy at the fact that he can see them at this present moment?

He glances, in a despairing fashion, at Clarissa; but she is plainly delighted at his discomfiture, and refuses to give him any assistance, unless a small approving nod can be accounted such.

Feeling himself, therefore, unsupported, he perforce, returns to the charge.

"It is a great pleasure to me to know that no changes have taken place during the past year, I hope"—(long pause)—"I hope we shall always have the same story to tell."

This is fearfully absurd, and he knows it, and blushes again.

"Well, at least," he goes on, "I hope we shall not part from each other without good cause,—such as a wedding, for instance."

Here he looks at the under-housemaid, who looks at the under-gardener, who looks at his boots, and betrays a wild desire to get into them forthwith.

"There is no occasion for me, I think, to make you a speech. I— —the fact is, I— —couldn't make you a speech, so you must excuse me. I wish you all a happy Christmas! I'm sure you all wish me the same. Eh?— —and— —"

Here he is interrupted by a low murmur from the servants, who plainly feel it their duty to let him know, at this juncture, that they do hope his Christmas will be a successful one.

"Well— —eh?— —thank you— —you know," says Mr. Peyton, at his wits' end as to what he shall say next.

"You are all very kind, very kind indeed— —very— —. Mrs. Lane,"— desperately,—"come here and take your Christmas-box."

The housekeeper advances, in a rounded stately fashion, and, with an elaborate courtesy and a smile full of benignity, accepts her gift and retires with it to the background. The others having all performed the same ceremony, and also retired, Mr. Peyton draws a deep sigh of relief, and turns to Clarissa, who, all through, has stood beside him.

"I think you might have put in a word or two," he says. "But you are a traitor; you enjoyed my discomfiture. Bless me, how glad I am that 'Christmas comes but once a year!'"

"And how sorry I am!" says Clarissa, making a slight grimace. "It is the one chance I get of listening to eloquence that I feel sure is unsurpassable."

They are still standing in the hall. At this moment a servant throws open the hall door and Dorian and Horace Branscombe, coming in, walk up to where they are, near the huge pine fire that is roaring and making merry on the hearth-stone; no grate defiles the beauty of the Gowran hall. They are flushed from the rapidity of their walk, and are looking rather more like each other than usual.

"Well, we have had a run for it," says Dorian. "Not been to breakfast, I hope? If you say you have finished that most desirable meal, I shall drop dead: so break it carefully. I have a wretched appetite, as a rule, but just now I feel as if I could eat you, Clarissa."

"We haven't thought of breakfast, yet," says Clarissa. "I am so glad I was lazy this morning! A happy Christmas, Dorian!"

"The same to you!" says Dorian, raising her hand and pressing it to his lips. "By what luck do we find you in the hall?"

"The servants have just been here to receive their presents. Now, why were you not a few minutes earlier, and you might have been stricken dumb with joy at papa's speech?"

"I don't believe it was half a bad speech," says Mr. Peyton, stoutly.

"Bad! It was the most enchanting thing I ever listened to!—in fact, faultless,—if one omits the fact that you looked as if you were in torment all the time, and seemed utterly hopeless as to what you were going to say next."

"James, is breakfast ready?" says Mr. Peyton, turning away to hide a smile, and making a strenuous effort to suppress the fact that he has heard one word of her last betrayal. "Come into the dining-room, Dorian," he says, when the man has assured him breakfast will be ready in two minutes: "it is ever so much more comfortable there."

Branscombe goes with him, and so presently, Clarissa and Horace find themselves alone.

Horace, going up to her, as in duty bound, places his arm round her, and presses his lips lightly, gently, to her cheek.

"You never wished *me* a happy Christmas," he says, in the low soft tone he always adopts when speaking to women. "You gave all your best wishes to Dorian."

"You knew what was in my heart," replies she, sweetly, pleased that he has noticed the omission.

"I wonder if I have brought you what you like," he says, laying in her little palm a large gold locket, oval-shaped, and with forget-me-nots in sapphires and diamonds, on one side. Touching a spring, it opens, and there, staring up at her, is his own face, wearing its kindliest expression, and seeming—to her—to breathe forth love and truth.

For a little minute she is silent; then she says softly, with lowered eyes, and a warm, tender blush,—

"Did you have this picture taken for me, alone?"

It is evident the face in the locket is even dearer to her than the locket itself.

"For you alone," says Horace, telling his lie calmly. "When it was finished I had the negative destroyed. I thought only of you. Was not that natural? There was one happy moment in which I assured myself that it would please you to have my image always near you. Was I wrong?— presumptuous?"

Into his tone he has managed to infuse a certain amount of uncertainty and anxious longing that cannot fail to flatter and do some damage to a woman's heart. Clarissa raises her trustful eyes to his.

"Please me!" she repeats, softly, tears growing beneath her lids: "it pleases me so much that it seems to me impossible to express my pleasure. You have given me the thing that, of all others, I have most wished for."

She blushes, vividly, as she makes this admission. Horace, lifting her hand, kisses it warmly.

"I am fortunate," he says, in a low tone. "Will you love the original, Clarissa, as you love this senseless picture? After long years, how will it be?" There is a touch of concern and doubt—and something more, that may be regret—in his tone.

"I shall always love you," says the girl, very earnestly, laying her hand on his arm, and looking at him with eyes that should have roused all tenderness and devotion in his breast:

> "For at each glance of those sweet eyes a soul
> Looked forth as from the azure gates of heaven."

He is spared a reply. Dorian, coming again into the hall, summons them gayly to breakfast.

In the little casemented window of the tiny chamber that calls her mistress, sits Ruth Annersley, alone.

The bells are ringing out still the blessed Christmas morn; yet she, with downcast eyes, and chin resting in her hand, heeds nothing, being wrapped in thought, and unmindful of aught but the one great idea that fills her to overflowing. Her face is grave—nay, almost sorrowful—and full of trouble; yet underlying all is gladness that will not be suppressed.

At this moment—perhaps for the first time—she wakes to the consciousness that the air is full of music, borne from the belfries far and near. She shudders slightly, and draws her breath in a quick unequal sigh.

"Another long year," she says wearily. "Oh that I could tell my father!"

She lifts her head impatiently, and once more her eyes fall upon the table on which her arm is resting. There are before her a few opened letters, some Christmas cards, a very beautiful Honiton lace handkerchief, on which her initials, "R. A.," are delicately worked, and—apart from all the rest—a ring, set with pearls and turquoises.

Taking this last up, she examines it slowly, lovingly, slipping it on and off her slender finger, without a smile, and with growing pallor.

A step upon the stairs outside! Hastily, and in a somewhat guilty fashion, she replaces the ring upon the table, and drops the lace handkerchief over it.

"Miss Ruth," says a tall, gawky country-girl, opening the door, "the maister he be waitin' breakfast for you. Do ee come down now." Then, catching sight of the handkerchief, "La! now," she says, "how fine that be! a beauty, surely, and real lace, too! La! Miss Ruth, and who sent you that, now? May I see it?"

She stretches out her hand, as though about to raise the dainty fabric from its resting-place; but Ruth is before her.

"Do not touch it," she says, almost roughly for her. Then, seeing the effect her words have caused, and how the girl shrinks back from her, she goes on, hurriedly and kindly, "You have been in the dairy, Margery, and perhaps your hands are not clean. Run away and wash them, and come to attend table. Afterwards you shall come up here and see my handkerchief and all my pretty cards."

She smiles, lays her hand on Margery's shoulder, and gently, but with determination, draws her towards the door.

Once outside, she turns, and, locking the door, carefully puts the key in her pocket.

Slowly, reluctantly, she descends the stairs, — slowly, and with a visible effort, presses her lips in gentle greeting to her father's care-worn cheek. The bells still ring on joyously, merrily; the sun shines; the world is white with snow, more pure than even our purest thoughts; but no sense of rest or comfort comes to Ruth. Oh, dull and heavy heart that holds a guilty secret. Oh, sad (even though yet innocent) is the mind that hides a hurtful thought! Not for you do Christmas bells ring out their happy greeting! Not for such as you does sweet peace reign triumphant.

CHAPTER XIII

"Is she not passing fair?" — *Two Gentlemen of Verona.*

The day at length dawns when Miss Broughton chooses to put in an appearance at Pullingham. It is Thursday evening on which she arrives, and as she has elected to go to the vicarage direct, instead of to Gowran, as Clarissa desired, nothing is left to the latter but to go down on Friday to the Redmonds' to welcome her.

She (Clarissa) had taken it rather badly that pretty Georgie will not come to her for a week or so before entering on her duties; yet in her secret soul she cannot help admiring the girl's pluck, and her determination to let nothing interfere with the business that must for the future represent her life. To stay at Gowran, — to fall, as it were, into the arms of luxury, — to be treated, as she knew she would be, by Clarissa, as an equal, even in worldly matters, would be only to unfit her for the routine that of necessity must follow. So she abstains, and flings far from her all thought of a happiness that would indeed be real, as Clarissa had been dear to her two years ago; and to be dear to Georgie once would mean to be dear to her forever.

The vicar himself opens the door for Clarissa, and tells her Miss Broughton has arrived, and will no doubt be overjoyed to see her.

"What a fairy you have given us!" he says, laughing. "Such a bewildering child; all golden hair, and sweet dark eyes, and mourning raiments. We are perplexed — indeed, I may say, dazed — at her appearance; because we have one and all fallen in love with her, — hopelessly, irretrievably, — and hardly know how to conduct ourselves towards her with the decorum that I have been taught to believe should be shown to the instructress of one's children. Now, the last young woman was so different, and — "

"Young," says Miss Peyton.

"Well, old, if you like it. She certainly, poor soul, did remind one of the 'sere and yellow.' But this child is all fire and life; and really," says the vicar, with a sigh that may be relief, "I think we all like it better; she is quite a break-in upon our monotony."

"I am so glad you all like her," says Clarissa, quite beaming with satisfaction. "She was such a dear little thing when last I saw her; so gentle, too, — like a small mouse."

"Oh, was she?" says the vicar, anxiously. "She is changed a little, I think. To me she is rather terrifying. Now, for instance, this morning at breakfast, she asked me, before the children, 'if I didn't find writing sermons a bore.' And when I said—as I was in duty bound to say, my dear Clarissa—that I did not, she laughed out quite merrily, and said she 'didn't believe me'! Need I say the children were in raptures? but I could have borne that, only, when Mrs. Redmond forsook me and actually laughed too, I felt the end of all things was come. Clarissa," (severely), "I do hope I don't see you laughing, too."

"Oh, no!—not—not much," says Miss Peyton, who is plainly enjoying the situation to its utmost. "It is very hard on you, of course."

"Well, it is," says the vicar, with his broad and rather handsome smile, that works such miracles in the parish and among the mining people, who look upon him as their own special property. "It is difficult for a man to hope to govern his own household when his nearest and dearest turn him into open ridicule. Your little friend is a witch. What shall we do with her?"

"Submit to her," says Clarissa. "Where is she? I want to see her."

"Cissy will find her for you. I dare say they are together, unless your 'Madam Quicksilver,' as I call her, has taken to herself wings and flown away."

He turns, as though to go with her.

"No, no," says Clarissa; "I shall easily find her by myself. Go, and do what you meant to do before I stopped you."

Moving away from him, she enters the hall, and seeing a servant, is conducted by her to a small room literally strewn with work of all kinds. Books, too, lie here in profusion, and many pens, and numerous bottles of ink, and a patriarchal sofa that never saw better days than it sees now, when all the children prance over it, and love it, and make much of it, as being their very own.

On this ancient, friend a tiny fairy-like girl is sitting, smiling sweetly at Cissy Redmond, who is chattering to her gayly and is plainly enchanted at having some one of her own age to converse with.

The fairy is very lovely, with red-gold hair, and large luminous blue eyes, soft and dark, that can express all emotions, from deepest love to bitterest scorn. Her nose is pure Greek; her lips are tender and mobile; her skin is neither white nor brown, but clear and warm, and somewhat destitute of color. Her small head is covered with masses of wavy, luxuriant, disobedient hair, that shines in the light like threads of living gold.

She is barely five feet in height, but is exquisitely moulded. Her hands and feet are a study, her pretty rounded waist a happy dream. She starts from the sofa to a standing position as Clarissa enters, and, with a low, intense little cry, that seems to come direct from her heart, runs to her and lays her arms gently round her neck.

Once again Clarissa finds herself in Brussels, with her chosen friend beside her. She clasps Georgie in a warm embrace; and then Cissy Redmond, who is a thoroughly good sort, goes out of the room, leaving the new governess alone with her old companion.

"At last I see you," says Miss Broughton, moving back a little, and leaning her hands on Clarissa's shoulders that she may the more easily gaze at her. "I thought you would never come. All the morning I have been waiting, and watching, and longing for you!"

Her voice is peculiar,—half childish, half petulant, and wholly sweet. She is not crying, but great tears are standing in her eyes as though eager to fall, and her lips are trembling.

"I didn't like to come earlier," says Clarissa, kissing her again. "It is only twelve now, you know; but I was longing every bit as much to see you as you could be to see me. Oh, Georgie, how glad I am to have you near me! and — —you have not changed a little scrap."

She says this in a relieved tone.

"Neither have you," says Georgie: "you are just the same. There is a great comfort in that thought. If I had found you changed,—different in any way,—what should I have done? I felt, when I saw you standing tall and slight in the doorway, as if time had rolled back, and we were together again at Madame Brochet's. Oh, how happy I was then! And now — —now — —"

The big tears in her pathetic eyes tremble to their fall, she covers her face with her hands.

"Tell me everything," says Clarissa, tenderly.

"What is there to tell?—except that I am alone in the world, and very desolate. It is more than a year ago now since— —since— —papa left me. It seems like a long century. At first I was apathetic; it was despair I felt, I suppose; indeed, I was hardly conscious of the life I was leading when with my aunt. Afterwards the reaction set in; then came the sudden desire for change, the intense longing for work of any kind; and then— —"

"Then you thought of me!" says Clarissa, pressing her hand.

"That is true. Then I thought of you, and how ready your sympathy had ever been. When—when he died, he left me a hundred pounds. It was all he had to leave." She says this hastily, passionately, as though it must be gone through, no matter how severe the pain that accompanies the telling of it. Clarissa, understanding, draws even closer to her. This gentle movement is enough. A heart, too full, breaks beneath affection's touch. Georgie bursts into tears.

"It was all on earth he *had* to give," she sobs, bitterly, "and I think he must have *starved* himself to leave me even that! Oh, shall I ever forget?"

"In time," whispers Clarissa, gently. "Be patient: wait." Then, with a sigh, "How sad for some this sweet world can be!"

"I gave my aunt forty pounds," goes on the fair-haired beauty, glad to find somebody in whom she can safely confide and to whom her troubles may be made known. "I gave it to her because I had lived with her some time, and she was not kind to me, and so I felt I should pay her something. And then I put a little white cross on *his* grave before I left him, lest he should think himself quite forgotten. It was all I could do for him," concludes she, with another heavy sob that shakes her slight frame.

Her heart seems broken! Clarissa, who by this time is dissolved in tears, places her arms round her, and presses her lips to her cheek.

"Try, *try* to be comforted," entreats she. "The world, they tell me, is full of sorrow. Others have suffered, too. And nurse used to tell me, long ago, that those who are unhappy in the beginning of their lives are lucky ever after. Georgie, it may be so with you."

"It may," says Georgie, with a very faint smile; yet, somehow, she feels comforted.

"Do you think you will be content here?" asks Clarissa, presently, when some minutes have passed.

"I think so. I am sure of it. It is such a pretty place, and so unlike the horrid little smoky town from which I have come, and to which" (with a heavy sigh), "let us hope, I shall never return."

"Never do," says Clarissa giving her rich encouragement. "It is ever so much nicer here." As she has never seen the smoky town in question, this is a somewhat gratuitous remark. "And the children are quite sweet, and very pretty; and the work won't be very much; and—and I am only just, an easy walking-distance from you."

At this termination they both laugh.

Georgie seems to have forgotten her tears of a moment since, and her passionate burst of grief. Her lovely face is smiling, radiant; her lips are parted; her great blue eyes are shining. She is a warm impulsive little creature, as prone to tears as to laughter, and with a heart capable of knowing a love almost too deep for happiness, and as surely capable of feeling a hatred strong and lasting.

The traces of her late emotion are still wet upon her cheeks. Perhaps she knows it not, but, "like some dew-spangled flower, she shows more lovely in her tears." She and Clarissa are a wonderful contrast. Clarissa is slight and tall and calm; she, all life and brightness, eager, excited, and unmindful of the end.

Cissy Redmond, at this juncture, summons up sufficient courage to open the door and come in again. She ignores the fact of Georgie's red eyes, and turns to Clarissa. She has Miss Peyton's small dog in her arms,—the terrier, with the long and melancholy face, that goes by the name of Bill.

"*Your* dog," she says to Clarissa, "and such a pet. He has eaten several legs off the tables, and all my fingers. His appetite is a credit to him. How do you provide for him at Gowran? Do you have an ox roasted whole occasionally, for his special benefit?"

"Oh, he is a worry," says Clarissa, penitently. "Billy, come here, you little reprobate, and don't try to look as if you never did anything bad in your life. Cissy, I wish you and Georgie and the children would all come up to Gowran to-morrow."

"We begin lessons to-morrow," says the new governess, gravely, who looks always so utterly and absurdly unlike a governess, or anything but a baby or a water-pixie, with her yellow hair and her gentian eyes. "It will be impossible for me to go."

"But lessons will be over at two o'clock," says Cissy, who likes going to Gowran, and regards Clarissa as "a thing of beauty." "Why not walk up afterwards?"

"I shall expect you," says Clarissa, with decision; and then the two girls tell her they will go with her as far as the vicarage gate, as she must now go home.

There she bids them good-by, and, passing through the gate, goes up the road. Compelled to look back once again, by some power we all know at times, she sees Georgie's small pale face pressed against the iron bars, gazing after her, with eyes full of lonely longing.

"Good-by, Clarissa," she says, a little sad imploring cadence desolating her voice.

"Until to-morrow" replies Clarissa, with an attempt at gayety, though in reality the child's mournful face is oppressing her. Then she touches the ponies lightly, and disappears up the road and round the corner, with Bill, as preternaturally grave as usual, sitting bolt upright beside her.

The next morning is soft and warm, and, indeed, almost sultry for the time of year. Thin misty clouds, white and shadowy, enwrap the fields and barren ghost-like trees and sweep across the distant hills. There is a sound as of coming rain,—a rushing and a rustling in the naked woods. "A still wild music is abroad," as though a storm is impending, that shall rise at night and shake the land the more fiercely because of its enforced silence all this day.

> "But now, at noon,
> Upon the southern side of the slant hill,
> And where the woods fence off the northern blast
> The season smiles, resigning all its rage,
> And has the warmth of May. The vault is blue,
> Without a cloud: and white without a speck,
> The dazzling splendor of the scene below."

The frost has gone, for the time being; no snow fell last night; scarcely does the wind blow. If, indeed, "there is in souls a sympathy with sounds," I fear Georgie and Cissy and the children must be counted utterly soulless, as they fail to hear the sobbing of the coming storm, but with gay voices and gayer laughter come merrily over the road to Gowran. Upon the warm sullen air the children's tones ring like sweet silver bells.

As they enter the gates of Gowran, the youngest child, Amy, runs to the side of the new governess, and slips her hand through her arm.

"I am going to tell you about all the pretty things as we go along," she says, patronizingly yet half shyly, rubbing her cheek against Miss Broughton's shoulder. She is a tall, slender child, and to do this has to stoop a little. "You fairy," she goes on, admiringly, encouraged perhaps by the fact that she is nearly as tall as her instructress, "you are just like Hans Andersen's tales. I don't know why."

"Amy! Miss Broughton won't like you to speak to her like that," says Cissy, coloring.

But Georgie laughs.

"I don't mind a bit," she says, giving the child's hand a reassuring pressure. "I am accustomed to being called that, and, indeed, I rather like it now. I suppose I *am* very small. But" (turning anxiously to Cissy, and speaking quite as shyly as the child Amy had spoken a moment since) "there is a name to which I am not accustomed, and I hate it. It is 'Miss Broughton.' Won't you call me 'Georgie?'"

"Oh, are you sure you won't mind?" says the lively Cissy, with a deep and undisguised sigh of relief. "Well, that is a comfort! it is all I can do to manage your name. You don't look a bit like a 'Miss Anything,' you know, and 'Georgie' suits you down to the ground."

"Look, look! There is the tree where the fairies dance at night," cries Amy, eagerly, her little, thin, spiritual face lighting with earnestness, pointing to a magnificent old oak-tree that stands apart from all the others, and looks as though it has for centuries defied time and storm and proved itself indeed "sole king of forests all."

"Every night the fairies have a ball there," says Amy, in perfect good faith. "In spring there is a regular wreath of blue-bells all round it, and they show where the 'good folks' tread."

"How I should like to see them!" says Georgie, gravely. I think, in her secret soul, she is impressed by the child's solemnity, and would prefer to believe in the fairies rather than otherwise.

"Well, *you* ought to know all about them," says Amy, with a transient but meaning smile: "you belong to them, don't you? Well" (dreamily), "perhaps some night we shall go out hand in hand and meet them here, and dance with them all the way to fairy-land."

"Miss Broughton,—there—through the trees! Do you see something gleaming white?" asks Ethel, the eldest pupil. "Yes? Well, there, in that spot, is a marble statue of a woman, and underneath her is a spring. It went dry ever so many years ago, but when Clarissa's great grandfather died the waters burst out again, and every one said the statue was crying for him, he was so good and noble and so well beloved."

"I think you might have let me tell that story," says Amy, indignantly. "You knew I wanted to tell her that story."

"I didn't," with equal indignation; "and, besides, you told her about the fairies' ball-room. I said nothing about that."

"Well, at all events," says Georgie, "they were two of the prettiest stories I ever heard in my life. I don't know which was the prettier."

"Now, look at that tree," breaks in Amy, hurriedly, feeling it is honestly her turn now, and fearing lest Ethel shall cut in before her. "King Charles the Second spent the whole of one night in that identical tree."

"Not the whole of it," puts in Ethel, unwisely.

"Now, I suppose this is my story, at all events," declares Amy, angrily, "and I shall just tell it as I like."

"Poor King Charles!" says Georgie, with a laugh, "If we are to believe all the stories we hear, half his lifetime must have been spent 'up a tree.'"

A stone balcony runs before the front of the house. On it stands Clarissa, as they approach, but, seeing them, she runs down the steps and advances eagerly to meet them.

"Come in," she says. "How late you are! I thought you had proved faithless and were not coming at all."

"Ah! what a lovely hall!" says Georgie, as they enter, stopping in a childishly delighted fashion to gaze round her.

"It's nothing to the drawing-room: that is the most beautiful room in the world," says the irrepressible Amy, who is in her glory, and who, having secured the unwilling but thoroughly polite Bill, is holding him in her arms and devouring him with unwelcome kisses.

"You shall see the whole house, presently," says Clarissa to Georgie, "including the room I hold in reserve for you when these children have driven you to desperation."

"That will be never," declares Amy, giving a final kiss to the exhausted Billy. "We like her far too much, and always will, I know, because nothing on earth could make me afraid of her!"

At this they all laugh. Georgie, I think, blushes a little; but even the thought that she is not exactly all she ought to be as an orthodox governess cannot control her sense of the ludicrous.

"Cissy, when is your father's concert to come off?" asks Clarissa, presently.

"At once, I think. The old organ is unendurable. I do hope it will be a success, as he has set his heart on getting a new one. But it is so hard to make people attend. They will pay for their tickets, but they won't come. And, after all, what the—the *others* like, is to see the county."

"Get Dorian Branscombe to help you. Nobody ever refuses him anything."

"Who is Dorian Branscombe?" asks Georgie, indifferently, more from want of something to say than an actual desire to know.

"Dorian?" repeats Clarissa, as though surprised; and then, correcting herself with a start, "I thought every one knew Dorian. But I forgot, you are a stranger. He is a great friend of mine; he lives near this, and you must like him."

"Every one likes him," says Cissy, cordially.

"Lucky he," says Georgie. "Is he your lover, Clarissa?"

"Oh, no," —with a soft blush, born of the thought that if he is not the rose he is very near to it. "He is only my friend, and a nephew of Lord Sartoris."

"So great as that?" —with a faint grimace. "You crush me. I suppose he will hardly deign to look at *me*?"

As she speaks see looks at herself in an opposite mirror, and smiles a small coquettish smile that is full of innocent childish satisfaction, as she marks the fair vision that is given back to her by the friendly glass.

"I hope he won't look at you too much, for his own peace of mind," says Cissy, at which Clarissa laughs again; and then, the children getting impatient, they all go out to see the pigeons and the gardens, and stay lingering in the open air until afternoon tea is announced.

CHAPTER XIV

"Where music dwells
Lingering, and wandering on, as loath to die,
Like thoughts whose very sweetness yieldeth proof
That they were born for immortality." —Wordsworth.

The parish church of Pullingham is as naught in the eyes of the parishioners, in that it is devoid of an organ. No sweet sounds can be produced from the awful and terrifying instrument that for years has served to electrify the ears of those unfortunate enough to possess sittings in the church. It has at last failed!

One memorable Sunday it groaned aloud, —then squeaked mildly; cr—r—r—k went something in its inside; there was a final shriek, more weird than the former, and then all was still! How thankful should they have been for that! I believe they were truly and devoutly so, but love for the "heavenly maid" still reigned in all their hearts, and with joy they hearkened to their vicar when he suggested the idea of a concert to be given for the purpose of raising funds wherewith to purchase a new organ, or, at least, to help to purchase it. The very thought was enough to raise high Jubilee within their musical hearts.

Now, the one good thing still belonging to Mrs. Redmond is the remains of what must once have been a very beautiful voice. With this she possesses the power of imparting to others her own knowledge of music, —a rather rare gift. With her own children, of course, she can do nothing; they are veritable dead-letters in her hands, —she being one of those women who spend their lives admonishing and thrusting advice upon the world, yet find themselves unequal to the government of their own household. But with the village choir all is different; here she reigns supreme, and is made much of, for Pullingham is decidedly musical, and all its young men and all its young women either sing, or think they sing, or long after singing.

Tenors, sopranos, and basses are to be met with round every corner; the very air is thick with them. The Pullinghamites *will* sing, whether they can or not, with a go and a gusto that speaks well for their lungs, if a trifle trying to the listeners.

Vocal music being the thing held highest in favor in the Methodist chapel, where Mr. Leatham, the "Methody" parson, holds unorthodox services, many were the seceders from the parish church to join the choir in the whitewashed chapel and shout the hymns of Moody and Sankey, just at the commencement of this story.

Such secessions went nigh to breaking Mr. Redmond's heart. The organ had failed him; it had wheezed, indeed, valiantly to the last, as though determined to die game; but a day had come, as I said, when it breathed its last sigh and the ancient bellows refused to produce another note.

What was to be done? The villagers should and would have music at any cost, and they never could be brought to see the enormity of worshipping in the whitewashed edifice that was, and is, as the temple of Belial in the eyes of their vicar.

It would take some time to procure funds for another and more satisfactory organ. In the mean time, the whilom choir was falling to pieces. The late organist had accepted a fresh and more lucrative post: there was literally no head to keep the members together. What was to be done?

In desperation, the vicar asked himself this, whilst looking vainly round for some one to help him drag back his flock from the vicious influence of the "American songsters," as he most irreverently termed Messrs. M. and S. And it was then, when he was at his wits' end, that Mrs. Redmond most unexpectedly came to the rescue. It was the first and the last time in her life she ever rose to the occasion: but this one solitary time she did it perfectly, and coming boldly to the front, carried all before her.

She would undertake a singing-class; she would arrange, and teach, and keep together a choir that should reduce to insignificance the poor pretensions of a man like Leatham! The vicar, dazzled by all this unlooked-for energy, gave his consent to her scheme, and never afterwards repented it; for in three short months she had regulated and coached a singing-class that unmistakably outshone its Methodistical rivals.

And then came the question of the new organ.

"We have some money, but not enough money," said the vicar, one evening, to the partner of his joys; "and something should be done to bring the want of an organ before the public."

"I should think it must be sufficiently brought before them every Sunday," said Mrs. Redmond, triumphantly laying her tenth mended sock in the basket near her.

"The parish is all very well, my dear, but the county ought to hear of it, and ought to help. I insist upon the county putting its hands in its pockets."

"I think you are quite right to insist," said Mrs. Redmond, placidly; "but how are you going to do it?"

"Let us give a concert," said the vicar, at last bringing to the light of day his great project, that fairly took his wife's breath away. "Yes, a concert, to which the whole county shall come and hear my—nay, your—choir surpass itself."

Mrs. Redmond was struck dumb by this bold proposition, but, finally giving in, she consented to teach the choir, assiduously twice a week, all the quartettes and trios and solos she knew; while still declaring, in a dismal fashion, that she knew the whole thing would be a dismal failure, and that the great cause would lose by it more than it would gain.

Many days, many hours, has Mr. Redmond spent arranging and disarranging all the details of the proposed concert.

The idea is in itself a "happy thought,"—far happier than any of Burnand's (so he tells himself); but a concert, however unpretentious, is a prodigious affair, and not to be conducted by half a dozen raw recruits.

Besides, the county admires the county, and would prefer seeing itself represented on the boards to listening to the warblings, be they never so sweet, of an outsider. It is so far more delicious to laugh behind one's fan at the people in one's own set than at those outside the pale of recognition. And, of course, the county must be humored.

The vicar grows nervous as he masters this fact, and strives diligently to discover some among the upper ten who will come forward and help to sweeten and gild the "great unwashed."

The duchess, unfortunately, is from home; but Lady Mary and Lady Patricia are at the Castle, and Lady Mary—when she can be heard, which, to do her justice, is very seldom, even in a very small room—can sing nice little songs very nicely. Indeed, she is fond of describing her own voice as "a sweet little voice," and certainly all truth is embodied in the word "little."

Then there is young Hicks, the surgeon's son, who boasts a good baritone, and is addicted to Molloy and Adams and all of their class, and who positively revels in Nancy Lees, and such gentle beings as those to whom the "Tar's Farewell" may be gently breathed.

Then there is the long gawky man staying with the Bellews, who can shout from afar, and make music of his own that will probably, nay, surely, go a long way towards bringing down the house, as far as the farmer class is concerned; and with him will come Miss Bellew, who can produce a very respectable second in any duet, and who is safe to go anywhere with the long gawky young man, if report speaks truly.

Mrs. McConkie, from the neighboring parish, will lend a helping hand, her husband being a brother clergyman; and there is, besides, Mr. Henly, who plays the violin, and Mr. Johnson, who can recite both comic and melancholy pieces with such success as to bring tears or laughter, as the case may be, into the eyes of any one with half a soul!

As nobody will confess to anything less than a whole soul, everybody in Pullingham laughs or cries immoderately whenever Mr. Johnson gives way to recitations.

And last, but not least, there is always Sarah Martin, the leader of the village choir, and the principal feature in it, whose strong if slightly ear-piercing soprano must prove her worthy of a new organ.

To the vicar's intense chagrin, Dorian Branscombe is absent,—has, indeed, been up in town since the day before Georgie Broughton's arrival, now a fortnight old.

Dorian would have been such a comfort! Not that he sings, or plays, or fiddles, or, indeed, does anything in particular, beyond cajoling the entire neighborhood; but that, as it happens, is, in this case, everything. To cajole, to entreat, to compel the people to come in and fill the empty benches, is all the vicar would require at his hands.

And Dorian could do all this. No one ever refuses him anything. Both old women and young women acknowledge his power, and give in to him, and make much of him, and hardly feel the worse because of their subservience,—he having a little way of his own that makes them believe, when they have been most ignominiously betrayed into saying "yes" to one of his wildest propositions, he has been conferring a favor upon them, more or less, for which he is just too generous to demand thanks.

But this invaluable ally is absent. The vicar, in the privacy of his own sanctum,—where no one can witness the ungodly deed,—stamps his feet with vexation as he thinks on this, and tells himself he is unlucky to the last degree, and acknowledges a worth in Dorian Branscombe never learned before!

Clarissa is perfectly delighted with the whole idea, and somewhat consoles him by her ready offers of assistance, and her determination to step into the absent Dorian's shoes and make love to the county in his stead.

She persists in calling it the "first concert of the season," which rather alarms the vicar, who is depressed by his wife's prognostications of failure, and sees nothing but ruin ahead. She declares her intention of publishing it in all the London papers, and offers the whole of the winter conservatories to decorate the school-house (where it is to be held), so that those accustomed to the sight of its white and somewhat barren walls will fail to recognize it in its new-born beauty.

"Then, shall we name the 4th as the day?" says the vicar, with some trepidation. It is now the end of January, and he is alluding to the first week in the ensuing month. "I wish you could sing, Clarissa! I dare say you would help me."

"Indeed I would. But Nature has proved unkind to me. And, after all, you want no one else. The choir, in itself, is very efficient; and if you must call for 'out-door relief,' why, you have Lady Mary, and the others. That fearful young-man at Bellew is a fortune in himself; and Mr. Johnson makes everybody cry—and it is so nice to cry."

"Yes,—yes,—I dare say," says the poor vicar, who is somewhat *distrait*, and, to say the truth, a little miserable about the whole undertaking. "Now, there is Sarah Martin. Do you think she will pull through? On her I build all my hopes; but some inward doubt about her oppresses me. Willie Bealman has a capital tenor; but he and Sarah don't speak,—she refused him, I think,—and so they won't sing their duet together. Then there is Lizzie Bealman, she might stand to me; but she loses her voice when nervous, and has a most uncomfortable trick of giggling when in the least excited."

"Put her in the background," says Clarissa. "She is of no use, except in a chorus."

"Her people wouldn't stand it. They look upon her as a rising prima donna. I assure you, my dear Clarissa," says the vicar, furtively wiping his brow, "only for the sin of it, there are moments when I could wish myself beneath the sod. The incessant worry is more than I can bear!"

"Oh, now, don't say that," says Miss Peyton, patting his arm lovingly. "It will be a great success, this concert: I know, I feel it will!"

CHAPTER XV

"As sweet and musical
As bright Apollo's lute, strung with his hair;
And when Love speaks, the voice of all the gods
Makes heaven drowsy with the harmony." —*Love's Labor's Lost.*

It is night, and the 4th of February. Already is Pullingham turning out, dressed in its very Sunday best, and is wending its way towards the school-house, where the concert is to be held.

For the last week it has been deep in the mysteries of solos, duets, and trios. Indeed, there is hardly a family in the whole village that does not know by heart every mortal thing that is going to be sung, each family possessing a son or a daughter engaged in the common work, and belonging to the choir; yet nevertheless it now goes in a body to the school-house, as possessed with curiosity as though music is an art unknown to them, and the piping of small trebles a thing unheard of.

Nothing can exceed the excitement and jealousy that reign everywhere, — principally in the hearts of Mr. Leatham's followers, who hope wildly, but secretly, that failure may be the only crop their rivals may reap.

It is a heavenly night, for which the Vicar is devoutly thankful. The moon is riding high in the dark-blue dome; the stars are all alight; the air, swift and keen, rushes along the high-roads, sweeping all before it. There is no sign of rain; the sky above, "star-inwrought," shows promise of many fair to-morrows. "There is no excuse for their non-attendance," murmurs the vicar to himself, as he stands inside the school-house door, wording his thought, as he might, were he thinking of the collecting together of his flock on Easter Sunday or to the Holy Communion.

"Vast night comes noiselessly up the eastern slope,
And so the eternal chase goes round the world."

But for the soughing wind, the world is still. One by one, or two by two, or sometimes as a whole family, the villagers drop in, arranging themselves modestly in the back rows, and exchanging greetings with each other in a subdued and whispered fashion.

A little while after the door is opened, the lower half of the hall is crowded to excess. The vicar is well beloved by his parishioners; but above and beyond all is the desire to see Maria, and Susan, and Ezekiel upon the boards, "a singing for the quality!"

The room itself is what reporters would term "a blaze of light." Much ingenuity has been exercised in the decoration of it; and certainly the designs in laurels, and the designs in moss, and the one grand design in paper roses, at the far end of the room, are all that heart can desire.

To Clarissa, I think, this last outburst on the part of the village is a heart-break; but, if so, she represses her grief valiantly, and even, with her own forgiving fingers, condescends to brighten the monstrosity with some hothouse flowers. But, when all is told, it remains an eyesore,—a regrettable blot, not to be eradicated under pain of bringing down the rage of the entire village upon the devoted head of him or her who should interfere.

Mrs. Redmond, seated on the small platform, with the piano before her, and the choir arranged, with careful regard to its different sizes, on each side of her, waits patiently the coming of the county. She is looking thinner, more miserable, than usual, and has a general air about her of being chilled to the bone. Her fingers, lying idly in her lap, clutch and unclutch each other aimlessly, as though vainly searching for the accustomed sock.

Miss Broughton, who is taking no part in the performance,—having suppressed the fact of her having a very beautiful voice, ever since her arrival at Pullingham,—is sitting on a side-seat, longing eagerly for Clarissa's arrival. The children have wandered a little away from her, and are gazing, as lost in admiration, at the huge rose-construction on the wall before them.

Presently, the Greys of Greymount come in, with a little shudder of disgust at finding themselves almost the first; followed closely by Lady Mary and Lady Patricia Hort, who do not shudder at all, but go straight up the small passage between the seats, with their patrician noses high in the air, and smile and nod cheerfully, and not at all condescendingly, at Mrs. Redmond, who, poor soul, is deeply relieved at sight of them.

Lady Mary goes on to the platform; Lady Patricia sinks into a front seat specially provided for her, whilst Lord Alfred, their brother,—who has been inveigled into coming, sorely against his will,—having conversed with Lady Patricia for a few minutes, and told her several lies about the arrangements for the evening,—not intentionally, but through ignorance, being under the false impression that a concert in a village is the same as a concert in town,— goes over to one side of the building, and plants himself listlessly with his back against a wall, from which position he gazes in a gloomy fashion at everything in general, but Miss Broughton in particular.

Then comes everybody, and makes a great fuss about its place,— Clarissa Peyton and her father excepted, who go straight to where Georgie is sitting, and stay with her all the evening.

Dorian Branscombe, who has come down expressly for the concert, at great trouble to himself, and simply to oblige the vicar, saunters leisurely up the room towards the middle of the evening, and looks round him dubiously, as though uncertain where to put in his time.

Seeing Clarissa, he goes up to her, and, with a faint sigh of relief, leans over the back of her chair and says, "Good-evening," in a languid tone.

"Ah! you, Dorian?" says Clarissa, very pleased. "Now, it *is* good of you to come."

"I'm always good," says Dorian. "I'm a model boy. It is so strange that people won't recognize the fact. They sort of give me to understand I'm quite the other thing, whatever that may be. Very full house, don't you think, and awfully swagger? What's Lady Patricia got on her? She is slightly terrifying, don't you think?"

"She isn't very well got up, certainly," says Clarissa, reluctantly.

"She's anyhow," says Mr. Branscombe, freely; and then his eyes fall upon Georgie, who is gazing, in her rapt, childish fashion, at the singer of the moment; and then he doesn't speak again for a little while.

"Is Horace quite well?" asks Clarissa, presently.

"Quite well. He always is, you know. Who— —who is the girl next your father?"

"That is my friend, Georgie Broughton. I think I told you about her. She is governess at the vicarage, now. Is she not lovely,—quite sweet?" asks Clarissa, eagerly.

But Mr. Branscombe does not answer her. He is still staring at the unconscious Georgie, and seems almost deaf to Clarissa's praise of her. At this Miss Peyton is somewhat disgusted, and declines any further attempt at laudation.

"A governess!" he says, at length, raising his brows, but without removing his eyes from the fair and perfect face that, even now, he tells himself, is without its equal.

"Yes. She is none the less sweet for that," says Clarissa, rather coldly. She tells herself it is unlike Dorian to look down upon any one because he or she may be in a worse position than his own.

"They are going to sing again," she says, in a tone she seldom uses to him: "we must not talk, you know." She had some faint idea of introducing him to Georgie, but she abandons it, and gives him to understand that she has at present nothing more to say to him.

Whether he quite comprehends all she intends to convey, I know not; but, raising himself slowly from his lounging position on the back of her chair, he takes a last look at Georgie's profile, and moves into the background.

"Good-evening, Branscombe," says Lord Alfred, presently; and Dorian, finding himself beside him, returns the greeting, and props himself up in his turn against the friendly wall, that shows its appreciation of them by giving them finely whitewashed coats.

The concert is getting on swimmingly. As yet no flaw has occurred to mark the brilliancy of its success. The opening chorus has been applauded to the echo, especially by Lord Alfred, who feels it his duty to do something, and who keeps on applauding, in the most open-hearted manner each thing and everything, until he discovers he has split his right glove all up the palm, when he caves in, and, having said something impossible, puts his hands behind his back and refuses to applaud again.

Lady Mary has come forward, and entreated her audience to "Love not," in the faintest and most plaintive of voices. The county is delighted with her, and smiles unrestrainedly behind its fans. "Dear Lady Mary is so funny, don't you know," says Miss Grey of Greymount, in an indescribable tone.

Then comes a solo on the violin, that charms all the back benches, and reduces the farmers' wives and daughters to tears, as it tells them how that the poor player's "lodging is on the cold ground."

Lord Alfred, who has not yet recovered his temper, says this is "disgusting," and "wonders what the—so-and-so—brought him here at all."

"I suppose the night brougham," says Dorian, equably, who is now engaged in a minute examination of Miss Broughton's head, round which her soft yellow hair is twisted in a loose artistic coil.

He is in quite a happy mood, if somewhat silent, and says the solo isn't half bad; and now Mr. Hastings, the curate, reads something from the "Ingoldsby Legends," that seems to displease Cissy Redmond extremely, as she will not lift her head during the reading, or even look at him, and expresses herself as quite charmed when it is at an end.

And now comes the event of the evening,—the thing that is to convince the county of the necessity for a good organ, and to show them the rare excellence of the Pullingham choir.

Sarah Martin, the leading soprano—all muslin and blue bows—comes forward, and begins the solo upon which all the vicar's hopes are centred.

"The shades of night are falling fast."

begins Sarah, nobly, and goes on in a hopeful manner to the end of the first verse.

The vicar draws a deep sigh of relief!

"His brow was sad, his eye beneath,"

goes on Sarah victoriously, her whole soul in the safe fulfilment of her task. She gets through to the end of the second verse as successfully as she did to the end of the first, and then pauses to draw breath.

The vicar exchanges a triumphant glance with Miss Peyton.

"In happy homes they saw the light,"

continues Sarah. And then—then! something horrible happens. A sound, very terrible to the vicar, smites upon his ear,—a sound that fills his clerical bosom with dismay. Sarah's voice—the voice of his chief prop—has proved false. It has given way; it has cracked upon a high note; and *the* solo of the evening has proved a dead failure.

Talk of failing for a million; talk of Isandula or Majuba Hill; talk of Mr. Parnell and the Coercion Bill! But was ever defeat so disastrous as this? The vicar, but for his sex, and the publicity of the thing, could thankfully have given way to tears. Miss Peyton flushes to her temples and feels as if she herself has been guilty of the miserable *fiasco*.

Of course it is hushed up. The piano comes out quite strong again, under Mrs. Redmond's bony fingers; the defaulter is gently pushed into the background, and a chorus introduced. Nevertheless, after the breakdown, things somehow seem to go wrong. The other singers are disheartened, and will not do their best; while Sarah, who is dissolved in tears in the cloak-room, and who has another song on the programme, obstinately refuses to try her powers again.

The vicar is in despair, although he walks about valiantly among the audience, trying, most unsuccessfully, to appear unconcerned; whilst the coughing and sneezing, that generally distinguish every place where silence is the thing most to be desired, seem now on the increase, to an alarming degree, and threaten to drown Lady Mary's second effort.

"Who *is* that blowing his nose?" demands the poor vicar, testily, looking daggers in the direction of the sound. Clarissa, who is the nearest to him as he makes this observation, just saves herself from laughing aloud.

"Things have taken a bad turn," says the vicar, regarding her reproachfully. "I am afraid my first attempt will only be remembered as a wretched failure; and that girl has another song, and she will not venture again, and there is no one to take her place."

"Mr. Redmond, I will sing for you, if you wish it," says a clear, childish voice, that has always something pathetic about it. Georgie has overheard his last speech, and has turned her soft, fair little face to his, and is speaking to him, with a flush and a smile.

"But, my dear, can you sing?" says the vicar, anxiously. Her face is full of music; but then he has never heard her sing. During her fortnight's stay at the vicarage she has never sung one note, has never betrayed the fact that she is a true daughter of Polyhymnia.

"I can, indeed,—really; I can sing very well," says Georgie, in her little earnest fashion, and without the very faintest suspicion of conceit. She is only eager to reassure him, to convince him of the fact that she is worthy to come to his relief.

"But the song?" says Mr. Redmond, still hesitating, and alluding to the second solo chosen by the defaulter.

"It is an old Irish song; I know it. It is 'Shule, agra,' and it begins, 'My Mary with the curling hair,'" says Georgie, with a slight nod. "I used to sing it long ago, and it is very pretty."

"Well, come," says the vicar, though with trepidation, and leads her on to the platform, and up to Mrs. Redmond, to that good woman's intense surprise.

Lady Mary has nearly brought her little vague whisper to an end. She has at last disclosed to a listening audience that she has discovered the real dwelling-place of the lost "Alice,"—who is uncomfortably ensconced "amidst the starshine," if all accounts be true,—and is now quavering feebly on a last and dying note.

"This is the song," says Mrs. Redmond, putting Sarah's rejected solo into her hand.

"Thank you," says Miss Broughton She looks neither frightened nor concerned, only a little pale, and with a great gleam in her eyes, born, as it were, of an earnest desire to achieve victory for the vicar's sake.

Then Lady Mary's final quaver dies, and she moves to one side, leaving the space before the piano quite clear.

There is a slight pause; and then the slight childish figure, in its gown of thin filmy black, comes forward, and stands before the audience. She is quite self-possessed, but rather white, which has the effect of rendering her large plaintive eyes darker and more lustrous than usual. Her arms are half bare; her throat and part of her neck can be seen gleaming white against the blackness of her dress. She is utterly unadorned. No brooch or ear-rings, or bracelets or jewels of any kind, can be seen. Yet she stands there before them a perfect picture, more sweet than words can tell.

She holds her small shapely head erect, and seems unconscious of the many eyes fixed upon her. Rarely has so fair a vision graced the dull daily life of Pullingham. Even the sturdy, phlegmatic farmers stir upon their seats, and nudge the partners of their joys, and wonder, in a stage whisper, who "you can be?"

Mrs. Redmond plays a few faint chords, and then Georgie begins the plaintive Irish air Sarah should have sung, and sings it as, perhaps, she never sang before.

During the second verse, borne away by her passionate desire to please, she forgets the music-sheet she holds, so that it flutters away from her down to the floor, and lies there; while her hands, seeking each other, grow entwined, and hang loosely before her, showing like little flakes of snow against the darkness of her gown.

Her voice is beautiful, sweet, and full, and quick with passion,—one of those exquisite voices that sink into the soul, and linger there forever, even when the actual earthly sound has died away. She carries the listeners with her, holding them as by a spell, and leaving them silent, almost breathless, when she has finished her "sweet song."

Now she has come to the end of "Shule, agra," and turns away somewhat abruptly to Mrs. Redmond, as though half frightened at the storm of applause that greets her.

"Did I really sing so well?" she asked the vicar, presently, when he has sought her out to thank her.

"Well?" repeats he. "What a word to use! It was divine; the whole room was spell-bound. What a gift you possess! My dear, you have saved the evening, and my honor, and the organ, and everything. I am deeply grateful to you."

"How glad I am!" says the girl, softly; "and don't thank me. I liked it, — the singing, the applause, the feeling that I was doing well. I will sing for you again later on, if you wish it."

"It is too much to ask," says the vicar; "but, if you really don't mind? Lady Patricia is in ecstasies, and says she could listen to you forever."

Georgie laughs.

"Well, at least she shall listen to me once more," she says, gayly.

Lady Patricia is not the only one enthralled by the beautiful singer. Dorian Branscombe has never once removed his eyes from her face: he is as one bewitched, and, even at this early moment, wonders vaguely within himself what can be the meaning of the strange pleasure, that is so near akin to pain, that is tugging at his heart-strings.

Lord Alfred, too, is plainly impressed, and stares at the pretty creature with the black gown and the snowy arms, until speech becomes a necessity.

"Well, I never in all my life," he begins, emphatically, and then stops. "Who is she, Branscombe?"

"Don't know, I'm sure," says Branscombe, rather shortly. What right has Hort — what right has any fellow — to see beauty in her, except himself? The words of her song are still running in his ears, — "My love, my pearl!" How well they suit her! What a little baby face she has, so pure and sweet! yet how full of feeling!

"What's her name?" asks Lord Alfred, nothing daunted.

"I have quite forgotten," returns Branscombe, even more coldly. His second answer hardly tallies with his first; but of this he is quite oblivious.

Lord Alfred raises his brows. "She has a magnificent voice, and is very beautiful," he says, evenly. "Yet — do you know? she reminds me somewhat of Harriet."

Harriet is a third and a favorite sister of Lord Alfred's, — a very estimable young woman, much given to the reformation of drunkards, who, though rather deficient in nose, makes up for it in prodigality of mouth.

"I can't say I see the likeness," says Dorian, with as little disgust as he can manage at so short a notice.

"My dear fellow," expostulates Lord Alfred, shifting his glass from one eye to the other and looking palpably amused, "there is no reason in the world why you should be grumpy because you are in love with the girl. *I* don't want to interfere with you."

"In love!" says Branscombe. "Nonsense! I never spoke a word to her in my life."

"Well, it is uncommon like it," says Lord Alfred.

"Is it? Well, I can't help that, you know. Nevertheless, I am not in love with any one."

"Then you ought to take that look off your face," persists his lordship, calmly.

"I'll take off anything you like," replies Dorian? somewhat nettled.

At this, Lord Alfred laughs beneath his breath, and tells him he will not keep him to this rash promise, as probably the Pullingham folk, being pre-Adamites, might object to the literal fulfilment of it.

"But she is a very lovely girl, and I don't wonder at your infatuation," he says, mildly.

"Foregone conclusions seem to be in your line," returns Dorian, with a shrug. "It seems a useless thing to tell you again I have *not* lost my heart to Miss Broughton."

"Oh, so you have remembered her name!" says his lordship, dryly.

Meantime, the concert has reasserted itself, and things once more are going on smoothly. The vicar, all smiles and sunshine, is going about accepting congratulations on all sides.

"Such a *charming* evening," says Mrs. Grey; "and *such* music! Really, London could not surpass it. And what a delicious face that girl has got— like Spring, or May, or—er——Morning, or that. I quite envy her to you. Now all *my* governesses are so unpleasant,—freckled, you know, or with a squint, or a crooked nose, or that. Some people have *all* the luck in this world," winds up Mrs. Grey, with a gentle sigh, who has ten thousand a year and no earthly care, and who always speaks in italics whenever she gets the slightest chance.

"So glad you are pleased," says the vicar, genially. "Yes, she is as beautiful as her voice. After all, I think the concert will prove a success."

"It *has* proved itself one," says Mrs. Grey, who adores the vicar, and would flirt with him if she dared. "But when do you fail in anything you undertake? Really, dear Mr. Redmond, you should not let the idea die out. You should give us a good time like this at least once in every month, and than see what *delicious* windows you could have. I for one" — coquettishly — "will promise to come to *every* one of them."

"At that rate, I should soon have no poor to look after," says the gratified vicar, gayly.

"And a good thing, too. The poor are always so oppressive, and — er — so *dirty*, but still" — seeing a change in his face — "*very* interesting, — *very*!"

And then the concert comes to an end, and adieux are said, and fresh congratulations poured out, so to speak, upon the Redmonds; and then every one goes home.

Dorian Branscombe climbs into his dog-cart, and drives swiftly homeward, under the glistening stars, whose "beauty makes unhappy," — his mind filled with many thoughts.

"'My love, my pearl!'" — the words of Georgie's song haunt him incessantly, and ring their changes on his brain. "What words could be more appropriate, more suited to her?" (Alas, when we come to pronouns it is generally all over with us!) "A pearl! so fair! so pure! so solitary! It just expressed her. By what right has Fate cast that pretty child upon the cruel world to take her chance, to live or die in it?

"How large her eyes are, and what a heavenly blue, and what a sad expression lies within them! 'Grandmamma, grandmamma, what big eyes you have!'" Here he rouses himself, and laughs a little, and wishes, with some petulance, that he could put her out of his head.

"'My love, my pearl!' Yes, it was a very pretty song, and haunts one somehow; but no doubt a good night's sleep will kill it. Hold up, you brute," — this to the kind and patient mare, who is doing her good nine miles an hour, and who has mildly objected to a sharp stone. "Why didn't Clarissa introduce me to her? I wish to goodness I hadn't to go back to town to-morrow!" And so on, until he reaches Sartoris, and flings himself, with some impatience, out of the trap, to the amazement of his groom, who is accustomed to think of his master as a young man to whom exertion is impossible.

Then he goes to bed, and spends the next four hours miserably, as he falls into a heavy slumber, and dreams that oysters, pearl-laden, are rushing boisterously over his body.

CHAPTER XVI

"There was a sound of revelry by night."—Byron.

So Dorian returns to town, and stays there until the annual hunt ball, of which he is a steward, summons him back to Pullingham.

It is, of course, the event of the season, this ball, and occurs early in March. Clarissa, going down to the vicarage,—where, now, indeed, she spends a good deal of her time,—speaks to the girls about it.

"I am so glad Georgie is in time for it," says Cissy, who is a warm-hearted little soul, and who desires good for every one. "There is something so nice about a real big ball."

"A ball!" says Georgie, growing a delicate pink, with excitement. "I never was at a real ball in my life. Oh, Clarissa, will you take me?"

"Georgie! As if it isn't a real joy to me to have you," says Clarissa, reproachfully. "I can't bear going anywhere by myself, and Mrs. Grey always insists on taking Cissy."

"Well, she is very kind, you know," says Cissy, with some regret. "But I do so wish she would let me go with *you*. However, mamma would not like me to refuse her, and, after all, I shall meet you both in the room. I wish we could manage to arrive just at the same moment."

"Well, I'll settle that with Mrs. Grey," says Clarissa. "Dorian will get me a ticket for Georgie."

"Who is Dorian?" asks Georgie, idly. Literally, she cares nothing about him, regarding him in this instance as merely a means to an end,—a person who can obtain for her an entrance into a desired haven. She has, indeed, forgotten that once before she asked this same question and received her answer.

"Why, I told you," says Clarissa. "He is Lord Sartoris's nephew,—the tall handsome young man who spoke to me at the concert."

"I didn't see him. When is this ball to be?"

"On the 5th. And now, about your dresses?"

"Mine goes without telling," says Cissy, in a resigned tone. "The whole county knows it by heart by this time. After all, there is a sort of comfort in everything, even in one's misfortune. Now, all *my* young men won't have the trouble of looking for me, they will know me directly, the instant their eyes light upon my gown, which is fast becoming an heirloom."

"If it is the gown you wore the other night at the Bellews', you look very sweet in it," says Clarissa, looking very sweet herself as she utters this comforting speech.

"You are an angel, you know," says Cissy, with a merry little laugh. "You see everybody through rose-colored spectacles."

"Isn't she rude?" says Clarissa. "One would think I was an old fogy of ninety-five. Spectacles, indeed!"

"I must run," says Miss Cissy. "I entirely forgot all about the dinner, and mamma left it to me, as she had to go and see old Mrs. Martin. Good-bye, dear, *dearest* Clarissa. How I wish I could go with you to this lovely ball!"

"Never mind; people always meet," says Clarissa, consolingly.

"Yes,—at Philippi," returns the irrepressible, and, with a faint grimace, she vanishes.

Georgie walks as far as the entrance-gate with Clarissa. When there, she looks at the iron bars wistfully, and then says, in her pretty childish way, "Let me go a little way with you, Clarissa, will you?"

Miss Peyton, who is walking, is delighted.

"As far as ever you will. Indeed, I want to speak to you. What—what is your dress like, Georgie?"

Georgie hesitates. Clarissa, misunderstanding her silence, says, gently, "Let me give you one, dearest?"

"Oh, no, no," says Miss Broughton, quickly. "I have one,—I have, indeed; and it is rather pretty."

"But you told me you had never been at a ball."

"Neither have I. The gown I speak of was bought for a musical party. It was given while I was with Aunt Elizabeth."

"Who gave it?"

"The gown?"

"Oh, no,—the party."

"Lady Lincoln. She has one son, Sir John, and I think it is he gives the parties. Aunt Elizabeth was so pleased that I was asked that she insisted on my going, though I cried, and prayed hard to be let stay at home. It was only" —dropping her voice, with a heavy sigh—"eleven months after papa had—had left me."

"It was cruel to force you to go against your will: but, when you were there, did you enjoy yourself?"

"I did," confesses Miss Broughton, with a blush. "I enjoyed myself more than I can say. I do not think I ever enjoyed myself so much in all my life. I forgot everything for the time being, and was quite happy. To me the flowers, the lights, the music, the pretty dresses, —everything,—were new and fresh, and helped to take me out of myself. And then, everybody was so kind, and Mr. Kennedy——"

"Who was he?" asks Clarissa, interested at once.

"A tall thin dark man, in the Guards,—the Coldstreams or the Grenadiers, I quite forget which. He talked to me all the evening; and, indeed, so did Sir John, Lady Lincoln's son; but I liked Mr. Kennedy best."

"Poor Sir John!"

"Oh, no. Of course he cared nothing. When I left, Mr. Kennedy, and Sir John, and Aunt Elizabeth's maid, walked home with me; and I think they were cross,—the men, I mean. When I got home I found one of my gloves was missing, and Aunt Elizabeth said I was very careless; and then she asked me where was the crimson rose I had on my bosom when starting, and, you see," —apologetically,—"I had given it to Mr. Kennedy, because he asked me for it; but when I told her so, she said I was very forward! Did you ever hear such a word?" says Miss Broughton, tears of indignation in her eyes. "Was it forward to give a dead rose to a man who had been very kind to me for a whole evening?"

"Certainly not," says Clarissa, emphatically. "I would give a rose to any one who was kind to me,—if they asked for it. Did you ever see Mr Kennedy again?"

"Yes; he called next day, to return me my glove, which, he declared, he had kept by mistake. But somehow I never got that glove again, so I suppose he took it away with him when he left."

"I suppose so. Well, I shall write to Dorian for your ticket."

"Perhaps 'Dorian' will think me a great bother."

"Let him," says Clarissa, impatiently: as yet she has not forgiven him that speech (so much mistaken) at the concert.

The 5th has arrived. The day has dawned, lived, grown to its full size, and then sunk, as we all must, into the arms of Death. The night has come, with sound of music and breath of dying flowers, and the drip, drip of the softly-flowing fountains.

The rooms are looking lovely; fair faces smile, and soft eyes gleam; and figures, round and *svelte* as Venus's own, sway with the music and mingle with the throng.

The ball is at its height, when Clarissa, seeing Dorian, beckons to him with her fan. It is a very slight invitation to her side, but one instantly obeyed.

"Keep one dance for a friend of mine," she says, earnestly.

"Let me keep one dance for you."

"That, too, if you wish it; but I have a little friend here to-night, and she knows nobody, and, though I know you won't like it" (calling to mind again his supposed disparaging tone at the concert), "still, for my sake, be kind to her."

"I shall be nectar to her, if you entreat me in that fashion. Who is she?"

"Well, she is only a governess," begins Clarissa, beating about the bush: she is quite determined, nevertheless, that Georgie shall not be neglected or left out in the cold at this her first ball.

"A governess!" says Dorian, unthinkingly. "Oh, Clarissa, don't let me in for that. I don't *mind* them a bit; but I'm afraid of them. She is safe to ask me if I don't think Murray's Grammar the most artfully compiled book in the world, and I shan't know what to say in reply."

"You need not be afraid of my governess," says Clarissa, earnestly: "she will not trouble you about Murray or his Grammar."

"Of course, if you say I must dance with her, I must," says Branscombe, with a heavy sigh.

"I see her now. Come, let me introduce you to her."

"But not for this dance. I am engaged—I am, I give you my word—to the prettiest girl in the room,—the prettiest child, I should say."

"You can dance with your child, of course; but at least let me introduce you to my friend."

With a faint and carefully subdued shrug he submits to the inevitable, and goes where Clarissa leads. He finds himself presently at the other end of the room, near where a little dainty black-robed figure stands, with three men before her, all evidently possessed with an overpowering desire to inscribe their names upon the morsel of tinted and gilded paper she holds in her hand.

Her large blue eyes are almost black with excitement; her lips are parted, and, like Herrick's "Julia," are like "rubies," soft and rich. She is glancing up, in a little puzzled fashion, at the tall fair man who is bending over her whilst going through the usual formula, "May I have the pleasure," etc.

"Well, where is this dreadful woman?" says Dorian, at this moment, almost impatiently; he is watching Georgie and the fair man, and feels distinctly savage.

"Why, here," says Clarissa.

"Here? Not the—the girl in black, talking to Bellew!"

"Yes; that is your dreadful woman."

"Oh, look here, you know, it is too absurd," says Dorian, with a low laugh. "I have danced twice with her already, and am engaged to her for this!"

"She is your 'child,' then?" asks Clarissa, opening her eyes.

"Yes; but a governess, my dear Clarissa?"

"She is teaching the Redmond children. I told you so at the concert."

"I quite forgot,—utterly. How could one think of her as that, you know?"

"Now, please, do try and write plainly," breaks in Georgie's voice, plaintively. "Up to this I have not been able to read a single name upon my card."

"I'll do my best," says the fair young man. "Is that legible?"

"Bellew, is it? Yes, I can read that. Thank you, so much. Do you know, I haven't the faintest idea who I am going to dance this with, because"— examining her card—"it looks like 'Barleycorn,' and it can't be that, you know?"

"There once was a John Barleycorn," says Mr. Bellew, thoughtfully.

Clarissa has been claimed by Horace Branscombe, and has disappeared. Dorian, coming to the front, goes up to the little beauty in black and silver, and says, in a contrite tone,—

"I am so sorry I can't write; yet nevertheless *I* am John Barleycorn, and this dance belongs to me."

"Why, so it does," says Georgie, recognizing him in a naïve manner, and placing her hand upon his arm. She performs this last act slowly and with hesitation, as though not entirely sure of his identity, which has the effect of piquing him, and therefore heightening his admiration for her.

"You have forgotten me," he says, reproachfully.

"Oh, no," —slowly. "It was with you I danced the last waltz, I think."

"No. The last polka." He is even more piqued now. "It has slipped your memory; yet there are some things one never forgets."

"Yes," says Miss Broughton, with a suppressed sigh; "but those are unhappy things. Why think of them now? Let us dance again, and forget while we can."

"You mistake me," says Dorian, hastily. "I thought of nothing unhappy. I thought of you. I shall never forget this night."

"Ah, neither shall I!" says Miss Broughton, very earnestly indeed. By an artificial observer, it might be thought somewhat sentimentally.

"Do you mean that?" says Dorian, hopefully, if curiously. "Am I to understand you mean to keep this particular ball forever in mind?"

"You may, indeed."

"But why?" —with much animation, and an over-increasing show of hope.

"Because it is my first," says Miss Broughton, confidentially, with a little quick-drawn sigh of utter content, and a soft, if rather too general, smile.

"I see," —disappointedly. "Is that your reason? What a curious one!"

"You think it ridiculous, don't you?" says Georgie, faintly, ashamed of herself; "but it is quite true, and I can't help it. I was eighteen last month, and never before was I at any ball. I shall never forget this room, —I know that, —or the lights, or the flowers, or the man over there beating time for the band, or—or anything."

"I think 'the man over there' has much the best of it," says Dorian. "I wish I was the leader of that band. Is there any chance that your partners of this evening will be remembered by you?"

"Well, I suppose I sha'n't quite forget you," says Georgie, seriously, after a moment's careful reflection.

"I'll take jolly good care you don't," says Mr. Branscombe, rather losing his head, because of her intense calmness, and speaking with more emphasis than as a rule belongs to him. "You are staying at the vicarage aren't you?"

"Yes," says Georgie.

"And I live just three miles from that— —." Here he pauses, as though afraid to make his insinuation too plain.

"At Sartoris, isn't it?" asks Georgie, sweetly. "Yes? Clarissa showed me the entrance-gate to it last week. It looks pretty."

"Some day will you come up and see it?" asks he, with more earnestness than he acknowledges even to himself; "and," with a happy thought, "bring the children. It will be a nice walk for them."

"But you are always in London, are you not?" says Georgie.

"Oh, no, not always: I sha'n't go there again, for ever so long. So promise, will you?"

"I'll ask Mrs. Redmond. But I know we can. She never refuses me anything," says this most unorthodox governess.

"I'm sure I'm not surprised at that," says Branscombe. "Who could?"

"Aunt Elizabeth could," says Miss Broughton.

"I haven't the misfortune to know your aunt Elizabeth, for which I am devoutly grateful, because if she 'could,' as you say, she must be too good for hanging. By the by, this is not *my* first ball; yet you have never taken the trouble to ask me (though I asked you) why I intend keeping this night as a white spot in my memory."

"Well, I ask you now," says Georgie, penitently.

"Do you care to know?"

"I do, indeed."

"Then it is because to-night I met you for the first time."

He bends his head a little, and looks into her eyes,—the beautiful eyes that smile back so calmly into his, and are so cold to him, and yet so full of fire,—eyes that somehow have power to charm him as no others have yet been able to.

He is strangely anxious to know how his words will be received, and is proportionately aggrieved in that she takes them as a matter of course.

"After all, my reason is better than yours," she says, in her sweet, petulant voice. "Come, let us dance: we are only wasting time."

Branscombe is at first surprised, then puzzled, then fascinated. Almost any other woman of his acquaintance would have accepted his remark as a challenge,—would have smiled, or doubted, or answered him with some speech that would have been a leading question. But with this girl all is different. She takes his words literally, and, while believing them, shows herself utterly careless of the belief.

Dorian, passing his arm round her waist, leads her out into the room, and again they waltz, in silence,—he having nothing to say to her, she being so filled with joy at the bare motion that she cares no more for converse. At last,

> "Like some tired bee that flags
> Mid roses over-blown,"

she grows languid in his arms, and stops before a door that leads into a conservatory. It has been exquisitely fitted up for the occasion, and is one glowing mass of green and white and crimson sweetness. It is cool and faintly lit. A little sad fountain, somewhere in the distance, is mourning sweetly, plaintively,—perhaps for some lost nymph.

"You will give me another dance?" says Branscombe, taking her card.

"If I have one. Isn't it funny?—I feared when coming I should not get a dance at all, because, of course, I knew nobody; yet I have had more partners than I want, and am enjoying myself so much."

"Your card is full," says Branscombe, in a tone that suggests a national calamity. "Would you—would you throw over one of these fellows for me?"

"I would, in a minute," says Miss Broughton, naïvely; "but, if he found me out afterwards, would he be angry?"

"He sha'n't find you out. I'll take care of that. The crowd is intense. Of course"—slowly—"I won't ask you to do it, unless you wish it. Do you?"

"There is one name on that card I can't bear," says Miss Broughton, with her eyes fixed upon a flower she holds. Her dark lashes have fallen upon her cheeks, and lie there like twin shadows. He can see nothing but her mobile lips and delicately pencilled brows. He is watching her closely, and now wonders vaguely if she is a baby or a coquette.

"Show me the man you would discard," he says, running her pencil down her programme.

"There,—stop there. The name is Huntley, is it not? Yes. Well, he is old, and fat, and horrid; and I know he can't dance. You may draw the pencil across his name,—if you are sure, *quite sure*, he won't find me out."

"He shall not. But I would far rather you condemned that fair-haired fellow you were talking to just now," says Dorian, who is vaguely, faintly jealous of young Bellew.

"But he is so much nicer than Mr. Huntley," declares Georgie, earnestly: "and he was my first partner, and I promised him so faithfully to keep this dance for him."

"He'll never see you in the crush," says Branscombe.

"But I told him exactly where to find me."

"It is the most difficult thing in the world to be anywhere at the precise moment stated."

"But I should *like* to dance with him again," declares Miss Broughton, innocently, being driven into a corner.

"Oh, of course that ends the matter," says Dorian, in an impossible tone, drawing the pencil with much uncalled-for energy across Mr. Huntley's name.

Then some other man comes up, and claims the little wilful beauty for the waltz then playing, and, carrying her off in triumph, leaves Branscombe alone.

CHAPTER XVII

"It is the hydra of calamities,
The sevenfold death: the jealous are the
Damn'd." —Young.

Having watched her until the last fold of her gown has disappeared, Branscombe turns abruptly away, and, passing through a glass door that leads into the gardens outside, paces slowly up and down the winding paths beneath the subdued light of countless Chinese lanterns, that, hanging amidst the foliage, contrast oddly with the cold white brilliancy of the stars overhead, that

"Rush forth in myriads, as to wage
War with the lines of darkness."

Cold as the night air is, not a breath of wind comes to disturb the strange calm that hangs over land and sea. Far down in the bay the ocean lies at rest. From the distance a faint sound of music from the band comes softly, seductively to the ear, but beyond and above it comes the song of the nightingale that, resting in yonder thicket, pours forth its heart in tender hurried melody, as though fearful the night will be

"Too short for him to utter forth his love-chant,
And disburthen his full soul of all its music."

The notes rise and fall, and tremble on the air. No other sound comes from the breast of nature to mar the richness of its tone. No earthly thing seems living but itself. For it the night appears created, and draws its "sable curtain stained with gold" over the sleeping world. This nightingale, of all the feathered tribes, is wakeful, and chants its hymn of praise at midnight, whilst all its brethren rest in peaceful slumber.

The intense and solemn stillness of all around renders more enchanting the trills and tender trembles that shake its tiny throat. There is

"No whispering but of leaves, on which the breath
Of heaven plays music to the birds that slumber."

Yet this one sweet bird refuses rest, and, as though one of those "small foules" that "slepen alle night with open eye," sings on courageously amidst the gloom.

Dorian, strolling absently through the walks, and into the shrubberies beyond, listens, and feels some sense of comfort (that has yet with it a touch of pain) creep through him as the nightingale's sweet song smites upon his ear.

Yet this is not the only sound that disturbs the quiet of the night. Sadly, mournfully, a half-suppressed sob falls upon the air.

Branscombe starts, and looks round suddenly, but can see nothing. No footsteps make themselves heard. The shrubs are sufficiently thick to conceal the presence of any one, yet it seems to him as if the thought of that sob was born of fancy, and that the earthly owner of it is unborn.

Then some ray from the brilliant moon opens his eyes, and he sees a woman's figure standing in a somewhat disconsolate attitude, with her back against a tall elm, and her eyes fixed wistfully upon the distant windows, through which the lights are streaming, and the passing to and fro of the dancing crowd may be distinctly seen.

Dorian, recognizing her, goes quickly up to her and lays his hand upon her shoulder. It is Ruth Annersley!

She stifles a low cry, and, turning to him, grows even a shade paler than she was a moment since.

"Ruth," says Dorian, "what on earth brings you here at this hour?"

For a moment she makes him no answer. She raises her hand to brush away the tears that still lie heavily upon her cheeks, and then moves a little away from him, so as to elude his touch.

"I came to see them dancing," she says, at length, with difficulty; "I thought it would be a pretty sight; and—it is—I have been so—so pleased."

The words seem to choke her. With a movement that is terribly pathetic she lays her hand upon her heart; and then Dorian, following the direction her eyes have taken, sees what they see.

In an open window, directly opposite to where they are standing, two figures can be seen in very close proximity to each other. Beyond are the forms of the dancers; the faint sweet strains of the band float out to meet the midnight air; but the two in the window seem lost to all but the fact of their own existence, and that they are together. At least, so it seems to the onlookers in the shrubberies.

See, now he takes her hand,—the kindly curtain hiding the act from those within; he stoops towards her; the girl leans a little forward; and then Dorian knows them; the man is Horace, and the girl Clarissa Peyton!

Instinctively he glances from them to Ruth. She, too, is leaning forward, her whole attention concentrated upon the picture before her. Her eyes are wide and miserable, her cheeks pale and haggard.

"You have seen enough of this ball, Ruth," says Branscombe, very gently. "Go home now."

"Yes; enough,—too much," says the girl, starting into life again. She draws her breath quickly, painfully: her brow contracts. As though unable to resist the movement, she again lays her hand upon her heart, and holds it there, as though in anguish.

"What is it?" asks Dorian. "Are you in pain? How white you are!"

"I am tired. I have a pain here," pressing her hand still more closely against her side. "This morning I felt well and strong—and now——. My mother died of heart-disease; perhaps I shall die of it too. I think so; I hope so!"

"You are talking very great nonsense," says Dorian, roughly, though in his soul shocked to the last degree by the girl's manner, which is full of reckless misery. "Nobody sees any amusement in dying. Come, let me see you home."

"Oh, no! Please do not come, Mr. Branscombe," entreats she, so earnestly that he feels she has a meaning in her words. "I have the key of the small gate, and can run home in five minutes once I pass that."

"Then at least I shall see you safely as far as the gate," says Branscombe, who is tender and gentle in his manner to all women.

Silently they walk through the damp night grass, neither speaking, until, coming to a curve in the way, she breaks silence.

"How beautiful Miss Peyton looks to-night," she says, in a tone impossible to translate.

"Very," says Dorian, unkindly, yet with very kindly intent. "But then she is always one of the most beautiful women I know."

"Is she—very much admired?"—this rather timidly.

"One can understand that at once," says Dorian, quietly. "Both her face and figure are perfect." As he says this, quite calmly, his heart bleeds for the girl beside him.

"Who has she been dancing most with?" Eagerly, almost painfully, this question is put. The utter simplicity of it touches Dorian to his heart's core.

"With my brother, of course. She—she would not care to dance very much with any one else now, on account of her engagement."

"Her engagement?"

"Yes. She is to be married to my brother some time next year."

He hates himself bitterly as he says this: but something within him compels him to the cruel deed, if only through pity for the girl who walks beside him.

They are now within the shade of trees, and he cannot see her face; though in very truth, if he could have seen it at this moment, he would not have looked at it. No word escapes her; she walks on steadily, as though actually made strong by the receiving of the blow.

Dorian would gladly believe that her silence means indifference; but to-night has forced a truth upon him that for months he has determinedly put behind him. Her tears, her agitation, the agony that shone in her eyes as she fixed them upon Horace's form in the window, have betrayed only too surely the secret she would so gladly hide.

She makes no further attempt at conversation, and, when they come to the little iron gate that leads on to the road, would have passed through, and gone on her homeward way mechanically, without bidding him even good-night, as if (which is indeed the case) she has forgotten the very fact of his near presence.

But he cannot let her go without a word.

"Good-night," he says, very kindly, his tone warmer because of his pity for her. "Take care of yourself. Are you sure you do not fear going alone?"

"Yes." Her voice is low, and sounds strange, even in her own ears.

"Wrap your shawl more closely round you. The night is cold. Is the pain in your side better?"

"Yes," — almost regretfully.

"That is right. Well, good-by. I shall stand here until I see you have safely turned the corner; then I shall know you are out of all danger." He has been holding her hand somewhat anxiously all this time, not quite liking the strained expression in her face. Now he presses it, and then drops it gently.

"Good-night," returns she, slowly, and then turns away from him, never remembering to thank him for his kindness, — hardly, indeed, conscious of having spoken the farewell word.

Her brain seems on fire; her body cold as death. Oh, to be in her own room, free from all watching eyes, where she can fling herself upon the ground, and moan and cry aloud against her fate, with only the friendly darkness to overhear her! She hurries rapidly onward, and soon the corner hides her from sight.

Dorian, when she has safely passed the spot agreed upon, goes back once more in the direction of the house. He has hardly, however, gone two hundred yards, when the voice of his uncle, Lord Sartoris, calling to him through the gloom, stays his steps, and rouses him from the painful revery into which he is fast falling.

"Who were you parting with at the gate?" asks Lord Sartoris, in so unusual a tone that Dorian looks at him in some surprise. He is a little sorry, for reasons that do not touch himself, that the question should have been asked at all.

"Ruth Annersley," he answers, without hesitation, feeling that any prevarication at this moment will only make matters worse for the unhappy girl. May not Arthur have seen and known her?

"Ruth Annersley?"

"Yes. You will, of course, say nothing about it. She was foolish enough to wish to see a few people dancing, so came here, and, standing among the shrubs, obtained her wish,—which, no doubt, proved as satisfactory as most of our desires, when gained."

"At this hour of the night to be here, alone!"

"Yes. Very imprudent of her, of course, and all that."

"There must have been some strong inducement to make a girl of her gentle nature undertake so bold, so daring, a step. It was a strictly improper action," says the old man, in his most stilted style.

"I dare say. Imprudent, however, was the word I used. I am rather glad I was the one to meet her, as she knew me; and, as a rule, people talk so much about nothing, and make such mountains out of mole-hills."

"It was fortunate, indeed, your meeting her. It might, in fact, almost be termed a curious coincidence, your managing to be on this deserted walk just at the required moment."

There is something so unpleasant, so sneering, about his tone that Dorian colors hotly.

"I confess I hardly see it in the light you do," he says, easily enough, but very coldly. "And I think I should term the coincidence 'lucky,' rather than curious. I see no difference between this walk and half a dozen others. People don't seem to affect any of them much."

"No," says Lord Sartoris.

"Any other fellow might have been here as well as me. You, for example."

"Just so!" says Lord Sartoris.

"Then why bring in the word curious?"

"It merely occurred to me at the moment," says his lordship, drily. "Been dancing much?"

"Yes,—no,—pretty well. Are you coming in?"

They are again in front of the house, and near the steps that lead to the conservatory.

"Not just yet, I think."

"Then I fear I must leave you. I am engaged for this dance."

So, for the first time, these two part coldly. The old man goes slowly, moodily, up and down the gravelled path beneath the brilliant moon, that—

> "From her clouded veil soft gliding,
> Lifts her silvery lamp on high,"

and thinks of many things in a humor more sad than bitter; while the young man, with angry brow and lips compressed, goes swiftly onward to the house.

As he regains the ball-room, the remembrance of the little partner he has come to claim rushes back upon him pleasantly, and serves to dissipate the gloomy and somewhat indignant thoughts that have been oppressing him. But where is she? He looks anxiously around; and, after five minutes' fruitless search, lo! there are her eyes smiling out at him from the arms of a gay and (doubtless) gallant plunger.

The next instant she is gone; but he follows her slight form with eager glance, and at length crosses the room to where she is now standing with her soldier. As he does so he flings from him all tormenting thoughts, forgetting—as it is his nature to do—the possible misery of the future in the certain happiness of the present.

"The next is ours, is it not?" he says; and she smiles at him, and—can it be?—willingly transfers her hand from the heavy's arm to his; and then they dance; and presently he takes her down to the Peytons' carriage and puts her carefully into it, and presses her hand, I think, ever so slightly, and then drives home, beneath the silent stars, with an odd sensation at his heart—half pain, half pleasure—he has never felt before.

CHAPTER XVIII

"Known mischiefs have their cure, but doubts have none;
And better is despair than friendless hope
Mixed with a killing fear."—May.

It is two o'clock on the following day. Horace,—who came down from town for the ball, and is staying with Dorian,—sauntering leisurely into the smoking-room at Sartoris, finds Branscombe there, overlooking some fishing-tackle.

This room is a mingled and hopelessly entangled mass of guns, pipes, whips, spurs, fishing-rods, and sporting pictures; there are, too, a few other pictures that might not exactly come under this head, and a various and most remarkable collection of lounging-chairs.

There is a patriarchal sofa, born to create slumber; and an ancient arm-chair, stuffed with feathers and dreams of many sleepers. Over the door stand out the skeleton remains of a horse's head, bleached and ghastly, and altogether hideous, that, even now, reminds its master of a former favorite hunter that had come to a glorious but untimely end upon the hunting-field. A stuffed setter, with very glassy eyes, sits staring, in an unearthly fashion, in one corner. Upon a window-sill a cat sits, blinking lazily at the merry spring sunshine outside.

"Are you really going back to town this evening, Horace?" asks the owner of all these gems, in a somewhat gloomy fashion, bending over a fishing line as he speaks.

"Yes. I feel I am bound to be back there again as soon as possible."

"Business?"

"Well, I can hardly say it is exactly press of business," says the candid Horace; "but if a man wants to gain any, he must be on the spot, I take it?"

"Quite so. Where have you been all the morning? Sleeping?"

"Nothing half so agreeable." By this time Horace is looking at him curiously, and with a gleam in his eyes that is half amusement, half contempt: Dorian, whose head is bent over his work, sees neither the amusement nor the scorn. "I did not go to bed at all. I walked down to to the farms to try to get some fresh air to carry back with me to the stifling city."

"Ah! past the mill? I mean in that direction? — towards the upper farms?"

"No; I went past Biddulph's," says Horace, easily, half closing his eyes, and Dorian believes him. "It is lighter walking that way; not so hilly. Did you put in a good time last night?"

"Rather so. I don't know when I enjoyed an affair of the kind so much."

"Lucky you!" yawns Horace, languidly. "Of all abominations, surely balls are the worst. One goes on when one ought to be turning in, and one turns in when one ought to be going out. They upset one's whole calculations. When I marry I shall make a point of forgetting that such things be."

"And Clarissa?" asks Dorian, dryly; "I can't say about the dancing part of it, — you may, I suppose, abjure that if you like, — but I think you will see a ball or two more before you die. She likes that sort of thing. By the by, how lovely she looked last night!"

"Very. She cut out all the other women, I thought; they looked right down cheap beside her."

"She had it very much her own way," says Dorian; yet, even as he speaks, there rises before him the vision of a little lithe figure gowned in black and crowned with yellow hair, whose dark-blue eyes look out at him with a smile and a touch of wistfulness that adds to their beauty.

"That little girl at the vicarage isn't bad to look at," says Horace, idly, beating a tattoo on the window-pane.

"Miss Broughton? I should call her very good to look at," says Dorian, for the first time making the discovery that there may be moments when it would be a sure and certain joy to kick even one's own brother.

"Here is Arthur," says Horace, presently, drawing himself up briskly from his lounging position. "A little of him goes a long way; and I should say, judging from the expression of his lips, that he is in his moodiest mood to day. You may interview him, Dorian: I feel myself unequal to the task. Give him my love and a kiss, and say I have gone for a ramble in the innocent woods."

He leaves the room, and, crossing the halls, makes his way into the open air through the conservatory; while Lord Sartoris, entering by the hall door, and being directed by a servant, goes on to Dorian's den.

He is looking fagged and care-worn, and has about him that look of extreme lassitude that belongs to those to whom sleep overnight has been a stranger. Strong and painful doubts of Dorian's honesty of purpose had kept him wakeful, and driven him now down from his own home to Sartoris.

A strange longing to see his favorite nephew again, to look upon the face he had always deemed so true, to hear the voice he loves best on earth, had taken possession of him; yet now he finds himself confronting Dorian with scarcely a word to say to him.

"I hardly hoped to find you at home," he says, with an effort.

"What a very flattering speech! Was that why you came? Sit here, Arthur: you will find it much more comfortable."

He pushes towards him the cosily-cushioned chair in which Horace had been sitting a minute ago.

"Do I look tired enough to require this?" says Sartoris, sinking, however, very willingly into the chair's embrace. As he does so, something lying on the ground (that has escaped Dorian's notice) attracts him.

"What is this?" he asks, stooping to pick it up.

It is a lace handkerchief, of delicate and exquisite workmanship, with some letters embroidered in one corner.

"You have been receiving gentle visitors very early," says Lord Sartoris, turning the pretty thing round and round curiously.

"Not unless you can count Horace as one," says Dorian, with a light laugh. "How on earth did that come here?" Stooping, he, too, examines minutely the fragile piece of lace and cambric his uncle is still holding. Sartoris turning it again, the initials in the corner make themselves known, and stand out, legibly and carefully worked, as "R. A."

Dorian's face changes. He knows the handkerchief only too well now. He himself had given it to Ruth at Christmas; but how had it come here? No one had entered the room to-day except himself and—Horace!

Notwithstanding the scene with Ruth the night before, when she had so unmistakably betrayed her love for Horace, Dorian had never for one moment suspected that things had gone farther than a mere foolish girlish liking for a man rather handsomer than the ordinary run of men. His brother's honor he had not doubted, nor did he deem him capable of any act calculated to bring misery upon one who had trusted him.

Now, in spite of himself, a terrible doubt arises, that will not be suppressed; like a blow conviction falls; and many past actions and past words crowd to his mind that, at the time of their occurrence, seemed as mere nothings, but now are "confirmations strong" of the truth that has just flashed upon him.

Had he lied to him when he told him a few minutes since he had been to Biddulph's farm and not anywhere in the direction of the Old Mill? Doubt, having once asserted itself, makes him now distrustful of his brother's every look and every tone. And the handkerchief! He must have had it from Ruth herself, and dropped it here inadvertently before leaving the room. To him the idea that Horace should have chosen a timid, fragile, gentle girl, like Ruth Annersley, upon whom to play off the fascinations and wiles taught him by a fashionable world, is nothing less than despicable. A deep sense of contempt for the man who, to pass away pleasantly a few dull hours in the country, would make a target of a woman's heart, fills his mind. He is frowning heavily, and his face has grown very white Looking up, he becomes aware that his uncle is watching him narrowly.

To the old man, the altered countenance of his nephew, his pallor and hesitation, all betoken guilt. Dorian's eyes are still clear and calm, as usual, but his expression has strangely altered.

"'R. A.,'" remarks Lord Sartoris, slowly. "Why, that might mean Ruth Annersley."

"It might," returns Dorian, absently. He dares not speak his inmost thoughts. After all, Horace may not be in the wrong: the girl's own vanity, or folly, may have led her to believe a few words spoken in jest to mean more than was ever intended. And, at all events, no matter what comes of it, he cannot betray his brother.

"How could it have come here?" asks Lord Sartoris, without raising his eyes from the luckless handkerchief. "Do you know anything of it?"

"Nothing; except that it belongs to Ruth. I gave it to her last Christmas."

"You! A curious gift to a girl in her rank in life?"

"She wished for it," returns Branscombe, curtly.

"Then she is no doubt heart-broken, imagining she has lost it. Return it to her, I advise you, without delay," says his uncle, contemptuously, throwing it from him to a table near. "I need not detain you any longer, now," —rising, and moving towards the door.

"Going so soon?" says the younger man, roused from his galling reflections, by his uncle's abrupt departure, to some sense of cordiality. "Why, you have hardly stayed a moment."

"I have stayed long enough, —too long," says Lord Sartoris, gloomily, fixing his dark eyes (that age have failed to dim) upon the man who has been to him as his own soul.

"Too long?" repeats Branscombe, coloring darkly.

"Yes. Have you forgotten altogether the motto of our race?—'Leal friend, leal foe.' Let me bring it to your memory."

"Pray do not trouble yourself. I remember it perfectly," says Dorian, haughtily, drawing up his figure to its fullest height. "I am sorry, my lord, you should think it necessary to remind me of it."

He bows and opens the door as he finishes his speech. Lord Sartoris, though sorely troubled, makes no sign; and, without so much as a pressure of the hand, they part.

CHAPTER XIX

> "Lock you, how she cometh, trilling
> Out her gay heart's bird-like bliss!
> Merry as a May-morn thrilling
> With the dew and sunshine's kiss.

> Ruddy gossips of her beauty
> Are her twin cheeks; and her mouth,
> In its ripe warmth, smileth fruity
> As a garden of the south." —Gerald Massey.

To Georgie the life at the vicarage is quite supportable, —is, indeed, balm to her wounded spirit. Mrs. Redmond may, of course, chop and change as readily as the east wind, and, in fact, may sit in any quarter, being somewhat erratic in her humors; but they are short-lived; and, if faintly trying, she is at least kindly and tender at heart.

As for the vicar, he is—as Miss Georgie tells him, even without a blush—"simply adorable;" and the children are sweet good-natured little souls, true-hearted and earnest, to whom the loss of an empire would be as dross in comparison with the gain of a friend.

They are young!

To Dorian Branscombe, Miss Broughton is "a thing of beauty, and a joy forever; her loveliness increases" each moment, rendering her more dear. Perhaps he himself hardly knows how dear she is to his heart, though day after day he haunts the vicarage, persecuting the vicar with parochial business of an outside sort. It ought, indeed, to be "had in remembrance," the amount of charity this young man expended upon the poor during all this early part of the year.

Then there is always Sunday, when he sits opposite to her in the old church, watching her pretty mischievous little face meditatively throughout the service, and listening to her perfect voice as it rises, clear and full of pathos, in anthem and in hymn.

The spring has come at last, though tardy and slow in its approach. Now—

> "Buds are bursting on the brier,
> And all the kindled greenery glows

And life hath richest overflows,
And morning fields are fringed with fire."

Winter is almost forgotten. The snow and frost and ice are as a dream that was told. No one heeds them now, or thinks of them, or feels aught about them, save a sudden chill that such things might have been.

To-day is beautiful beyond compare. The sun is high in the heavens; the birds are twittering and preening their soft feathers in the yellow light that Phœbus flings broadcast upon the loving earth. The flowers are waking slowly into life, and stud the mossy woods with colorings distinct though faint:

"Nooks of greening gloom
Are rich with violets that bloom
In the cool dark of dewy leaves."

Primroses, too, are all alive, and sit staring at the heavens with their soft eyes, as though in their hearts they feel they are earth's stars. Each subtle green is widening, growing. All nature has arisen from its long slumber, and "beauty walks in bravest dress."

Coming up the road, Dorian meets Georgie Broughton, walking with quick steps, and in evident haste, towards the vicarage. She is lilting some merry little song of her own fancy, and has her hat pushed well back from her forehead, so that all her sunny hair can be seen. It is a lovely hat,—inexpensive, perhaps, but lovely, nevertheless, in that it is becoming to the last degree. It is a great big hat, like a coal-scuttle,—as scuttles used to be,—and gives her all the appearance of being the original of one of Kate Greenaway's charming impersonations.

"Good-morning," says Dorian, though, in truth, he hardly takes to heart the full beauty of the fair morning that has been sent, so rapt he is in joy at the very sight of her. "Going back to the vicarage now?"

"Yes." She is smiling sweetly at him,—the little, kind, indifferent smile that comes so readily to her red lips.

"Well, so am I," says Dorian, turning to accompany her.

Miss Broughton glances at him demurely.

"You can't want to go to the vicarage again?" she says, lifting her brows.

"How do you know I have been there at all to-day?" says Dorian.

"Oh, because you are always there, aren't you?" says Georgie, shrugging her shoulders, and biting a little flower she has been holding, into two clean halves.

"As you know so much, perhaps you also know *why* I am always there," says Branscombe, who is half amused, half offended, by her wilfulness.

"No, I don't," replies she, easily, turning her eyes, for the first time, full upon his. "Tell me."

She is quite calm, quite composed; there is even the very faintest touch of malice beneath her long lashes. Dorian colors perceptibly. Is she coquette, or unthinking, or merely mischievous?

"No, not now," he says, slowly. "I hardly think you would care to hear. Some day, if I may—. What a very charming hat you have on to-day!"

She smiles again,—what true woman can resist a compliment—and blushes faintly, but very sweetly, until all her face is like a pale "rosebud brightly blowing."

"This old hat?" she says, with a small attempt at scorn and a very well got-up belief that she has misunderstood him: "why, it has seen the rise and fall of many generations. You can't mean *this* hat?"

"Yes, I do. To me it is the most beautiful hat in the world, no matter how many happy generations have been permitted to gaze upon it. It is yours!"

"Oh, yes; I bought it in the dark ages," says Miss Broughton, disdaining to notice the insinuation, and treating his last remark as a leading question. "I am glad you like it."

"Are you? I like something else, too: I mean your voice."

"It is too minor,—too discontented, my aunt used to say."

"Your aunt seems to have said a good deal in her time. She reminds me of Butler's talker: 'Her tongue is always in motion, though very seldom to the purpose;' and again, 'She is a walking pillory, and punishes more ears than a dozen standing ones.' But I wasn't talking exactly of your everyday voice: I meant your singing: it is quite perfect."

"Two compliments in five minutes!" says Miss Georgie, calmly. Then, changing her tone with dazzling, because unexpected, haste, she says, "Nothing pleases me so much as having my singing praised. Do you know," with hesitation,—"I suppose—I am afraid it is very great vanity on my part, but I love my own voice. It is like a friend to me,—the thing I love best on earth."

"Are you always going to love it best on earth?"

"Ah! Well, that, perhaps, was an exaggeration. I love Clarissa. I am happier with her than with any one else. You"—meditatively—"love her too?"

"Yes, very much indeed. But I know somebody else with whom I am even happier."

"Well, that is the girl you are going to marry, I suppose," says Georgia, easily, — so easily that Dorian feels a touch of disappointment, that is almost pain, fall on his heart. "But as for Clarissa," — in a puzzled tone, — "I cannot understand her. She is going to marry a man utterly unsuited to her. I met him at the ball the other night, and" — thoughtlessly — "I don't like him."

"Poor Horace!" says Dorian, rather taken aback. Then she remembers, and is in an instant covered with shame and confusion.

"I beg your pardon," she says, hurriedly. "I quite forgot. It never occurred to me he was your brother, — never, really. You believe me, don't you? And don't think me rude. I am not" — plaintively — "naturally rude, and — and, after all," — with an upward glance full of honest liking, — "he is not a *bit* like *you*!"

"If you don't like him, I am glad you think he isn't," says Dorian; "but Horace is a very good fellow all through, and I fancy you are a little unjust to him."

"Oh, not unjust," says Georgie, softly. "I have not accused him of any failing; it is only that something in my heart says to me, 'Don't like him.'"

"Does something in your heart ever say to you, '*Like* some one'?"

"Very often." She is (to confess the honest truth) just a little bit coquette at heart, so that when she says this she lifts her exquisite eyes (that always seem half full of tears) to his for as long as it would take him to know they had been there, and then lowers them. "I shall have to hurry," she says; "it is my hour for Amy's music-lesson."

"Do you like teaching?" asks he, idly, more for the sake of hearing her plaintive voice again, than from any great desire to know.

"Like it?" She stops short on the pretty woodland path, and confronts him curiously: "Now, do you *think* I could like it? I don't, then! I perfectly hate it! The perpetual over and over again, the knowledge that to-morrow will always be as to-day, the feeling that one can't get away from it, is maddening. And then there are the mistakes, and the false notes, and everything. What a question to ask me! Did any one ever like it, I wonder!"

There is some passion, and a great deal of petulance, in her tone; and her lovely flower-like face flushes warmly, and there is something besides in her expression that is reproachful. Dorian begins to hate himself. How could he have asked her such a senseless question? He hesitates, hardly knowing what to say to her, so deep is his sympathy; and so, before he has time to decide on any course, she speaks again.

"It is so monotonous," she says, wearily. "One goes to bed only to get up again; and one gets up with no expectation of change except to go to bed again."

"'One dem'd horrid grind,'" quotes Mr. Branscombe, in a low tone. He is filled with honest pity for her. Instinctively he puts out his hand, and takes one of hers, and presses it ever so gently. "Poor child!" he says, from his heart. To him, with her baby face, and her odd impulsive manner, that changes and varies with every thought, she is merely a child.

She looks at him, and shakes her head.

"You must not think me unhappy," she says, hastily. "I am not that. I was twice as unhappy before I came here. Everybody now is so kind to me,—Clarissa, and the Redmonds, and"—with another glance from under the long lashes—"you, and——Mr. Hastings."

"The curate?" says Dorian, in such a tone as compels Miss Broughton, on the instant, to believe that he and Mr. Hastings are at deadly feud.

"I thought you knew him," she says, with some hesitation.

"I have met him," returns he, "generally, I think, on tennis-grounds. He can run about a good deal, but it seems a pity to waste a good bat on him. He never hits a ball by any chance, and as for serving—I don't think I swore for six months until the last time I met him."

"Why, what did he do?"

"More than I can recall in a hurry. For one thing, he drank more tea than any four people together that ever I knew."

"Was that all? I see no reason why any one should be ashamed of liking tea."

"Neither do I. On the contrary, one should be proud of it. It betrays such meekness, such simplicity, such contentment. I myself am not fond of tea,—a fact I deplore morning, noon, and night."

"It is a mere matter of education," says Georgie, laughing. "I used not to care for it, except at breakfast, and now I love it."

"Do you? I wish with all my heart I was good souchong," says Mr. Branscombe, at which she laughs again.

"One can't have all one's desires," she says. "Now, with me music is a passion; yet I have never heard any of the great singers of the age. Isn't that hard?"

"For you it must be, indeed. But how is it you haven't?"

"Because I have no time, no money, no—no anything."

"What a hesitation! Tell me what the 'anything' stands for."

"Well, I meant no home,—that is, no husband, I suppose," says Georgie. She is quite unconcerned, and smiles at him very prettily as she says it. Of the fact that he is actually in love with her, she is totally unaware.

"That is a regret likely to be of short standing," he says, his eyes on hers. But her thoughts are far away, and she hardly heeds the warmth of his gaze or the evident meaning in his tone.

"I suppose if I did marry somebody he would take me to hear all the great people?" she says, a little doubtfully, looking at him as though for confirmation of her hope.

"I should think he would take you wherever you wanted to go, and to hear whatever you wished to hear," he says, slowly.

"What a charming picture you conjure up!" says Georgie, looking at him. "You encourage me. The very first rich man that asks me to marry him, I shall say 'Yes' to."

"You have made up your mind, then, to marry for money?" He is watching her closely, and his brow has contracted a good deal, and his lips show some pain.

"I have made up my mind to nothing. Perhaps I haven't one to make up,"—lightly. "But I hate teaching, and I hate being poor. That is all. But we were not talking of that. We were thinking of Mr. Hastings. At all events, you must confess he reads well, and that is something! Almost everybody reads badly."

"They do," says Branscombe, meekly. "I do. Unless in words of one syllable, I can't read at all. So the curate has the pull over me there. Indeed, I begin to feel myself nowhere beside the curate. He can read well, and drink tea well, and I can't do either."

"Why, here we are at the vicarage," says Georgie, in a tone of distinct surprise, that is flattering to the last degree. "I didn't think we were half so close to it. I am so glad I met you, because, do you know, the walk hasn't seemed nearly so long as usual. Well, good-by."

"May I have those violets?" says Branscombe, pointing to a little bunch of those fair comers of the spring that lies upon her breast.

"You may," she says, detaching them from her gown and giving them to him willingly, kindly, but without a particle of the tender confusion he would gladly have seen in her. "They are rather faded," she says, with some disappointment; "you could have picked yourself a sweeter bunch on your way home."

"I hardly think so."

"Well, good-by again," she says, turning up to him the most bewitching and delicious of small faces, "and be sure you put my poor flowers in water. They will live the longer for it."

"They shall live forever. A hundred years hence, were you to ask me where they were, I swear I should be able to show them."

"A very safe oath," says Miss Broughton; and then she gives him her hand, and parts from him, and runs all the way down the short avenue to the house, leaving him to turn and go on to Gowran.

CHAPTER XX

"There have been hearts whose friendship gave
Them thoughts at once both soft and grave."

In the drawing-room he finds Clarissa sitting among innumerable spring offerings. The whole place seems alive with them. "The breath of flowers is on the air." Primroses and violets shine out from tiny Etruscan vases, and little baskets of pale Belleek are hidden by clustering roses brought from the conservatory to make sweet the sitting-room of their mistress.

"I am so glad you have come," says Clarissa, rising with a smile to welcome him, as he comes up to her. "The day was beginning to drag a little. Come over here, and make yourself comfortable."

"That will I, right willingly, so it pleases you, madam," says Dorian, and straightway, sinking into the desirable lounging-chair she has pointed out, makes himself thoroughly happy.

A low bright fire is burning merrily; upon the rug a snow-white Persian cat sinks blinking; while Billy, the Irish terrier, whose head is bigger than his body, and whose hair is of the shabbiest, reclines gracefully upon an ottoman near. Clarissa, herself, is lying back upon a cushioned chair, looking particularly pretty, if a trifle indolent.

"Now for your news," she says, in the tone one adopts when expecting to be amused.

Dorian, lifting his arms, lays them behind his head.

"I wonder if ever in all my life I had any news," he says, meditatively. "After all, I begin to think I'm not much. Well, let me see: would it be news to say I met and talked with, and walked with your 'lassie wi' the lint-white locks'?"

"Georgie? You— —. She was with me all the morning."

"So she told me."

"Ah? And how far did you go with her?"

"To the vicarage. As I had been there all the morning, I couldn't well go in again,—a fact I felt and deplored."

"I am glad you walked back with her," says Miss Peyton; but she doesn't look glad. "I hope you were nice to her?"

"Extremely nice: ask her if I wasn't. And our conversation was of the freshest. We both thought it was the warmest spring day we had ever known, until we remembered last Thursday, and then we agreed *that* was the warmest spring day we had ever known. And then we thought spring was preferable to summer. And, then, that Cissy Redmond would be very pretty if she hadn't a cocked nose. Don't look so amazed, my dear Clarissa: it was Miss Broughton's expression, not mine, and a very good one too, I think. We say a cocked hat; therefore why not a cocked nose? And then we said all education was a bore and a swindle, and then— —. How old is she, Clarissa?"

"You mean Georgie?"

"Yes."

"Neither nineteen nor twenty."

"So much! Then I really think she is the youngest-looking girl I ever met at that age. She looks more like sweet seventeen."

"You think her pretty?"

"Rather more than that: she reminds me always of 'Maggie Lauder:'

"'Her face is as the summer cloud, whereon
The dawning sun delights to rest his rays.'

And, again, surely Apollo loves to

"Play at hide-and-seek amid her golden hairs.'"

"Dorian, don't—don't make her unhappy," says Clarissa, blushing hotly.

"I wish I could," says Dorian. He laughs as he speaks, but there is truth hidden in his jesting tone. Oh, to make her feel something,—that cold indifferent child!

"No, no. I am in earnest," says Clarissa, a little anxiously. "Don't pay her too much attention, if you don't mean it."

"Perhaps I do mean it." ·

"She is very young,"—ignoring his last speech altogether. "She is a perfect baby in some ways. It isn't kind of you, I think."

"My dear child, what am I doing? If I hand Miss Broughton a chair, or ask her if she would like another cup of tea, is that 'making her unhappy'? I really begin to think society is too moral for me. I shall give it up, and betake myself to Salt Lake City."

"You won't understand me," begins she, sitting more upright, as though desirous of argument; but he interrupts her.

"There you mistake me," he says. "My motives are quite pure. I am dying to understand you, only I can't. If you would try to be a little more lucid, all would be well; but why I am to be sat upon, and generally maltreated, because I walked a mile or so with a friend of yours, is more than I can grasp."

"I don't want to sit upon you," says Clarissa a little vexed.

"No! I dare say that chair is more comfortable."

"I don't want anything; I merely ask you to be careful. She is very young, and has seen few men; and if you persist in your attentions she may fall in love with you."

"I wish to goodness she would," says Branscombe; and then something in his own mind strikes him, and he leans back in his chair, and laughs aloud. There is, perhaps, more bitterness than mirth in his laugh; yet Miss Peyton hears only the mirth.

"I hope she won't," she says, severely. "Nothing would cause me greater sorrow. Underneath her childish manner there lies a passionate amount of feeling that, once called into play, would be impossible to check. Amuse yourself elsewhere, Dorian, unless you mean to marry her."

"Well, why shouldn't I marry her?" says Dorian.

"I see no reason why you shouldn't. I only know you have no intention whatever of doing so."

"If you keep on saying that over and over again, I dare say I *shall* want to marry her," says Dorian. "There is nothing like opposition for that kind of thing; you go and tell a fellow he can't and sha'n't marry such-and-such a girl, and ten to one but he goes and does it directly."

"Don't speak like that," says Clarissa, entreatingly: she is plainly unhappy.

"Like what? What nonsense you have been talking all this time! Has it never occurred to you that though, no doubt, I am endowed with many qualities above the average, still I am not an 'Adonis,' or an 'Apollo,' or an 'Admirable Crichton,' or any thing of that sort, and that it is probable your Miss Broughton might be in my society from this till the day she dies without experiencing a pang, as far as I am concerned."

"I don't know about 'Apollo' or 'Crichton,'" says Clarissa; "but let her alone. I want her to marry Mr. Hastings."

"The curate?" says Dorian, for the second time to day.

"Yes. Why should you be so amazed? He is very charming, and I think she likes him. He is very kind-hearted, and would make her happy; and she doesn't like teaching."

"I don't believe she likes Hastings," says Dorian; yet his heart dies within him as he remembers how she defended him about his unlimited affection for the cup that "cheers but not inebriates."

"I believe she does," says Clarissa.

"Can't you do something for *me*, Clarissa?" says Dorian, with a rather strained laugh: "you are evidently bent on making the entire country happy, yet you ignore my case. Even when I set my heart upon a woman, you instantly marry her to the curate. I hate curates! They are so mild, so inoffensive, so abominably respectable. It is almost criminal of you to insist on handing over to one of them that gay little friend of yours with the yellow hair. She will die of Hastings, in a month. The very next time I have the good fortune to find her alone, I shall feel it my duty to warn her off him."

"Does anybody ever take advice unless it falls in with their own wishes?" says Clarissa. "You may warn her as you will."

"I sha'n't warn her at all," says Dorian.

When he has left Clarissa, and is on his homeward way, this thought still haunts him. Can that pretty child be in love with the lanky young man in the long-tailed coat? She can't! No; it is impossible! Yet, how sure Clarissa seemed! and of course women understand each other, and perhaps Georgie had been pouring confidences of a tender nature into her ears. This last is a very unpleasant idea, and helps to decapitate three unoffending primroses.

Certainly she had defended that fellow very warmly (the curate is now "that fellow"), and had spoken of him a though she felt some keen interest in him. After all, what is it to him? (This somewhat savagely, and with the aid of a few more flowers.) If he was in love with her, it would be another thing; but as it is,—yes, as it *is*.

How often people have advised him to marry and settle down! Well, hang it all, he is surely as good to look at as the curate, and his position is better; and only a few hours ago she had expressed a desire to see something of life. What would Arthur think of — —

His thoughts change. Georgie's *riante* lovely face fades into some deeper recess of his heart, and a gaunt old figure, and a face stern and disappointed, rises before him. Ever since that day at Sartoris, when the handkerchief had been discovered, a coldness, a nameless but stubborn shadow, had fallen between him and his uncle,—a shadow impossible to lift until some explanation be vouchsafed by the younger man.

Such an explanation it is out of Dorian's power to give. The occurrence altogether was unhappy, but really nothing worthy of a violent quarrel. Branscombe, as is his nature, pertinaciously thrusts the whole affair out of sight, refusing to let it trouble him, except on such occasions as the present, when it pushes itself upon him unawares, and will not be suppressed.

Horace has never been to Pullingham since the night of the ball, and his letters to Clarissa have been many and constant, so that Dorian's suspicions have somewhat languished, and are now, indeed, almost dead, he being slow to entertain evil thoughts of any one.

Ruth Annersley, too, though plainly desirous of avoiding his society ever since his meeting with her in the shrubberies, seems happy and content, if very quiet and subdued. Once, indeed, coming upon her unexpectedly, he had been startled by an expression in her eyes foreign to their usual calm; it was a look half terrified, half defiant, and it haunted him for some time afterwards. But the remembrance of that faded, too; and she had never afterwards risked the chance of a *tête-à-tête* with him.

Meantime, Miss Peyton's little romance about the Broughton-Hastings affair rather falls to bits. Georgie, taking advantage of an afternoon that sees the small Redmonds on the road to a juvenile party, goes up to Gowran, and, making her way to the morning room, runs to Clarissa and gives her a dainty little hug.

"Aren't you glad I have come?" she says, with the utmost *naïveté*. "I'm awfully glad myself. The children have all gone to the Dugdales', and so I am my own mistress."

"And so you came to me," says Clarissa.

"Yes, of course."

"And now, to make you happy," says Clarissa, meditatively.

"Don't take any thought about that. It is already an accomplished fact. I am with *you*, and therefore I am perfectly happy."

"Still, you so seldom get a holiday," goes on Clarissa, regretfully, which is a little unfair, as the Redmonds are the easiest-going people in the world, and have a sort of hankering after the giving of holidays and the encouragement of idleness generally. The vicar, indeed, is laden with a suppressed and carefully hidden theory that children should never do anything but laugh and sit in the sun. In his heart of hearts he condemns all

Sunday-schools, as making the most blessed day one of toil, and a wearying of the flesh, to the little ones.

"Why,—why," said he, once, in an unguarded moment, bitterly repented of afterwards, "forbid them their rest on the Sabbath day?"

"What a pity the afternoon is so uncertain!" says Clarissa. "We might have gone for a nice long drive."

She goes over to the window, and gazes disconsolately at the huge shining drops that fling themselves heavily against the panes, and on the leaves and flowers outside; while

"The thirsty earth soaks up the rain,
And drinks, and gapes for drink again."

"I cannot feel anything to be a pity to-day," says Georgie. "I can feel only a sense of freedom. Clarissa, let us play a game of battledore and shuttlecock. I used to beat you at Brussels; try if you can beat me now."

Into the large hall they go, and, armed with battledores, commence their fray. Hither and thither flies the little white bird, backwards and forwards move the lithe figures of the girls. The game is at its height: it is just the absorbing moment, when 199 has been delivered, and received, and returned, when Georgie, stopping short suddenly, cries "Oh!" and 200 flutters to the ground.

Clarissa, who is standing with her back to the hall door, turns instinctively towards it, and sees Dorian Branscombe.

"I have disturbed you. I have come in at the wrong moment?" asks that young man, fearfully.

"Ah! you have spoiled our game. And we were so well into it. Your sudden entrance startled Georgie, and she missed her aim."

"I am sorry my mere presence should reduce Miss Broughton to a state of abject fright," says Dorian, speaking to Clarissa, but looking at Georgie.

Her arm is still half raised, her color deep and rich, her eyes larger, darker than usual; the excitement of the game is still full upon her. As Dorian speaks, her lips part, and a slow sweet smile creeps round them, and she looks earnestly at him, as though to assure him that she is making him a free present of it,—an assurance that heightens her beauty, to his mind. Gazing at her with open and sincere admiration, he tells himself that

"Nature might no more her child advance."

"Your presence would not frighten me," she says, shaking her head; "but it was—I don't know what; I only know that I forgot myself for the moment and missed my aim. Now, that was hard, because we were so near our second hundred. Why did you not come a little sooner or a little later?"

"Because 'a thoughtless animal is man,'" quotes he, his blue eyes full of contrition. "And the door was wide open, and the picture before me put all other thoughts out of my head. I wish I was a girl! I should do nothing but play battledore and shuttlecock from morning till night." Then, reproachfully, "I think you might both shake hands with me, especially as I can say only 'how d'ye do' and 'good-by' in one breath: I am bound to meet Arthur at three precisely."

"What a comfort!" says Clarissa, devoutly. "Then there is some faint chance we may be allowed to end our afternoon in peace!"

"If there is one thing on earth for which I have a keen admiration, it is candor," says Branscombe; "I thank you, Clarissa, for even this small touch of it. Miss Broughton, be candid too, and say you, at least, will regret me."

"I shall," says Georgie, with decided—and, it must be confessed, unexpected—promptness.

"Ha!" says Dorian, victoriously. "Now I am content to go. A fig for your incivility, Clarissa! At least I leave one true mourner behind."

"Two," says Clarissa, relentingly.

"Too late now; apology is useless! Well, I'm off. Can I do anything for either of you?"

"Yes; bring me up that little dog you promised me,—one of Sancho's puppies."

"You shall have the very prettiest to-morrow, in spite of your ill-treatment. And you, Miss Broughton, what can I do for you?"

He is looking tenderly at the small childish face, framed in gold, that is gazing at him smilingly from the distance.

"Me?" she says, waking, as if from a revery, with a faint blush. "Oh! give me my liberty." She says it jestingly, but with a somewhat sad shrug of her rounded shoulders, as she remembers the dismal school-room, and the restraint that, however gentle, is hateful to her gay, petulant nature. Her smile dies, and tears creep into her eyes.

In another moment she is laughing again; but months go by before Dorian forgets the sad little petition and the longing glance that accompanied it, and the sigh that was only half repressed.

"I like Mr. Branscombe so much," says Georgie, a little later on, when Dorian has disappeared. They have forsaken their late game, and are now in Clarissa's own room, standing in a deep oriel window that overlooks the long sweep of avenue on one side, and the parterre beneath where early spring flowers are gleaming wet with the rain that fell so heavily an hour ago.

"Every one likes Dorian," says Clarissa, pleasantly, but without her usual warmth when speaking of Branscombe. "He is a general favorite, and I think he knows it. He is like a spoiled child; he says what he likes to everyone, but nobody takes anything he says *seriously*."

This friendly hint is utterly thrown away. Miss Broughton understands it not at all.

"Yet sometimes he looks quite grave," she says,—"nearly as grave as Mr. Hastings when in his surplice, only not so solemn. That is all the difference."

"I like Mr. Hastings in his surplice," says Clarissa; "I think him very handsome: don't you?"

"Well—yes—. Only I wish his ears didn't stick out so much. Why do they? He always, somehow, makes me think of Midas."

"But you like him," persists Clarissa, feeling, however, a little crestfallen. It doesn't sound promising, this allusion to Mr. Hastings's ears.

"Ever so much," says Georgie, enthusiastically; "and really, you know, he can't help his ears. After all, how much worse a crooked eye would be!"

"Of course. And his eyes are really beautiful."

"You are not in love with him, are you?" says Miss Georgie, with an amused laugh; and again Clarissa's hopes sink to zero.

"No. But I am glad you are a friend of his. Does he—like you?"

"Yes, I think so: I am sure of it. Clarissa,"—with hesitation,—"if I tell you something, will you promise me faithfully not to tell it again?"

"I promise faithfully, darling, if you wish it."

"It is something Mr. Hastings said to me last night, and though I was not told in words to keep it secret, still I think he would wish me to be silent about it for—for a while. There can't be any harm in confiding it to you, can there? You are such an old friend of both."

"Not the slightest harm," says Miss Peyton, with conviction. Woman-like, she is burning with curiosity. Not for an instant does she doubt that one of her greatest wishes is about to be fulfilled: Mr. Hastings, who has a small though not insignificant income of his own, independent of the Church, is about to marry her dearest Georgie.

"Her dearest Georgie," raising herself a little from her recumbent position, leans her arm upon Clarissa's knee, and looks up into her face: there is importance largely mingled with delight in her fair features.

"Well, then," she says, slowly, as though loath to part all at once with her treasured news, "last night—he told me—that he—was in love!"

"Did he?"—with suppressed excitement. "And—and you—what did you say?"

"I didn't say much," says Miss Broughton, regretfully. "I might have said a great deal more, something kinder, more encouraging, you know; but I was so surprised and so——"

"Pleased?"—tenderly.

"Pleased! I should think so," with so much *empressement* that even Clarissa is taken aback. "I was never so delighted in my life, only, as I said before, a little confused, and couldn't think of anything pretty to say."

"I think it was far nicer your saying nothing," says Clarissa, very gently. She is a little disappointed in Georgie; a woman may be glad to marry a man, but she shouldn't say so, at least not exactly in such a cold-blooded fashion. "I can quite understand"—with sufficient hesitation to convince herself, at least, that she does not understand—"how you felt nervous in spite of your happiness."

"Oh, you always know everything," says Georgie, so lovingly that Clarissa hates herself for thinking even one unpleasant thought of her. "Well, he went on to say he never loved before. Now, honestly, Clarissa,"—in a thoroughly matter-of-fact tone,—"do you think that could be true?"

"Why shouldn't it be true?" says Clarissa, wishing with all her heart the other would be a little more sentimental over her own first love-affair, as she believes it to be.

"Well, yes, of course; he is rather young, and beauty goes a long way with some men."

Again Clarissa stares. She hadn't thought Georgie vain of her own charms. How difficult it is to know any one, even one's chiefest friend!

"Then he went on to say he could never feel real happiness again until he knew he was loved in return."

"Well?"—breathlessly,—"and then——?"

"I said,"—with the gayest little laugh imaginable,—"I thought he *was* loved in return."

"You *thought*, Georgie? What a strange answer! I do think you are a little bit coquette! I am so glad, though. Do you know, I guessed all along how it would be?"

"So did I. I knew very well how it would end. I felt he would fall a victim sooner or later. It is rather soon, isn't it? But of course it is only natural I should know about it?"

"Yes, only natural." Clarissa can think of nothing else to say. Not like this had *she* felt when——. To talk of him as a victim!

"I hope everything will be settled soon," goes on Miss Broughton, gayly, "'Happy is the wooing that isn't long adoing.' And I should like the marriage to be soon; wouldn't you? I think next time I see him I shall ask him about it."

"Oh, Georgie, don't! Indeed I would not, if I were you," exclaims Clarissa, in an agony. Good gracious! Is she lost to all sense of shame? "He won't like it. It is surely the man's part to speak first about that."

"Oh, very well,"—amicably. "But there couldn't be any harm in my speaking about it." "Just as much as in any other woman's."

"Not so much as if it was Cissy?"

"Twice as much. What has she got to do with it?"

"Well, a great deal, I take it,"—laughing again.

"As a friend she may feel some interest in him, I suppose. But *she* is not going to marry him."

"Well, I think she is. You don't think she will refuse him, do you?"— anxiously.

"Cissy Redmond!"

"Cissy Redmond."

"Do you mean to tell me," says Clarissa, growing very red, "that it is Cissy you have been talking about all this time, and not—yourself?"

"Myself! What on earth are you thinking of?" It is now Georgie's turn to blush crimson, and she does it very generously. Then she breaks into wild mirth, and, laying her head on Clarissa's knees, laughs till she nearly cries. "Oh, when I think of all I have said!" she goes on, the keenest enjoyment in her tone,—"how I praised myself, and how cavalierly I treated his proposal, and—what was it I said about asking him to name the wedding-day? Oh, Clarissa, what a dear you are!—and what a *goose!*"

"Well, certainly, I never was so taken in in my life," confesses Miss Peyton, and then she laughs too, and presently is as deeply interested in Cissy's lover as if he had indeed been Georgie's.

CHAPTER XXI

"Sin and shame are ever tied together
With Gordian knots, of such a strong thread spun,
They cannot without violence be undone." —Webster.

"Sharper than the stings of death!" —Reynolds.

Upon Pullingham a great cloud has descended. It has gathered in one night, —swiftly, secretly, —and has fallen without warning, crushing many hearts beneath it. Shame, and sin, and sorrow, and that most terrible of all things—uncertainty—have come together to form it, while doubt and suspicion lie in its train.

Ruth Annersley is missing! She has disappeared, —utterly! entirely!—leaving no trace behind her, no word, no line to relieve the heart of the old man, her father, and which is slowly beginning to break, as the terrible truth dawns upon him.

Only yester eve she had poured out his tea as usual, had bidden him good night, —lovingly, indeed, but not as one would bid an eternal farewell. Afterwards, he remembered, she had not given him—on that night of all others—the customary kiss, but had passed away from him coldly, callously—or was it that she feared?

Tired out with his day's work, the miller had gone to bed The girl, as was her habit ever since the longer evenings had set in, had gone for a little walk into the dewy woods, where we are told "every bough that moves over our head has an oracular wisdom." Alas! that they should have taught her so little. She had crossed the road before the very eyes of her household, had entered the green forest of early-breaking leaves, had faded from sight, and never came back again.

The old man, who rises and goes to bed with the sun (most constant companion of simple minds), had slept peacefully all night, never doubting that the child of his heart lay dreaming calm and happy dreams in her own room. Not until the morning was far advanced did he discover that Ruth's bed had known no occupant the night before.

Afterwards, too, he remembered how little this thought had jarred upon him just at first. It was strange, vexing; she should have told him where she meant to spend her evening; but, beyond that, it caused him no pang, no suspicion.

Her aunt lived in a neighboring town,—probably she had gone there. It was only four miles away,—a walk Ruth had taken many a day, and thought nothing of it; but it was imprudent starting on such a journey so late in the evening; and, besides, there was always the old mare to drive her there and back.

Messengers were despatched to her aunt's house, but they returned bringing no tidings. She was not there—had not been for over a fortnight.

Day wanes; twilight is descending,—

> "Melting heaven with earth,
> Leaving on craggy hills and running streams
> A softness like the atmosphere of dreams."

All day the miller has sat apart, his snow-white head upon his arms, in the room her hands had beautified and made so dear. With passionate indignation he has thrust from him all the attempts at sympathy, all the hurtful, though well-meant, offers of assistance held out to him by kindly neighbors. Silent, and half maddened by his thoughts, he sits dogged and silent, refusing food, and waiting only for her who never comes.

But when, at length, the gloaming comes, and day is over, without bringing to him the frail form of her he so desires, he rises, and, pushing back his chair, goes up to Hythe, and into the presence of Lord Sartoris.

"*You* will find me my girl," he says, and then he tells him all the story.

Sartoris listens, and, as he does so, sickens with doubt that is hardly a doubt, and fear that is nearly a certainty. Is this the end he has so dreaded? Is this the creeping horror that has of late so tortured him? Alas for the unblemished honor of the old name that for centuries has held itself *sans peur et sans reproche*.

How can he dare to offer consolation to old Annersley? He covers his face with his hands, and bends forward over the table. There is something in his attitude that denotes despair, and renders more keen the agony in Annersley's bosom.

"Why do you do that?" he cries, fiercely. "What is there to groan about? Nothing, I tell you! The child has gone too far,—has lost her way. She didn't understand. She cannot find her road home.—No more—no more!"

His excitement and grief are pitiful to see. He wrings his hands; his whole bearing and expression are at variance with his hopeful words. "She will come back in an hour or two, mayhap," he says, miserably, "and then I shall feel that I have disturbed your lordship: but I am in a hurry, you see: I want her, and I cannot wait."

"What do you want me to do for you?" says Sartoris, very humbly. He feels that he can hardly lift his eyes in this man's presence.

"Find her! That is all I ask of you. Find her, dead or alive! You are a great man,—high in authority, with power, and servants at command. Find me my child! Oh, *man*, help me, in some way!"

He cries this in an impassioned tone. He is totally overcome. His poor old white head falls helplessly upon his clasped arms.

Sartoris, pale as death, and visibly affected, can make no reply. He trembles, and stands before the humble miller as one oppressed with guilt.

Annersley mistakes his meaning, and, striding forward, lays his hand upon his arm.

"You are silent," he says, in a terrible tone, made up of grief and anguish more intense than words can tell. "You do not think she is in the wrong, do you? You believe her innocent? Speak!—speak!"

"I do," responds Sartoris, and only his own heart knows that he lies. Yet his tone is so smothered, so unlike his usual one, that he hardly recognizes it himself.

"If Mr. Branscombe were only here," says Annersley, in a stricken voice, after a lengthened pause, "he would help me. He has always been a kind friend to me and mine."

Lord Sartoris draws a deep breath, that is almost a sob.

"When does he return, my lord?"

"On Saturday. He said so, at least, when leaving."

"A long time," murmurs the old man, mournfully. "She will be home before that,—if she ever comes at all." His head sinks upon his breast. Then he rouses himself, and, glancing at Lord Sartoris, says entreatingly, "Won't you write to him, my lord? Do, I implore of you, and conjure him to return. If any one can help me it will be Mr. Dorian."

"I shall write to him now,—now,—at once," says Sartoris, mechanically, feeling how hideous is the mockery of this promise, knowing what he thinks he knows. Even yet he clings to the hope that he has been mistaken.

Thus he soothes the old man with vain promises, and so gets rid of him, that he may be left alone with his own thoughts.

Shall he go to Dorian? This is the first engrossing idea. Yet it affords but little consolation. To see him, to hear him, to listen to a denial from his lips; that is what it holds out to him, and it is all insufficient. How shall he believe him, knowing the many things that have occurred? How treat his very most eager denial as anything but a falsehood?

For hours he paces to and fro, pondering on what is the best course to pursue. He is not his father, that he can coerce him. By nature suspicious (though tender-hearted and indulgent in other ways), it comes easily to him to believe that even the man in whom he has trusted has been found wanting.

"To doubt is worse than to have lost," says Massinger; and surely he is right. Sartoris, in deep perplexity, acknowledges the truth of this line, and tells himself that in his old age he has been sorely tried. The whole world seems changed. Sunshine has given place to gloom; and he himself stands alone, —

> "Stoynde and amazde at his own shade for dreed,
> And fearing greater daungers than was nede."

Not until he is thoroughly exhausted, both in mind and body, does he decide on leaving for town by the mid-day train next day.

In the mean time he will telegraph to Claridge's, some faint remembrance lingering with him of Dorian's having made mention of that hotel as being all any one's fancy could possibly paint it.

But the morrow brings its own tidings.

It is almost noon, and Sartoris, sitting in his library, writing some business letters, — preparatory to catching the up train to town, — is disturbed by a light knock at the door.

"Come in," he calls out, impatiently; and Simon Gale, opening the door, comes slowly in.

He is a very old man, and has been butler in the family for more years than he himself can count. His head is quite white, his form a little bent; there is, at this moment, a touch of deep distress upon his face that makes him look even older than he is.

"Are you busy, my lord?" asks he, in a somewhat nervous tone.

"Yes; I am very much engaged. I can see no one, Gale. Say I am starting for town immediately."

"It isn't that, my lord. It is something I myself have to say to you. If you could spare me a few minutes——." He comes a little nearer, and speaks even more earnestly. "It is about Ruth Annersley."

Lord Sartoris, laying down his pen, looks at him intently.

"Close the door, Simon," he says, hurriedly, something in the old servant's manner impressing him. "I will hear you. Speak, man: what is it?"

"A story I heard this morning, my lord, which I feel it my duty to repeat to you. Not that I believe one word of it. You will remember that, my lord, — *not one word*." The grief in his tone belies the truth of his avowal. His head is bent. His old withered hands clasp and unclasp each other nervously.

"You are trembling," says Lord Sartoris. "Sit down. This news, whatever it is, has unstrung you."

"It has," cries Simon, with vehemence. "I *am* trembling; I *am* unstrung. How can I be otherwise when I hear such a slander put upon the boy I have watched from his cradle?"

"You are speaking of— —?" demands Sartoris, with an effort.

"Mr. Dorian." He says this in a very low tone; and tears, that always come so painfully and so slowly to the old, shine in his eyes. "His sad complexion wears grief's mourning livery." He covers his face with his hands.

Sartoris, rising from his seat, goes over to the window, and so stands that his face cannot be seen.

"What have you got to say about Mr. Branscombe?" he asks, in a harsh, discordant tone.

"My lord, it is an impertinence my speaking at all," says Gale.

"Go on. Let me know the worst. I can hardly be more miserable than I am," returns Sartoris.

"It was Andrews, the under-gardener, was telling me," begins Simon, without any further attempt at hesitation. "This morning, early, I met him near the Ash Grove. 'Simon,' he says, 'I want to speak wi'ye. I have a secret on my mind.'

"'If you have, my man, keep it,' says I. 'I want none o' your secrets.' For in truth he is often very troublesome, my lord, though a well-meaning youth at bottom.

"'But it is on my conscience,' says he, 'and if I don't tell it to you I shall tell it to some one else, because tell it I must, or bust!'

"So when he went that far, my lord, I saw as how he was real uneasy, and I made up my mind to listen. And then he says, —

"'Night before last feyther was coming through the copse wood that runs t'other side o' the fence from Master Annersley's, and there, in the thickest part o' it, he saw Miss Ruth a standing, and wi' her was Mr. Branscombe.'

"'Which Mr. Branscombe?' says I.

"'Mr. Dorian,' he says, 'He seen him as plain as life, though it was dusk, standing wi' his back half turned towards him, but not so turned but what he could see his ear and part o' his face. He had a hold o' Miss Ruth's hands; and was speaking very earnest to her, as though he were persuading her to something she were dead against. And she were crying very bitter, and trying to draw her hands away; but presently she got quiet like; and then they went away together, slowly at first, but quicker afterwards, in the direction of the wood that leads to Langham. He did not stir a peg until they was out o' sight, he was so afeard o' being seen. And now it is on his conscience that he did not speak sooner, ever since he saw old Mr. Annersley yesterday, like a mad creature, looking for his girl.'

"That was his story, my lord. And he told it as though he meant it. I said to him as how Mr. Dorian was in Lonnun, and that I didn't believe one word of it; and then he said, —

"'Lonnun or no Lonnun, there is no mistake about it. If, as you say, he did go up to Lonnun, he must ha' come down again by the Langham train, for he see him wi' his two eyes.'

"'Mr. Horace is very like Mr. Dorian,' I said. (Forgive me, my lord, but there was a moment when I would gladly have believed the blame might fall on Mr. Horace.) 'There are times when one can hardly know them asunder;' but he scouted this notion.

"'Feyther seen him,' he said. 'He had one o' them light overcoats on he is so fond o' wearing. It was him, and no other. He noticed the coat most perticler. And a damn'd shame it is for him! If you don't believe me, I can't help you. I believe it: that is enough for me.'"

Gale ceases speaking. And silence follows that lasts for several minutes. Then he speaks again:

"I ask your pardon, my lord, for having so spoken about any member of the family. But I thought it was only right you should know."

"You have acted very kindly." Even to himself his tone is strained and cold. "This Andrews must be silenced," he says, after a little pause, full of bitterness.

"I have seen to that, my lord. After what I said to him, he will hardly speak again to any one on the subject."

"See to it, Simon. Let him fully understand that dismissal will be the result of further talk."

"I will, my lord." Then, very wistfully, "Not that any one would distrust Mr. Dorian in this matter. I feel—I know, he is innocent."

Lord Sartoris looks at him strangely; his lips quiver; he seems old and worn, and as a man might who has just seen his last hope perish.

"I envy you your faith," he says, wearily; "I would give half—nay, all I possess, if I could say that honestly."

Just at this moment there comes an interruption.

"A telegram, my lord," says one of the men, handing in a yellow envelope.

Sartoris, tearing it open, reads hurriedly.

"I shall not go to town, Gale," he says, after a minute or two of thought. "Counter-order the carriage. Mr. Branscombe comes home to-night."

CHAPTER XXII

"When there is a great deal of smoke, and no clear flame,
it argues much moisture in the matter, yet it witnesseth,
certainly, that there is fire there." —Leighton.

Long before the night has set in he comes; and, as he enters the room where his uncle sits awaiting him, Lord Sartoris tells himself that never before has he seen him so handsome, so tall, so good to look at.

"Your telegram made me uneasy," he says, abruptly, "so I came back sooner than I had intended. Had you mine?"

"Yes; some hours ago."

"Did you want me, Arthur?"

"Yes; but not your return here. I sent my telegram principally to learn your address, as I had made up my mind to go up to town. You have frustrated that plan."

There is a meaning in his tone that puzzles Dorian.

"You going to trust yourself alone in our great Babylon?" he says, raising his brows. "Why, the world must be coming to an end. What business had you there that I could not have managed for you?"

"My business was with you."

"Anything wrong?" says the young man, impatiently, tapping a table lightly with his fingers, and frowning somewhat heavily. "Your tone implies as much. Has anything happened in my absence to cause you annoyance? If so, let me know at once, and spare me any beating about the bush. Suspense is unpleasant."

"It is," says Sartoris, rising from his chair, and moving a few steps nearer to him. "It is slowly murdering poor old John Annersley!"

"I am still hopelessly in the dark," says Dorian, shrugging his shoulders. "What has suspense got to do with old Annersley?"

"Are you really ignorant of all that has occurred? Have you not heard of Ruth's mysterious disappearance?"

"'Ruth's disappearance?' I have heard nothing. Why, where can she have gone?"

"That is exactly what no one knows, except she herself, of course, and—one other." Then, turning impulsively to face his nephew, "I thought you could have told me where she is," he says, without giving himself time to think of all the words may convey to Dorian.

"What do you mean?" demands Branscombe, throwing up his head, and flushing darkly. His eyes flash, his nostrils dilate. "Am I to infer from your last remark that you suspect *me* of having something to do with her disappearance?"

"I do," returns Sartoris, slowly, but with his eyes upon the ground. "How can I do otherwise when I call to mind all the causes you have given me to doubt you? Have you forgotten that day, now some months ago, when I met you and that unhappy girl together on the road to the village? I, at least, shall never forget the white misery of her face, and the unmistakable confusion in her manner, as I greeted her. Even then the truth began to dawn upon me."

"The truth?" says Branscombe, with a short and bitter laugh.

"At that time I was unwilling to harbor unkind doubts of you in my breast," goes on Sartoris, unmoved, nay, rather confirmed in his suspicions by Branscombe's sneer; "but then came the night of the Hunt ball, when I met you, alone with her, in the most secluded part of the grounds, and when you were unable to give me any reasonable explanation of her presence there; and then, a little later, I find a handkerchief (which you yourself acknowledge having given her) lying on your library floor; about that, too, you were dumb: no excuse was ready to your lips. By your own actions I judge you."

"Your suspicions make you unjust, my lord," says the young man, haughtily. "They overrule your better judgment. Are such paltry evidences as you have just put forward sufficient to condemn me, or have you further proofs?"

"I have,—a still stronger one than any other I have mentioned. The last place in which Ruth Annersley was seen in this neighborhood was in Hurston Wood, at eight o'clock on the evening of her departure, and—you were with her!"

"*I* was?"

"The man who saw you will swear to this."

"He must be rather a clever fellow. I congratulate you on your 'man.'"

"Do you deny it?" There is something that is almost hope in his tone. "If not there last Tuesday, at that hour, where were you?"

"Well, really, it would take me all my time to remember. Probably dining: got to my fish by that time, no doubt. Later on I was at Lady Chetwoode's crush; but that"—with a sarcastic laugh—"is a very safe thing to say, is it not? One can hardly prove the presence of any one at a gathering together of the clans, such as there was at her 'at home.' I *wouldn't* believe I was there, if I were you."

He laughs again. Sartoris flushes hotly all over his lean earnest face.

"It is needless lying," he says, slowly. "The very coat you wore—a light overcoat,—probably" (pointing to it) "the one you are now wearing—was accurately described." Dorian starts visibly. "Do you still hope to brave it out?"

"A coat like this, do you say?" asks Branscombe, with a nervous attempt at unconcern, laying his hand upon his sleeve.

"A light overcoat. Such was the description. But" (with a longing that is terribly pathetic) "many overcoats are alike. And—and I dare say you have not worn that one for months."

"Yes, I have. I wear it incessantly: I have taken rather a fancy to it," replies Branscombe, in an uncompromising tone. "My persistent admiration for it has driven my tailor to despair. I very seldom (except, perhaps, at midnight revels or afternoon bores) appear in public without it."

"Then you deny nothing?"

"Nothing!"—contemptuously, making a movement as though to depart. "Why should I? If, after all these years that you have known me, you can imagine me capable of evil such as you describe so graphically, it would give me no pleasure to vindicate myself in your eyes. Think of me as you will: I shall take no steps to justify myself."

"You dare not!" says Sartoris, in a stifled tone, confronting him fully for the first time.

"That is just as you please to think," says Branscombe, turning upon him with flashing eyes. He frowns heavily, and, with a little gesture common to him, raises his hand and pushes the end of his fair moustache between his teeth. Then, with a sudden effort, he controls himself, and goes on more quietly: "I shall always feel regret in that you found it so easy a matter to believe me guilty of so monstrous a deed. I think we can have nothing further to say to each other, either now or in the future. I wish you good-evening."

Sartoris, standing with his back almost turned to his nephew, takes no heed of this angry farewell; and Dorian, going out, closes the door calmly behind him.

Passing through the Long Hall, as it has been called from time immemorial, he encounters Simon Gale, the old butler, and stops to speak to him, kindly, as is his wont, though in truth his heart is sore.

"Ah, Simon! How warm the weather grows!" he says, genially brushing his short hair back from his forehead. The attempt is praiseworthy, as really there is no hair to speak of, his barber having provided against that. He speaks kindly, carelessly—if a little wearily. His pulses are throbbing, and his heart beating hotly with passionate indignation and disappointment.

"Very warm, sir," returns the old man, regarding him wistfully. He is not thinking of the weather, either of its heat or cold. He is only wondering, with a foreboding sadness, whether the man before him—who has been to him as the apple of his eye—is guilty or not of the crime imputed to him. With an effort he recovers himself, and asks, hastily, though almost without purpose, "Have you seen my lord?"

"Yes; I have only just left him."

"You will stay to dinner, Mr. Dorian?" He has been "Mr. Dorian" to him for so many years that now the more formal Mr. Branscombe is impossible.

"Not to-night. Some other time when my uncle—" He pauses.

"You think him looking well?" asks the old man, anxiously, mistaking his hesitation.

"Well! Oh, that doesn't describe him," says Branscombe, with a shrug, and a somewhat ironical laugh. "He struck me as being unusually lively,—in fact, 'strong as Boreas on the main.' I thought him very well indeed."

"Ay, he is so! A godly youth brings a peaceful age; and his was that. He has lived a good life, and now is reaping his reward."

"Is he?" says Dorian, with a badly-suppressed yawn. "Of course I was mistaken, but really it occurred to me that he was in an abominable temper. Is a desire to insult every one part of the reward?"

"You make light of what I say," returns Simon, reproachfully, "yet it is the very truth I speak. He has no special sin to repent, no lasting misdeed to haunt him, as years creep on. It were well to think of it," says Simon, with a trembling voice, "while youth is still with us. To you it yet belongs. If you have done aught amiss, I entreat you to confess, and make amends for it, whilst there is yet time."

Dorian, laying his hands upon the old servant's shoulders, pushes him gently backwards, so that he may look the more readily into his face.

"Why, Simon! How absolutely in earnest you are!" he says, lightly. "What crime have I committed, that I should spend the rest of my days in sackcloth and ashes!"

"I know nothing," says old Gale, sadly. "How should I be wiser than my masters? All I feel is that youth is careless and headstrong, and things once done are difficult of undoing. If you would go to your grave happy, keep yourself from causing misery to those who love you and—*trust* in you."

His voice sinks, and grows tremulous. Dorian, taking his hands from his shoulders, moves back from the old man, and regards him meditatively, stroking his fair moustache slowly, in a rather mechanical fashion, as he does so.

"The whole world seems dyspeptic to-day," he says, ironically. Then, "It would be such a horrid bore to make any one miserable that I daresay I sha'n't try it. If, however, I do commit the mysterious serious offence at which you broadly hint, and of which you plainly believe me fully capable, I'll let you know about it."

He smiles again,—a jarring sort of smile, that hardly accords with the beauty of the dying day,—and, moving away from the old man, crosses the oaken flooring to the glass door that lies at the farther end of the room, and that opens on to a gravelled path outside, on which lilacs are flinging broadcast their rich purple bloom. As he moves, with a pale face and set lips (for the bitter smile has faded), he tramples ruthlessly, and without thought for their beauty, upon the deep soft patches of coloring that are strewn upon the flooring from the stained-glass windows above.

Throwing open the door, he welcomes gladly the cool evening air that seems to rush to meet him.

"Pah!" he says, almost aloud, as he strides onwards beneath the budding elms. "To think, after all these years, they should so readily condemn! Even that old man, who has known me from my infancy, believes me guilty."

Then a change sweeps over him. Insults to himself are forgotten, and his thoughts travel onward to a fear that for many days has been growing and gaining strength.

Can Horace have committed this base deed? This fear usurps all other considerations. Going back upon what he has just heard, he examines in his mind each little detail of the wretched history imparted to him by his uncle.

All the suspicions—lulled to rest through lack of matter wherewith to feed them—now come to life again, and grow in size and importance in spite of his intense desire to suppress them.

On Tuesday night the girl had left her home. On Tuesday morning he had been to Horace's rooms, had found him there, had sat and conversed with him for upwards of an hour on different subjects,—chiefly, he now remembers, of Clarissa Peyton.

The day had been warm, and he had taken off his coat (the light overcoat he had affected for the past month), and had thrown it on a chair, and—*left it there when going*!

The next morning he had called again and found the coat in the very self-same place where he had thrown it. But in the mean time, during all the hours that intervened between the afternoon of one day and the forenoon of another, where had it been?

"The very coat you wore was minutely described."—The words come back upon him with a sudden rush, causing him a keener pang than any he has ever yet known. Must he indeed bring himself to believe that his own brother had made use of the coat with the deliberate intention (should chance fling any intruder in the way) of casting suspicion upon him— Dorian?

In the dusk of the evening any one might easily mistake one brother for the other. They are the same height; the likeness between them is remarkable. He almost hates himself for the readiness with which he pieces his story together, making doubt merge with such entirety into conviction.

The evening is passing fair, yet it brings no comfort to his soul; the trees towering upwards lie heavily against the sky; the breath of many flowers makes rich the air. Already the faint moon arising, throws her "silver light o'er half the world," and makes more blue the azure depths above:

> "Star follows star, though yet day's golden light
> Upon the hills and headlands faintly streams."

The far-off grating sound of the corncrake can be heard; the cuckoo's tuneless note, incessant and unmusical, tires the early night. The faint sweet chirrups of many insects come from far and near, and break upon the sense with a soft and lulling harmony:

> "There is no stir, nor breath of air; the plains
> Lie slumbering in the close embrace of night."

All nature seems sinking into one grand repose, wherein strife and misery and death appear to have no part.

To Dorian the tender solemnity of the scene brings no balm. To go again to town by the night mail — to confront Horace and learn from him the worst — is his one settled thought, among the multitude of disordered ones; and upon it he determines to act.

But what if he shall prove innocent, or deny all knowledge of the affair? What then can clear Dorian in his uncle's eyes? And even should he acknowledge the fact that he had enticed the girl from her home, how can it benefit Dorian? He is scarcely the one to defend himself at another's expense; and to betray Horace to clear himself would be impossible to him.

He grows bewildered and heart-sick. Reaching home, he orders his dog-cart to be brought round, and, by taking it a good deal out of his good gray mare, he manages to catch the evening train to town.

Lord Sartoris, sitting brooding over miserable thoughts in the library at Hythe, has tidings brought him of his nephew's speedy return to London, and endures one stab the more, as he feels now more than ever convinced of his duplicity.

Arrived in town, Branscombe drives to Horace's rooms, hoping against hope that he may find him at home. To his surprise he does so find him, — in the midst of papers, and apparently up to his eyes in business.

"Working so late?" says Dorian, involuntarily, being accustomed to think of Horace, at this hour, as one of a chosen band brought together to discuss the lighter topics of the day over soup and fish and flesh. In truth, now he is on the spot and face to face with his brother, the enormity of his errand makes itself felt, and he hardly knows what to say to him.

"You, Dorian?" Horace, raising his eyes, smiles upon him his usual slow impenetrable smile. "Working? Yes; we others, the moneyless ones, must work or die; and death is unpopular nowadays. Still, law is dry work when all is confessed." He presses his hand to his forehead with affected languor, and for an instant conceals his face. "By the by, it is rather good of you to break in so unexpectedly upon my monotony. Anything I can do for you?"

"Let me speak to you," says Dorian, impulsively, laying his hand upon his arm. "If I am wronging you in my thoughts I shall never forgive myself, and you, in all probability, will never forgive me either; yet I must get it off my mind."

"My dear fellow, how you have flung away undoubted talent! Your tone out-Irvings Irving: it is ultra-tragic. Positively, you make my blood run cold. Don't stand staring at me in that awful attitude, but tell me, as briefly as you can, what I have done."

He laughs lightly.

Dorian regards him fixedly. Has he wronged him? Has instinct played him false?

"Where is Ruth Annersley?" he asks, awkwardly, as though getting rid of the question at any price and without preamble. He has still his hand upon his brother's arm, and his eyes upon his face.

"Ruth Annersley?" reiterates Horace, the most perfect amazement in his tone. If purposely done, the surprise is very excellent indeed. "Why? What has happened to her?"

"Have you heard nothing?"

"My dear fellow, how could I? I have not been near Pullingham for a full month; and its small gossips fail to interest our big city. What has happened?"

"The girl has left her home; has not been heard of since last Tuesday. They fear she has wilfully flung up happiness and honor to gain—misery."

"What a charitable place is a small village!" says Horace, with a shrug. "Why should the estimable Pullinghamites imagine so much evil? Perhaps, finding life in that stagnate hole unendurable, Ruth threw up the whole concern, and is now seeking a subsistence honorably. Perhaps, too, she has married. Perhaps——"

"Why do you not suppose her dead?" says Dorian, tapping the table with his forefinger, his eyes fixed moodily on the pattern of the maroon-colored cloth. "All such speculations are equally absurd. I hardly came to London to listen to such vain imaginings."

"Then—I think I barely understand you," says Horace, amicably; "you came because——?"

"Because I fancied I had here the best chance of hearing about her," interrupts Dorian, bluntly, losing patience a little.

"How fearfully you blunder!" returns Horace, still quite calmly,—nay, in even a tone that might be called amused. "If you mean that I have had anything to do with her vamoose, I beg to say your imagination has run wild. You can search the place if you like. The old lady who attends to my wants will probably express some faint disapprobation when you invade the sanctity of her chamber, but beyond that no unpleasantness need be anticipated. This is her favorite hour for imbibing brandy—*my* brandy, you will understand (she takes it merely as a tonic, being afflicted—as she tells me—with what she is pleased to term 'nightly trimbles'): so if, in the course of your wanderings, you chance to meet her, and she openly molests you, don't blame me."

"Is that all you can tell me?"

"All about my old lady, certainly."

"And of Ruth?"

"I know nothing, as *you* should understand." He laughs significantly.

"What do you mean?" demands Dorian, a little fiercely. His eyes are dark and flashing, his lips compressed.

"What can I mean, except that you are ridiculously absurd?" says Horace, rising. "What is it you expect me to say? I can't get you out of it. I always knew you had a *penchant* for her, but never thought it would carry you so far. If you will take my advice, however, you will be milder about it, and take that look off your face. If you go in for society with that cut-up expression in your eyes, people will talk."

"Then you know nothing?" repeats Branscombe, taking no notice of— perhaps not even hearing—the foregoing speech.

"Absolutely nothing. How should I?" says Horace, with his soft smooth smile. "Have a brandy-and-soda, Dorian, or a little curaçoa? Perhaps, indeed, the brandy will be best (always allowing Mrs. McGinty has left me any), you look so thoroughly done up."

"Thank you,—nothing." He gazes at his brother long and earnestly. "The Branscombe word *ought* to be sure," he says, moodily.

"Still unconvinced!" says Horace, with an airy laugh. "I know I ought to take you by the shoulders, Dorian, and pitch you down the stairs; but, somehow, I haven't the pluck to-night. I am overdone through this abominable law, and—you are such a tremendous fellow when compared with me. Must you really be off so soon? Stay and have a cup of coffee? No? Well, if it must be, good-night."

Dorian goes down the stairs,—puzzled, bewildered, almost convinced. At the foot of the staircase he looks up again, to see Horace standing above him still, candle in hand, radiant, smiling, *débonnaire*, apparently without a care in the world.

He nods to him, and Dorian, returning the salute in grave and silent fashion, goes out into the lighted streets, and walks along in momentary expectation of a hansom, when a well known voice smites upon his ear:

"What in the name of wonder, Branscombe, brings you here?"

Turning, he finds himself face to face with Sir James Scrope.

"My presence is hardly an eighth wonder," he says, wearily. "But how is it you are not in Paris?"

"Fate ordained it so, and probably fortune, as I just want a friend with whom to put in an evening."

"You have chosen a dull companion," says Dorian, stupidly. "What brought you home so soon? or, rather, what took you to Paris originally?"

"Business partly, and partly because—er—that is, I felt I needed a little change."

"Ah! just so," says Branscombe. But he answers as one might who has heard nothing. Sir James casts upon him a quick penetrating glance.

"Anything wrong with you, Branscombe?" he asks, quietly. "Anything in which I can be of use to you?"

"Thank you, no. I'm just a little down on my luck, that's all." Then, abruptly, "I suppose you have heard of the scandal down in Pullingham?"

"About that poor little girl?" says Sir James. "Oh, yes. 'Ill news flies apace;' and this morning Hodges, who came to town to see me about Bennett's farm, gave me a garbled account of her disappearance. I think I hardly understand even now. How did it happen?"

For a full minute Dorian makes no reply. He is looking earnestly in James Scrope's face, to see if in it there lurks any hidden thought, any carefully concealed expression of mistrust. There is, indeed, none. No shadow, no faintest trace of suspicion, lies in Scrope's clear and honest eyes. Branscombe draws a deep breath. Whatever in the future this friend may come to believe, now, at least, he holds him—Dorian—clear and pure from this gross evil that has been imputed to him.

He throws up his head with a freer air, and tries, with a quick effort, to conquer the morbid feeling that for hours past has been pressing upon him heavily.

"I know nothing," he says, presently, in answer to Sir James's last remark.

"It is such an unaccountable story," says Scrope, lifting his brows. "Where did she go? and with whom? Such a quiet little mouse of a girl, one hardly understands her being the heroine of a tragedy. But how does it particularly affect you?"

Branscombe hesitates. For one brief moment he wonders whether he shall or shall not reveal to Scrope the scene that has passed between him and his uncle. Then his whole sympathies revolt from the task, and he determines to let things rest as they now are.

"Arthur has tormented himself needlessly about the whole business," he says, turning his face from Scrope. "He thinks me—that is, every one—to blame, until the girl is restored to her father."

"Ah! I quite see," says James Scrope.

CHAPTER XXIII

"Her eyes were deeper than the depth
Of waters stilled at even."

"Dorian?" says Clarissa.

"Clarissa!" says Dorian.

"I really think I shall give a ball."

"What?" cries a small, sweet, plaintive voice from the corner, and Georgie, emerging from obscurity and the tremendous volume she has been studying, comes to the front, in her usual vehement fashion, and stands before Miss Peyton, expectation in every feature. "Oh, Clarissa, do say it again."

"Papa says I must entertain the county in some way," says Clarissa, meditatively, "and I really think a ball will be the best way. Don't you?"

"Don't I, though?" says Miss Broughton, with much vivacity. "Clarissa, you grow sweeter daily. Let me offer you some small return for your happy thought."

She laughs, and, stooping, presses her warm ripe lips against her friend's cheek. She blushes as she performs this graceful act, and a small, bright, mischievous gleam grows within her eye. The whole action is half mocking, half tender:

"A rosebud set with little wilfulthorns,
And sweet as English air can make her, she."

The lines come hurriedly to Branscombe's mind, and linger there. Raising her head again, her eyes meet his, and she laughs, for the second time, out of the pure gladness of her heart.

"I think it was my happy thought," says Branscombe, mildly. "*I* suggested this dance to Clarissa only yesterday. Might not I, too, partake of the 'small return'?"

"It no longer belongs to me; I have given it all away,—here," says Georgie, touching Clarissa's cheek with one finger; "but for that," with a slow adorable glance, "I should be charmed."

"I think I shall get pencil and paper and write down the names," says Clarissa, energetically, rising and going towards the door. "Dorian, take care of Georgie until I return."

"I wish I knew how," says Branscombe, in a tone so low that only Georgie can hear it. Then, as the door closes he says, "Did you mean your last speech?"

"My last? What was it? I never remember anything." She very seldom blushes, but now again a soft delicate color creeps into her face.

"If you *hadn't* given it all away, would you have given me a little of that small return?"

"No."

"Not even if *I* were to give a ball for you?"

"N-o—no."

"Not if I were to do for you the one thing you most desired?"

"No—no—no!" She speaks hastily, and glances at him somewhat confusedly from beneath her long lashes.

"Well, of course, it is too much to expect," says Branscombe; "yet I would do a good deal for you, even without hope of payment."

He comes a little nearer to her, and lays his hand upon the table close to hers.

"If you really made the suggestion to Clarissa, you deserve some reward," says Georgie, nodding her head. "Now, what shall it be?"

"Dance half the night with me."

"That would bore you,—and me. No; but if dancing delights you—sir— may I have the pleasure of the first quadrille?"

"Madam," says Branscombe, laying his hand upon his heart, "you do me too much honor; I am at your service now and forever."

"It is too large a promise."

"A true one, nevertheless."

A little earnest shade shows itself upon his face, but Georgie laughs lightly, and moves away from him over to the window, and at this moment Clarissa returns, armed with paper and pencils and a very much pleased smile.

"Can't I have the gardens lighted?" she says, "with Chinese lanterns, and that? I have been thinking of it."

"I don't know about 'that,'" says Dorian. "I'm not sure but it might blow us all to atoms; but the celestial lights will be quite 'too, too!' It must be a splendid thing, Clarissa, to have a brain like yours. Now, neither Miss Broughton nor I have a particle between us."

"Speak for yourself, please," says Miss Broughton, very justly incensed.

"I'm doing even more than that, I'm speaking for you too. Don't put up too many Chinese lanterns, Clarissa, or it will be awkward: we shall be seen."

"What matter? I love light," says Georgie, innocently. "How I do hope there will be a moon! Not a mean effort at one, but a good, round, substantial, vast old moon, such as there was two months ago."

She has her wish: such another moonlight night as comes to Pullingham on the night of Miss Peyton's ball has been rarely, if ever, seen. It breaks over the whole place in a flood of light so whitely brilliant that the very sleeping flowers lift up their heads, as though believing the soft mystic light to be the early birth of morn.

All around is calm and drowsy sweet. The stars come forth to light the world, and, perhaps, to do homage to Clarissa on this the night of her first ball.

About six weeks have passed since Ruth Annersley left her home, and as yet no tidings of her have reached Pullingham. Already people are beginning to forget that such an *esclandre* ever occurred in their quiet village. The minutest inquiries have been made (chiefly by Lord Sartoris, who is now very seldom at home); rewards offered; numerous paragraphs, addressed to "R. A.," have appeared in the London papers, but without result. The world is growing tired of the miserable scandal, and Ruth's disappearance ceases to be the one engrossing topic of conversation at village teas and bar-room revelries.

To-night is fair enough to make one believe sin impossible. It is touched by heaven; great waves of light, sent by the "silver queen of night," lie languidly on tree and bower; the very paths are bright with its stray beams.

"Bats and grisly owls on noiseless wings" flit to and fro, "and now the nightingale, not distant far, begins her solitary song."

Within, music is sounding, and laughter, and the faint sweet dropping of fountains. Clarissa, moving about among her guests, is looking quite lovely in a pale satin trimmed heavily with old gold. She is happy and quite content, though her eyes, in spite of her, turn anxiously, every now and then, to the doorway.

Every one is smiling, radiant. Even Dorian, who is waltzing with any one but the woman he desires, is looking gracious all through, and is creating havoc in the bosom of the damsel who has rashly intrusted herself to his care.

Cissy Redmond, in the arms of a cavalry-man, is floating round the room, her unutterable little *nez retroussé* looking even more pronounced than usual. Her face is lit up with pleasurable excitement; to her—as she tells the cavalry-man without hesitation—the evening is "quite too awfully much, don't you know!" and the cavalry-man understands her perfectly, and is rather taking to her, which is undoubtedly clever of the cavalry-man.

He is now talking to her in his very best style, and she is smiling,—but not at him.

Within the shelter of a door, directly opposite, stands Mr. Hastings, and he is answering back her smile fourfold. He will not dance himself,—conscience forbidding,—yet it pleases him to see his Cissy (as she now is) enjoying herself. The band is playing "Beautiful Ferns" dreamily, languidly; and I think at this very moment Mr. Hastings's reverend toes are keeping excellent time to the music. But this, of course, is barest supposition; for what human eye can penetrate leather?

The waltz comes to an end, and Dorian, having successfully rid himself of his late partner, draws Georgie's hand within his arm and leads her into a conservatory.

Her late partner was a fat, kindly squire, who *will* dance, but who, at the expiration of each effort to eclipse Terpsichore, feels devoutly thankful that his task has come to an end. He is, to say the mildest least of him, exceedingly tiring, and Georgie is rather glad than otherwise that Dorian should lead her into the cool recess where flowers and perfumed fountains hold full sway. She sinks into a seat, and sighs audibly, and looks upwards at her companion from under half-closed lids, and then, letting them drop suddenly, plays, in a restless fashion, with the large black fan she holds.

Branscombe is stupidly silent; indeed, it hardly occurs to him that speech is necessary. He is gazing earnestly, tenderly, at the small face beside him,—

"A face o'er which a thousand shadows go."

The small face, perhaps, objects to this minute scrutiny, because presently it raises itself, and says, coquettishly,—

"How silent you are! What are you thinking of?"

"Of you," says Dorian, simply. "What a foolish question! You are a perfect picture in that black gown, with your baby arms and neck."

"Anything else?" asks Miss Broughton, demurely.

"Yes. It also seems to me that you cannot be more than fifteen. You look such a little thing, and so young."

"But I'm not young," says Georgie, hastily. "I am quite old. I wish you would remember I am nearly nineteen."

"Quite a Noah's Ark sort of person,—a fossil of the pre-Adamite period. How I envy you! You are, indeed, unique in your way. Don't be angry with me because I said you looked young; and don't wish to be old. There is no candor so hateful, no truth so unpleasing, as age."

"How do you know?" demands she, saucily, sweetly, half touched by his tone. "You are not yet a Methuselah." Then, "Do you know your brother has come at last? He is very late, isn't he?"

"He always is," says Dorian.

"And he has brought a friend with him. And who do you think it is?"

"I haven't the faintest idea," says Branscombe, turning a vivid red.

"Why, *my* Mr. Kennedy!"

"*Your* Mr. Kennedy?" reiterates he, blankly, his red becoming a crimson of the liveliest hue.

"Yes, the dark thin young man I met at Sir John Lincoln's. I dare say I told you about him?"

"Yes, you did," says Dorian, grimly.

"I see him over there," pointing airily with her fan through the open conservatory door to a distant wall where many young men are congregated together.

"The man with the nose?" asks Branscombe, slightingly, feeling sure in his soul he is *not* the man with the nose.

"He has a nose," says Miss Broughton, equably, "though there isn't much of it. He is very like a Chinese pug. Don't you see him? But he *is* so nice."

Dorian looks again in the desired direction, and as he does so a tall young man, with a somewhat canine expression, but very kindly, advances towards him, and, entering the conservatory, comes up to Miss Broughton with a smile full of delight upon his ingenuous countenance.

"Miss Broughton," he says, in a low musical voice, that has unmistakable pleasure in it. "Can it really be you? I didn't believe life could afford me so happy a moment as this."

"I saw you ten minutes ago," says Georgie, in her quick bright fashion.

"And made no sign? that was cruel," says Kennedy, with some reproach in his tone. He is looking with ill-suppressed admiration upon her fair uplifted face. "Now that I have found you, what dance will you give me?"

"Any one I have," she says, sweetly.

"The tenth? The dance after next,—after this, I mean?"

Branscombe, who is standing beside her, here turns his head to look steadfastly at her. His blue eyes are almost black, his lips are compressed, his face is very pale. Not an hour ago she had promised him this tenth dance. He had asked it of her in haste, even as he went by her with another partner, and she had smiled consent. Will she forget it?

"With pleasure," she says, softly, gayly, her usual lovely smile upon her lips. She is apparently utterly unconscious of any one except her old-new friend. Kennedy puts her name down upon his card.

At this Dorian makes one step forward, as though to protest against something,—some iniquity done; but, a sudden thought striking him, he draws back, and, bringing his teeth upon his under lip with some force, turns abruptly away. When next he looks in her direction, he finds both Georgie and her partner have disappeared.

The night wanes. Already the "keen stars that falter never" are dropping, one by one, to slumber, perfect and serene. Diana, tired of her ceaseless watch, is paling, fading, dying imperceptibly, as though feeling herself soon to be conquered by the sturdy morn.

Dorian, who has held himself carefully aloof from Miss Broughton ever since that last scene, when she had shown herself so unmindful of him and his just claim to the dance then on the cards, now, going up to her, says, coldly,—

"I think the next is our dance, Miss Broughton."

Georgie, who is laughing gayly with Mr. Kennedy, turns her face to his, some surprise mixed with the sweetness of her regard. Never before has he addressed her in such a tone.

"Is it?" she says, gently. "I had forgotten; but of course my card will tell."

"One often forgets, and one's card doesn't always tell," replies he, with a smile tinctured with bitterness.

She opens her eyes, and stares at him blankly. There is some balm in Gilead, he tells himself, as he sees she is totally unaware of his meaning. Perhaps, after all, she *did* forget about that tenth dance, and did not purposely fling him over for the man now beside her, who is grinning at her in a supremely idiotic fashion. How he hates a fellow who simpers straight through everything, and looks always as if the world and he were eternally at peace!

She flushes softly,—a gentle, delicate flush, born of distress, coldness from even an ordinary friend striking like ice upon her heart. She looks at her card confusedly.

"Yes, the next is ours," she says, without raising her eyes; and then the band begins again, and Dorian feels her hand upon his arm, and Kennedy bows disconsolately and disappears amid the crowd.

"Do you particularly want to dance this?" asks Dorian, with an effort.

"No; not much."

"Will you come out into the gardens instead? I want—I must speak to you."

"You may speak to me here, or in the garden, or any where," says Georgie, rather frightened by the vehemence of his tone.

She lets him lead her down the stone steps that lead to the shrubberies outside, and from thence to the gardens. The night is still. The waning moonlight clear as day. All things seem calm and full of rest,—that deepest rest that comes before the awakening.

"Who is your new friend?" asks he, abruptly, when silence any longer has become impossible.

"Mr. Kennedy. He is not exactly a friend. I met him one night before in all my life, and he was very kind to me——"

"One night!" repeats Dorian, ignoring the fact that she yet has something more to say. "One night! What an impression"—unkindly—"he must have made on that memorable occasion, to account for the very warm reception accorded to him this evening!"

She turns her head away from him, but makes no reply.

"Why did you promise me that dance if you didn't mean giving it?" he goes on, with something in his voice that resembles passion, mixed with pain. "I certainly believed you in earnest when you promised it to me."

"You believed right: I did mean it. Am I not giving it?" says Georgie, bewildered, her eyes gleaming, large and troubled, in the white light that illumines the sleeping world. "It is your fault that we are not dancing now. I, for my part, would much rather be inside, with the music, than out here with you, when you talk so unkindly."

"I have no doubt you would rather be anywhere than with me," says Dorian, hastily; "and of course this new friend is intensely interesting."

"At least he is not rude," says Miss Broughton, calmly, plucking a pale green branch from a laurestinus near her.

"I am perfectly convinced he is one of the few faultless people upon earth," says Branscombe, now in a white heat of fury. "I shouldn't dream of aspiring to his level. But yet I think you needn't have given him the dance you promised me."

"I didn't," says Miss Broughton, indignantly, in all good faith.

"You mean to tell me you hadn't given me the tenth dance half an hour before?"

"The tenth! You might as well speak about the hundred and tenth! If it wasn't on my card how could I remember it?"

"But it was on your card: I wrote it down myself."

"I am sure you are making a mistake," says Miss Broughton, mildly; though in her present frame of mind, I think she would have dearly liked to tell him he is lying.

"Then show me your card. If I have blundered in this matter I shall go on my knees to beg your pardon."

"I don't want you on your knees," —pettishly. "I detest a man on his knees, he always looks so silly. As for my card," —grandly,—"here it is."

Dorian, taking it, opens it, and, running his eyes down the small columns, stops short at number ten. There, sure enough, is "D. B." in very large capitals indeed.

"You see," he says, feeling himself, as he says it, slightly ungenerous.

"I am very sorry," says Miss Broughton, standing far away from him, and with a little quiver in her tone. "I have behaved badly, I now see. But I did not mean it." She has grown very pale; her eyes are dilating; her rounded arms, soft and fair and lovable as a little child's, are gleaming snow-white against the background of shining laurel leaves that are glittering behind her in the moonlight. Her voice is quiet, but her eyes are full of angry tears, and her small gloved hands clasp and unclasp each other nervously.

"You have proved me in the wrong," she goes on, with a very poor attempt at coolness, "and, of course, justice is on your side. And you are quite right to say anything that is unkind to me; and—and I *hate* people who are always in the right."

With this she turns, and, regardless of him, walks hurriedly, and plainly full of childish rage, back to the house.

Dorian, stricken with remorse, follows her.

"Georgie, forgive me! I didn't mean it; I swear I didn't!" he says, calling her by her Christian name for the first time, and quite unconsciously. "Don't leave me like this; or, at least let me call to-morrow and explain."

"I don't want to see you to-morrow or any other day," declares Miss Broughton, with cruel emphasis, not even turning her head to him as she speaks.

"But you shall see me to-morrow," exclaims he, seizing her hand, as she reaches the conservatory door, to detain her. "You will be here; I shall come to see you. I entreat, I implore you not to deny yourself to me." Raising her hand, he presses it with passionate fervor to his lips.

Georgie, detaching her hand from his grasp, moves away from him.

"'Must is for the queen, and shall is for the king,'" quotes she, with a small pout, "and to-morrow—catch me if you can!"

She frowns slightly, and, with a sudden movement, getting behind a large flowering shrub, disappears from his gaze for the night.

CHAPTER XXIV

"But sweeter still than this, than these, than all,
Is first and passionate love: it stands alone." — Byron.

Next day is born, lives, grows, deepens; and, as the first cold breath of even declares itself, Dorian rides down the avenue that leads to Gowran.

Miss Peyton is not at home (he has asked first for her, as in duty bound), and Miss Broughton is in the grounds somewhere. This is vague. The man offers warmly to discover her and bring her back to the house to receive Mr. Branscombe; but this Mr. Branscombe will not permit. Having learned the direction in which she is gone, he follows it, and glides into a region wherein only fairies should have right to dwell.

A tangled mass of grass, and blackberry, and fern; a dying sunlight, deep and tender; soft beds of tawny moss. Myriad bluebells are alive, and, spreading themselves, far and wide, in one rich carpeting (whose color puts to shame the pale blue of the heavenly vault above), make one harmonious blending with their green straight leaves.

Far as the eye can reach they spread, and, as the light and wanton wind stoops to caress them, shake their tiny bells with a coquettish grace, and fling forth perfume to him with a lavish will.

The solemn trees, that "seem to hold mystical converse with each other," look down upon the tranquil scene that, season after season, changes, fades away, and dies, only to return again, fairer and fresher than of yore. The fir-trees tower upwards, and gleam green-black against the sky. Upon some topmost boughs the birds are chanting a pæan of their own; while through this "wilderness of sweets" — far down between its deep banks (that are rich with trailing ivy and drooping bracken) — runs a stream, a slow, delicious, lazy stream, that glides now over its moss-grown stones, and anon flashes through some narrow ravine dark and profound. As it runs it babbles fond love-songs to the pixies that, perchance, are peeping out at it, through their yellow tresses, from shady curves and sun-kissed corners.

It is one of May's divinest efforts, — a day to make one glad and feel that it is well to be alive. Yet Branscombe, walking through this fairy glen, though conscious of its beauty, is conscious, too, that in his heart he knows a want not to be satisfied until Fate shall again bring him face to face with the girl with whom he had parted so unamicably the night before.

Had she really meant him not to call to-day? Will she receive him coldly? Is it even possible to find her in such an absurd place as this, where positively everything seems mixed up together in such a hopeless fashion that one can't see farther than one's nose? Perhaps, after all, she is not here, has returned to the house, and is now — —

Suddenly, across the bluebells, there comes to him a fresh sweet voice, that thrills him to his very heart. It is hers; and there, in the distance, he can see her, just where the sunlight falls athwart the swaying ferns.

She is sitting down, and is leaning forward, having taken her knees well into her embrace. Her broad hat is tilted backward, so that the sunny straggling hair upon her forehead can be plainly seen. Her gown is snow-white, with just a touch of black at the throat and wrists; a pretty frill of soft babyish lace caresses her throat.

Clear and happy, as though it were a free bird's her voice rises on the wind and reaches Branscombe, and moves him as no other voice ever had — or will ever again have — power to move him.

> "There has fallen a splendid tear
> From the passion-flower at the gate;
> She is coming, my dove, my dear;
> She is coming, my life, my fate."

The kind wind brings the tender passionate love-song to him, and repeats it in his ear as it hurries onward: "My dove, my dear." How exactly the words suit her! he says them over and over again to himself, almost losing the rest of the music which she is still breathing forth to the evening air.

"My life! my fate!" Is she his life, — his fate? The idea makes him tremble. Has he set his whole heart upon a woman who perhaps can never give him hers in return? The depth, the intensity of the passion with which he repeats the words of her song astonishes and perplexes him vaguely. Is she indeed his fate?

He is quite close to her now; and she, turning round to him her lovely flower-like face, starts perceptibly, and, springing to her feet, confronts him with a little frown, and a sudden deepening of color that spreads from chin to brow.

At this moment he knows the whole truth. Never has she appeared so desirable in his eyes. Life with her means happiness more than falls to the lot of most; life without her, an interminable blank.

"Love lights upon the hearts, and straight we feel
More worlds of wealth gleam in an upturned eye
Than in the rich heart or the miser sea."

"I thought I told you not to come," says Miss Broughton, still frowning.

"I am sure you did not," contradicts he, eagerly; "you said, rather unkindly, I must confess,—but still you said it,—'Catch me if you can.' That was a command. I have obeyed it. And I have caught you."

"You knew I was not speaking literally," says Miss Broughton, with some wrath. "The idea of your supposing I really meant you to catch me! You couldn't have thought it."

"Well, what was I to think? You certainly said it. So I came. I believed"—humbly—"it was the best thing to do."

"Yes; and you found me sitting—as—I was, and singing at the top of my voice. How I dislike people"—says Miss Broughton, with fine disgust—"who steal upon other people unawares!"

"I didn't steal; I regularly trampled"—protests Branscombe, justly indignant—"right over the moss and ferns and the other things, as hard as ever I could. If bluebells won't crackle like dead leaves it isn't my fault, is it? *I* hadn't the ordering of them!"

"Oh, yes, it is, every bit your fault," persists she, wilfully, biting, with enchanting grace largely tinctured with viciousness, the blade of grass she is holding.

Silence, of the most eloquent, that lasts for a full minute, even until the unoffending grass is utterly consumed.

"Perhaps you would rather I went away," says Mr. Branscombe, stiffly, seeing she will not speak. He is staring at her, and is apparently hopelessly affronted.

"Well, perhaps I would," returns she, coolly, without condescending to look at him.

"Good-by,"—icily.

"Good-by,"—in precisely the same tone, and without changing her position half an inch.

Branscombe turns away with a precipitancy that plainly betokens hot haste to be gone. He walks quickly in the home direction, and gets as far as the curve in the glen without once looking back. So far the hot haste lasts, and is highly successful; then it grows cooler; the first deadly heat dies away, and, as it goes, his steps grow slower and still slower. A severe struggle with pride ensues, in which pride goes to the wall, and then he comes to a standstill.

Though honestly disgusted with his own want of firmness, he turns and gazes fixedly at the small white-gowned figure standing, just as he had left her, among the purple bells.

Yet not exactly as he had left her: her lips are twitching now, her lids have fallen over her eyes. Even as he watches, the soft lips part, and a smile comes to them,—an open, irrepressible smile, that deepens presently into a gay, mischievous laugh, that rings sweetly, musically upon the air.

It is too much. In a moment he is beside her again, and is gazing down on her with angry eyes.

"Something is amusing you," he says. "Is it me?"

"Yes," says the spoiled beauty, moving back from him, and lifting her lids from her laughing eyes to cast upon him a defiant glance.

"I dare say I do amuse you," exclaims he, wrathfully, goaded to deeper anger by the mockery of her regard. "I have no doubt you can find enjoyment in the situation, but I cannot! I dare say"—passionately—"you think it capital fun to make me fall in love with you,—to play with my heart until you can bind me hand and foot as your slave,—only to fling me aside and laugh at my absurd infatuation when the game has grown old and flavorless."

He has taken her hand whether she will or not, and, I think, at this point, almost unconsciously, he gives her a gentle but very decided little shake.

"But there is a limit to all things," he goes on, vehemently, "and here, now, at this moment, you shall give me a plain answer to a plain question I am going to ask you."

He has grown very pale, and his nostrils are slightly dilated. She has grown very pale, too, and is shrinking from him. Her lips are white and trembling; her beautiful eyes are large and full of an undefined fear. The passion of his tone has carried her away with it, and has subdued within her all desire for mockery or mirth. Her whole face has changed its expression, and has become sad and appealing. This sudden touch of fear and entreaty makes her so sweet that Dorian's anger melts before it, and the great love of which it was part again takes the upper hand.

Impulsively he takes her in his arms, and draws her close to him, as though he would willingly shield her from all evil and chase the unspoken fear from her eyes.

"Don't look at me like that," he says, earnestly. "I deserve it, I know. I should not have spoken to you as I have done, but I could not help it. You made me so miserable—do you know how miserable?—that I forgot myself. Darling, don't turn from me; speak to me; forgive me!"

This sudden change from vehement reproach to as vehement tenderness frightens Georgie just a little more than the anger of a moment since. Laying her hand upon his chest, she draws back from him; and he, seeing she really wishes to get away from him, instantly releases her.

As if fascinated, however, she never removes her gaze from his, although large tears have risen, and are shining in her eyes.

"You don't hate me? I won't believe that," says Branscombe, wretchedly. "Say you will try to love me, and that you will surely marry me."

At this—feeling rather lost, and not knowing what else to do—Georgie covers her face with her hands, and bursts out crying.

It is now Branscombe's turn to be frightened, and he does his part to perfection. He is thoroughly and desperately frightened.

"I won't say another word," he says, hastily; "I won't, indeed. My dearest, what have I said that you should be so distressed? I only asked you to marry me."

"Well, I'm sure I don't know what more you could have said," sobs she, still dissolved in tears, and in a tone full of injury.

"But there wasn't any harm in that," protests he, taking one of her hands from her face and pressing it softly to his lips. "It is a sort of thing" (expansively) "one does every day."

"Do you do it every day?"

"No: I never did it before. And" (very gently) "you will answer me, won't you?"

No answer, however, is vouchsafed.

"Georgie, say you will marry me."

But Georgie either can't or won't say it; and Dorian's heart dies within him.

"Am I to understand by your silence that you fear to pain me?" he says, at length, in a low voice. "Is it impossible to you to love me? Well, do not speak. I can see by your face that the hope I have been cherishing for so many weeks has been a vain one. Forgive me for troubling you: and believe I shall never forget how tenderly you shrank from telling me you could never return my love."

Again he presses her hand to his lips; and she, turning her face slowly to his, looks up at him. Her late tears were but a summer shower, and have faded away, leaving no traces as they passed.

"But I didn't mean one word of all that," she says, naïvely, letting her long lashes fall once more over her eyes.

"Then what did you mean?" demands he, with some pardonable impatience. "Quite the contrary, all through?"

"N—ot quite,"—with hesitation.

"At least, that some day you will be my wife?"

"N—ot altogether."

"Well, you can't be half my wife," says Mr. Branscombe promptly. "Darling, *darling*, put me out of my misery, and say what I want you to say."

"Well, then, yes." She gives the promise softly, shyly, but without the faintest touch of any deeper, tenderer emotion. Had Dorian been one degree less in love with her, he could have hardly failed to notice this fact. As it is, he is radiant, in a very seventh heaven of content.

"But you must promise me faithfully never to be unkind to me again," says Georgie, impressively, laying a finger on his lips.

"Unkind?"

"Yes; *dreadfully* unkind: just think of all the terrible things you said, and the way you said them. Your eyes were as big as half-crowns, and you looked exactly as if you would like to eat me. Do you know, you reminded me of Aunt Elizabeth!"

"Oh, Georgie!" says Branscombe, reproachfully. He has grown rather intimate with Aunt Elizabeth and her iniquities by this time, and fully understands that to be compared with her hardly tends to raise him in his beloved's estimation.

There is silence between them after this, that lasts a full minute,—a long time for lovers freshly made.

"What are you thinking of?" asks Dorian, presently, bending to look tenderly into her downcast eyes. Perhaps he is hoping eagerly that she has been wasting a thought upon him.

"I shall never have to teach those horrid lessons again," she says, with a quick sigh of relief.

If he is disappointed, he carefully conceals it. He laughs, and, lifting her exquisite face, kisses her gently.

"Never," he says, emphatically. "When you go home, tell Mr. Redmond all about it; and to-morrow Clarissa will go down to the vicarage and bring you up to Gowran, where you must stay until we are married."

"I shall like that," says Georgie, with a sweet smile. "But, Mr. Branscombe——"

"Who on earth is Mr. Branscombe?" asks Dorian. "Don't you know my name yet?"

"I do. I think it is almost the prettiest name I ever heard,—Dorian."

"*Darling!* I never thought it a nice name before; but now that you have called me by it, I can feel its beauty. But I dare say if I had been christened Jehoshaphat I should, under these circumstances, think just the same. Well, you were going to say——?"

"Perhaps Clarissa will not care to have me for so long."

"So long? How long? By the by, perhaps she wouldn't; so I suppose we had better be married as soon as ever we can."

"I haven't got any clothes," says Miss Broughton; at which they both laugh gayly, as though it were the merriest jest in the world.

"You terrify me," says Branscombe. "Let me beg you will rectify such a mistake as soon as possible."

"We have been here a long time," says Georgie, suddenly, glancing at the sun, that is almost sinking out of sight behind the solemn firs.

"It hasn't been ten minutes," says Mr. Branscombe, conviction making his tone brilliant.

"Oh, nonsense!" says Georgie. "I am sure it must be quite two hours since you came."

As it has been barely one, this is rather difficult to endure with equanimity.

"How long you have found it!" he says, with some regret. He is honestly pained, and his eyes grow darker. Looking at him, she sees what she has done, and, though ignorant of the very meaning of the word "love," knows that she has hurt him more than he cares to confess.

"I have been happy,—quite happy," she says, sweetly, coloring warmly as she says it. "You must not think I have found the time you have been with me dull or dreary. Only, I am afraid Clarissa will miss me."

"I should think any one would miss you," says Dorian, impulsively. He smiles at her as he speaks; but there is a curious mingling of sadness and longing and uncertainty in his face. Laying one arm round her, with his other hand he draws her head down on his breast.

"At least, before we go, you will kiss me once," he says, entreatingly. All the gayety—the gladness—has gone from his voice; only the deep and lasting love remains. He says this, too, hesitatingly, as though half afraid to demand so great a boon.

"Yes; I think I should like to kiss you," says Georgie, kindly; and then she raises herself from his embrace, and, standing on tiptoe, places both hands upon his shoulders, and with the utmost calmness lays her lips on his.

"Do you know," she says, a moment later, in no wise disconcerted because of the warmth of the caress he has given her in exchange for hers,— "do you know, I never remember kissing any one in all my life before, except poor papa, and Clarissa, and you."

Even at this avowal she does not blush. Were he her brother, or an aged nurse, she could scarcely think less about the favor she has just conferred upon the man who is standing silently regarding her, puzzled and disappointed truly, but earnestly registering a vow that sooner or later, if faithful love can accomplish it, he will make her all his own, in heart and soul.

Not that he has ever yet gone so deeply into the matter as to tell himself the love is all on his own side. Instinctively he shrinks from such inward confession. It is only when he has parted from her, and is riding quietly homeward through the wistful gloaming, that he remembers, with a pang, how, of all the thousand and one things asked and answered, one alone has been forgotten. He has never desired of her whether she loves him.

CHAPTER XXV

"Love set me up on high: when I grew vain
Of that my height, love brought me down again.

"The heart of love is with a thousand woes
Pierced, which secure indifference never knows.

"The rose aye wears the silent thorn at heart,
And never yet might pain for love depart." — Trench.

When Mrs. Redmond, next morning, is made aware of Georgie's engagement to Dorian Branscombe, her curiosity and excitement know no bounds. For once she is literally struck dumb with amazement. That Dorian, who is heir to an earldom, should have fixed his affections upon *her* governess, seems to Mrs. Redmond like a gay continuation of the "Arabian Nights' Entertainments." When she recovers her breath, after the first great shock to her nervous system, she lays down the inevitable sock she is mending, and says as follows:

"My dear Georgina, are you quite sure he meant it? Young men, nowadays, say so many things without exactly knowing why, — more especially after a dance, as I have been told."

"I am quite sure," says Georgie, flushing hotly. She has sufficient self-love to render this doubt very unpalatable.

Something that is not altogether remote from envy creeps into Mrs. Redmond's heart. Being a mother, she can hardly help contrasting her Cissy's future with the brilliant one carved out for her governess. Presently, however, being a thoroughly good soul, she conquers these unworthy thoughts, and when next she speaks her tone is full of heartiness and honest congratulation. Indeed, she is sincerely pleased. The fact that the future Lady Sartoris is at present an inmate of her house is a thought full of joy to her.

"You are a very happy and a very fortunate girl," she says, gravely.

"Indeed yes, I think so," returns Georgie, in a low tone, but with perfect calmness. There is none of the blushing happiness about her that should of right belong to a young girl betrothed freshly to the lover of her heart.

"Of course you do," says Mrs. Redmond, missing something in her voice, though she hardly knows what. "And what we are to do without you, I can't conceive; no one to sing to us in the evening, and we have got so accustomed to that."

"I can still come and sing to you sometimes," says Georgie, with tears in her eyes and voice.

"Ah, yes,—sometimes. That is just the bad part of it; when one has known an 'always,' one does not take kindly to a 'sometimes.' And now here come all my governess troubles back upon my shoulders once more. Don't think me selfish, my dear, to think of that just now in the very morning of your new happiness, but really I can't help it. I have been so content with you, it never occurred to me others might want you too."

"I will ask Clarissa to get you some one else nicer than me," says Georgie, soothingly.

"Will you? Yes, do, my dear: she will do anything for you. And, Georgina,"—from the beginning she has called her thus,—nothing on earth would induce Mrs. Redmond to call her anything more frivolous,—"tell her I should prefer somebody old and ugly, if at all bearable, because then she may stay with me. Dear, dear! how Cissy will miss you! And what will the vicar say?"

And so on. She spends the greater part of the morning rambling on in this style, and then towards the evening despatches Georgie to Gowran to tell Clarissa, too, the great news.

But Clarissa knows all about it before her coming, and meets her in the hall, and kisses her then and there, and tells her she is so glad, and it is the very sweetest thing that could possibly have happened.

"He came down this morning very early and told me all about it," she says, looking as pleased as though it is her own happiness and not another's she is discussing.

"Now, what a pity!" says Georgie: "and I did so want to tell you myself, after the disgraceful way in which you tried to wed me to Mr. Hastings."

"He could not sleep; he confessed that to me. And you had forbidden him to go to the vicarage to see you to-day. What else then could he do but come over and put in a good time here? And he did. We had quite a splendid time," says Miss Peyton, laughing; "I really don't know which of us was the most delighted about it. We both kept on saying pretty things about you all the time,—more than you deserved, I think."

"Now, don't spoil it," says Georgie: "I am certain I deserved it all, and more. Well, if he didn't sleep, I did, and dreamed, and dreamed, and dreamed all sorts of lovely things until the day broke. Oh, Clarissa,"— throwing out her arms with a sudden swift gesture of passionate relief,—"I am free! Am I not lucky, fortunate, to have deliverance sent so soon?"

"Lucky, fortunate;" where has the word "happy" gone, that she has forgotten to use it? Clarissa makes no reply. Something in the girl's manner checks her. She is standing there before her, gay, exultant, with all a child's pleasure in some new possession; "her eyes as stars of twilight fair," flashing warmly, her whole manner intense and glad; but there are no blushes, no shy half-suppressed smiles, there is no word of love; Dorian's name has not been mentioned, except as a secondary part of her story, and then with the extremest unconcern.

Yet there is nothing in her manner that can jar upon one's finer feelings; there is no undue exultation at the coming great change in her position,—no visible triumph at the fresh future opening before her; it is only that in place of the romantic tenderness that should accompany such a revelation as she has been making, there has been nothing but a wild passionate thankfulness for freedom gained.

"When are you coming to stay with me altogether?—I mean until the marriage?" asks Clarissa, presently.

"I cannot leave Mrs. Redmond like that," says Georgie, who is always delightfully indefinite. "She will be in a regular mess now until she gets somebody to take my place. I can't leave her yet."

"Dorian will not like that."

"He must try to like it. Mrs. Redmond has been very good to me, and I couldn't bear to make her uncomfortable. I shall stay with her until she gets somebody else. I don't think, when I explain it to him, that Dorian will mind my doing this."

"He will think it very sweet of you," says Clarissa, "considering how you detest teaching, and that."

While they are at tea, Dorian drops in, and, seeing the little yellow-haired fairy sitting in the huge lounging-chair, looks so openly glad and contented that Clarissa laughs mischievously.

"Poor Benedick!" she says, mockingly: "so it has come to this, that you know no life but in your Beatrice's presence!"

"Well, that's hardly fair, I think," says Branscombe; "you, at least, should not be the one to say it, as you are in a position to declare I was alive and hearty at half-past twelve this morning."

"Why, so you were," says Clarissa, "terribly alive,—but only on one subject. By the by, has any one seen papa lately? He had some new books from town to-day,—some painfully *old* books, I mean,—and has not been found since. I am certain he will be discovered some day buried beneath ancient tomes; perhaps, indeed, it will be this day. Will you two forgive me if I go to see if it is yet time to dig him out?"

They forgive her; and presently find themselves alone.

"Is it all true, I wonder?" says Dorian, after a little pause. He is holding her hand, and is looking down at her with a fond sweet smile that betrays the deep love of his heart.

"Quite true; at least, I hope so," with an answering smile. Then, "I am so glad you are going to marry me," she says, without the faintest idea of shyness; "more glad than I can tell you. Ever since—since I was left alone, I have had no one belonging to me,—that is, no one quite my own; and now I have you. You will always be fonder of me than of anybody else in the world, won't you?"

She seems really anxious as she asks this.

"My darling, of course I shall. How could you ask me such a question? And you, Georgie, do you love me?"

"Love you? Yes, I suppose so; I don't know,"—with decided hesitation. "I am certain I like you very, very much. I am quite happy when with you, and you don't bore me a bit. Is that it?"

This definition of what love *may* be, hardly comes up to the mark in Mr. Branscombe's estimation.

She has risen, and is now looking up at him inquiringly, with eyes earnest and beautiful and deep, but so cold. They chill him in spite of his efforts to disbelieve in their fatal truthfulness.

"Hardly, I think," he says, with an attempt at gayety. "Something else is wanting, surely. Georgie, when I asked you to marry me yesterday, and when you gave the promise that has made me so unutterably happy ever since, what was it you thought of?"

"Well, I'll tell you," says Miss Broughton, cheerfully. "First, I said to myself, 'Now I shall never again have to teach Murray's Grammar.'"

"Was that your *first* thought?" He is both surprised and pained.

"Yes, my very first. You look as if you didn't believe me," says Miss Broughton, with a little laugh. "But if you had gone through as many moods and tenses as I have during the past week, you would quite understand. Well, then I thought how good it would be to have nothing to do but amuse myself all day long. And then I looked at you, and felt so glad you had no crooked eyes, or red hair, or anything that way. And then, above all things, I felt how sweet it was to know I had found somebody who would have to look after me and take care of me, so that I need never trouble about myself any more."

"Did you never once think of me?" asks he, in a curious tone.

"Of you? Oh, no! You are quite happy," says Georgie, with a sigh. "You have nothing to trouble you."

"Nothing! Of course not." Going up to her, he takes her dear little face between both his hands, and looks long and earnestly into her clear unconscious eyes. How gladly would he have seen them droop and soften beneath his gaze! "Now let me tell you how I feel towards you," he says, smoothing her soft hair back from her forehead.

"I don't think I am a bit pretty with my hair pushed back," she says, moving away from the caressing hand, and, with a touch, restoring her "amber locks" to their original position. She smiles as she says this,—indeed, ill temper, in any form, does not belong to her,—and, when her hair is once more restored to order, she again slips her fingers into his confidingly, and glances up at him. "Now tell me all about it," she says.

"What am I to tell you?—that when I am away from you I am restless, miserable; when with you, more than satisfied. I know that I could sit for hours contentedly with this little hand in mine" (raising it to his lips), "and I also know that, if fate so willed it, I should gladly follow you through the length and breadth of the land. If you were to die, or—or forsake me, it would break my heart. And all this is because I love you."

"Is it?"—in a very low tone. "Does all that mean being in love? Then"—in a still lower tone—"I know I am not one bit in love with *you*."

"Then why are you marrying me?" demands he, a little roughly, stung to pained anger by her words.

"Because I promised papa, when—when he was leaving me, that I would marry the very first rich man that asked me," replies she, again lifting her serious eyes to his. "I thought it would make him happier. And it did. I am keeping my promise now," with a sigh that may mean regret for her dead, or, indeed, anything.

"Are you not afraid to go too far?" demands he, very pale, moving back from her, and regarding her with moody eyes. "Do you quite know what you are saying—what you are compelling me, against my will, to understand?"

She is plainly not listening to him. She is lost in a mournful revery, and, leaning back in her chair, is staring at her little white fingers in an absent fashion, and is twisting round and round upon her third finger an old worn-out gold ring. Poor little ring, so full of sweet and moving memories!

"It was very fortunate," she says, suddenly, with a smile, and without looking up at him, being still engrossed in her occupation of twisting the ring round her slender finger,—"it was *more* than fortunate that the first rich man should be *you*."

"Much more," he says, in an indescribable tone. Then with an effort, "Would you have thrown me over had I been poor?"

"I shouldn't have consented to marry you, I think," says Miss Broughton, quite calmly.

"As I said before, to be candid is your *forte*," exclaims he, with extreme bitterness. "I wonder even if you loved a man to distraction (I am not talking of myself, you know,—that is quite evident, is it not?) would you reject him if he was not sufficiently—*bon parti*?"

"I don't think I could love any one to distraction," replies she, quite simply. It seems the very easiest answer to this question.

"I believe you speak the very honest truth when you say that," says Dorian, drawing his breath quickly. "You are indeed terribly honest. You don't even shrink from telling the man you have elected to marry that he is no more to you than any other man might be who was equally possessed of filthy—if desirable—lucre!"

He turns from her, and, going to the window, stares out blindly upon the dying daylight, and the gardens stretched beneath, where dying flowers seem breathing of, and suggesting, higher thoughts.

He is unutterably wretched. All through his short courtship he had entertained doubts of her affection; but now, to have her so openly, so carelessly, declare her indifference is almost more than he can bear. "We forgive so long as we love." To Dorian, though his love is greater than that of most, forgiveness now seems difficult. Yet can he resign her? She has so woven herself into his very heart-strings—this cold, cruel, lovely child—that he cannot tear her out without a still further surrender of himself to death. To live without her—to get through endless days and interminable nights without hope of seeing her, with no certain knowledge that the morrow will bring him sure tidings of her—seems impossible. He sighs; and then, even as he sighs, five slim cold little fingers steal within his.

"I have made you angry," says the plaintive voice, full of contrition. A shapely yellow head pushes itself under one of his arms, that is upraised, and a lovely sorrowful pleading face looks up into his. How can any one be angry with a face like that?

"No, not angry," he says. And indeed the anger has gone from his face,—her very touch has banished it,—and only a great and lasting sadness has replaced it. Perhaps for the first time, at this moment she grasps some faint idea of the intensity of his love for her. Her eyes fill with tears.

"I think—it will be better for you—to—give me up," she says, in a down-hearted way, lowering her lids over her tell-tale orbs, that are like the summer sea now that they shine through their unwonted moisture

"Tears are trembling in her blue eyes,
Like drops that linger on the violet,"

and Dorian, with a sudden passionate movement, takes her in his arms and presses her head down upon his breast.

"Do you suppose I can give you up now," he says, vehemently, "when I have set my whole heart upon you? It is too late to suggest such a course. That you do not love me is my misfortune, not your fault. Surely it is misery enough to know that,—to feel that I am nothing to you,—without telling me that you wish so soon to be released from your promise?"

"I don't wish it," she says, earnestly, shaking her head. "No, indeed! It was only for your sake I spoke. Perhaps by and by you will regret having married some one who does not love you altogether. Because I know I could not sit contentedly for hours with my hand in any one's. And there are a great many things I would not do for you. And if *you* were to die——"

"There! that will do," he says, with sudden passion. "Do you know how you hurt, I wonder? Are you utterly heartless?"

Her eyes darken as he speaks, and, releasing herself from his embrace,—which, in truth, has somewhat slackened,—she moves back from him. She is puzzled, frightened; her cheeks lose their soft color, and—

"With that, the water in her eie
Arose, that she ne might it stoppe;
And, as men sene the dew be droppe
The leves and the floures eke,
Right so upon her white cheke
The wofull salt teres felle."

"I don't want to hurt you," she says, with a sob; "and I know I am *not* heartless." There is a faint tinge of indignation in her tone.

"Of course you are not. It was a rather brutal thing my saying so. Darling, whatever else may render me unhappy, I can at all events find comfort in the thought that you never loved any other man."

"But I did," says Miss Broughton, still decidedly tearful: "you must always remember that. There was one; and"—she is plainly in the mood for confessions—"I shall never love you or any one as I loved him."

"What are you going to tell me now?" says Dorian, desperately. He had believed his cup quite full, and only now discovers his mistake. Is there a still heavier amount of misery in store for him? "Is the worst to be told me yet?" he says, with the calmness of despair, being quite too far gone for vehemence of any description. "Why did you keep it from me until now?"

"I didn't keep anything," cries she: "I told you long ago—at least, I——"

"What is the name?" demands he, gloomily, fully expecting the hated word "Kennedy" to fall from her lips. "Better let me know it. Nothing you can possibly say can make me feel more thoroughly stranded than I am."

"I think you are taking it very unreasonably," says Miss Broughton, with quivering lips. "If I cannot bring myself to love anybody as well as poor papa, I can't help it—and it isn't my fault—and you are very unkind to me—and——"

"Good gracious! what a fright all about nothing!" says Mr. Branscombe, with a sigh of intense relief. "I don't mind your poor father, you know,—I rather admire your faithfulness there,—but I thought—er—it doesn't in the least matter what I thought," hastily: "every one has silly fancies at times." He kisses her lids warmly, tenderly, until the heavy drops beneath press through and run all down her charming childish face. "I am sure of this, at least," he says, hopefully, "that you like me better than any living man."

"Well, I do, indeed," replies she, in a curious tone, that might be suggestive of surprise at her own discovery of this fact. "But, then, how bad you are to me at times! Dear Dorian,"—laying one hand, with a pathetic gesture, on his cheek,—"do not be cross to me again."

"My sweetest!—my best beloved!" says Mr. Branscombe, instantly, drawing his breath a little quickly, and straining her to his heart.

CHAPTER XXVI

"The wisdom of this world is idiotism." — Decker.

"If thou desirest to be borne with, thou must bear also with others." — Kempis.

It takes some time to produce another governess suited to the Redmonds' wants. At length, however, the desired treasure is procured, and forwarded, "with care," to the vicarage.

On inspection, she proves to be a large, gaunt, high-cheek-boned daughter of Caledonia, with a broad accent, a broader foot, and uncomfortably red hair. She comes armed with testimonials of the most severely complimentary description, and with a pronounced opinion that "salary is not so much an object as a comfortable home."

Such a contrast to Georgie can scarcely be imagined. The Redmonds, in a body, are covered with despair, and go about the house, after her arrival, whispering in muffled tones, and casting blanched and stricken glances at each other. Dire dismay reigns in their bosoms; while the unconscious Scot unlocks her trunks, and shakes out her gowns, and shows plainly, by her behavior, that she has come to sit down before the citadel and carry on a prolonged siege.

To tea she descends with a solemn step and slow, that Amy designates as a "thud." But yet at this first tea she gains a victory. Arthur, the second boy, who has been wicked enough to get measles at school, and who is now at home to recruit himself and be the terror of his family, is at this time kept rather on short commons by his mother because of his late illness. This means bread-and-butter *without* jam, — a meaning the lively Arthur rather resents. Seeing which, the Caledonian, opening her lips almost for the first time, gives it as her opinion that jam, taken moderately, is wholesome.

She goes even farther, and insinuates it may assist digestion, which so impresses Mrs. Redmond that Arthur forthwith finds himself at liberty to "tuck into" (his own expression) the raspberry jam without let or hindrance.

This marvellous behavior on the part of the bony Scot tells greatly in her favor, so far as the children go. They tell each other later on that she can't be altogether an unpleasant sort, Master Arthur being specially loud in her praise. He even goes so far as to insinuate that Miss Broughton would never have said as much; but this base innuendo is sneered down by the faithful children who have loved and lost her. Nevertheless, they accept their fate; and, after a week or two, the new-comer gains immense ground, and is finally pronounced by her pupils to be (as she herself would probably express it) "no' that bad." Thus, Miss McGregor becomes governess at the vicarage, vice Georgie Broughton promoted.

To be married at once, without any unnecessary delay, is Dorian's desire; and when, with some hesitation, he broaches the subject to Georgie, to his surprise and great content he finds her quite willing to agree to anything he may propose. She speaks no word of reluctance, appears quite satisfied with any arrangement he or Clarissa may think proper, makes no shrinking protest against the undue haste. She betrays no shyness, yet no unseemly desire for haste. It seems to her a matter of perfect indifference. She is going to be married, sooner or later, as the case may be. Then why not the sooner?

This is, perhaps, the happiest time of her life. She roams all day among the flowers and in the pleasure-grounds, singing, laughing, talking gayly to any one she may meet at Gowran, where, since Miss McGregor's advent, she has been. When at length it is finally settled that the marriage is to take place next month, she seems rather pleased than otherwise, and is openly delighted at the prospect held out to her by Dorian of so soon seeing, with her own eyes, all the foreign lands and romantic scenes her fancy has so often depicted.

Just now, even as the tiny clock inside the room is chiming four, Dorian is standing outside the low French window of Miss Peyton's morning-room, and, leaning half in, half out of it, is conversing with her, alone. Georgie, for the time being, is lost to sight,—happy, somewhere, no doubt, in the warm sunshine she loves so well.

"Clarissa," he is saying, in a somewhat halting fashion,—he is coloring hotly, and is looking as uncomfortable as a man can look, which is saying a good deal,—"look here."

An ignominious break-down.

"I'm looking," says Clarissa, somewhat unkindly; "and I don't see much."

"Well, 'tis this, you know. You won't think it queer of me, will you?"

"I won't; I promise that. Though I haven't the faintest idea whether I shall or not."

"When she is getting her things, her *trousseau*,—I want her to have every earthly thing she can possibly fancy," he says, at last, desperately. "Can't you manage that for me? Do; and make any use you like of this."

He flings a cheque-book into her lap through the open window as he speaks.

"She shall have everything she wants," says Clarissa; "but I don't think"—taking up the book—"we shall require this."

"Nevertheless, keep it. You must want it; and don't mention me in the matter at all. And—look here again—what do you think she would like as a wedding-present?"

Of course he has given her long ago the orthodox engagement ring, the locket, the bracelet, and so forth.

"Why don't you ask her?" says Miss Peyton.

"Because the other day she said she adored surprises. And I am sure she doesn't care about being asked what she likes."

"You have your mother's diamonds."

"Oh, of course"—airily—"all my mother's things will be hers; that goes without telling; but I hate old rubbish. I want to give her something from myself to wear on her marriage morning. Don't you see? or is it that you grow imbecile in your old age, my good Clarissa?"

"No; it only means that you are growing extravagant in your dotage, my good Dorian. Well, mention something, that I may object to it."

"Emeralds, then?"

"No: papa has set his heart on giving her those."

"Rubies?"

"Oh, nothing red: they would not suit her."

"Opals?"

"Too unlucky, she would die or run away from you."

"Pearls? But of course,"—quickly: "why did I not think of them before?"

"Why, indeed? They will be charming. By the by, Dorian, have you told Lord Sartoris of your engagement?"

Dorian's brow darkens.

"No. He has been from home, you know, either in Paris or the Libyan desert, or somewhere. He only turned up again two days ago. Seen him since?"

"He was here, but I was out. Have you seen him?"

"Well, yes,—at a distance."

"Dorian, there is certainly something wrong between you and Lord Sartoris. I have noticed it for some time. I don't ask you what it is, but I entreat you to break through this coldness and be friends with him again." She stoops towards him, and looks earnestly into his face. He laughs a little.

"I'm tremendous friends with him, really," he says, "if you would only try to believe it. I think him no end of a good fellow, if slightly impossible at times. When he recovers from the attack of insanity that is at present rendering him very obnoxious, I shall be delighted to let by-gones be by-gones. But until then——"

"You will tell him of your engagement?"

"Perhaps: if occasion offers."

"No, not perhaps. Go to-day, this very evening, and tell him of it."

"Oh, I can't, really, you know," says Mr. Branscombe, who always finds a difficulty in refusing any one anything.

"You must,"—with decision: "he surely deserves so much at your hands."

"But how few of us get our deserts!" says Dorian, still plainly unimpressed.

"Well, then, I think you should speak of it openly to him,—if only for Georgie's sake."

"For her sake?" He colors again, and bites his lips. "If you really think I owe it to her, of course I shall do it, however distasteful the task may be; though I cannot see how it will benefit her."

"He is your uncle; you will wish your own family to receive her?"

"I dare say you are right," says Branscombe, with a shrug. "People always are when they suggest to you an unpleasant course."

"What is unpleasant now? How can there be anything to distress any one on such a heavenly day as this?" cries the soft petulant voice he loves so well, calling to them across a flower-bed near.

Springing over it, she comes up to the window, and, leaning her elbows on the sill close to him, laughs gayly up into his face.

"There shall be nothing to distress you, at all events, my 'amber witch,'" returns he, gayly, too. "Come, show me once more these gardens you love so well."

A promise with Dorian is not made of pie-crust: though sorely against his will, he goes up to Hythe after dinner to acquaint his uncle formally of his approaching marriage. The evening is calm and full of rest and quiet, a fit ending to the perfect day that has gone before:

"The long day wanes, the broad fields fade; the night—
The sweet June night—is like a curtain drawn.
The dark lanes know no faintest sound, and white
The pallid hawthorn lights the smooth-bleached lawn;
The scented earth drinks from the silent skies
Soft dews, more sweet than softest harmonies."

Going through the woods that lie upon his right, he walks silently onward, impressed by the beauty of the swift-coming night, yet too restless in mind to take in all its charms that are rich enough to satisfy a hungry soul. A soft wind is sighing; beneath its touch the young and tender branches are swaying lightly to and fro; all the "feathery people of mid-air" are preening their downy plumage and murmuring sleepy hymns ere sinking to their rest.

Scarce a sound can be heard, save the distant lowing of cattle, and the drowsy drone of a slumberous bee as it floats idly by. The very sound of Dorian's footsteps upon the soft grass can be distinctly heard, so deadly is the calm that ushers in the night; when, lo! from out some thicket, the nightingale,—

"Who is silent all day long;
But when pale eve unseals her clear throat, looses
Her twilight music on the dreaming boughs
Until they waken"—

bursts into song. High and clear and exquisite rise the notes one above the other, each vying in beauteous harmony with the last, until one's very heart aches for love and admiration of their sweetness.

Dorian, though oppressed with many discordant thoughts, still pauses to listen, until silence following upon the passionate burst of melody, he draws his breath quickly and goes on to Hythe, and into the dining-room there, where he finds Lord Sartoris still over his wine.

He is sitting at the head of the long table, looking strangely solitary, and very much aged, considering the short time that has elapsed since last he left Pullingham.

"So you are home again, Arthur," says Dorian, coldly, but with apparent composure. They have not been face to face since that last meeting, when bitter words, and still more bitter looks, had passed between them.

Now, letting the quickly spoken sentence take the place of a more active greeting, they nod coolly to each other, and carefully refuse to let their hands touch.

"Yes," says Sartoris, evenly; "I returned two days ago. Business recalled me; otherwise I was sufficiently comfortable where I was to make me wish to remain there."

"And Constance, is she quite well?"

"Quite well, thank you. Your other cousins desired to be remembered to you. So did she, of course."

A pause, prolonged and undesirable.

"You will take some claret?" says Sartoris, at last, pushing the bottle towards him.

"No, thank you; I have only just dined. I came up to-night to tell you what I dare say by this you have heard from somebody else; I am going to be married on the 9th of next month."

Lord Sartoris turns suddenly to confront him.

"I had not heard it," he says, with amazement. "To be married! This is very sudden." Then, changing his tone, "I am glad," he says, slowly, and with an unmistakable sneer, "that at last it has occurred to you to set that girl right in the eyes of the world. As a man of honor there was no other course left open to you."

"To whom are you alluding?" asks Branscombe, growing pale with anger, an ominous flash betraying itself in his gray eyes.

"I hope I understand you to mean to offer full, though tardy, reparation to Ruth Annersley."

With an effort Branscombe restrains the fierce outburst of wrath that is trembling on his lips.

"You still persist, then, in accusing me of being accessory to that girl's disappearance?"

"You have never yet denied it," exclaims Sartoris, pushing back his glass, and rising to his feet. "Give me the lie direct, if you *can*,—if you *dare*,—and I will believe you."

"I never will," returns Dorian, now thoroughly roused,—"*never!* If my own character all these past years is not denial enough, I shall give no other. Believe what you will. Do you imagine I shall come to you, like a whipped school-boy, after every supposed offence, to say, 'I did do this,' or, 'I did not do that'? I shall contradict nothing, assert nothing: therefore judge me as it may please you. I shall not try to vindicate my actions to any living man."

His tone, his whole bearing, should have carried conviction to the hearts of most men; but to the old lord, who has seen so much of the world in its worst phases,—its cruelties and falsehoods,—and who has roughed it so long among his fellowmen, faith, in its finer sense, is wanting.

"Enough," he says, coldly, with a slight wave of his hand. "Let us end this subject now and forever. You have come to tell me of your approaching marriage; may I ask the name of the lady you intend making your wife?"

"Broughton; Georgie Broughton," says Branscombe, briefly.

"Broughton,—I hardly fancy I know the name; and yet am I wrong in thinking there is a governess at the vicarage of that name?"

"There *was*. She is now staying with Clarissa Peyton, I am to be married to her, as I have already told you, early next month."

"A *governess!*" says Sartoris. There is a world of unpleasant meaning in his tone. "Really,"—with slow contempt,—"I can hardly congratulate you on your *tastes*! You, who might have chosen your wife almost anywhere, can find nothing to suit you but an obscure governess."

"I don't think there is anything particularly obscure about Georgie," replies Dorian, with admirable composure, though he flushes hotly. "Have you ever seen her? No? Then, of course, you are not in a position to judge of either her merits or demerits. I shall thank you, therefore,"—surveying his uncle rather insolently, from head to heel,—"to be silent on the subject."

After a slight pause, he turns again to Sartoris, and, forcing him to meet his gaze, says haughtily,—

"May we hope you will be present at our wedding, my lord?"

"I thank you, no. I fear not," returns the older man, quite as haughtily. "I hope to be many miles from here before the end of next week."

Dorian smiles unpleasantly.

"You will at least call upon Miss Broughton before leaving the neighborhood?" he says, raising his brows.

At this Sartoris turns upon him fiercely, stung by the apparent unconcern of his manner.

"Why should I call?" he says, his voice full of indignant anger. "Is it to congratulate her on her coming union with you? I tell you, were I to do so, the face of another woman would rise before me and freeze the false words upon my lips. To you, Dorian, in my old age, all my heart went out. My hopes, my affections, my ambitions, began and ended with you. And what a reward has been mine! Yours has been the hand to drag our name down to a level with the dust. Disgrace follows hard upon your footsteps. Were I to go, as you desire, to this innocent girl, do you imagine I could speak fair words to her? I tell you, no! I should rather feel it my duty to warn her against entering a house so dishonored as yours. I should——"

"Pshaw!" says Branscombe, checking him with an impatient gesture. "Don't let us introduce tragedy into this very commonplace affair. Pray don't trouble yourself to go and see her at all. In your present mood, I rather think you would frighten her to death. I am sorry I intruded my private matters upon you: but Clarissa quite made a point of my coming to Hythe to-night for that purpose, and, as you know, she is a difficult person to refuse. I'm sure I beg your pardon for having so unwarrantably bored you."

"Clarissa, like a great many other charming people, is at times prone to give very unseasonable advice," says Sartoris, coldly.

"Which, interpreted, means that I did wrong to come. I feel you are right." He laughs faintly again, and, taking up his hat, looks straight at his uncle. He has drawn himself up to his full height, and is looking quite his handsomest. He is slightly flushed (a dark color that becomes him), and a sneer lies round the corners of his lips. "I hardly know how to apologize," he says, lightly, "for having forced myself upon you in this intrusive fashion. The only amends I can possibly make is to promise you it shall never occur again, and to still further give you my word that, for the future, I shall not even annoy you by my presence."

So saying, he turns away, and, inclining his head, goes out through the door, and, closing it gently after him, passes rapidly down the long hall, as though in haste to depart, and, gaining the entrance-door, shuts it, too, behind him, and breathes more freely as he finds the air of heaven beating on his brow.

Not until he has almost reached Sartoris once more does that sudden calm fall upon him that, as a rule, follows hard upon all our gusts of passion. The late interview has hurt him more than he cares to confess even to himself. His regard—nay, his affection—for Sartoris is deep and sincere; and, though wounded now, and estranged from him, because of his determination to believe the worst of him, still it remains hidden in his heart, and is strong enough to gall and torture him after such scenes as he has just gone through.

Hitherto his life has been unclouded,—has been all sunshine and happy summer and glad with laughter. Now a dark veil hangs over it, threatening to deaden all things and dim the brightness of his "golden hours."

"He who hath most of heart knows most of sorrow." To Dorian, to be wroth with those he loves is, indeed, a sort of madness that affects his heart, if not his brain.

He frowns as he strides discontentedly onward through the fast-falling night: and then all at once a thought comes to him—a fair vision seems to rise almost in his path—that calms him and dulls all resentful memories. It is Georgie,—his love, his darling! She, at least, will be true to him. He will teach her so to love him that no light winds of scandal shall have power to shake her faith. Surely a heart filled with dreams of her should harbor no miserable thoughts. He smiles again; his steps grow lighter! he is once more the Dorian of old; he will—he must—be, of necessity, utterly happy with her beside him during all the life that is to come.

Alas that human hopes should prove so often vain!

CHAPTER XXVII

"Tis now the summer of your youth; time has not cropt the roses from your cheek, though sorrow long has washed them." — *The Gamester.*

The wedding—a very private one—goes off charmingly. The day breaks calm, smilingly, rich with beauty. "Lovely are the opening eyelids of the morn."

Georgie, in her wedding garments, looking like some pale white lily, is indeed "passing fair." She is almost too pallid, but the very pallor adds to the extreme purity and childishness of her beauty, and makes the gazer confident "there's nothing ill can dwell in such a temple." Dorian, tall and handsome, and unmistakably content, seems a very fit guardian for so fragile a flower.

Of course the marriage gives rise to much comment in the county, Branscombe being direct heir to the Sartoris title, and presumably the future possessor of all his uncle's private wealth. That he should marry a mere governess, a positive nobody, horrifies the county, and makes its shrug its comfortable shoulders and give way to more malicious talk than is at all necessary. With some, the pretty bride is an adventuress, and, indeed,—in the very softest of soft whispers, and with a gentle rustling of indignant skirts,—not *altogether* as correct as she might be. There are a few who choose to believe her of good family, but "awfully out-at-elbows, don't you know;" a still fewer who declare she is charming all round and fit for anything; and hardly one who does not consider her, at heart, fortunate and designing.

One or two rash and unsophisticated girls venture on the supposition that perhaps, after all, it is a real *bonâ fide* love-match, and make the still bolder suggestion that a governess may have a heart as well as other people. But these silly children are pushed out of sight, and very sensibly pooh-poohed, and are told, with a little clever laugh, that they "are quite too sweet, and quite dear babies, and they must try and keep on thinking all that sort of pretty rubbish as long as ever they can. It is so successful, and so very taking nowadays."

Dorian is regarded as an infatuated, misguided young man, who should never have been allowed out without a keeper. Such a disgraceful flinging away of opportunities, and birth, and position, to marry a woman so utterly out of his own set! No wonder his poor uncle refused to be present at the ceremony,—actually ran away from home to avoid it. And—so—by the by, talking of running away, what was that affair about that little girl at the mill? Wasn't Branscombe's name mixed up with it unpleasantly? Horrid low, you know, that sort of thing, when one is found out.

The county is quite pleased with its own gossip, and drinks innumerable cups of choicest tea over it, out of the very daintiest Derby and Sèvres and "Wooster," and is actually merry at the expense of the newly-wedded. Only a very few brave men, among whom is Mr. Kennedy, who is staying with the Luttrels, give it as their opinion that Branscombe is a downright lucky fellow and has got the handsomest wife in the neighborhood.

Towards the close of July, contrary to expectation, Mr. and Mrs. Branscombe return to Pullingham, and, in spite of censure, and open protest, are literally inundated with cards from all sides.

The morning after her return, Georgie drives down to Gowran, to see Clarissa, and tell her "all the news," as she declares in her first breath.

"It was all too enchanting," she says, in her quick, vivacious way. "I enjoyed it *so*. All the lovely old churches, and the lakes, and the bones of the dear saints, and everything. But I missed you, do you know,—yes, really, without flattery, I mean. Every time I saw anything specially desirable, I felt I wanted you to see it too. And so one day I told Dorian I was filled with a mad longing to talk to you once again, and I think he rather jumped at the suggestion of coming home forthwith; and—why, here we are."

"I can't say how glad I am that you *are* here," says Clarissa. "It was too dreadful without you both. I am so delighted you had such a really good time and were so happy."

"Happy!—I am quite that," says Mrs. Branscombe, easily. "I can always do just what I please, and there is nobody now to scold or annoy me in any way."

"And you have Dorian to love," says Clarissa, a little gravely, she hardly knows why. It is perhaps the old curious want in Georgie's tone that has again impressed her.

"Love, love, love," cries that young woman, a little impatiently. "Why are people always talking about love? Does it really make the world go round, I wonder? Yes, of course I have Dorian to be fond of now." She rises impulsively, and, walking to one of the windows, gazes out upon the gardens beneath. "Come," she says, stepping on to the veranda; "come out with me. I want to breathe your flowers again."

Clarissa follows her, and together they wander up and down among the heavy roses and drooping lilies, that are languid with heat and sleep. Here all the children of the sun and dew seem to grow and flourish.

> "No daintie flowre or herbe that growes on grownd,
> No arborett with painted blossoms drest
> And smelling sweete, but there it might be fownd
> To bud out faire and throwe her sweete smels al arownd."

Dorian, coming up presently to meet his wife and drive her home, finds her and Clarissa laughing gayly over one of Georgie's foreign reminiscences. He walks so slowly over the soft green grass that they do not hear him until he is quite close to them.

"Ah! you have come, Dorian," says Dorian's wife, with a pretty smile, "but too soon. Clarissa and I haven't half said all we have to say yet."

"At least I have said how glad I am to have you both back," says Clarissa. "The whole thing has been quite too awfully dismal without you. But for Jim and papa I should have gone mad, or something. I never put in such a horrid time. Horace came down occasionally,—very occasionally,—out of sheer pity, I believe; and Lord Sartoris was a real comfort, he visited so often; but he has gone away again."

"Has he? I suppose our return frightened him," says Branscombe, in a peculiar tone.

"I have been telling Clarissa how we tired of each other long before the right time," says Georgie, airily, "and how we came home to escape being bored to death by our own dulness."

Dorian laughs.

"She says what she likes," he tells Clarissa. "Has she yet put on the dignified stop for you? It would quite subdue any one to see her at the head of her table. Last night it was terrible. She seemed to grow several inches taller, and looked so severe that, long before it was time for him to retire, Martin was on the verge of nervous tears. I could have wept for him, he looked so disheartened."

"I'm perfectly certain Martin adores me," says Mrs. Branscombe, indignantly, "and I couldn't be severe or dignified to save my life. Clarissa, you must forgive me if I remove Dorian at once, before he says anything worse. He is quite untrustworthy. Good-by, dearest, and be sure you come up to see me to-morrow. I want to ask you ever so many more questions."

"Cards from the duchess for a garden-party," says Georgie, throwing the invitations in question across the breakfast-table to her husband. It is quite a week later, and she has almost settled down into the conventional married woman, though not altogether. To be entirely married—that is, sedate and sage—is quite beyond Georgie. Just now some worrying thought is oppressing her, and spoiling the flavor of her tea; her kidney loses its grace, her toast its crispness. She peeps at Dorian from behind the huge silver urn that seeks jealously to conceal her from view, and says, plaintively,—

"Is the duchess a very grand person, Dorian?"

"She is an awfully fat person, at all events," says Dorian, cheerfully. "I never saw any one who could beat her in that line. She'd take a prize, I think. She is not a bad old thing when in a good temper, but that is so painfully seldom. Will you go?"

"I don't know,"—doubtfully. Plainly, she is in the lowest depths of despair. "I—I—think I would rather not."

"I think you had better, darling."

"But you said just now she was always in a bad temper."

"Always? Oh, no; I am sure I couldn't have said that. And, besides, she won't go for you, you know, even if she is. The duke generally comes in for it. And by this time he rather enjoys it, I suppose,—as custom makes us love most things."

"But, Dorian, really now, what is she like?"

"I can't say that: it is a tremendous question. I don't know what she is; I only know what she is not."

"What, then?"

"'Fashioned so slenderly, young and so fair,'" quotes he, promptly. At which they both laugh.

"If she is an old dowdy," says Mrs. Branscombe, somewhat irreverently, "I sha'n't be one scrap afraid of her, and I do so want to go right over the castle. Somebody—Lord Alfred—would take me, I dare say. Yes,"—with sudden animation,—"let us go."

"I shall poison Lord Alfred presently," says Dorian, calmly. "Nothing shall prevent me. Your evident determination to spend your day with him has sealed his doom. Very well: send an answer, and let us spend a 'nice long happy day in the country.'"

"We are always spending that, aren't we?" says Mrs. Branscombe, adorably. Then, with a sigh, "Dorian, what shall I wear?"

He doesn't answer. For the moment he is engrossed, being deep in his "Times," busy studying the murders, divorces, Irish atrocities, and other pleasantries it contains.

"Dorian, do put down that abominable paper," exclaims she again, impatiently, leaning her arms on the table, and regarding him anxiously from the right side of the very forward urn that still will come in her way. "What shall I wear?"

"It can't matter," says Dorian: "you look lovely in everything, so it is impossible for you to make a mistake."

"It is a pity you can't talk sense,"—reproachfully. Then, with a glance literally heavy with care, "There is that tea-green satin trimmed with Chantilly."

"I forget it," says Dorian, professing the very deepest interest, "but I know it is all things."

"No, it isn't: I can't bear the sleeves. Then"—discontentedly—"there is that velvet."

"The very thing,"—enthusiastically.

"Oh, Dorian, dear! What are you thinking of? Do remember how warm the weather is."

"Well, so it is,—grilling," says Mr. Branscombe, nobly confessing his fault.

"Do you like me in that olive silk?" asks she, hopefully, gazing at him with earnest intense eyes.

"Don't I just?" returns he, fervently, rising to enforce his words.

"Now, don't be sillier than you can help," murmurs she, with a lovely smile. "Don't! I like that gown myself, you know: it makes me look so nice and old, and that."

"If I were a little girl like you," says Mr. Branscombe, "I should rather hanker after looking nice and young."

"But not too much so: it is frivolous when one is once married." This pensively, and with all the air of one who has long studied the subject.

"Is it? Of course you know best, your experience being greater than mine," says Dorian, meekly, "but, just for choice, I prefer youth to anything else."

"Do you? Then I suppose I had better wear white."

"Yes, do. One evening, in Paris, you wore a white gown of some sort, and I dreamt of you every night for a week afterwards."

"Very well. I shall give you a chance of dreaming of me again," says Georgie, with a carefully suppressed sigh, that is surely meant for the beloved olive gown.

The sigh is wasted. When she does don the white gown so despised, she is so perfect a picture that one might well be excused for wasting seven long nights in airy visions filled all with her. Some wild artistic marguerites are in her bosom (she plucked them herself from out the meadow an hour agone); her lips are red, and parted; her hair, that is loosely knotted, and hangs low down, betraying the perfect shape of her small head, is "yellow, like ripe corn." She smiles as she places her hand in Dorian's and asks him how she looks; while he, being all too glad because of her excessive beauty, is very slow to answer her. In truth, she is "like the snow-drop fair, and like the primrose sweet."

At the castle she creates rather a sensation. Many, as yet, have not seen her; and these stare at her placidly, indifferent to the fact that breeding would have it otherwise.

"What a peculiarly pretty young woman," says the duke, half an hour after her arrival, staring at her through his glasses. He had been absent when she came, and so is only just now awakened to a sense of her charms.

"Who?—what?" says the duchess, vaguely, she being the person he has rashly addressed. She is very fat, very unimpressionable, and very fond of argument. "Oh! over there. I quite forget who she is. But I do see that Alfred is making himself, as usual, supremely ridiculous with her. With all his affected devotion to Helen, he runs after every fresh face he sees."

"'There's nothing like a plenty,'" quotes the duke, with a dry chuckle at his own wit; indeed he prides himself upon having been rather a "card" in his day, and anything but a "k'rect" one, either.

"Yes, there is,—there is propriety," responds the duchess, in an awful tone.

"That wouldn't be a bit like it," says the duke, still openly amused at his own humor; after which—thinking it, perhaps, safer to withdraw while there is yet time—he saunters off to the left, and, as he has a trick of looking over his shoulder while walking, nearly falls into Dorian's arms at the next turn.

"Ho, hah!" says his Grace, pulling himself up very shortly, and glancing at his stumbling-block to see if he can identify him.

"Why, it is you, Branscombe," he says, in his usual cheerful, if rather fussy, fashion. "So glad to see you!—so glad." He has made exactly this remark to Dorian every time he has come in contact with him during the past twenty years and more. "By the by, I dare say you can tell me,—who is that pretty child over there, with the white frock and the blue eyes?"

"That pretty child in the frock is my wife," says Branscombe, laughing.

"Indeed! Dear me! dear me! I beg your pardon. My dear boy, I congratulate you. Such a face,—like a Greuze; or a—h'm—yes." Here he grows slightly mixed. "You must introduce me, you know. One likes to do homage to beauty. Why, where could you have met her in this exceedingly deficient county, eh? But you were always a sly dog, eh?"

The old gentleman gives him a playful slap on his shoulder, and then, taking his arm, goes with him across the lawn to where Georgie is standing talking gayly to Lord Alfred.

The introduction is gone through, and Georgie makes her very best bow, and blushes her very choicest blush; but the duke will insist upon shaking hands with her, whereupon, being pleased, she smiles her most enchanting smile.

"So glad to make your acquaintance. Missed you on your arrival," says the duke, genially. "Was toiling through the conservatories, I think, with Lady Loftus. Know her? Stout old lady, with feathers over her nose. She always will go to hot places on hot days."

"I wish she would go to a final hot place, as she affects them so much," says Lord Alfred, gloomily. "I can't bear her; she is always coming here bothering me about that abominable boy of hers in the Guards, and I never know what to say to her."

"Why don't you learn it up at night and say it to her in the morning?" says Mrs. Branscombe, brightly. "I should know what to say to her at once."

"Oh! I dare say," says Lord Alfred. "Only that doesn't help me, you know, because I don't."

"Didn't know who you were, at first, Mrs. Branscombe," breaks in the duke. "Thought you were a little girl—eh?—eh?"—chuckling again. "Asked your husband who you were, and so on. I hope you are enjoying yourself. Seen everything, eh? The houses are pretty good this year."

"Lord Alfred has just shown them to me. They are quite too exquisite," says Georgie.

"And the lake, and my new swans?"

"No; not the swans."

"Dear me! why didn't he show you those? Finest birds I ever saw. My dear Mrs. Branscombe, you really must see them, you know."

"I should like to, if you will show them to me," says the little hypocrite, with the very faintest, but the most successful, emphasis on the pronoun, which is wine to the heart of the old beau; and, offering her his arm, he takes her across the lawn and through the shrubberies to the sheet of water beyond, that gleams sweet and cool through the foliage. As they go, the county turns to regard them; and men wonder who the pretty woman is the old fellow has picked up; and women wonder what on earth the duke can see in that silly little Mrs. Branscombe.

Sir James, who has been watching the duke's evident admiration for his pretty guest, is openly amused.

"Your training!" he says to Clarissa, over whose chair he is leaning. "You ought to be ashamed of yourself and your pupil. Such a disgraceful little coquette I never saw. I really pity that poor duchess: see there, how miserably unhappy she is looking, and how— —er— —pink."

"Don't be unkind: your hesitation was positively cruel. The word 'red' is unmistakably the word for the poor duchess to-day."

"Well, yes, and yesterday, and the day before, and probably to-morrow," says Sir James, mildly. "But I really wonder at the duke,—at his time of life, too! If I were Branscombe I should feel it my duty to interfere."

He is talking gayly, unceasingly, but always with his grave eyes fixed upon Clarissa, as she leans back languidly on the uncomfortable garden-chair, smiling indeed every now and then, but fitfully, and without the gladness that generally lights up her charming face.

Horace had promised to be here to-day,—had faithfully promised to come with her and her father to this garden-party; and where is he now? A little chill of disappointment has fallen upon her, and made dull her day. No smallest doubt of his truth finds harbor in her gentle bosom, yet grief sits heavy on her, "as the mildews hang upon the bells of flowers to blight their bloom!"

Sir James, half divining the cause of her discontent, seeks carefully, tenderly, to draw her from her sad thoughts in every way that occurs to him; and his efforts, though not altogether crowned with success, are at least so far happy in that he induces her to forget her grievance for the time being, and keeps her from dwelling too closely upon the vexed question of her recreant lover.

To be with Sir James is, too, in itself a relief to her. With him she need not converse unless it so pleases her; her silence will neither surprise nor trouble him; but with all the others it would be so different: they would claim her attention whether she willed it or not, and to make ordinary spirited conversation just at this moment would be impossible to her. The smile dies off her face. A sigh replaces it.

"How well you are looking to-day!" says Scrope, lightly, thinking this will please her. She is extremely pale, but a little hectic spot, born of weariness and fruitless hoping against hope, betrays itself on either cheek. His tone, if not the words, does please her, it is so full of loving kindness.

"Am I?" she says. "I don't feel like looking well; and I am tired, too. They say, —

'A merry heart goes all the day,
Your sad tires in a mile-a;'

I doubt mine is a sad one, I feel so worn out. Though," —hastily, and with a vivid flush that changes all her pallor into warmth, —"if I were put to it, I couldn't tell you why."

"No? Do you know I have often felt like that," says Scrope, carelessly. "It is both strange and natural. One has fits of depression that come and go at will, and that one cannot account for; at least, I have, frequently. But you, Clarissa, you should not know what depression means."

"I know it to day." For the moment her courage fails her. She feels weak; a craving for sympathy overcomes her; and, turning, she lifts her large sorrowful eyes to his.

She would, perhaps, have spoken; but now a sense of shame and a sharp pang that means pride come to her, and, by a supreme effort, she conquers emotion, and lets her heavily-lashed lids fall over her suffused eyes, as though to conceal the tell-tale drops within from his searching gaze.

"So, you see," —she says, with a rather artificial laugh, —"your flattery falls through: with all this weight of imaginary woe upon my shoulders, I can hardly be looking my best."

"Nevertheless, I shall not allow you to call my true sentiments flattery," says Scrope: "I really meant what I said, whether you choose to believe me or not. Yours is a

'Beauty truly blent, whose red and white
Nature's own sweet and cunning hand laid on.'"

"What a courtier you become!" she says, laughing honestly for almost the first time to-day. It is so strange to hear James Scrope say anything high-flown or sentimental. She is a little bit afraid that he knows why she is sorry, yet, after all, she hardly frets over the fact of his knowing. Dear Jim! he is always kind, and sweet, and thoughtful! Even if he does understand, he is quite safe to look as if he didn't. And that is always such a comfort!

And Sir James, watching her, and marking the grief upon her face, feels a tightening at his heart, and a longing to succor her, and to go forth—if need be—and fight for her as did the knights of old for those they loved, until "just and mightie death, whom none can advise," enfolded him in his arms.

For long time he has loved her,—has lived with only her image in his heart. Yet what has his devotion gained him? Her liking, her regard, no doubt, but nothing that can satisfy the longing that leaves desolate his faithful heart. Regard, however deep, is but small comfort to him whose every thought, waking and sleeping, belongs alone to her.

> "Full little knowest thou, that hast not tride,
> What hell it is, in swing long to bide;
> To loose good dayes that might be better spent,
> To wast long nights in pensive discontent;
> To speed to-day, to be put back to-morrow;
> To feed on hope, to pine with feare and sorrow;
> To fret thy soul with crosses and with cares;
> To eate thy heart through comfortlesse dispaires."

He is quite assured she lives in utter ignorance of his love. No word has escaped him, no smallest hint, that might declare to her the passion that daily, hourly, grows stronger, and of which she is the sole object. "The noblest mind the best contentment has," and he contents himself as best he may on a smile here, a gentle word there, a kindly pressure of the hand to-day, a look of welcome to-morrow. These are liberally given, but nothing more. Ever since her engagement to Horace Branscombe he has, of course, relinquished hope; but the surrender of all expectation has not killed his love. He is silent because he must be so, but his heart wakes, and

> "Silence in love bewrays more woe
> Than words, though ne'er so witty."

"See, there they are again," he says now, alluding to Georgie and her ducal companion, as they emerge from behind some thick shrubs. Another man is with them, too,—a tall, gaunt young man, with long hair, and a cadaverous face, who is staring at Georgie as though he would willingly devour her—but only in the interest of art. He is lecturing on the "Consummate Daffodil," and is comparing it unfavorably with the "Unutterable Tulip," and is plainly boring the two, with whom he is walking, to extinction. He is Sir John Lincoln, that old-new friend of Georgie's, and will not be shaken off.

"Long ago," says Georgie, tearfully, to herself, "he was not an æsthete. Oh, how I *wish* he would go back to his pristine freshness!"

But he won't: he maunders on unceasingly about impossible flowers, that are all very well in their way, but whose exaltedness lives only in his own imagination, until the duke, growing weary (as well he might, poor soul), turns aside, and greets with unexpected cordiality a group upon his right, that, under any other less oppressive circumstances, would be abhorrent to him. But to spend a long hour talking about one lily is not to be borne.

Georgie follows his example, and tries to escape Lincoln and the tulips by diving among the aforesaid group. She is very successful,—groups do not suit æsthetics,—and soon the gaunt young man takes himself, and his long hair, to some remote region.

"How d'ye do, Mrs. Branscombe?" says a voice at her elbow, a moment later, and, turning, she finds herself face to face with Mr. Kennedy.

"Ah! you?" she says, with very flattering haste, being unmistakably pleased to see him. "I had no idea you were staying in the country."

"I am staying with the Luttrells'. Molly asked me down last month."

"She is a great friend of yours, I know," says Mrs. Branscombe; "yet I hadn't the faintest notion I should meet you here to-day."

"And you didn't care either, I dare say," says Mr. Kennedy, in a tone that is positively sepulchral, and, considering *all* things, very well done indeed.

"I should have cared, if I had even once thought about it," says Mrs. Branscombe, cheerfully.

Whereupon he says,—

"*Thank* you!" in a voice that is *all* reproach.

Georgie colors. "I didn't mean what *you* think," she says, anxiously. "I didn't *indeed*."

"Well, it sounded exactly like it," says Mr. Kennedy, with careful gloom. "Of course it is not to be expected that you ever *would* think of me, but——I haven't seen you since that last night at Gowran, have I?"

"No."

"I think you might have told me then you were going to be married."

"I wasn't going to be married then," says Georgie, indignantly: "I hadn't a single idea of it. Never thought of it, until the next day."

"I quite thought you were going to marry me," says Mr. Kennedy, sadly; "I had quite made up my mind to it. I never" —forlornly—"imagined you as belonging to any other fellow. It isn't pleasant to find that one's pet doll is stuffed with sawdust, and yet—"

"I can't think what you are talking about," says Mrs. Branscombe, coldly, and with some fine disgust; she cannot help thinking that she must be the doll in question, and to be filled with sawdust sounds anything but dignified.

Kennedy, reading her like a book, nobly suppresses a wild desire for laughter, and goes on in a tone, if possible, more depressed than the former one.

"My insane hope was the doll," he says: "it proved only dust. I haven't got over the shock yet that I felt on hearing of your marriage. I don't suppose I ever shall now."

"Nonsense!" says Georgie, contemptuously. "I never saw you look so well in all my life. You are positively fat."

"That's how it always shows with me," says Kennedy, unblushingly. "Whenever green and yellow melancholy marks me for its own, I sit on a monument (they always keep one for me at home) and smile incessantly at grief, and get as fat as possible. It is a refinement of cruelty, you know, as superfluous flesh is not a thing to be hankered after."

"How you must have fretted," says Mrs. Branscombe, demurely, glancing from under her long lashes at his figure, which has certainly gained both in size and in weight since their last meeting.

At this they both laugh.

"Is your husband here to-day?" asks he, presently.

"Yes."

"Why isn't he with you?"

"He has found somebody more to his fancy, perhaps."

As she says this she glances round, as though for the first time alive to the fact that indeed he is not beside her.

"Impossible!" says Kennedy. "Give any other reason but that, and I may believe you. I am quite sure he is missing you terribly, and is vainly searching every nook and corner by this time for your dead body. No doubt he fears the worst. If you were my— —I mean if ever I were to marry (which of course is quite out of the question now), I shouldn't let my wife out of my sight."

"Poor woman! what a time she is going to put in!" says Mrs. Branscombe, pityingly. "Don't go about telling people all that, or you will never get a wife. By this time Dorian and I have made the discovery that we can do excellently well without each other sometimes."

Dorian coming up behind her just as she says this, hears her, and changes color.

"How d'ye do!" he says to Kennedy, civilly, if not cordially, that young man receiving his greeting with the utmost bonhommie and an unchanging front.

For a second, Branscombe refuses to meet his wife's eyes, then, conquering the momentary feeling of pained disappointment, he turns to her, and says, gently,—

"Do you care to stay much longer? Clarissa has gone, and Scrope, and the Carringtons."

"I don't care to stay another minute: I should like to go home now," says Georgie, slipping her hand through his arm, as though glad to have something to lean on; and, as she speaks, she lifts her face and bestows upon him a small smile. It is a very dear little smile, and has the effect of restoring him to perfect happiness again.

Seeing which, Kennedy raises his brows, and then his hat, and, bowing, turns aside, and is soon lost amidst the crowd.

"You are sure you want to come home?" says Dorian, anxiously. "I am not in a hurry, you know."

"I am. I have walked enough, and talked enough, to last me a month."

"I am afraid I rather broke in upon your conversation just now," says Branscombe, looking earnestly at her. "But for my coming, Kennedy would have stayed on with you; and he is a—a rather amusing sort of fellow, isn't he?"

"Is he? He was exceedingly stupid to-day, at all events. I don't believe he has a particle of brains, or else he thinks other people haven't. I enjoyed myself a great deal more with the old duke, until that ridiculous Sir John Lincoln came to us. I don't think he knew a bit who the duke was, because he kept saying odd little things about the grounds and the guests, right under his nose; at least, right behind his back: it is all the same thing."

"What is? His nose and his back?" asks Dorian; at which piece of folly they both laugh as though it was the best thing in the world.

Then they make their way over the smooth lawns, and past the glowing flower-beds, and past Sir John Lincoln, too, who is standing in an impossible attitude, that makes him all elbows and knees, talking to a very splendid young man—all bone and muscle and good humor—who is plainly delighted with him. To the splendid young man he is nothing but one vast joke.

Seeing Mrs. Branscombe, they both raise their hats, and Sir John so far forgets the tulips as to give it as his opinion that she is "Quite too, too intense for every-day life." Whereupon the splendid young man, breaking into praise too, declares she is "Quite too awfully jolly, don't you know," which commonplace remark so horrifies his companion that he sadly and tearfully turns aside, and leaves him to his fate.

Georgie, who has been brought to a standstill for a moment, hears both remarks, and laughs aloud.

"It is something to be admired by Colonel Vibart, isn't it?" she says to Dorian; "but it is really very sad about poor Sir John. He has bulbous roots on the brain, and they have turned him as mad as a hatter."

CHAPTER XXVIII

"There's not a scene on earth so full of lightness
That withering care
Sleeps not beneath the flowers and turns their brightness
To dark despair."—Hon. Mrs. Norton.

It is a day of a blue and goldness so intense as to make one believe these two are the only colors on earth worthy of admiration. The sky is cloudless; the great sun is wide awake; the flowers are drooping, sleeping,—too languid to lift their heavy heads.

"The gentle wind, that like a ghost doth pass,
A waving shadow on the cornfield keeps."

And Georgie descending the stone steps of the balcony, feels her whole nature thrill and glow beneath the warmth and richness of the beauty spread all around with lavish hand. Scarcely a breath stirs the air; no sound comes to mar the deep stillness of the day, save the echo of the "swallows' silken wings skimming the water of the sleeping lake."

As she passes the rose-trees, she puts out her hand, and, from the very fulness of her heart, touches some of the drowsy flowers with caressing fingers. She is feeling peculiarly happy to-day: everything is going so smoothly with her; her life is devoid of care; only sunshine streams upon her path; storm and rain and nipping frosts seem all forgotten.

Going into the garden, she pulls a flower or two and places them in the bosom of her white gown, and bending over the basin of a fountain, looks at her own image, and smiles at it, as well she may.

Then she blushes at her own vanity, and, drawing back from nature's mirror, tells herself she will go a little farther, and see what Andrews, the under-gardener (who has come to Sartoris from Hythe), is doing in the shrubbery.

The path by which she goes is so thickly lined with shrubs on the right-hand side that she cannot be seen through them, nor can she see those beyond. Voices come to her from the distance, that, as she advances up the path, grow even louder. She is not thinking of them, or, indeed, of anything but the extreme loveliness of the hour, when words fall upon her ear that make themselves intelligible and send the blood with a quick rush to her heart.

"It is a disgraceful story altogether; and to have the master's name mixed up with it is shameful!"

The voice, beyond doubt, belongs to Graham, the upper-housemaid, and is full of honest indignation.

Hardly believing she has heard aright, and without any thought of eaves-dropping, Georgie stands still upon the walk, and waits in breathless silence for what may come next.

"Well, I think it is shameful," says another voice, easily recognized as belonging to Andrews. "But I believe it is the truth for all that. Father saw him with his own eyes. It was late, but just as light as it is now, and he saw him plain."

"Do you mean to tell me," says Graham, with increasing wrath (she is an elderly woman, and has lived at Sartoris for many years), "that you really think your master had either hand, act, or part in inducing Ruth Annersley to leave her home?"

"Well, I only say what father told me," says Andrews, in a half-apologetic fashion, being somewhat abashed by her anger. "And he ain't one to lie much. He saw him with her in the wood the night she went to Lunnun, or wherever 'twas, and they walked together in the way to Langham Station. They do say, too, that——"

A quick light footstep, a putting aside of branches, and Georgie, pale, but composed, appears before them. Andrews, losing his head, drops the knife he is holding, and Graham grows a fine purple.

"I don't think you are doing much good here, Andrews," says Mrs. Branscombe, pleasantly. "These trees look well enough: go to the eastern walk, and see what can be done there."

Andrews, only too thankful for the chance of escape, picks up his knife again and beats a hasty retreat.

Then Georgie, turning to Graham, says slowly,—

"Now, tell me every word of it, from beginning to end."

Her assumed unconsciousness has vanished. Every particle of color has flown from her face, her brow is contracted, her eyes are shining with a new and most unenviable brilliancy. Perhaps she knows this herself, as, after the first swift glance at the woman on Andrews's departure, she never lifts her eyes again, but keeps them deliberately fixed upon the ground during the entire interview. She speaks in a low concentrated tone, but with firm compressed lips.

Graham's feelings at this moment would be impossible to describe. Afterwards — many months afterwards — she herself gave some idea of them when she declared to the cook that she thought she should have "swooned right off."

"Oh, madam! tell you what?" she says, now, in a terrified tone, shrinking away from her mistress, and turning deadly pale.

"You know what you were speaking about just now when I came up."

"It was nothing, madam, I assure you, only idle gossip, not worth——"

"Do not equivocate to me. You were speaking of Mr. Branscombe. Repeat your 'idle gossip.' I will have it word for word. Do you hear?" She beats her foot with quick impatience against the ground.

"Do not compel me to repeat so vile a lie," entreats Graham, earnestly. "It is altogether false. Indeed, madam," —confusedly, —"I cannot remember what it was we were saying when you came up to us so unexpectedly."

"Then I shall refresh your memory. You were talking of your master and — and of that girl in the village who——" The words almost suffocate her; involuntarily she raises her hand to her throat. "Go on," she says, in a low, dangerous tone.

Graham bursts into tears.

"It was the gardener at Hythe—old Andrews—who told it to our man here," she sobs, painfully. "You know he is his father, and he said he had seen the master in the copsewood the evening—Ruth Annersley ran away."

"He was in London that evening."

"Yes, madam, we all know that," says the woman, eagerly. "That alone proves how false the whole story is. But wicked people will talk, and it is wise people only who will not give heed to them."

"What led Andrews to believe it was your master?" She speaks in a hard constrained voice, and as one who has not heard a word of the preceding speech. In truth, she has not listened to it, her whole mind being engrossed with this new and hateful thing that has fallen into her life.

"He says he saw him, —that he knew him by his height, his figure, his side-face, and the coat he wore, —a light overcoat, such as the master generally uses."

"And how does he explain away the fact of—of Mr. Branscombe's being in town that evening?"

At this question Graham unmistakably hesitates before replying. When she does answer, it is with evident reluctance.

"You see, madam," she says, very gently, "it would be quite possible to come down by the mid-day train to Langham, to drive across to Pullingham, and get back again to London by the evening train."

"It sounds quite simple," says Mrs. Branscombe, in a strange tone. Then follows an unbroken silence that lasts for several minutes and nearly sends poor Graham out of her mind. She cannot quite see her mistress's face as it is turned carefully aside, but the hand that is resting on a stout branch of laurel near her is steady as the branch itself. Steady,—but the pretty filbert nails show dead-white against the gray-green of the bark, as though extreme pressure, born of mental agitation and a passionate desire to suppress and hide it, has compelled the poor little fingers to grasp with undue force whatever may be nearest to them.

When silence has become positively unbearable, Georgie says, slowly,—

"And does all the world know this?"

"I hope not, ma'am. I think not. Though, indeed,"—says the faithful Graham, with a sudden burst of indignation,—"even if they did, I don't see how it could matter. It would not make it a bit more or less than a deliberate lie."

"You are a good soul, Graham," says Mrs. Branscombe, wearily.

Something in her manner frightens Graham more than all that has gone before.

"Oh, madam, do not pay any attention to such a wicked tale," she says, anxiously, "and forgive me for ever having presumed to lend my ears to it. No one knowing the master could possibly believe in it."

"Of course not." The answer comes with unnatural calmness from between her white lips. Graham bursts into fresh tears, and flings her apron over her head.

Mrs. Branscombe, at this, throws up her head hastily, almost haughtily, and, drawing her hand with a swift movement across her averted eyes, breathes a deep lingering sigh. Then her whole expression changes; and, coming quite near to Graham, she lays her hand lightly on her shoulder, and laughs softly.

Graham can hardly believe her ears: has that rippling, apparently unaffected laughter come from the woman who a moment since appeared all gloom and suppressed anger?

"I am not silly enough to fret over a ridiculous story such as you have told me," says Georgie, lightly. "Just at first it rather surprised me, I confess, but now—now I can see the absurdity of it. There; do not cry any more; it is a pity to waste tears that later on you may long for in vain."

But when she has gained the house, and has gone up to her own room, and carefully locked her door, her assumed calmness deserts her. She paces up and down the floor like some chained creature, putting together bit by bit the story just related to her. Not for a moment does she doubt its truth: some terrible fear is knocking at her heart, some dread that is despair and that convinces her of the reality of Andrews's relation.

Little actions of Dorian's, light words, certain odd remarks, passed over at the time of utterance as being of no importance, come back to her now, and assert themselves with overwhelming persistency, until they declare him guilty beyond all dispute.

When she had gone to the altar and sworn fidelity to him, she had certainly not been in love with her husband, according to the common acceptation of that term. But at least she had given him a heart devoid of all thought for another, and she had fully, utterly, believed in his affection for her. For the past few months she had even begun to cherish this belief, to cling to it, and even to feel within herself some returning tenderness for him.

It is to her now, therefore, as the bitterness of death, this knowledge that has come to her ears. To have been befooled where she had regarded herself as being most beloved,—to have been only second, where she had fondly imagined herself to be first and dearest,—is a thought bordering upon madness.

Passionate sobs rise in her throat, and almost overcome her. An angry feeling of rebellion, a vehement protest against this deed that has been done, shakes her slight frame. It cannot be true; it shall not; and yet—and yet—why has this evil fallen upon her of all others? Has her life been such a happy one that Fate must needs begrudge her one glimpse of light and gladness? Two large tears gather in her eyes, and almost unconsciously roll down her cheeks that are deadly white.

Sinking into a chair, as though exhausted, she leans back among its cushions, letting her hands fall together and lie idly in her lap.

Motionless she sits, with eyes fixed as if riveted to earth, while tears insensibly steal down her pensive cheeks, which look like weeping dew fallen on the statue of despair.

For fully half an hour she so rests, scarce moving, hardly seeming to breathe. Then she rouses herself, and, going over to a table, bathes her face with eau-de-Cologne. This calms her in a degree, and stills the outward expression of her suffering, but in her heart there rages a fire that no waters can quench.

Putting her hat on once again, she goes down-stairs, feeling eager for a touch of the cool evening air. The hot sun is fading, dying; a breeze from the distant sea is creeping stealthily up to the land. At the foot of the staircase she encounters Dorian coming towards her from the library.

"I have been hunting the place for you," he says, gayly. "Where on earth have you been hiding? Visions of ghastly deaths rose before me, and I was just about to have the lake dragged and the shrubberies swept. Martin is nearly in tears. You really ought to consider our feelings a little. Why, where are you off to now?"—for the first time noticing her hat.

"Out," returns she, coldly, looking straight over his head: she is standing on the third step of the stairs, while he is in the hall below. "I feel stifled in this house."

Her tone is distinctly strange, her manner most unusual. Fearing she is really ill, he goes up to her and lays his hand upon her arm.

"Anything the matter, darling? How white you look," he begins, tenderly; but she interrupts him.

"I am quite well," she says, hardly, shrinking away from his touch as though it is hateful to her. "I am going out because I wish to be alone."

She sweeps past him through the old hall and out into the darkening sunlight, without a backward glance or another word. Amazed, puzzled, Branscombe stands gazing after her until the last fold of her dress has disappeared, the last sound of her feet has echoed on the stone steps beyond; then he turns aside, and, feeling, if possible, more astonished than hurt, goes back to the library.

From this hour begins the settled coldness between Dorian and his wife that is afterwards to bear such bitter fruit. She assigns no actual reason for her changed demeanor; and Dorian, at first, is too proud to demand an explanation,—though perhaps never yet has he loved her so well as at this time, when all his attempts at tenderness are coldly and obstinately rejected.

Not until a full month has gone by, and it is close upon the middle of August, does it dawn upon him why Georgie has been so different of late.

Sir James Scrope is dining with them, and, shortly after the servants have withdrawn, he makes some casual mention of Ruth Annersley's name.

No notice is taken of it at the time, the conversation changes almost directly into a fresh channel, but Dorian, happening to glance across the table at his wife, sees that she has grown absolutely livid, and really, for the instant, fears she is going to faint. Only for an instant! Then she recovers herself, and makes some careless remark, and is quite her usual self again.

But he cannot forget that sudden pallor, and like a flash the truth comes to him, and he knows he is foul and despicable in the eyes of the only woman he loves.

When Sir James has gone, he comes over to her, and, leaning his elbow on the chimney-piece, stands in such a position as enables him to command a full view of her face.

"Scrope takes a great interest in that girl Ruth," he says, purposely introducing the subject again. "It certainly is remarkable that no tidings of her have ever since reached Pullingham."

Georgie makes no reply. The nights have already grown chilly and there is a fire in the grate, before which she is standing warming her hands. One foot,—a very lovely little foot,—clad in a black shoe relieved by large silver buckles, is resting on the fender, and on this her eyes are riveted, as though lost in admiration of its beauty, though in truth she sees it not at all.

"I can hardly understand her silence," persists Dorian. "I fear, wherever she is, she must be miserable."

Georgie raises her great violet eyes to his, that are now dark and deep with passionate anger and contempt.

"She is not the only miserable woman in the world," she says, in a low, quick tone.

"No, I suppose not. But what an unsympathetic tone you use! Surely you can feel for her?"

"Feel for her! Yes. No woman can have as much compassion for her as I have."

"That is putting it rather strongly, is it not? You scarcely know her; hardly ever spoke to her. Clarissa Peyton, for instance, must think more pitifully of her than you can."

"I hope it will never be Clarissa's lot to compassionate any one in the way I do her."

"You speak very bitterly."

"Do I? I think very bitterly."

"What do you mean?" demands he, suddenly, straightening himself and drawing up his tall figure to its fullest height. His tone is almost stern.

"Nothing. There is nothing to be gained by continuing this conversation."

"But I think there is. Of late, your manner towards me has been more than strange. If you complain of anything, let me know what it is, and it shall be rectified. At the present moment, I confess, I fail to understand you. You speak in the most absurdly romantic way about Ruth Annersley (whom you hardly knew), as though there existed some special reason why you, above all women, should pity her."

"I do pity her from my heart; and there is a special reason: she has been deceived, and so have I."

"By whom?"

"I wish you would discontinue the subject, Dorian: it is a very painful one to me, if—if not to you." Then she moves back a little, and, laying her hand upon her chest, as though a heavy weight, not to be lifted, is lying there, she says, slowly, "You compel me to say what I would willingly leave unsaid. When I married you, I did not understand your character; had I done so——"

"You would not have married me? You regret your marriage?" He is very pale now, and something that is surely anguish gleams in his dark eyes. Perhaps had she seen his expression her answer would have been different, or, at least, more merciful.

"I do," she says, faintly.

"Why?" All heart seems gone from his voice. He is gazing mournfully upon the girlish figure of his wife as she stands at some little distance from him. "Have I been such a bad husband to you, Georgie?" he says, brokenly.

"No, no. But it is possible to be cruel in more ways than one."

"It is, indeed!" Then he sighs wearily; and, giving up all further examination of her lovely unforgiving face, he turns his gaze upon the fire. "Look here," he says, presently; "I heard unavoidably what you said to Kennedy that afternoon at the castle, that we could manage to get on without each other excellently well on occasion: you alluded to yourself, I suppose. Perhaps you think we might get on even better had we never met."

"I didn't say that," says Georgie, turning pale.

"I understand,"—bitterly: "you only meant it. Well, if you are so unhappy with me, and if—if you wish for a separation, I think I can manage it for you. I have no desire whatever"—coldly—"to keep you with me against your will."

"And have all the world talking?" exclaims she, hastily. "No. In such a case the woman goes to the wall: the man is never in fault. Things must now remain as they are. But this one last thing you can do for me. As far as is possible, let us live as utter strangers to each other."

"It shall be just as you please," returns he, haughtily.

Day by day the dark cloud that separates them widens and deepens, drifting them farther and farther apart, until it seems almost impossible that they shall ever come together again.

Dorian grows moody and irritable, and nurses his wrongs in sullen morbid silence. He will shoot whole days without a companion, or go for long purposeless rides across country, only to return at nightfall weary and sick at heart.

"Grief is a stone that bears one down." To Dorian, all the world seems going wrong; his whole life is a failure. The two beings he loves most on earth—Lord Sartoris and his wife—distrust him, and willingly lend an open ear to the shameless story unlucky Fate has coined for him.

As for Georgie, she grows pale and thin, and altogether unlike herself. From being a gay, merry, happy little girl, with "the sun upon her heart," as Bailey so sweetly expresses it, she has changed into a woman, cold and self-contained, with a manner full of settled reserve.

Now and again small scenes occur between them that only render matters more intolerable. For instance, coming into the breakfast-room one morning, Georgie, meeting the man who brings the letters, takes them from him, and, dividing them, comes upon one directed to Dorian, in an unmistakable woman's hand, bearing the London post-mark, which she throws across the table to her husband.

Something in the quickness of her action makes him raise his head to look at her. Catching the expression of her eyes, he sees that they are full of passionate distrust, and at once reads her thoughts aright. His brow darkens; and, rising, he goes over to her, and takes her hands in his, not with a desire to conciliate, but most untenderly.

"It is impossible you can accuse me of this thing," he says, his voice low and angry.

"Few things are impossible," returns she, with cold disdain. "Remove your hands, Dorian: they hurt me."

"At least you shall be convinced that in this instance, as in all the others, you have wronged me."

Still holding her hands, he compels her to listen to him while he reads aloud a letter from the wife of one of his tenants who has gone to town on law business and who has written to him on the matter.

Such scenes only help to make more wide the breach between them. Perhaps, had Georgie learned to love her husband before her marriage, all might have been well; but the vague feeling of regard she had entertained for him (that, during the early days of their wedded life, had been slowly ripening into honest love, not having had time to perfect itself) at the first check had given in, and fallen—hurt to death—beneath the terrible attack it had sustained.

She fights and battles with herself at times, and, with passionate earnestness, tries to live down the growing emptiness of heart that is withering her young life. All night long sometimes she lies awake, waiting wearily for the dawn, and longing prayerfully for some change in her present stagnation.

And, even if she can summon sleep to her aid, small is the benefit she derives from it. Bad dreams, and sad as bad, harass and perplex her, until she is thankful when her lids unclose and she feels at least she is free of the horrors that threatened her a moment since.

> "Thou hast been called, O sleep! the friend of woe;
> But, 'tis the happy that have called thee so!"

CHAPTER XXIX

"The waves of a mighty sorrow
Have whelmed the pearl of my life;
And there cometh to me no morrow
Shall solace this desolate strife.

"Gone are the last faint flashes,
Set in the sun of my years,
And over a few poor ashes
I sit in darkness and tears." —Gerald Massey.

All night the rain has fallen unceasingly; now the sun shines forth again, as though forgetting that excessive moisture has inundated the quiet uncomplaining earth. The "windy night" has not produced a "rainy morrow;" on the contrary, the world seems athirst for drink again, and is looking pale and languid because it comes not.

"Moist, bright, and green, the landscape laughs around:
Full swell the woods."

Everything is richer for the welcome drops that fell last night. "The very earth, the steamy air, is all with fragrance rife;" the flowers lift up their heads and fling their perfume broadcast upon the flying wind;

"And that same dew, which sometime within buds
Was wont to swell, like round and Orientpearls,
Stood now within the pretty flowerets' eyes,
Like tears that did their own disgrace bewail."

Georgie, with scarcely any heart to see their beauty, passes by them, and walks on until she reaches that part of Hythe wood that adjoins their own. As she passes them, the gentle deer raise their heads and sniff at her, and, with their wild eyes, entreat her to go by and take no notice of them.

Autumn, with his "gold hand," is

"Gilding the falling leaf,
Bringing up winter to fulfil the year,
Bearing upon his back the ripéd sheaf."

All nature seems lovely, and, in coloring, intense. To look upon it is to have one's heart widen and grow stronger and greater as its divinity fills one's soul to overflowing. Yet to Georgie the hour gives no joy: with lowered head and dejected mien she goes, scarce heeding the glowing tints that meet her on every side. It is as though she tells herself the world's beauty can avail her nothing, as, be the day

"Foul, or even fair,
Methinks her hearte's joy is stainéd with some care."

Crossing a little brook that is babbling merrily, she enters the land of Hythe; and, as she turns a corner (all rock, and covered with quaint ferns and tender mosses), she comes face to face with an old man, tall and lean, who is standing by a pool, planted by nature in a piece of granite.

He is not altogether unknown to her. At church she has seen him twice, and once in the village, though she has never been introduced to him, has never interchanged a single word with him: it is Lord Sartoris.

He gazes at her intently. Perhaps he too knows who she is, but, if so, he makes no sign. At last, unable to bear the silence any longer, she says, naïvely and very gently, —

"I thought you were in Paris."

At this extraordinary remark from a woman he has never spoken to before, Sartoris lifts his brows, and regards her, if possibly, more curiously.

"So I was," he says; "but I came home yesterday." Then, "And you are Dorian's wife?"

Her brows grow clouded.

"Yes," she says, and no more, and, turning aside, pulls to pieces the flowering grasses that grow on her right hand.

"I suppose I am unwelcome in your sight," says the old man, noting her reserve. "Yet if, at the time of your marriage, I held aloof, it was not because you were the bride."

"Did you hold aloof?" says Georgie, with wondering eyes. "Did our marriage displease you? I never knew: Dorian never told me." Then, with sudden unexpected bitterness, "Half measures are of no use. Why did you not forbid the wedding altogether? That would have been the wisest and kindest thing, both for him and me."

"I don't think I quite follow you," says Lord Sartoris, in a troubled tone. "Am I to understand you already regret your marriage? Do not tell me that."

"Why should I not?" says Georgie, defiantly. His tone has angered her, though why, she would have found a difficulty in explaining. "You are his uncle," she says, with some warmth: "why should you not know? Why am I always to pretend happiness that I never feel?"

"Do you know what your words convey?" says Sartoris, more shocked than he can express.

"I think I do," says the girl, half passionately; and then she turns aside, and moves as though she would leave him.

"This is terrible," says Sartoris, in a low voice full of pain. "And yet I cannot believe he is unkind to you."

"Unkind? No," with a little scornful smile: "I hear no harsh words, my lightest wish is law; yet the veriest beggar that crawls the road is happier than I am."

"It seems impossible," says Sartoris, quietly, looking intently at her flower-like face and lovely wistful eyes,—"seeing you, it seems impossible to me that he can do anything but love you."

"Do not profane the words," she says, quickly. Then she pauses, as though afraid to continue, and presently says, in a broken voice, "Am I—the only woman he has—loved?"

Something in the suppressed passion of her tone tells Lord Sartoris that she too is in possession of the secret that for months has embittered his life. This discovery is horrible to him.

"Who has been cruel enough to make you wise on that subject?" he says, impulsively, and therefore unwisely.

Georgie turns upon him eyes brilliant with despair and grief. "So"—she says, vehemently—"it is the world's talk. You know it: it is, indeed, common property, this disgraceful story." Something within her chokes her words; she can say no more. Passion overcomes her, and want of hope, and grief too deep for expression. The gentle wells that nature supplies are dead within her; her eyes, hot and burning, conceal no water wherewith to cool the fever that consumes them.

"You are a stranger to me," she says, presently. "Yet to you I have laid bare my thoughts. You think, perhaps, I am one to parade my griefs, but it is not so; I would have you——"

"I believe you," he interrupts her hastily. He can hardly do otherwise, she is looking so little, so fragile, with her quivering lips, and her childish pleading eyes, and plaintive voice.

"Take courage," he says, softly: "you are young: good days may yet be in store for you; but with me it is different. I am on the verge of the grave,—

am going down into it with no one to soothe or comfort my declining years. Dorian was my one thought: you can never know how I planned, and lived, and dreamed for him alone; and see how he has rewarded me! For youth there is a future, and in that thought alone lies hope; for age there is nothing but the flying present, and even that, for me, has lost its sweetness. I have staked my all, and—lost! surely, of we two, I should be the most miserable."

"Is that your belief?" says Mrs. Branscombe, mournfully. "Forgive me if I say I think you wrong. You have but a little time to endure your grief, I have my life, and perhaps"—pathetically—"it will be a long one. To know I must live under his roof, and feel myself indebted to him for everything I may want, for many years, is very bitter to me."

Sartoris is cut to the heart: that it should have gone so far that she should shrink from accepting anything at Dorian's hands, galls him sorely. And what a gentle tender boy he used to be, and how incapable of a dishonest thought or action! At least, something should be done for his wife,—this girl who has grown tired and saddened and out of all heart since her luckless marriage. He looks at her again keenly, and tells himself she is sweet enough to keep any man at her side, so dainty she shows in her simple linen gown, with its soft Quakerish frillings at the throat and wrists. A sudden thought at last strikes him.

"I am glad I have met you," he says, quietly. "By and by, perhaps, we shall learn to be good friends. In the mean time will you do me a small favor? will you come up to Hythe on Thursday at one o'clock?"

"If you want me to come," says Georgie, betraying through her eyes the intense surprise she feels at this request.

"Thank you. And will you give Dorian a written message from me?"

"I will," she says again. And tearing a leaf from his pocket-book, he writes, as follows:

"When last we parted, it was with the expressed determination on your part never again to enter my doors until such time as I should send for you. I do so now, and beg you will come up to Hythe on Thursday next at half-past one o'clock. I should not trouble you so far, but that business demands your presence. I give you my word not to detain you longer than is absolutely necessary."

Folding up this note, he gives it to her, and pressing her hand warmly, parts from her, and goes back again to Hythe.

When in answer to his uncle's summons, Dorian walks into the library at Hythe on Thursday afternoon, he is both astonished and disconcerted to find his wife there before him. She had given the letter not to him, but to one of the men-servants to deliver to him: so that he is still in utter ignorance of her meeting in the wood with his uncle.

"You here?" he says to her, after he has acknowledged Lord Sartoris's presence by the coldest and haughtiest of salutations.

She says, "Yes," in a low tone, without raising her eyes.

"I was not aware you and Lord Sartoris were on such intimate terms."

"We met by chance last Monday for the first time," returns she, still without troubling herself to turn her eyes in his direction.

"You will sit down?" says Sartoris, nervously pushing a chair towards him. Dorian is looking so pale and haggard, so unlike himself, that the old man's heart dies within him. What "evil days" has he not fallen on!

"No, thank you: I prefer standing. I must, however, remind you of your promise not to detain me longer than you can help."

"Nor shall I. I have sent for you to-day to let you know of my determination to settle upon your wife the sum of twenty thousand pounds, to be used for her own exclusive benefit, to be hers absolutely to do with as may seem best to her."

"May I ask what has put this quixotic idea into your head?" asks Dorian, in a curious tone.

Georgie, who, up to this time, has been so astounded at the disclosure of the earl's scheme as to be unable to collect her ideas, now feels a sudden light break in upon her. She rises to her feet, and comes a little forward, and, for the first time since his entrance, turns to confront her husband.

"Let me tell you," she says, silencing Lord Sartoris by a quick motion of the hand. "On Monday I told your uncle how—how I hated being indebted to you for everything I may require. And he has thought of this plan, out of his great kindness," turning eyes dark with tears upon Lord Sartoris,—"to render me more independent. I thank you," she says, going up to Sartoris and slipping her icy cold little hands into his, "but it is far—far too much."

"So you have been regaling Lord Sartoris (an utter stranger to you) with a history of all our private griefs and woes!" says Dorian, slowly, utter contempt in his tone and an ominous light in his eyes.

"You wrong her, Dorian," says his uncle, gently. "It is not as you represent it. It was by the merest chance I discovered your wife would feel happier if more her own mistress."

"And by what right, may I inquire, do you seek to come between my wife and me?" says Dorian, white with anger, standing, tall and strong, with his arms folded and his eyes fixed upon his uncle. "Is it not my part to support and keep her? Whose duty is it, if not mine? I wish to know why you, of all men, have dared to interfere."

"I have not come between you: I seek no such ungracious part," replies Sartoris, with quiet dignity. "I am only doing now what I should have done on her marriage morning had—had things been different."

"It seems to me that I am brought up here as a criminal before my judge and accuser," says Branscombe, very bitterly. "Let me at least have the small satisfaction of knowing of what it is I am accused,—wherein lies my crime. Speak," he says, turning suddenly to his wife.

She is awed more than she cares to confess by his manner, which is different from anything she has ever seen in him before. The kind-hearted, easy-going Dorian is gone, leaving a stern, passionate, disappointed man in his place.

"Have I ill-used you?" he goes on, vehemently. "Have I spoken harsh words to you, or thwarted you in any way? Ever since the first hour that saw you my wife have I refused to grant your lightest wish? Speak, and let us hear the truth of this matter. I am a bad husband, you say,—so infamous that it is impossible for you to receive even the common necessaries of life at my hands! How have I failed in my duty towards you?"

"In none of the outward observances," she says, faintly. "And yet you have broken my heart!"

There is a pause. And then Dorian laughs aloud,—a terrible, sneering, embittered laugh, that strikes cold on the hearts of the hearers.

"Your heart!" he says, witheringly. "Why, supposing for courtesy's sake you did possess such an inconvenient and unfashionable appendage, it would be still absurd to accuse me of having broken it, as it has never been for five minutes in my possession."

Taking out his watch, he examines it leisurely. Then, with an utter change of manner, addressing Lord Sartoris, he says, with cold and studied politeness,—

"If you have quite done with me, I shall be glad, as I have another appointment at three."

"I have quite done," says his uncle, wistfully, looking earnestly at the handsome face before him that shows no sign of feeling whatsoever. "I thank you much for having so far obliged me."

"Pray do not mention it. Good-morning."

"Good-morning," says Sartoris, wearily. And Branscombe, bowing carelessly, leaves the room without another word.

When he has gone, Georgie, pale and trembling, turns to Sartoris and lays her hand upon his arm.

"He hates me. He will not even look at me," she says, passionately. "What was it he said, that I had no heart? Ah! what would I not give to be able to prove his words true?"

She bursts into tears, and sobs long and bitterly.

"Tears are idle," says Sartoris, sadly. "Have you yet to learn that? Take comfort from the thought that all things have an end."

CHAPTER XXX

"Oh that the things which have been were not now
In memory's resurrection! But the past
Bears in her arms the present and the future." —Bailey.

Of course it is quite impossible to hide from Clarissa Peyton that everything is going wrong at Sartoris. Georgie's pale unsmiling face (so different from that of old), and Dorian's evident determination to absent himself from all society, tell their own tale.

She has, of course, heard of the uncomfortable gossip that has connected Ruth Annersley's mysterious disappearance with Dorian, but—stanch friend as she is—has laughed to scorn all such insinuations: that Georgie can believe them, puzzles her more than she cares to confess. For a long time she has fought against the thought that Dorian's wife can think aught bad of Dorian; but time undeceives her.

To-day, Georgie, who is now always feverishly restless, tells herself she will go up to Gowran and see Clarissa. To her alone she clings,—not outwardly, in any marked fashion, but in her inmost soul,—as to one who at her worst extremity will support and comfort her.

The day is warm and full of color. Round her "flow the winds from woods and fields with gladness laden:" the air is full of life. The browning grass rustles beneath her feet. The leaves fall slowly one by one, as though loath to leave their early home; the wind, cruel, like all love, wooes them only to their doom.

"The waves, along the forest borne," beat on her face and head, and half cool the despairing thoughts that now always lie hidden deep down within her breast.

Coming to Gowran and seeing Clarissa in the drawing room window, she beckons to her, and Clarissa, rising hastily, opens the hall door for her, herself, and leads her by the hand into another cosier room, where they may talk without interruption.

It so happens that Georgie is in one of her worst moods; and something Clarissa says very innocently brings on a burst of passion that compels Clarissa to understand (in spite of all her efforts to think herself in the wrong) that the dissensions at Sartoris have a great deal to do with Ruth Annersley.

"It is impossible," she says, over and over again, walking up and down the room in an agitated manner. "I could almost as soon believe Horace guilty of this thing!"

Georgie makes no reply. Inwardly she has conceived a great distaste to the handsome Horace, and considers him a very inferior person, and quite unfit to mate with her pretty Clarissa.

"In your heart," says Miss Peyton, stopping before her, "I don't believe you think Dorian guilty of this thing."

"Yes I do," says Mrs. Branscombe, with dogged calmness. "I don't ask you to agree with me. I only tell you what I myself honestly believe." She has given up fighting against her fate by this time.

"There is some terrible mistake somewhere," says Clarissa, in a very distressed voice, feeling it wiser not to argue the point further. "Time will surely clear it up sooner or later, but it is very severe on Dorian while it lasts. I have known the dear fellow all my life, and cannot now begin to think evil of him. I have always felt more like a sister to him than anything else, and I cannot believe him guilty of this thing."

"*I* am his wife, and I *can*," says Mrs. Branscombe, icily.

"If you loved him as you ought, you could not." This is the one rebuke she cannot refrain from.

Georgie laughs unpleasantly, and then, all in a little moment, she varies the performance by bursting into a passionate and most unlooked-for flood of tears.

"Don't talk to me of love!" she cries, miserably. "It is useless. I don't believe in it. It is a delusion, a mere mockery, a worn-out superstition. You will tell me that Dorian loved me; and yet in the very early days before our marriage, when his so-called love must have been at its height, he insulted me beyond all forgiveness."

"You are making yourself wretched about nothing," says Clarissa, kneeling beside her, and gently drawing her head down on her shoulder. "Don't, darling,—don't cry like that. I know, I feel, all will come right in the end. Indeed, unless Dorian were to come to me and say, 'I have done this hateful thing,' I should not believe it."

"I would give all the world to be able to say that from my heart," says Mrs. Branscombe, with excessive sadness.

"Try to think it. Afterwards belief will be easy. Oh, Georgie, do not nourish hard thoughts; tear them from your heart, and by and by, when all this is explained away, think how glad you will be that, without proof, you had faith in him. Do you know, unless my own eyes saw it, I should never for any reason lose faith in Horace."

A tender, heavenly smile creeps round her beautiful lips as she says this. Georgie, seeing it, feels heart-broken. Oh that she could have faith like this!

"It is too late," she says, bitterly: "and I deserve all I have got. I myself have been the cause of my own undoing. I married Dorian for no other reason than to escape the drudgery of teaching. Yet now" —with a sad smile—"I know there are worse things than Murray's Grammar. I am justly punished." Her lovely face is white with grief. I have tried, *tried*, TRIED to disbelieve, but nothing will raise this cloud of suspicion from my breast. It weighs me down and crushes me more cruelly day by day. "I wish—I wish" —cries poor little Georgie, from her very soul—"that I had never been born, because I shall never know a happy moment again."

The tears run silently down her cheeks one by one. She puts up her small hands to defend herself, and the action is pitiable in the extreme.

"How happy you were only a month ago!" says Clarissa, striken with grief at the sight of her misery.

"Yes, I have had my day, I suppose," says Mrs. Branscombe, wearily. "One can always remember a time when

'Every morning was fair,
And every season a May!'

But how soon it all fades!"

"Too soon for you," says Clarissa, with tears in her eyes. "You speak as though you had no interest left in life."

"Yes, I have," says Georgie, with a faint smile. "I have the school-children yet. You know I go to them every Sunday to oblige the dear vicar. He would have been so sorry if I had deserted them, because they grew fond of me, and he said, for that reason, I was the best teacher in the parish, because I didn't bore them." Here she laughs quite merrily, as though grief is unknown to her; but a minute later, memory returning, the joy fades from her face, leaving it sadder than before. "I might be Irish," she says, "emotion is so changeable with me. Come down with me now to the village, will you? It is my day at the school."

"Well, come up-stairs with me while I put on my things," says Clarissa; and then, though really sad at heart, she cannot refrain from smiling. "You are just the last person in the world," she says, "one would accuse of teaching Scripture, or the Catechism, or that."

"What a very rude remark!" said Georgie, smiling naturally for the first time to-day. "Am I such a *very* immoral young woman?"

"No. Only I could not teach Genesis, or the Ten Commandments, or Watts, to save my life," says Clarissa. "Come, or we shall be late, and Pullingham Junior without Watts would, I feel positive, sink into an abyss of vice. They might bark and bite, and do other dangerous things."

Mrs. Branscombe (with Clarissa) reaching the school-house just in time to take her class, the latter sits down in a disconsolate fashion upon a stray bench, and surveys the scene before her with wondering eyes.

There sits Georgie, a very fragile teacher for so rough a class; here sits the vicar with the adults before him, deep in the mysteries of the Thirty-nine Articles.

The head teacher is nearly in tears over the Creed, because of the stupidity of her pupils; the assistant is raging over the Ten Commandments. All is gloom! Clarissa is rather delighted than otherwise, and, having surveyed everybody, comes back to Georgie, she being the most refreshing object on view.

At the top of the class, facing the big window, sits John Spriggs (*ætat.* ten) on his hands. He has utterly declined to bestow his body in any other fashion, being evidently imbued with the belief that his hands were made for the support of the body,—a very correct idea, all things considered.

He is lolling from side to side in a reckless way, and his eyes are rolling in concert with him, and altogether his behavior is highly suggestive of fits.

Lower down, Amelia Jennings is making a surreptitious cat's cradle, which is promptly put out of sight, behind her back, every time her turn comes to give an answer; but, as she summarily dismisses all questions by declaring her simple ignorance of every matter connected with Biblical history, the cradle progresses most favorably, and is very soon fit to sleep in.

Mrs. Branscombe, having gone through the seventh chapter of St. Luke without any marked success, falls back upon the everlasting Catechism, and swoops down upon Amelia Jennings with a mild request that she will tell her her duty to her neighbor.

Amelia, feeling she has no neighbors at this trying moment, and still less catechism, fixes her big round blue eyes on Mrs. Branscombe, and, letting the beloved cradle fall to the ground behind her back, prepares to blubber at a second's notice.

"Go on," says Georgie, encouragingly.

Miss Jennings, being thus entreated, takes heart, and commences the difficult injunction in excellent hope and spirits. All goes "merry as a marriage bell," until she comes to the words "Love your neighbor as yourself," when John Spriggs (who is not by nature a thoroughly bad boy, but whose evil hour is now full upon him) says audibly, and without any apparent desire to torment, "and paddle your own canoe."

There is a deadly pause, and then Amelia Jennings giggles out loud, and Spriggs follows suit, and, after a bit, the entire class gives itself up to merriment.

Spriggs, instead of being contrite at this flagrant breach of discipline, is plainly elated with his victory. No smallest sign of shame disfigures his small rubicund countenance.

Georgie makes a praiseworthy effort to appear shocked, but, as her pretty cheeks are pink, and her eyes great with laughter, the praiseworthy effort rather falls through.

At this moment the door of the school-house is gently pushed open, and a new-comer appears on the threshold: it is Mr. Kennedy.

Going up unseen, he stands behind Georgie's chair, and having heard from the door-way all that has passed, instantly bends over and hands the notorious Spriggs a shilling.

"Ah! you again?" says Mrs. Branscombe, coloring warmly, merely from surprise. "You are like Sir Boyle Roche's bird: you can be in two places at the same moment. But it is wrong to give him money when he is bad. It is out of all keeping; and how shall I manage the children if you come here, anxious to reward vice and foster rebellion?"

She is laughing gayly now, and is looking almost her own bright little self again, when, lifting her eyes, she sees Dorian watching her. Instantly her smile fades; and she returns his gaze fixedly, as though compelled to do it by some hidden instinct.

He has entered silently, not expecting to find any one before him but the vicar: yet the very first object his eyes meet is his wife, smiling, radiant, with Kennedy beside her. A strange pang contracts his heart, and a terrible amount of reproach passes from his eyes to hers.

He is sad and dispirited, and full of melancholy. His whole life has proved a failure; yet in what way has he fallen short?

Kennedy, seeing Mrs. Branscombe's expression change, raises his head, and so becomes aware of her husband's presence. Being a wise young man in his own generation, he smiles genially upon Dorian, and, going forward, shakes his hand as though years of devotion have served to forge a link likely to bind them each to each forever.

"Charming day, isn't it?" he says, with a beatific smile. "Quite like summer."

"Rather more like January, I think," says Dorian, calmly, who is in his very worst mood. "First touch of winter, I should say." He laughs as he says this; but his laugh is as wintry as the day, and chills the hearer. Then he turns aside from his wife and her companion, and lays his hand upon the vicar's shoulder, who has just risen from his class, having carried it successfully through the best part of Isaiah.

"My dear boy,—you?" says the vicar, quite pleased to see him. "But in bad time: the lesson is over, so you can learn nothing. I don't like to give them too much Scripture on a week-day. It has a disheartening effect, and——"

"I wish they could hear you," says Branscombe, with a slight shrug.

"It is as well they cannot," says the vicar; "though I doubt if free speaking does much harm; and, really, perpetual grinding does destroy the genuine love for our grand old Bible that we should all feel deep down in our souls."

"Feeling has gone out of fashion," says Dorian, so distinctly that Georgie in the distance hears him, and winces a little.

"Well, it has," says the vicar. "There can't be a doubt of it, when one thinks of the alterations they have just made in that fine old Book. There are innovations from morning till night, and nothing gained by them. Surely, if we got to heaven up to this by the teaching of the Bible as it *was*, it serves no cause to alter a word here and there, or a sentence that was dear to us from our childhood. It brings us no nearer God, but only unsettles beliefs that, perhaps, up to this were sound enough. The times are not to be trusted."

"Is anything worthy of trust?" says Dorian, bitterly.

"I doubt I'm old-fashioned," says the dear vicar, with a deprecating smile. "I dare say change is good, and works wonders in many ways. We old people stick fast, and can't progress. I suppose I should be content to be put on one side."

"I hope you will be put on my side," says Dorian: "I should feel pretty safe then. Do you know, I have not been in this room for so many years that I am afraid to count them? When last here, it was during a holiday term; and

I remember sitting beside you and thinking how awfully jolly glad I was to be well out of it, when other children were doing their lesson."

"Comfortable reflection, and therefore, as a rule, selfish," says the vicar, with a laugh.

"Was it selfish? I suppose so." His face clouds again: a sort of reckless defiance shadows it. "You must not expect much from me," he says, slowly: "they don't accredit me with any good nowadays."

"My dear fellow," says the vicar, quietly, "there is something wrong with you, or you would not so speak. I don't ask you now what it is: you shall tell me when and where you please. I only entreat you to believe that no one, knowing you as I do, could possibly think anything of you but what is kind and good and true."

Branscombe draws his breath quickly. His pale face flushes; and a gleam, that is surely born of tears, shines in his eyes. Clarissa, who, up to this, has been talking to some of the children, comes up to him at this moment and slips her hand through his arm. Is he not almost her brother?

Only his wife stands apart, and, with white lips and dry eyes and a most miserable heart, watches him without caring—or daring—to go near to him. She is silent, *distraite*, and has altogether forgotten the fact of Kennedy's existence (though he still stands close beside her),—a state of things that young gentleman hardly affects.

"Has your class been too much for you? Or do other things—or people— distress you?" he asks, presently, in a meaning tone. "Because you have not uttered one word for quite five minutes."

"You have guessed correctly: some people do distress me—after a time," says Mrs. Branscombe, so pointedly that Kennedy takes the hint, and, shaking hands with her somewhat stiffly, disappears through the door-way.

"Oh, yes," the vicar is saying to Clarissa, in a glad tone, that even savors of triumph, "the Batesons have given up the Methodist chapel and have come back to me. They have forgiven about the bread, though they made a heavy struggle for it. Mrs. Redmond and I put our heads together and wondered what we should do, and if we couldn't buy anything there so as to make up for the loss of the daily loaves, because she would not consent to poison the children."

"And you would!" says Clarissa, reproachfully. "Oh, what a terrible admission!"

"We won't go into that, my dear Clarissa, if you please," says the vicar, contritely. "There are moments in every life that one regrets. But the end of our cogitations was this: that we went down to the village,—Mrs. Redmond and I,—and, positively, for one bar of soap and a package of candles we bought them all back to their pew in church. You wouldn't have thought there was so much grace in soap and candles, would you?" says the vicar, with a curious gleam in his eyes that is half amusement, half contempt.

Even Georgie laughs a little at this, and comes nearer to them, and stands close beside Clarissa, as if shy and uncertain, and glad to have a sure partisan so near to her,—all which is only additional pain to Dorian, who notices every lightest word and action of the woman he has married.

"How did you get on to-day with your little people?" asks Mr. Redmond, taking notice of her at once,—something, too, in her downcast attitude appealing to his sense of pity. "Was that boy of the Brixton's more than usually trying?"

"Well, he was bad enough," says Georgie, in a tone that implies she is rather letting off the unfortunate Brixton from future punishment. "But I have known him worse; indeed, I think he improves."

"Indeed, I think a son of his father could never improve," says the vicar, with a melancholy sigh. "There isn't an ounce of brains in all that family. Long ago, when first I came here, Sam Brixton (the father of your pupil) bought a cow from a neighboring farmer called George Gilbert, and he named it John. I thought that an extraordinary name to call a cow, so I said to him one day, 'Sam, why on earth did you christen that poor inoffensive beast John?' 'John?' said he, somewhat indignantly, 'John? Why wouldn't I call him John, when I bought him from George Gilbert?' I didn't see his meaning then,—and, I confess, I haven't seen it since,—but I was afraid to expose my stupidity, so I held my tongue. Do you see it?" He turns to Dorian.

"Not much," says Dorian, with a faint laugh.

CHAPTER XXXI

"One woe doth tread upon another's heel,
So fast they follow." —*Hamlet.*

"One, that was a woman, sir." —*Hamlet.*

Across the autumn grass, that has browned beneath the scorching summer rays, and through the fitful sunshine, comes James Scrope.

Through the woods, under the dying beech-trees that lead to Gowran, he saunters slowly, thinking only of the girl beyond, who is not thinking of him at all, but of the man who, in his soul, Sir James believes utterly unworthy of her.

This thought so engrosses him, as he walks along, that he fails to hear Mrs. Branscombe, until she is close beside him, and until she says, gently, —

"How d'ye do, Sir James?" At this his start is so visible that she laughs, and says, with a faint blush, —

"What! is my coming so light that one fails to hear it?"

To which he, recovering himself, makes ready response:

"So light a foot
Will ne'er wear out the everlasting flint."

Then, "You are coming from Gowran?"

"Yes; from Clarissa."

"She is well?"

"Yes, and, I suppose, happy," —with a shrug. "She expects Horace to-morrow." There is a certain scorn in her manner, that attracts his notice.

"Is that sufficient to create happiness?" he says, some what bitterly, in spite of himself. "But of course it is. You know Horace?"

"Not well, but well enough," says Mrs. Branscombe, with a frown. "I know him well enough to hate him."

She pauses, rather ashamed of herself for her impulsive confidence, and not at all aware that by this hasty speech she has made a friend of Sir James for life.

"Hate him?" he says, feeling he could willingly embrace her on the spot were society differently constituted. "Why, what has he done to you?"

"Nothing; but he is not good enough for Clarissa," protests she, energetically. "But then who is good enough? I really think," says Mrs. Branscombe, with earnest conviction, "she is far too sweet to be thrown away upon any man."

Even this awful speech fails to cool Sir James's admiration for the speaker. She has declared herself a non-admirer of the all-powerful Horace, and this goes so far a way with him that he cannot bring himself to find fault with her on any score.

"I don't know why I express my likes and dislikes to you so openly," she says, gravely, a little later on; "and I don't know, either, why I distrust Horace. I have only a woman's reason. It is Shakespeare slightly altered: 'I hate him so, because I hate him so.' And I hope, with all my heart, Clarissa will never marry him."

Then she blushes again at her openness, and gives him her hand, and bids him good-by, and presently he goes on his way once more to Gowran.

On the balcony there stands Clarissa, the solemn Bill close beside her. She is leaning on the parapet, with her pretty white hands crossed and hanging loosely over it. As she sees him coming, with a little touch of coquetry, common to most women, she draws her broad-brimmed hat from her head, and, letting it fall upon the balcony, lets the uncertain sunlight touch warmly her fair brown hair and tender exquisite face.

Bill, sniffing, lifts himself, and, seeing Sir James, shakes his shaggy sides, and, with his heavy head still drooping, and his most hang-dog expression carefully put on, goes cautiously down the stone steps to greet him.

Having been patted, and made much of, and having shown a scornful disregard for all such friendly attentions, he trots behind Sir James at the slow funeral pace he usually affects, until Clarissa is reached.

"Better than my ordinary luck to find you here," says Sir James, who is in high good humor. "Generally you are miles away when I get to Gowran. And—forgive me—how exceedingly charming you are looking this morning!"

Miss Peyton is clearly not above praise. She laughs,—a delicious rippling little laugh,—and colors faintly.

"A compliment from you!" she says. "No wonder I blush. Am I really lovely, Jim, or only commonly pretty? I should hate to be commonly pretty." She lifts her brows disdainfully.

"You needn't hate yourself," says Scrope, calmly. "Lovely is the word for you."

"I'm rather glad," says Miss Peyton, with a sigh of relief. "If only for—Horace's sake!"

Sir James pitches his cigar over the balcony, and frowns. Always Horace! Can she not forget him for even one moment?

"What brought you?" asks she, presently.

"What a gracious speech!"—with a rather short laugh. "To see you, I fancy. By the by, I met Mrs. Branscombe on my way here. She didn't look particularly happy."

"No." Clarissa's eyes grow sad. "After all, that marriage was a terrible mistake, and it seemed such a satisfactory one. Do you know," in a half-frightened tone, "I begin to think they hate each other?"

"They don't seem to hit it off very well, certainly," says Sir James, moodily. "But I believe there is something more on Branscombe's mind than his domestic worries: I am afraid he is getting into trouble over the farm, and that, and nothing hits a man like want of money. That Sawyer is a very slippery fellow, in my opinion: and of late Dorian has neglected everything and taken no interest in his land, and, in fact, lets everything go without question."

"I have no patience with Georgie," says Clarissa, indignantly. "She is positively breaking his heart."

"She is unhappy, poor little thing," says Scrope, who cannot find it in his heart to condemn the woman who has just condemned Horace Branscombe.

"It is her own fault if she is. I know few people so lovable as Dorian. And now to think he has another trouble makes me wretched. I do hope you are wrong about Sawyer."

"I don't think I am," says Scrope; and time justifies his doubt of Dorian's steward.

> "Sartoris, Tuesday, four o'clock.
>
> "Dear Scrope,—
>
> "Come up to me at *once*, if possible. Everything here is in a deplorable state. You have heard, of course, that Sawyer bolted last night; but perhaps you have *not* heard that he has left things in a ruinous state. I must see you with as little delay as you can manage. Come straight to the library, where you will find me alone.

"Yours ever,

"D. B."

Sir James, who is sitting in his sister's room, starts to his feet on reading this letter.

"Patience, I must go at once to Sartoris," he says, looking pale and distressed.

"To see that mad boy?"

"To see Dorian Branscombe."

"That is quite the same thing. You don't call him sane, do you? To marry that chit of a girl without a grain of common sense in her silly head, just because her eyes were blue and her hair yellow, forsooth. And then to go and get mixed up with that Annersley affair—"

"My dear Patience!"

"Well, why not? Why should I not talk? One must use one's tongue, if one isn't a dummy. And then there is that man Sawyer: he could get no one out of the whole country but a creature who——"

"Hush!" says Sir James, hastily and unwisely. "Better be silent on that subject." Involuntarily he lays his hand upon the letter just received.

"Ha!" says Miss Scrope, triumphantly, with astonishing sharpness. "So I was right, was I? So that pitiful being has been exposed to the light of day, has he? I always said how it would be; I knew it!—ever since last spring, when I sent to him for some cucumber-plants, and he sent me instead (with wilful intent to insult me) two vile gourds. I always knew how it would end."

"Well, and how has it ended?" says Sir James, with a weak effort to retrieve his position, putting on a small air of defiance.

"Don't think to deceive me," says Miss Scrope, in a terrible tone; whereupon Sir James flies the apartment, feeling in his heart that in a war of words Miss Scrope's match is yet to be found.

Entering the library at Sartoris, he finds Dorian there, alone, indeed, and comfortless, and sore at heart.

It is a dark dull day. The first breath of winter is in the air. The clouds are thick and sullen, and are lying low, as if they would willingly come down to sit upon the earth and there rest themselves,—so weary they seem, and so full of heaviness.

Above them a wintry sun is trying vainly to recover its ill temper. Every now and then a small brown bird, flying hurriedly past the windows, is almost blown against them by the strong and angry blast.

Within, a fire is burning, and the curtains are half drawn across the windows and the glass door, that leads, by steps, down into the garden. No lamps are lit, and the light is sombre and severe.

"You have come," says Dorian, advancing eagerly to meet him. "I knew I could depend upon you, but it is more than good of you to be here so soon. I have been moping a good deal, I am afraid, and forgot all about the lamps. Shall I ring for some one now to light them?"

"No: this light is what I prefer," says Scrope, laying his hand upon his arm. "Stir up the fire, if you like."

"Even that I had not given one thought to," says Branscombe, drearily. "Sitting here all alone, I gave myself up a prey to evil thoughts."

The word "alone" touches Sir James inexpressibly. Where was his wife all the time, that she never came to him to comfort and support him in his hour of need?

"Is everything as bad as you say?" he asks, presently, in a subdued tone.

"Quite as bad; neither worse nor better. There are no gradations about utter ruin. You heard about Sawyer, of course? Harden has been with me all last night and to-day, and between us we have been able to make out that he has muddled away almost all the property,—which, you know, is small. As yet we hardly know how we stand. But there is one claim of fifteen thousand pounds that must be paid without delay, and I have not one penny to meet it, so am literally driven to the wall."

"You speak as if——"

"No, I am speaking quite rationally. I know what you would say; but if I was starving I would not accept one shilling from Lord Sartoris. That would be impossible. You can understand why, without my going into that infamous scandal. I suppose I can sell Sartoris, and pay my—that is, Sawyer's—debts; but that will leave me a beggar." Then, in a low tone, "I should hardly care, but for her. That is almost more than I can bear."

"You say this debt of fifteen thousand pounds is the one that presses hardest?"

"Yes. But for that, I might, by going in for strict economy, manage to retrieve my present position in a year or two."

"I wish you would explain more fully," says Sir James; whereupon Dorian enters into an elaborate explanation that leaves all things clear.

"It seems absurd," says Scrope, impatiently, "that you, the heir to an earldom and unlimited wealth, should be made so uncomfortable for the sake of a paltry fifteen thousand pounds."

"I hardly think my wealth unlimited," says Branscombe; "there is a good deal of property not entailed, and the ready money is at my uncle's own disposal. You know, perhaps, that he has altered his will in favor of Horace,—has, in fact, left him everything that it is possible to leave?"

"This is all new to me," says Sir James, indignantly. "If it is true, it is the most iniquitous thing I ever heard in my life."

"It is true," says Branscombe, slowly. "Altogether, in many ways, I have been a good deal wrong; and the money part of it has not hurt me the most."

"If seven thousand pounds would be of any use to you," says Scrope, gently, delicately, "I have it lying idle. It will, indeed, be a great convenience if you will take it at a reasonable— —"

"That is rather unkind of you," says Dorian, interrupting him hastily. "Don't say another word on that subject. I shall sink or swim without aid from my friends,—aid, I mean, of that sort. In other ways you can help me. Harden will, of course, see to the estate; but there are other, more private matters, that I would intrust to you alone. Am I asking too much?"

"Don't be unkind in your own turn," says Scrope, with tears in his eyes.

"Thank you," says Dorian, simply. His heart seems quite broken.

"What of your wife?" asks Sir James, with some hesitation. "Does she know?"

"I think not. Why should she be troubled before her time? It will come fast enough. She made a bad match, after all, poor child! But there is one thing I must tell you, and it is the small drop of comfort in my cup. About a month ago, Lord Sartoris settled upon her twenty thousand pounds, and that will keep her at least free from care. When I am gone, I want you to see to her, and let me know, from time to time, that she is happy and well cared for."

"But will she consent to this separation from you, that may last for years?"

"Consent!" says Dorian, bitterly. "That is not the word. She will be glad, at this chance that has arisen to put space between us. I believe from my heart that— —"

"What is it you believe?" says a plaintive voice, breaking in upon Dorian's speech with curious energy. The door leading into the garden is wide open: and now the curtain is thrust aside, and a fragile figure, gowned in some black filmy stuff, stands before them. Both men start as she advances in the uncertain light. Her face is deadly pale; her eyes are large, and almost black, as she turns them questioningly upon Sir James Scrope. It is impossible for either man to know what she may, or may not, have heard.

"I was in the garden," she says, in an agitated tone, "and I heard voices; and something about money; and Dorian's going away: and— —" (she puts her hand up to her throat) "and about ruin. I could not understand: but you will tell me. You must."

"Tell her, Dorian," says Sir James. But Dorian looks doggedly away from her, through the open window, into the darkening garden beyond.

"Tell me, Dorian," she says, nervously, going up to him, and laying a small white trembling hand upon his arm.

"There is no reason why you should be distressed," says Branscombe, very coldly, lifting her hand from his arm, as though her very touch is displeasing to him. "You are quite safe. Sawyer's mismanagement of the estate has brought me to the verge of ruin; but Lord Sartoris has taken care that you will not suffer."

She is trembling violently.

"And you?" she says.

"I shall go abroad until things look brighter." Then he turns to her for the first time, and, taking both her hands, presses them passionately. "I can hardly expect forgiveness from you," he says: "you had, at least, a right to expect position when you made your unhappy marriage, and now you have nothing."

I think she hardly hears this cruel speech. Her thoughts still cling to the word that has gone before.

"Abroad?" she says, with quivering lips.

"Only for a time," says Sir James, taking pity upon her evident distress.

"Does he owe a great deal?" asks she, feverishly. "Is it a very large sum? Tell me how much it is."

Scrope, who is feeling very sorry for her, explains matters, while Dorian maintains a determined silence.

"Fifteen thousand pounds, if procured at once, would tide him over his difficulties," says Sir James, who does her the justice to divine her thoughts correctly. "Time is all he requires."

"I have twenty thousand pounds," says Georgie, eagerly. "Lord Sartoris says I may do what I like with it. Dorian," — going up to him again, — "take it, — do, *do*. You will make me happier than I have been for a long time if you will accept it."

A curious expression lights Dorian's face. It is half surprise, half contempt: yet, after all, perhaps there is some genuine gladness in it.

"I cannot thank you sufficiently," he says, in a low tone. "Your offer is more than kind: it is generous. But I cannot accept it. It is impossible I should receive anything at your hands."

"Why?" she says, her lips white, her eyes large and earnest.

"Does that question require an answer?" asks Dorian, slowly. "There was a time, even in our short married life, when I believed in your friendship for me, and then I would have taken anything from you, — from my wife; but now, I tell you again, it is impossible. You yourself have put it out of my power."

He turns from her coldly, and concentrates his gaze once more upon the twilit garden.

"Don't speak to me like that, — at least now," says Georgie, her breath coming in short quick gasps. "It hurts me so! Take this wretched money, if — if you still have any love for me."

He turns deliberately away from the small pleading face.

"And leave you penniless," he says.

"No, not that. Some day you can pay me back, if you wish it. All these months you have given me every thing I could possibly desire, let me now make you some small return."

Unfortunately, this speech angers him deeply.

"We are wasting time," he says, quickly. "Understand, once for all, I will receive nothing from you."

"James," says Mrs. Branscombe, impulsively, going up to Scrope and taking his hand. She is white and nervous, and, in her agitation, is hardly aware that, for the first time, she has called him by his Christian name. "Persuade him. Tell him he should accept this money. Dear James, speak for me: *I* am nothing to him."

For the second time Branscombe turns and looks at her long and earnestly.

"I must say I think your wife quite right," says Scrope, energetically. "She wants you to take this money; your not taking it distresses her very much, and you have no right in the world to marry a woman and then make her unhappy." This is faintly quixotic, considering all the circumstances, but nobody says anything. "You ought to save Sartoris from the hammer no matter at what price,—pride or anything else. It isn't a fair thing, you know, Branscombe, to lift the roof from off her head for a silly prejudice."

When he has finished this speech, Sir James feels that he has been unpardonably impertinent.

"She will have a home with my uncle," says Branscombe, unmoved,—"a far happier and more congenial home than this has ever been." A faint sneer disfigures his handsome mouth for a moment. Then his mood changes, and he turns almost fiercely upon Georgie. "Why will you fight against your own good fortune?" he says. "See how it is favoring you. You will get rid of me for years, perhaps—I hope—forever, and you will be comfortable with him."

"No, I shall not," says Mrs. Branscombe, a brilliant crimson has grown upon her pale cheeks, her eyes are bright and full of anger, she stands back from him and looks at him with passionate reproach and determination in her gaze. "You think I will consent to live calmly here while you are an exile from your home? In so much you wrong me. When you leave Sartoris, I leave it too,—to be a governess once more."

"I forbid you to do that," says Branscombe. "I am your husband, and, as such, the law allows me some power over you. But this is only an idle threat," he says, contemptuously. "When I remember how you consented to marry even me to escape such a life of drudgery, I cannot believe you will willingly return to it again."

"Nevertheless I shall," says Georgie, slowly. "You abandon me: why, then, should you have power to control my actions? And I will not live at Hythe, and I will not live at all in Pullingham unless I live here."

"Don't be obstinate, Dorian," says Sir James, imploringly. "Give in to her: it will be more manly. Don't you see she has conceived an affection for the place by this time, and can't bear to see it pass into strange hands? In the name of common sense, accept this chance of rescue, and put an end to a most unhappy business."

Dorian leans his arms upon the mantel-piece, and his head upon his arms. Shall he, or shall he not, consent to this plan? Is he really behaving, as Scrope has just said, in an unmanly manner?

A lurid flame from the fire lights up the room, and falls warmly upon Georgie's anxious face and clasped hands and sombre clinging gown; upon Dorian's bowed head and motionless figure, and upon Sir James, standing tall and silent within the shadow that covers the corner where he is. All is sad, and drear, and almost tragic!

Georgie, with both hands pressed against her bosom, waits breathlessly for Dorian's answer. At last it comes. Lifting his head, he says, in a dull tone that is more depressing than louder grief, —

"I consent. But I cannot live here just yet. I shall go away for a time. I beg you both to understand that I do this thing against my will for my wife's sake, — not for my own. Death itself could not be more bitter to me than life has been of late." For the last time he turns and looks at Georgie. "You know who has embittered it," he says. And then, "Go: I wish to be alone!"

Scrope, taking Mrs. Branscombe's cold hand in his, leads her from the room. When outside, she presses her fingers on his in a grateful fashion, and, whispering something to him in a broken voice, — which he fails to hear, — she goes heavily up the staircase to her own room.

When inside, she closes the door, and locks it, and, going as if with a purpose to a drawer in a cabinet, draws from it a velvet frame. Opening it, she gazes long and earnestly upon the face it contains: it is Dorian's.

It is a charming, lovable face, with its smiling lips and its large blue honest eyes. Distrustfully she gazes at it, as if seeking to discover some trace of duplicity in the clear open features. Then slowly she takes the photograph from the frame, and with a scissors cuts out the head, and, lifting the glass from a dull gold locket upon the table near her, carefully places the picture in it.

When her task is finished, she looks at it once again, and then laughs softly to herself, — a sneering unlovable laugh full of self-contempt. Her whole expression is unforgiving, yet suggestive of deep regret. Somehow, at this moment his last words came back to her and strike coldly on her heart: "I wish to be alone!"

"Alone!" How sadly the word had fallen from his lips! How stern his face had been, how broken and miserable his voice! Some terrible grief was tearing at his heart, and there was no one to comfort or love him, or — —

She gets up from her chair, and paces the room impatiently, as though inaction had ceased to be possible to her. An intense craving to see him again fills her soul. She must go to him, if only to know what he has been doing since last she left him. Acting on impulse, she goes quickly down the stairs, and across the hall to the library, and enters with a beating heart.

All is dark and dreary enough to chill any expectant mind. The fire, though warm and glowing still, has burned to a dull red, and no bright flames flash up to illumine the gloom. Blinded by the sudden change from light to darkness, she goes forward nervously until she reaches the hearth-rug: then she discovers that Dorian is no longer there.

CHAPTER XXXII

"Shake hands forever, cancel all our vows;
And when we meet at any time again,
Be it not seen in either of our brows
That we one jot of former love retain." —Drayton.

Not until Mrs. Branscombe has dismissed her maid for the night does she discover that the plain gold locket in which she had placed Dorian's picture is missing. She had (why, she hardly cares to explain even to herself) hung it round her neck; and now, where is it?

After carefully searching her memory for a few moments, she remembers that useless visit to the library before dinner, and tells herself she must have dropped it then. She will go and find it. Slipping into a pale-blue dressing-gown, that serves to make softer and more adorable her tender face and golden hair, she thrusts her feet into slippers of the same hue, and runs down-stairs for the third time to-day, to the library.

Opening the door, the brilliant light of many lamps greets her, and, standing by the fire is her husband, pale and haggard, with the missing locket in his hand. He has opened it, and is gazing at his own face with a strange expression.

"Is this yours?" he asks, as she comes up to him. "Did you come to look for it?"

"Yes." She holds out her hand to receive it from him, but he shows some hesitation about giving it.

"Let me advise you to take this out of it," he says, coldly, pointing to his picture. "Its being here must render the locket valueless. What induced you to give it such a place?"

"It was one of my many mistakes," returns she, calmly, making a movement as though to leave him; "and you are right. The locket is, I think, distasteful to me. I don't want it any more: you can keep it."

"I don't want it, either," returns he, hastily; and then, with a gesture full of passion, he flings it deliberately into the very heart of the glowing fire. There it melts, and grows black, and presently sinks, with a crimson coal, utterly out of sight.

"The best place for it," says he, bitterly. "I wish I could as easily be obliterated and forgotten."

Is it forgotten? She says nothing, makes no effort to save the fated case that holds his features, but, with hands tightly clenched, watches its ruin. Her eyes are full of tears, but she feels benumbed, spiritless, without power to shed them.

Once more she makes a movement to leave him.

"Stay," he says, gently; "I have a few things to say to you, that may as well be got over now. Come nearer to the fire: you must be cold."

She comes nearer, and, standing on the hearth-rug, waits for him to speak. As she does so, a sharp cough, rising to her throat, distresses her sufficiently to bring some quick color into her white cheeks. Though in itself of little importance, this cough has now annoyed her for at least a fortnight, and shakes her slight frame with its vehemence.

"Your cough is worse to-night," he says, turning to regard her more closely.

"No, not worse."

"Why do you walk about the house so insufficiently clothed?" asks he, angrily, glancing at her light dressing-gown with great disfavor. "One would think you were seeking ill health. Here, put this round you." He tries to place upon her shoulders the cashmere shawl she had worn when coming in from the garden in the earlier part of the evening. But she shrinks from him.

"No, no," she says, petulantly; "I am warm enough; and I do not like that thing. It is black,—the color of Death!"

Her words smite cold upon his heart. A terrible fear gains mastery over him. Death! What can it have to do with one so fair, so young, yet, alas! so frail?

"You will go somewhere for change of air?" he says, entreatingly, going up to her and laying his hand upon her shoulder. "It is of this, partly, I wish to speak to you. You will find this house lonely and uncomfortable (though doubtless pleasanter) when I am gone. Let me write to my aunt, Lady Monckton. She will be very glad to have you for a time."

"No; I shall stay here. Where are you going?"

"I hardly know; and I do not care at all."

"How long will you be away?"

"How can I answer that question either? There is nothing to bring me home."

"How soon do you go?" Her voice all through is utterly without expression, or emotion of any kind.

"Immediately," he answers, curtly. "Are you in such a hurry to be rid of me? Be satisfied, then: I start to-morrow." Then, after an unbroken pause, in which even her breathing cannot be heard, he says, in a curious voice, "I suppose there will be no occasion for me to write to you while I am away?"

She does not answer directly. She would have given half her life to be able to say, freely, "Write to me, Dorian, if only a bare line, now and then, to tell me you are alive;" but pride forbids her.

"None, whatever," she says, coldly, after her struggle with her inner self. "I dare say I shall hear all I care to hear from Clarissa or Sir James."

There is a long silence. Georgie's eyes are fixed dreamily upon the sparkling coals. His eyes are fixed on her. What a child she looks in her azure gown, with her yellow hair falling in thick masses over her shoulders. So white, so fair, so cruelly cold! Has she no heart, that she can stand in that calm, thoughtful attitude, while his heart is slowly breaking?

She has destroyed all his happy life, this "amber witch," with her loveliness, and her pure girlish face, and her bitter indifference; and yet his love for her at this moment is stronger, perhaps, than it has ever been. He is leaving her. Shall he ever see her again?

Something at this moment overmasters him. Moving a step nearer to her, he suddenly catches her in his arms, and, holding her close to his heart, presses kisses (unforbidden) upon her lips and cheek and brow.

In another instant she has recovered herself, and, placing her hands against his chest, frees herself, by a quick gesture, from his embrace.

"Was that how you used to kiss *her*?" she says, in a choked voice, her face the color of death. "Let me go: your touch is contamination."

Almost before the last word has passed her lips, he releases her, and, standing back, confronts her with a face as livid as her own.

In the one hurried glance she casts at him, she knows that all is, indeed, over between them now; never again will he sue to her for love or friendship. She would have spoken again,—would, perhaps, have said something to palliate the harshness of her last words,—but by a gesture he forbids her. He points to the door.

"Leave the room," he says, in a stern commanding tone; and, utterly subdued and silenced by his manner, she turns and leaves him.

CHAPTER XXXIII

"A goodly apple, rotten at the heart.
Oh, what a goodly outside falsehood hath!" —*Merchant of Venice.*

"No hinge nor loop
To hang a doubt on." —*Othello.*

Dorian has been two months gone, and it is once again close on Christmas-tide. All the world is beginning to think of gifts, and tender greetings, and a coming year. Clarissa is dreaming of wedding garments white as the snow that fell last night.

The post has just come in. Clarissa, waking, stretches her arms over her head with a little lazy delicious yawn, and idly turns over her letters one by one. But presently, as she breaks the seal of an envelope, and reads what lies inside it, her mood changes, and, springing from her bed, she begins to dress herself with nervous rapidity.

Three hours later, Sir James, sitting in his library, is startled by the apparition of Clarissa standing in the door-way with a very miserable face.

"What on earth has happened?" says Sir James, who is a very practical young man and always goes at once to the root of a mystery.

"Horace is ill," says Miss Peyton, in a tone that might have suited the occasion had the skies just fallen. "Oh, Jim, what shall I do?"

"My dearest girl," says Scrope, going up to her and taking her hands.

"Yes, he is very ill! I had not heard from him for a fortnight, and was growing wretchedly uneasy, when to-day a letter came from Aunt Emily telling me he has been laid up with low fever for over ten days. And he is very weak, the doctor says, and no one is with him. And papa is in Paris, and Lord Sartoris is with Lady Monckton, and Dorian—no one knows where Dorian is!"

"Most extraordinary his never getting any one to write you a line!"

"Doesn't that only show how fearfully ill he must be? Jim, you will help me, won't you?"

This appeal is not to be put on one side.

"Of course I will," says Scrope: "you know that—or you ought. What do you want me to do?"

"To take me to him. I want to see him with my own eyes."

"To go yourself?" says Sir James, extreme disapprobation in his tone. "You must be out of your mind."

"I am not," returns she, indignantly. "I never was more in it. And I am going, any-way."

"What will your father say?"

"He will say I was quite right. Dear, *dear*, DEAR Jim,"—slipping her hand through his arm, and basely descending from *hauteur* to coaxing,— "do say you will take me to him. It can't be wrong! Am I not going to be his wife in a month's time?"

Sir James moves a chair out of his way with most unnecessary vehemence.

"How that alters the case I can't see," he says, obstinately.

"You forsake me!" says Miss Peyton, her eyes filling with tears. "Do. I can't be much unhappier than I am, but I did depend on you, you were always so much my friend." Here two large tears run down her cheeks, and they, of course, decide everything.

"I will take you," he says, hastily. "To-day?—The sooner the better, I suppose."

"Yes; by the next train. Oh, how obliged to you I am! Dear Jim, I shall never forget it to you!"

This is supposed to be grateful to him, but it is quite the reverse.

"I think you are very foolish to go at all," he says, somewhat gruffly.

"Perhaps I am," she says, with a rueful glance. "But you cannot understand. Ah! if you loved, yourself, you could sympathize with me."

"Could I?" says Sir James, with a grimace that is meant for a smile, but as such is a most startling specimen of its class.

So they go up to town, and presently arrive at the house where Horace lies unconscious of all around him. The door is opened to them by an unmistakable landlady,—a fat, indolent person, with sleepy eyes, and a large mouth, and a general air about her suggestive of perpetual beef-steaks and bottled stout.

This portly dame, on being questioned, tells them, "Mr. Branscum has just bin given his draft, and now he is snoozin' away as peaceable as a hinfant, bless 'im."

"Is he—in bed?" asks Sir James, diffidently, this large person having the power to reduce him to utter subjection.

"Lawks! no, sir. He wouldn't stay there he's that contrairy. Beggin' yore parding, sir, he's yore brother?"

Sir James nods. She may prove difficult, this stout old lady, if he declares himself no relative.

"To be shore!" says she. "I might 'a' knowed by the speakin' likeness between you. You're the born himage of 'im. After his draft we laid 'im on the sofy, and there he is now, sleepin' the sleep of the just. Just step up and see him; do, now. He is in a state of comus, and not expectit to get out of it for two hours."

"The young—lady—will go up," says Sir James, feeling, somehow, as if he has insulted Clarissa by calling her "a young lady." "She would like" (in a confidential tone that wins on the stout landlady) "to see him alone, just at first."

"Just so," says Mrs. Goodbody, with a broad wink; and Clarissa is forthwith shown up-stairs, and told to open the first door she comes to.

"And you," says Mrs. Goodbody to Sir James, "will please just to step in 'ere and wait for her, while I see about the chicking broth!"

"What a charming room!" says Sir James, hypocritically; whereupon the good woman, being intensely flattered, makes her exit with as much grace as circumstances and her size will permit.

Clarissa opening the door with a beating heart, finds herself in a pretty, carefully-shaded room, at the farther end of which, on a sofa, Horace lies calmly sleeping. He is more altered than even her worst fears had imagined, and as she bends over him she marks, with quick grief, how thin and worn and haggard he has grown.

The blue veins stand out upon his nerveless hands. Tenderly, with the very softest touch, she closes her own fingers over his. Gently she brushes back the disordered hair from his flushed forehead, and then, with a quick accession of coloring, stoops to lay a kiss upon the cheek of the man who is to be her husband in one short month.

A hand laid upon her shoulder startles and deters her from her purpose. It is a light, gentle touch, but firm and decided and evidently meant to prevent her from giving the caress. Quickly raising herself, Clarissa draws back, and, turning her head, sees — —

Who is it? Has time rolled backwards? A small, light, gray-clad figure stands before her, a figure only too well remembered! The brown hair brushed back from the white temples with the old Quakerish neatness, the dove-like eyes, the sensitive lips, cannot be mistaken. Clarissa raises her hands to her eyes to shut out the sight.

Oh! not that! Anything but that! Not Ruth Annersley!

A faint sick feeling overcomes her; involuntarily she lays a hand upon the back of a chair near her, to steady herself; while Ruth stands opposite to her, with fingers convulsively clinched, and dilated nostrils, and eyes dark with horror.

"What brings you here?" asks Ruth, at length, in a voice hard and unmusical.

"To see the man whose wife I was to have been next month," says Clarissa, feeling compelled to answer. "And" —in a terrible tone—"who are you?"

"The woman who ought to be his wife," says Ruth, in the same hard tone, still with her hands tightly clasped.

Clarissa draws her breath hard, but returns no answer; and then there falls upon them a long, long silence, that presently becomes unbearable. The two women stand facing each other, scarcely breathing. The unnatural stillness is undisturbed save by the quick irregular gasps of the sick man.

Once he sighs heavily, and throws one hand and arm across his face. Then Ruth stirs, and, going swiftly and noiselessly to his side, with infinite tenderness draws away the arm and replaces it in its former position. She moves his pillows quietly, and passes her cool hand across his fevered brow.

"Ruth?" he moans, uneasily, and she answers, "I am here, darling," in the faintest, sweetest whisper.

Something within Clarissa's heart seems to give way. At this moment, for the first time, she realizes the true position in which he has placed her. A sensation of faintness almost overcomes her, but by a supreme effort she conquers her weakness, and crushes back, too, the rising horror and anger that have sprung into life. A curious calm falls upon her, —a state that often follows upon keen mental anguish. She is still completing the victory she has gained over herself, when Ruth speaks again.

"This is no place for you!" she says, coldly, yet with her hand up to her cheek, as though to shield her face from the other's gaze.

Clarissa goes up to her then.

"So you are found at last," she says, somewhat monotonously. "And, of all places, here! Is there any truth in the world, I wonder? Was it shame kept you from writing, all these months, to your unhappy father? Do you know that an innocent man—his brother"—pointing with a shivering gesture to the unconscious Horace—"has been suffering all this time for his wrong-doing?"

"I know nothing," replies Ruth, sternly. "I seek to know nothing. My intercourse with the world ceased with my innocence."

"You knew of my engagement to him?" says Clarissa, again motioning towards the couch.

"Yes."

"Before you left Pullingham?"

"No! oh, no!—not then," exclaims Ruth, eagerly. "I did not believe it then. Do not judge me more harshly than you can help."

The dull agony that flashes into her eyes quickens into life some compassionate feeling that still lies dormant in Clarissa's breast.

"I do not judge you at all," she says, with infinite gentleness. Then, with an impulsive movement, she turns and lays her hand upon her shoulder. "Come home with me—now!" she says. "Leave this place, Ruth, I implore you, listen to me!"

"Do not," says Ruth, shrinking from her grasp; "I am not fit for you to touch. Remember all that has passed."

"Do you think I shall ever forget!" says Clarissa, slowly. "But for your father's sake: he is ill,—perhaps dying. Come. For his sake you will surely return?"

"It is too late!" says the girl, in a melancholy voice. And then, again, "It is impossible." Yet it is apparent that a terrible struggle is taking place within her breast: how it might have ended, whether the good or bad angel would have gained the day, can never now be said; a sigh, a broken accent, decided her.

"My head!" murmurs the sick man, feebly, drawing his breath wearily, and as if with pain. "Ruth, Ruth, are you there?" The querulous dependent tone rouses into instant life all the passionate tenderness that is in Ruth's heart. Having soothed him by a touch, she turns once more to Clarissa.

"He too is sick,—perhaps dying," she says, feverishly. "I cannot leave him! I have sacrificed all for him, and I shall be faithful unto the end. Leave me: I have done you the greatest wrong one woman can do another. Why should you care for my salvation?" Through all the defiance there is bitter misery in her tone.

"I don't know why; yet I do," says poor Clarissa, earnestly.

"You are a saint," says Ruth, with white lips. And then she falls upon her knees. "Oh, if it be in your heart," she cries, "grant me your forgiveness!"

Clarissa bursts into tears.

"I do grant it," she says. "But I would that my tongue possessed such eloquence as could induce you to leave this house." She tries to raise Ruth from her kneeling position.

"Let me remain where I am," says Ruth, faintly. "It is my right position. I tell you again to go; this is no place for you. Yet stay you, sweet woman," — she cries, with sudden fervor, catching hold of the hem of Clarissa's gown and pressing it to her lips, —"let me look at you once again! It is my final farewell to all that is pure; and I would keep your face fresh within my heart."

She gazes at her long and eagerly.

"What! tears?" she says; "and for me? Oh, believe me, though I shall never see you again, the recollection of these tears will soothe my dying hours, and perhaps wash out a portion of my sins!"

Her head drops upon her hands. So might the sad Magdalen have knelt. Her whole body trembles with the intensity of her emotion, yet no sound escapes her.

"Ruth, for the last time, I implore you to come with me," says Clarissa, brokenly. And once more the parched lips of the crouching woman frame the words, "It is too late!"

A moment after, the door is opened, and closed again and Clarissa has looked her last upon Ruth Annersley.

How she makes her way down to the room where Sir James sits awaiting her, Clarissa never afterwards remembers.

"It is all over: take me away!" she says, quietly, but somewhat incoherently.

"He isn't dead?" says Sir James, who naturally conceives the worst from her agitation.

"No: it is even worse," she says. And then she covers her face with her hands, and sinks into a chair. "Ruth Annersley is here!" When she has said this, she feels that life has almost come to an end. How shall she make this wretched revelation to her father, to Georgie, to all the rest of the world?

As for Sir James, he stands at some distance from her, literally stunned by the news. Words seem to fail him. He goes up to her and takes one of her small icy-cold hands in his.

"Did you see her?"

"Yes."

"The scoundrel!" says Sir James, in a low tone. Then, "Is he very ill?" There is unmistakable meaning in his tone.

"Very." And here she falls to bitter weeping again.

It is a cruel moment: Sir James still holds her hand, but can find no words to say to comfort her; indeed, where can comfort lie?

At this instant a heavy footfall resounds along the passage outside. It warns them of the sylph-like approach of Mrs. Goodbody. Sir James going quickly to the door, intercepts her.

"My—my sister is quite upset," he says, nervously. "Mr. Branscombe was—was worse than she expected to find him."

"Upset!—and no wonder, too," says Mrs. Goodbody, with heavy sympathy, gazing approvingly at Miss Peyton. "There's no denying that he's so worn out, the pore dear, as it's quite dispiritin' to see 'im, what with his general appearings and the fear of a bad turn at any mingit. For myself, I take my meals quite promiscuous like, since he fell ill,—just a bit here and a bit there, it may be, but nothing reg'lar like. I ain't got the 'art. Howsoever, 'hope on, hope never,' is my motter, miss; and we must allus hope for the best, as the sayin' is."

"Just so," says Sir James, who doesn't know, in the very least, what to say.

"A good wife, sir, I allus say, is half the battle; and that lady up-stairs, she is a reg'lar trump, she is, and so devoted, as it's quite affectin' to witness. Good-mornin' sir—thank you, sir. I'll see to him, you be bound; and, with his good lady above, there ain't the smallest——"

Sir James, opening the hall door in despair, literally pushes Clarissa out and into the cab that is awaiting them. For a long time she says nothing; and just as he is beginning to get really anxious at her determined silence, she says, with some difficulty,—

"Jim, promise me something?"

"Anything," says Jim.

"Then never again allude to this day, or to anything connected with it; and never again mention—his—name to me, unless I first speak to you."

"Never!" returns he, fervently. "Be sure of it."

"Thank you," she says, like a tired child; and then, sinking back in her corner of the cab, she cries long and bitterly.

CHAPTER XXXIV

"Our doubts are traitors,
And make us lose the good we oft might win." —
Shakespeare.

"The day goeth down red darkling,
The moaning waves dash out the light,
And there is not a star of hope sparkling
On the threshold of my night." —Gerald Massey.

The morning after her unfortunate visit to town, Clarissa sends to Mrs. Branscombe, asking her to come to her without delay. The secret that is in her heart weighs heavily, and Georgie must be told. Yet, now, when the door opens, and Georgie stands before her, she is dumb, and cold, and almost without power to move.

"What is it?" says Mrs. Branscombe, suddenly. The sad little smile that of late has been peculiar to her fades at sight of Clarissa's grief-stricken face. She advances, and lays a hand upon her arm. "You look positively ill, Clarissa: something dreadful has happened. I can see it in your eyes. It is bad news. Dorian,—he is not — —"

She puts her hand to her throat, and leans on a chair.

"It is no bad news for you," says Clarissa, faintly, "but for me." She pauses.

"Are you in trouble, dearest?" says Mrs. Branscombe, sadly. "I thought you the happiest girl alive. Is there nothing but misery in this wretched world?"

"I was in town yesterday," Clarissa begins, with an effort, and then stops. How is she to betray her lover's falseness?

"And you saw Horace, and he is ill?" says Georgie, anxiously. "Tell me all, Clarissa."

"It is so hard to tell," says poor Clarissa; and then she turns her face to the wall, and wishes honestly that all things for her might now be at an end:

"Love, art thou bitter?
Sweet is death to me."

At this moment she could have gladly welcomed death.

"There are many things," she says, "but this worst of all. He does not love me; he has never loved me. And there is some one else; and— —"

"Who is it?" asks Georgie, breathlessly, though the truth as yet is far from her.

"Ruth Annersley! She was there,—in his rooms!" says Clarissa; and, after this, there is a silence that lasts for several minutes.

The unhappy truth is told. Clarissa, shamed and heartbroken, moves away, that her companion may not see her face. As for Mrs. Branscombe, at first intense wonder renders her motionless; and then, as the exact meaning of this terrible story breaks in upon her, a great and glorious gleam of unmistakable rapture lights all her face, and, sinking upon a *prie-Dieu* near her, she presses her hands tightly together. That Dorian is exonerated, is her first thought; that he will never forgive her, is her second; and this drives all the blood from her cheeks, and the gladness from her heart, and brings her back again to the emptiness and barrenness that have made life a wilderness to her for so many months.

Going over to Clarissa, she lays her arms gently round her neck. There seems to be a new bond, born of grief, between them now.

"Do not pity me," says Clarissa, entreatingly.

"Pity you? no! There is no occasion for it. You are fortunate in having escaped such a fate as was in store for you. In time you will forget all this, and be happy in some other way."

"Shall I?" says Clarissa, drearily. "But, in the mean time, what shall I do? How shall I fill the blank here?" She lays her hand upon her heart.

"He is a wretch," says Georgie, with sudden fire. "If I were a man, I should kill him."

"You should rather be thankful to him," says Clarissa, with some bitterness. "My misery has proved your joy. The shadow has been raised from Dorian."

"Clarissa, if you speak to me like that you will break my heart," says Georgie, deeply grieved. "How could I know joy when you are unhappy? And—and, besides, there is no joy for me anywhere. Dorian will never forgive me. How could he? I, his wife, was the one who most heartily condemned him and believed in his guilt."

"When you see him, all will be well. But he should be told; you will see to that."

"Of course, darling. He is coming home next week. But how shall I meet him and say all this to him! The very thought of it is terrible."

"Next week?—so soon?"

"Yes; I had a line from him this morning,—the only one he wrote me since his departure; but that was my own fault. I am almost sorry he is coming now," says Mrs. Branscombe, nervously. "I shall dread the look in his eyes when I confess to him how readily I believed in that false rumor."

"You hardly deserve pity," says Clarissa, suddenly, turning upon her with some just anger. "You undervalued him all through. Instead of going 'down on your knees to thank heaven, fasting, for a good man's love,' you deliberately flung it away. How different it has been with me! I trusted blindly, and see my reward! Even yet I cannot realize it. It seems like some strange horrible nightmare, from which I must awake. Yesterday I was so happy; to-day——"

She breaks down, and bursts into bitter weeping.

Georgie throws herself on her knees before her.

"Is this your luggage, sir? Glad to see you back again, sir."

"Thank you, Jeffers. Yes, that is mine. All right at home, I hope? Your mistress quite well?"

"Quite well, sir. She is at home, awaiting you."

Dorian turns away with a bitter smile. "At home, awaiting him!" What a wretched fool he once was, when he used to really picture to himself a fair fond woman waiting and longing for his return, whenever Fate had called him from her side!

Arriving at Sartoris, he runs up the stairs to his own room, meeting no one on his way. He smiles again—the same unlovely smile—as he tells himself that Jeffers exaggerated the case a little,—as, plainly, Georgie has taken special pains to be out of the way to avoid meeting him on his first arrival.

Opening his door, he goes in, closing it firmly behind him. Everything in the room is just as he had left it. Nothing has been changed; the very book he had been reading is lying now open at the page he had last looked into. A glorious fire is burning in the grate. A delicate Bohemian vase is filled with some rare sweet flowers.

Whose hand had gathered them? If it was one of the servants, it was very thoughtful. He is very fond of flowers. He moves listlessly about, wondering vaguely how everything can look, after some months' absence, so exactly as if he had seen it only yesterday, when a small object lying on a side-table attracts his notice.

It is a little gray glove, soiled, finger-pressed, warm as if its owner but just a minute since had drawn it from her hand. It is yet almost a part of the white, soft flesh it had covered. His brow contracts, and a pained expression crosses his face. Taking it up, he lays it in his open palm, and regards it earnestly; he hesitates, and then, as though unable to prevent himself, he raises it and presses it passionately to his lips. An instant later, with a contemptuous gesture and an inward anathema upon his own weakness, he flings it far from him through the open window down on to the balcony beneath,—where it flutters to Mrs. Branscombe's feet!

Mechanically she stoops and picks it up. She has been hurrying towards the house, having only just heard of her husband's arrival, she not having expected him for some time later, trains at Pullingham being none of the most punctual.

Gazing at the luckless glove, her whole expression changes. She is beneath his window: was it his hand flung it so disdainfully to the ground,—the glove she had worn such a short time before, when gathering the flowers that are now making his room so sweet? Clasping the unoffending bit of kid closely in her hand, she enters the house, by a wide French window, and goes straight into Dorian's room.

At the door she hesitates, and then knocks somewhat nervously.

"Come in." His voice has been so long a stranger to her that she almost starts on hearing it, and the last remnant of her courage vanishes. She opens the door and goes slowly in.

Dorian's back is turned to her. His coat is off, and he is brushing his hair before a glass in the furious fashion men, as a rule, affect. As she enters, he turns, and putting down the brushes, regards her with undisguised surprise. Plainly, he has not expected her.

"How d'ye do?" he says, presently. It is perfectly absurd; yet neither of them laughs. It is the most ridiculous greeting he could possibly have made her, considering all things; yet no sense of ridicule touches them. They are too near to tragedy to harbor a thought of comedy.

"I did not expect you until five," says Georgie, in a constrained tone. "If I had known, I should have been ready to receive you."

"Pray do not apologize," he says, coldly. "It is very good of you to come here now. It is more than I expected."

"I came," says Georgie, with an effort, "because I have something to tell you, that should be told without delay."

"What is it?" he asks, quickly. "Is my uncle well?"

"Quite well. I saw him yesterday. It has nothing to do with him; though, of course, it must touch him very nearly."

"You will be tired," he says, with grave but distant politeness. "Sit down while you tell me your news."

"No; I prefer standing." She clasps one hand tightly over the other, and leans against the wall; she cannot, try as she will, remove her eyes from his face. "What I want to say is this: I have heard of Ruth Annersley!"

"Have you?" with an ominous calm in look and tone. "Where is she?"

"With—your brother!"

Dorian walks abruptly to the window, and stands there so that his face cannot be seen. He is distressed beyond measure. So his old suspicions have proved true, after all, and Horace's protestations were as basest lies. He feels sick at heart for his brother's honor,—that miserable remnant of a once fair thing, that costly garment, now reduced to rags. After a while he forces himself to speak again.

"Who found her there?" he asks, huskily.

"Clarissa."

"Clarissa?" He is now thoroughly shocked. "What cruel fate made her the discoverer?"

"Chance. He was ill, and she went to see him, out of pure love for him. She was rewarded by a sight of Ruth Annersley!"

"Poor girl!" says Branscombe, sadly. "So true,—so trusting."

Georgie draws her breath quickly. Are not his words a reflection upon her?—she, who has so failed in faith and love?

"I suppose that is all you have to tell me," says Dorian, presently, in an absent, weary way.

"Not quite all," she says, with a trembling voice. She forces herself to come nearer to him, and now stands before him like a small pale culprit, unable to lift her eyes to his. "I want to tell you how deeply I regret the injustice, the—"

"No, no," interrupts he, impatiently. "Let nothing be said about that. It would be worse than useless. Why waste words over what can never be undone?"

Still she perseveres bravely, although her breath is coming quicker, and her lips are trembling.

"I must tell you how sorry I am," she says, with a suppressed sob. "I want to ask you, if possible, to forg— —"

"Believe me, it will be better to leave all this unsaid," he interrupts her, gravely.

"Then you do not care to hear how I have regretted the wrong I did you, and— —?"

"As you ask me the question, I will answer you. No, I do not. Had you, at any time, felt one particle of affection for me, you could never have so misunderstood me. Let things now remain as they are. Though I think that perhaps, for the short time I shall remain at home, it will be better for your sake that we should appear before the world, at least, as friends."

"You are leaving home again?" she asks, timidly. Now, as he stands before her, so tall, and strong, and unforgiving, with this new-born dignity upon him, she fully realizes, for the first time, all she has recklessly resigned. He had loved her at one time, surely, and she had trampled on that love, until she had crushed out of it all life and sweetness:

"For it so falls out
That what we have we prize not to the worth
While we enjoy it; but, being lacked and lost,
Why, then we rack the value; then we find
The virtue that possession would not show us
While it was ours."

"Yes, as soon as I can finish the business that has brought me back. I fear that will keep me two months, at least. I wish I could hasten it, but it would be impossible." He grows slightly *distrait*, but, after a moment, rouses himself with a start, and looks at her. "Am I keeping you?" he asks, courteously. (To her the courtesy is a positive cruelty.) "Do not let me detain you any longer. Is there anything more you wish to say to me?"

"Nothing." His last words have frozen within her all desire for reconciliation. Is he, indeed, in such great haste to be gone? Without another word, she goes to the door, but, as she puts out her hand to open it, something within her grasp becomes known to her. It is the glove she had picked up on the balcony half an hour ago, and has held ever since almost unconsciously.

"Was it—was it you that threw this from the window?" she says, suddenly, for the last time raising her beautiful eyes to her husband's face.

"Yes. This was no place for it," returns he, sternly.

Going down the staircase, full of grief and wounded pride, she encounters Lord Sartoris.

"He has come?" asks the old man, in an agitated manner, laying his hand on her arm.

"He has. If you wish to see him, he is in his own room," replies she, in a singularly hard tone.

"Have you told him everything?" asks Sartoris, nervously. "It was a fatal mistake. Do you think he will forgive me?"

"How can I say?" says Mrs. Branscombe, with a bitter smile. "I can only tell you he has not forgiven me."

"Bless me!" says Lord Sartoris; "then, I suppose, I haven't a chance."

He is disheartened by her words, and goes very slowly on his way towards his nephew's room. When they are once more face to face, they pause and look with uncertainty upon each other. Then the older man holds out his hands beseechingly.

"I have come to demand your forgiveness," he says, with deep entreaty. "Dorian—grant it!—I am very old——"

In an instant Dorian's arm is round his neck, as it used to be in the days long ago, before the dark cloud had rolled between them.

"Not another word, or I shall never forgive you!" says Branscombe, tenderly, with the old smile upon his lips. And Sartoris, strong, obstinate, self-willed man that he is, lays his head down upon his "boy's" shoulder, and sobs aloud.

CHAPTER XXXV

"Oh, what a deal of scorn looks beautiful
In the contempt and anger of her lips." —*Twelfth Night.*

The dark day is growing colder and more drear. The winds are sighing sadly. A shivering sobbing breeze, that rushes in a mournful fashion through the naked twigs, tells one the year is drawing to a close, and that truly it is "faint with cold, and weak with old."

Clarissa, riding along the forest path that leads to Sartoris, feels something akin to pleasure in the sound of the rushing torrent that comes from above and falls headlong into the river that runs on her right hand.

There is, too, a desolation in the scene that harmonizes with her own sad thoughts. She has watched the summer leaves and flowers decay, but little thought her own hopes and longings should have died with them. Is she never to know peace, or joy, or content again? On her "rests remembrance like a ban:" she cannot shake it off.

"Rest! rest! Oh, give me rest and peace!" she cries aloud to her soul, but no rest cometh. The world seems colorless, without tint or purpose. She would gladly forget, if that might be, but it seems impossible to her.

"Ourselves we cannot recreate,
Nor get our souls to the same key
Of the remembered harmony."

The past—that is, her happy past—seems gone; the present is full of grief; the future has nothing to offer. This fact comes to her, and, with her eyes full of tears, she turns the corner and finds herself face to face with Horace Branscombe.

The old smile is on his face; he comes to her and holds out both his hands to take hers. He is worn and thin, and very handsome.

"I am too fortunate to meet you so soon," he says. "Yet I hardly think I should shake hands with you." Evidently, some thought unknown to her is in his mind.

"I am glad you have come to that conclusion," she says, "as there is no desire whatever on my part that our hands should meet."

He is plainly puzzled.

"What a strange welcome!" he says, reproachfully. "My letters during the past week should have explained everything to you."

"I have had none," says Clarissa, shortly.

"No? Was that why I received no answers? I have risen from a sick-bed to come to you, and demand the reason of your silence."

"I am sorry you troubled yourself so far. Ruth Annersley could have given you the answer you require."

His face blanches perceptibly; and his eyes, in their usual stealthy fashion, seek the ground.

"What have I to do with her?" he says, sullenly.

"Coward!" says Miss Peyton, in a low tone. "Do you, then, deny even all knowledge of the woman you have so wronged?"

"Take care! do not go too far," cries he, passionately, laying his hand upon her bridle, close to the bit. "Have you no fear?"

"Of you? none!" returns she, with such open contempt as stings him to the quick. "Remove your hand, sir."

"When I have said all I wish to say," returns he, coarsely, all his real brutality coming to the surface. "You shall stay here just as long as I please, and hear every word I am going to say. You shall——"

"Will you remove your hand?"

"When it suits me," returns he; "not before."

Passionate indignation conquers her self-control. Raising her arm, she brings down her riding-whip, with swift and unexpected violence, upon his cheek. The blow is so severe that, for the moment, he loses his presence of mind, and, swaying backward, lets the bridle go. Clarissa, finding herself free, in another moment is out of his reach and on her way to Sartoris.

As she reaches the gate, she meets James Scrope coming out, and, drawing rein, looks at him strangely.

"Have you seen a ghost?" asks he, slipping from his saddle, and coming up to her. "Your face is like death."

"I have, the ghost of an old love, but, oh, how disfigured! Jim, I have seen Horace."

She hides her face with her hands. She remembers the late scene with painful distinctness, and wonders if she has been unwomanly, coarse, undeserving of pity. She will tell him,—that is, Scrope,—and, if he condemns her, her cup will be indeed full.

Sir James—who, as a rule, is the most amiable of men—is now dark with anger.

"Branscombe—here?" he says, indignantly.

"Yes. He had evidently heard nothing. But I told him; and—and then he said things he should not have said; and he held my reins; and I forgot myself," says poor Clarissa, with anguish in her eyes; "and I raised my whip, and struck him across the face. Jim, if you say I was wrong in doing this thing, you will kill me."

"Wrong!" says Scrope. "Hanging would be too good for him. Oh, to think you should have been alone on such an occasion as that!"

"But it was a hateful thing to do, wasn't it?" says Miss Peyton, faintly.

"Hateful? Why? I only wish you had laid his cheek open," says Sir James, venomously. "But of course this poor little hand could not manage so much." Stooping involuntarily, he presses his lips to the hand that rests upon her knee.

"That wasn't the hand at all," says Miss Peyton, feeling inexpressibly consoled by his tone and manner.

"Wasn't it? Then I shall kiss the right one now," says Sir James, and caresses the other hand right warmly.

"I can't go on to Sartoris to-day," says Clarissa, in a troubled tone, checking her horse in the middle of the broad avenue.

"No; come home instead," says Scrope; and, turning, they go slowly, and almost silently, back to Gowran.

Horace, rousing himself after his encounter with Clarissa, puts his hand impulsively to his face, the sting of the blow still remaining. His illness has left him somewhat prostrate and weak; so that he feels more intensely than he otherwise would the pain that has arisen from the sudden stroke. A bitter execration rises to his lips; and then, feeling that all hope of reconciliation with Clarissa is at an end, he returns to Langham Station, and, with a mind full of evil thoughts and bitter revenge, goes back to town.

Wild and disturbed in appearance, he breaks in upon Ruth as she sits reading alone in the very room where she had last seen Clarissa. As he enters, she utters a glad little cry of welcome, and, springing to her feet, goes over to him.

"So soon returned?" she says, joyfully; and then something she sees in his face freezes within her all further expressions of pleasure: his eyes are dark, his whole face is livid with rage.

"So you betrayed me?" he says, pushing her away from him. "Now, no lies! I saw Clarissa Peyton to-day, and I know everything."

"You have been to Pullingham?" exclaims she, with a little gasp. "Horace, do not blame me. What was I to do? When she came in here, and saw me——"

"Clarissa, here?"

"Yes, here. I was afraid to tell you of it before, you seemed so weak, so fretful. Last Tuesday week—the day you had the sleeping-draught from Dr. Gregson—she came; she entered the room, she came near you, she touched you, she would"—faintly—"have kissed you. But how could I bear that? I stepped forward just in time to prevent her lips from meeting yours."

"And so," he says, with slow vindictiveness, taking no notice of her agony, "for the sake of a mere bit of silly sentimentality you spoiled every prospect I have in life."

"Horace, do not look at me like that," she entreats, painfully. "Remember all that has passed. If for one moment I went mad and forgot all, am I so much to be blamed? You had been mine—altogether mine—for so long that I had not strength in one short moment to relinquish you. When she would have kissed you, it seemed to me more than I could endure."

"Was it? It is but a little part of what you will have to endure for the future," he says, brutally. "You have wilfully ruined me, and must take the consequences. My marriage with Clarissa Peyton would have set me straight with the world once more, and need not have altered our relations with each other one iota."

"You would have been false to your wife?" murmurs she, shrinking back from him. "Oh, no! that would have been impossible!"

He laughs ironically.

"I tell you candidly," he says, with reckless emphasis, "I should have been false to one or other of you, and it certainly would not have been to you."

"You malign yourself," she says, looking at him with steadfast love.

"Do I? What a fool you are!" he says, roughly. "Well, by your own mad folly you have separated us irretrievably. Blame yourself for this, not me. My affairs are so hopelessly entangled that I must quit the country without delay. Your own mad act has rolled an ocean between us."

He turns, and goes towards the door. Wild with grief and despair, she follows him, and lays a detaining hand upon his arm.

"Not like this, Horace!" she whispers, desperately. "Do not leave me like this. Have pity. You shall not go like this! Be merciful: you are my all!"

"Stand out of my way," he says, between his teeth: and then, as she still clings to him in her agony, he raises his hand and deliberately strikes her. Not violently, not severely, but still with sufficient force to make her stagger backwards and catch hold of a chair to keep her from falling.

He is gone: and she, stunned, quivering, half blind with nervous horror, still stands by the chair and tries to realize all that has passed. As she draws a deep breath, she places her hand, with a spasmodic movement, to her left side, as though to quell some darting pain that lies there. The action brings back consciousness, and that saddest of all things, memory.

"He did not mean it," she whispers to herself, with white set lips. "It was not a blow; it was only that he wished to put me to one side, and I was in his way, no doubt: I angered him by my persistency. Darling! How could I think that he would hurt me?"

Languid, heart-broken, she creeps to her bed, and, flinging herself upon it, dressed as she is, sleeps heavily until the morn, "diffusing round a trembling flood of light," wakes her to grief once more.

CHAPTER XXXVI

"Have mind that eild aye follows youth;
Death follows life with gaping mouth;
Sen erdly joy abidis never,
Work for the joy that lastis ever;
For other joy is all but vain,
And erdly joy returns in pain." — W. Dunbar.

Something within her knows he will return. Yet all the next day long she sits in terrible suspense, not being certain of the end. Towards noon he comes, sullen, disdainful, and dark with depression.

He sinks into a chair, looking tired and careworn.

"You have over-fatigued yourself?" she says, gently, going over to him and touching his hand lightly.

"No. I have been to Pullingham again and back; that is all."

"There again?" she says. "And you saw — —?"

"Only Dorian. Don't trouble yourself about Clarissa," he says, with an unpleasant laugh: "that game is played out. No, Dorian, alone, I went to see." He shades his face with his hand, and then goes on: "There are few like him in the world. In spite of all that has come and gone, he received me kindly, and has given me what will enable me to commence life afresh in a foreign land." There is remorse and deep admiration in his tone.

But Ruth makes no reply: she cannot. Those last words, "a foreign land," have struck like a dying knell upon her heart. She watches him in despairing silence, as he walks restlessly up and down the room in the uncertain twilight.

Presently he stops close to her.

"I suppose there is some orthodox way of breaking bad news," he says, "but I never learned it. Ruth, your father is dead."

The girl shrinks back, and puts her hand to her forehead in a dazed, pitiful fashion.

"Not dead!" she says, imploringly, as though her contrition could bring him back to life. "Not altogether gone beyond recall. Sick, perhaps,—nay, dying,—but not dead!"

"Yes, he is dead," says Horace, though more gently. "He died a week ago."

A terrible silence falls upon the room. Presently, alarmed at her unnatural calm, he lays his hand upon her shoulder to rouse her.

"There is no use in fretting over what cannot be recalled," he says, quickly, though still in his gentler tone. "And there are other things I must speak to you about to-night. My remaining time in this country is short, and I want you to understand the arrangements I have made for your comfort before leaving you."

"You will leave me?" cries she, sharply. A dagger seems to have reached and pierced her heart. Falling upon her knees before him, she clasps him, and whispers, in a voice that has grown feeble through the intensity of her emotion, "Horace, do not forsake me. Think of all the past, and do not let the end be separation. What can I do? Where can I go?—with no home, no aim in life! Have pity! My father is dead; my friends, too, are dead to me. In all this wide miserable world I have only you!"

"Only me!" he echoes, with a short bitter laugh. "A prize, surely. You don't know what folly you are talking. I give you a chance of escape from me,—an honorable chance, where a new home and new friends await you."

"I want no friends, no home." (She is still clinging to his knees, with her white earnest face uplifted to his.) "Let me be your slave,—anything; but do not part from me. I cannot live without you now. It is only death you offer me."

"Remember my temper," he says, warningly. "Only last night I struck you. Think of that. I shall probably strike you again. Be advised in time, and forsake me, like all the others."

"You torture me," she says, still in the same low panting whisper. "You are my very heart,—my life. Take me with you. Only let me see your face sometimes, and hear your voice. I will not trouble you, or hinder you in any way; only let me be near you." She presses her pale lips to his hand with desperate entreaty.

"Be it so," he says, after a moment's hesitation. "If ever, in the days to come, you repent your bargain, blame yourself, not me. I have offered you liberty, and you have rejected it. I shall leave this country in a week's time; so be prepared. But before going, as you are so determined to cast in your lot with mine, I shall marry you."

She starts to her feet.

"Marry me?" she says, faintly. "Make me your wife! Oh, no! you don't know what you are saying."

She trembles violently, and her head falls somewhat heavily against his arm.

"It isn't worth a fainting fit," he says, hastily enough; but his arm, as he places it round her, is strong and compassionate. "Can anything be more absurd than a woman? Sit down here, and try to be reasonable. You must be quick with your preparations, as we start on Tuesday. I will see about a special license, and we can get the marriage ceremony over to-morrow. I know a fellow who will manage it all for me."

"You are quite sure you will never regret this step?" she says, earnestly, even at this supremely happy moment placing his happiness before her own.

"I don't suppose so. If it is any satisfaction to you to know it," he says, with a shrug, "you are the only woman I have ever loved, and probably the only one I ever shall love."

A smile—radiant, perfect—lights her face. Surely, just then, the one moment of utter happiness, that they tell us is all that is ever allowed to poor mortals, is hers. It is broken by the clock of a neighboring church clanging out the hour.

"So late!" says Horace, hurriedly. "I must go. Until to-morrow, Ruth, good-by."

"Good-by!" She places her hands upon his shoulders, and, throwing back her head, gazes long and earnestly into his face, as though reading once again each line in the features she loves with such devotion. "Before you go," she says, solemnly, "call me what I shall be so soon. Say, 'Good-by, my wife!'"

"Good-by, my wife!" returns he, with more love in his accents than she has heard for months.

She presses her lips passionately to his, and again, for the last time, breathes the word "Farewell!"

His rapid footsteps descend the stairs. She listens to them until they have ceased and all is still. Then she goes to the window, and presses her forehead against the cold pane, that she may once more see him as he crosses the street. The lamps are all alight, and a lurid glare from one falls full upon her as she stands leaning eagerly forward to catch the last glimpse of him she loves.

Presently she sinks into a seat, always with her eyes fixed upon the spot where she last has seen him, and sits motionless, with her fingers twisted loosely in her lap; she is so quiet that only the red gleam from the world without betrays the fact of her presence.

Once her lips part, and from them slowly, ecstatically, come the words, "His wife." Evidently her whole mind is filled with this one thought alone. She thinks of him, and him only,—of him who has so cruelly wronged her, yet who, in his own way, has loved her, too.

The moments fly, and night comes on apace, clothed in her "golden dress, on which so many stars like gems are strewed;" yet still she sits before the window silently. She is languid, yet happy,—weak and spent by the excitement of the past hour, yet strangely full of peace. Now and again she presses her hand with a gesture that is almost convulsive to her side; yet whatever pain she feels there is insufficient to drown the great gladness that is overfilling her.

To-morrow,—nay, even now, it is to-day,—and it is bringing her renewed hope, fresh life, restored honor! He will be hers forever! No other woman will have the right to claim him. Whatever she may have to undergo at his hands, at least he will be her own. And he has loved her as he never loved another. Oh, what unspeakable bliss lies in this certainty! In another land, too, all will be unknown. A new life may be begun in which the old may be swallowed up and forgotten. There must be hope in the good future.

> "When we slip a little
> Out of the way of virtue, are we lost?
> Is there no medicine called sweet mercy?"

Only this morning she had deemed herself miserable beyond her fellows; now, who can compete with her in utter content? In a few short hours she will be his wife! Oh that her father could but— —

Her father! Now, all at once, it rushes back upon her; she is a little dazed, a good deal unsettled, but surely some one had said that her—her father—was—dead!

The lamps in the street die out. The sickly winter dawn comes over the great city. The hush and calm still linger; only now and then a dark phantom form issues from a silent gateway, and hurries along the pavement, as though fearful of the growing light.

Ruth has sunk upon her knees, and is doing fierce battle with the remorse that has come to kill her new-born happiness. There is a terrible pain at her heart, even apart from the mental anguish that is tearing it. Her slight frame trembles beneath the double shock; a long shivering sob breaks from her; she throws her arms a little wildly across the couch before which she is kneeling, and gradually her form sinks upon her arms. No other sob comes to disturb the stillness. An awful silence follows. Slowly the cold gray morning fills the chamber, and the sun, —

"Eternal painter, now begins to rise,
And limn the heavens in vermilion dyes."

But within deathly silence reigns. Has peace fallen upon that quiet form? Has gentle sleep come to her at last?

Horace, ascending the stairs cautiously, before the household is astir, opens the room where last he had seen Ruth, and comes gently in. He would have passed on to the inner chamber, thinking to rouse her to prepare in haste for their early wedding, when the half-kneeling half-crouching figure before the lounge attracts his notice.

"Ruth," he says, very gently, fearful lest he shall frighten her by too sudden a summons back to wakefulness; but there is no reply. How can she have fallen asleep in such an uncomfortable position? "Ruth," he calls again, rather louder, some vague fear sending the blood back to his heart; but again only silence greets his voice. And again he says, "Ruth!" this time with passionate terror in his tone; but, alas! there is still no response. For the first time she is deaf to his entreaty.

Catching her in his arms, he raises her from her kneeling posture, and, carrying her to the window, stares wildly into her calm face, — the poor, sad, pretty face of her who had endured so much, and borne so long, and loved so faithfully.

She is dead! — quite dead! Already the limbs are stiffening, the hands are icy cold, the lips, that in life would so gladly have returned kiss for kiss, are now silent and motionless beneath the despairing caresses he lavishes upon them in the vain hope of finding yet some warmth remaining.

But there is none. She is gone, past recall, past hearing all expressions of remorseful tenderness. In the terrible lonely dawn she had passed away, with no one near to hold her dying hand, without a sigh or moan, leaving no farewell word of love or forgiveness to the man who is now straining her lifeless body to his heart, as though to make one last final effort to bring her back to earth.

There is a happy smile upon her lips, her eyes are quite closed, almost she seems as one that sleepeth. The awful majesty of death is upon her, and no voice of earth, however anguished and imploring, can reach her ice-bound heart. As the first faint touch of light that came to usher in her wedding morn broke upon the earth, she had died, and gone somewhere

"Above the smoke and stir of this dim spot
Which men call earth."

CHAPTER XXXVII

"Was I deceived, or did a sable cloud
Turn forth her silver lining on the night?"—Milton.

The two months that Dorian has given himself in which to finish the business that, he said, had brought him home, have almost come to an end. Already winter is passing out of mind, and "Spring comes up this way."

The "checkered daffodil" and the soft plaintive primrose are bursting into bloom. The gentle rain comes with a passing cloud, and sinks lovingly into the earth's bosom and into the hearts of the opening buds.

The grass is springing; all the world is rich with fresh young life. The very snowdrops—pale blossoms, born of bitter winds and sunless skies—have perished out of sight.

Ruth is lying in her grave, cold and forgotten save by two,—the man who has most wronged her, and the woman who had most to forgive her. As yet, Clarissa cannot rise out of the depression that fell upon her when Horace's treachery was first made known to her. Her love had seemed so good, so tender, it had so brightened all her life, and had been so much a part of her existence, that it seemed to carry to the grave with it all her youth and gladness. However untrue this young love of her life had been, still, while she believed in it, it had been beautiful to her, and it is with bitterest grief she has laid it aside; to her it had been a living thing, and even as it fades from her she cries to it aloud to stay, and feels her arms empty in that it no longer fills them.

"But, oh, not yet, not yet
Would my lost soul forget
How beautiful he was while he did live,
Or, when his eyes were dewy and lips wet,
What kisses, tenderer than all regret,
My love would give.

"Strew roses on his breast,—
He loved the roses best;
He never cared for lilies or for snow.
Let be this bitter end of his sweet quest;

Let be the pallid silence, that is rest,
And let all go!"

Mr. Winter's exquisite words come often to her; and yet, when the first great pang is over, a sensation that may be almost called relief raises her soul and restores her somewhat to her old self.

She is graver—if possible, gentler, more tender—than in the days before grief had touched her. And, though her love has really died beyond all reawakening, still the memory of what once had been has left its mark upon her.

To Sir James she has never since mentioned the name of the man in whom she had once so firmly believed, though oftentimes it has occurred to her that relief might follow upon the bare asking of a question that might serve to make common the actual remembrance of him.

To-day, as Scrope comes up the lawn to meet her, as she bends over the "bright children of the sun," a sense of gladness that he is coming fills her. She feels no nervousness or weariness with him, only rest and peace, and something that is deeper still, though yet vague and absolutely unknown to her own heart.

She goes forward to meet him, a smile upon her lips, treading lightly on the young grass, that is emerald in hue,—as the color of my own dear land,—and through which

"The meek daisies show
Their breasts of satin snow,
Bedecked with tiny stars of gold mid perfume sighs."

"You again?" she says, with a lovely smile. He was here only yesterday.

"What an uncivil speech! Do I come too often?" He has her hand in his, and is holding it inquiringly, but it is such a soft and kind inquiry.

"Not half often enough," she says, and hardly knows why his face flushes at her words, being still ignorant of the fact that he loves her with a love that passeth the love of most.

"Well, you sha'n't have to complain of that any longer," he says, gayly. "Shall I take up my residence here?"

"Do," says Miss Peyton, also in jest.

"I would much rather you took up yours at Scrope," he says, unthinkingly, and then he flushes again, and then silence falls between them.

Her foot is tapping the sward lightly, yet nervously. Her eyes are on the "daisies pied." Presently, as though some inner feeling compels her to it, she says,—"Why do you never speak to me of—Horace?"

"You forbade me," he says: "how could I disobey you? He is well, however, but, I think, not altogether happy. In his last letter, to me he still spoke remorsefully of—her." It is agony to him to say this, yet he does it bravely, knowing it will be the wisest thing for the woman he himself loves.

"Yes," she says, quite calmly. At this instant she knows her love for Horace Branscombe is quite dead. "Her death was terrible."

"Yet easy, I dare say. Disease of the heart, when it carries one off, is seldom painful. Clarissa, this is the very first time you have spoken of her, either."

"Is it?" She turns away from him, and, catching a branch, takes from it a leaf or two. "You have not spoken to me," she says.

"Because, as I said, you forbade me. Don't you know your word to me is law?"

"I don't think I know much," says Miss Peyton, with a sad little smile; but she lets her hand lie in his, and does not turn away from him. "Horace is in Ceylon," she says presently.

"Yes, and doing very well. Do you often think of him now?"

"Very often. I am glad he is getting on successfully."

"Have you forgotten nothing, Clarissa?"

"I have forgotten a great deal. How could it be otherwise? I have forgotten that I ever loved any one. It seems to me now impossible that I could have felt all that I did two months ago. Yet something lingers with me,—something I cannot explain." She pauses, and looks idly down upon her white hands, the fingers of which are twining and intertwining nervously.

"Do you mean that you have ceased to think of Horace in the light of a lover?" he asks, with an effort certainly, yet with determination. He will hear the truth now or never.

"What! wouldst thou have a serpent sting thee twice?" she says, turning to him with some passion; and then her anger fades, and her eyes fill with tears.

"If you can apply such a word to him, your love must be indeed dead," he says, in a curious tone, and, raising one of her hands, he lays it upon his breast.

"I wish it had never been born," she says, with a sigh, not looking at him.

"But is it dead?" persists he, eagerly.

"Quite. I buried it that day you took me—to his—rooms: you remember?"

"How could I forget? Clarissa, if you are unhappy, so am I. Take pity upon me."

"You unhappy?" She lifts her eyes to his.

"Yes. All my life I have loved you. Is your heart quite beyond my reach?"

She makes him no answer.

"Without you I live but half a life," he goes on, entreatingly. "Every hour is filled with thoughts of you. I have no interests apart from you. Clarissa, if there is any hope for me, speak; say something."

"Would not his memory be a shadow between us always?" whispers she, in trembling accents. "Forgiveness is within our power, forgetfulness is beyond us! Jim, is this thing wise, that you are doing? Have you thought of it?"

"I have thought of it for more than a long year," says Sir James. "I think all my life, unconsciously, I have loved you."

"For so long?" she says, softly; and then, "How faithful you have been!"

"When change itself can give no more,
'Tis easy to be true,"

quotes he, tenderly; and then she goes nearer to him,—tears in her eyes.

"You are too good for me," she says.

"Darling," says Scrope, and after that, somehow, it seems but a little thing that his arms should close around her, and that her head should lie contentedly upon his shoulder.

CHAPTER XXXVIII

"There is no life on earth but being in love!"—Ben Jonson.

"Love framed with Mirth a gay fantastic round;
And he, amidst his frolic play,
As if he would the charming air repay,
Shook thousand odors from his dewy wing."—Collins.

It is the afternoon of the same day, and Dorian, with a keeper behind him, is trudging through the woods of Hythe, two trusty setters at his heels. He cannot be said to be altogether unhappy, because he has had a real good day with his gun, as his bag can testify, and, be a man never so disturbed by conflicting emotions, be he five fathoms deep in a hopeless attachment, still he will tramp through his heather, or ride to hounds, or smoke his favorite cigars, with the best, and find, indeed, pleasure therein. For, truly,—

"Man's love is of man's life a thing apart;
'Tis woman's whole existence."

The sun is sinking to rest; the chill of a spring evening is in the air. Dismissing the man who holds his bag, he sends him home to the house by a nearer route, and, lighting a fresh cigar, follows the path that leads through the fragrant wood into the grounds of Sartoris. The breath of the bluebells is already scenting the air; the ferns are growing thick and strong. He has come to a turn, that is all formed of rock, and is somewhat abrupt, because of the sharp angle that belongs to it, over which hart's-tongues and other graceful weeds fall lazily, when, at a little distance from him, he sees Georgie sitting on the fallen trunk of a tree, her head leaning against an oak, her whole expression full of deep dejection.

As he comes nearer to her, he can see that she has been crying, and that even now two tears are lying heavily upon her cheeks.

A troubled expression crosses his face. She looks so childish, so helpless, with her hat upon the ground beside her, and her hands lying listlessly upon her lap, and no one near to comfort her or to kiss the melancholy from her large mournful eyes.

As she hears him coming, she starts to her feet, and, turning aside, hastily dries the tears upon her cheeks, lest he shall mark her agitation.

"What is the matter with you?" asks he, with quick but suppressed concern.

"Nothing," returns she, in a low tone.

"You can't be crying for nothing," says Dorian; "and even your very voice is full of tears! Are you unhappy about anything?"

"What a question to ask me!" says Mrs. Branscombe, reproachfully, with a fresh irrepressible sob, that goes to his heart. He shifts his gun uneasily from one shoulder to the other, hardly knowing what to say. Is it his fault that she is so miserable? Must he blame himself because she has found it impossible to love him?

"I beg your pardon," he says, in a low tone. "Of course I have no right to ask you any questions."

"Yet I would answer you if I knew how," returns she, in a voice as subdued as his own.

The evening is falling silently, yet swiftly, throwing "her dusky veil o'er nature's face." A certain chill comes from the hills and damps the twilight air.

"It is getting late," says Branscombe, gently. "Will you come home with me?"

"Yes, I will go home," she says, with a little troubled submissive sigh, and, turning, goes with him down the narrow pathway that leads to the avenue.

Above them the branches struggle and wage a goblin war with each other, helped by the night-wind, which even now is rising with sullen purpose in its moan.

Dorian strides on silently, sad at heart, and very hopeless. He is making a vigorous effort to crush down all regretful memories, and is forcing himself to try and think with gladness of the time, now fast approaching, when he shall be once more parted from her who walks beside him with bent head and quivering lips. His presence is a grief to her. All these past weeks have proved this to him: her lips have been devoid of smiles; her eyes have lost their light, her voice its old gay ring. When he is gone, she may, perhaps, recover some of the gayety that once was hers. And, once gone, why should he ever return? And— —

And then—then! A little bare cold hand creeps into the one of his that is hanging loosely by his side, and, nestling in it, presses it with nervous warmth.

Dorian's heart beats madly. He hardly dares believe it true that she should, of her own accord, have given her hand to him; yet he holds it so closely in his own that his clasp almost hurts her. They do not speak; they do not turn even to look at each other, but go on their way, silent, uncertain, but no longer apart. By that one tender touch they have been united.

"You are going abroad again?" she says, in a tone so low that he can scarcely hear her.

"I was going," he says, and then their fingers meet again and press each other gently.

Coming to the stile that leads into the next path, he lays down his gun, and, mounting the steps, holds out his hand to help her to gain the top.

Then, springing down to the other side, he takes her in his arms to bring her to the ground beside him.

But when his arms have closed round her he leaves them there, and draws her to his heart, and lays his cheek against hers. With a little soft happy sob she lifts her arms and lays them round his neck; and then, he tells himself, there is nothing more on earth to be wished for.

"My wife!—my darling!" he says, unsteadily.

The minutes pass; then she looks up at him with soft speaking eyes. There are no tears upon her cheeks, but her face is pale as moonlight, and on it is a new deep meaning that Dorian has never seen there in all his life before,—a gentle light, as kind as death, and as soft as holy love!

As she so stands, gazing solemnly into his face, with all her heart in her eyes, Dorian stoops and lays his lips on her. She colors a lovely trembling crimson, and then returns the caress.

"You do love me at last?" he says. And then she says,—

"I do, with all my soul,"—in a tone not to be mistaken. Afterwards, "Are you happy now?"

"Yes. How can I be otherwise? For

'Thou with softest touch transfigurest
This toil-worn earth into a heaven of rest.'

How could you so far have misjudged me?" he says, reproachfully, referring to the old wound. "What had I done to you, that you should believe me capable of such a thing?"

"It was my one sin," whispers she, nervously. "Is it too bad to be forgiven?"

"I wonder what you could do, I wouldn't forgive," replies he, tenderly, "now I know you love me."

"I think you needn't have thrown my poor glove out of the window!" she says, with childish reproach. "That was very unkind, I think."

"It was brutal," says Branscombe. "But I don't believe you did love me then."

"Well, I did. You broke my heart that day. It will take you all you know"—with an adorable smile—"to mend it again."

"My own love," says Dorian, "what can I do? I would offer you mine in exchange, but, you see, you broke it many a month ago, so the bargain would do you no good. Let us both make up our minds to heal each other's wounds, and so make restitution."

"Sweet heart, I bid you be healed," says Georgie, laying her small hand, with a pretty touch of tenderest coquetry, upon his breast. And then a second silence falls upon them, that lasts even longer than the first. The moments fly; the breezes grow stronger, and shake with petulant force the waving boughs. The night is falling, and "weeps perpetual dews, and saddens Nature's scene."

"Why do you not speak?" says Georgie, after a little bit, rubbing her cheek softly against his. "What is it that you want?"

"Nothing. Don't you know that 'Silence is the perfectest herald of joy: I were but little happy, if I could say how much'?"

"How true that is! yet somehow, I always want to talk," says Mrs. Branscombe,—at which they both laugh.

"Come home," says Dorian: "it grows cold as charity, and I'm getting desperately hungry besides. Are you?"

"I'm starving," says Georgie, genially. "There, now; they say people never want to eat anything when they are in love and when they are filled with joy. And I haven't been hungry for weeks, until this very moment."

"Just shows what awful stuff some fellows will talk," says Mr. Branscombe, with an air of very superior contempt. After which they go on their homeward journey until they reach the shrubbery.

Here voices, coming to them from a side-path, attract their notice.

"That is Clarissa," says Georgie: "I suppose she has come out to find me. Let us wait for her here."

"And Scrope is with her. I wish she would make up her mind to marry him," says Branscombe. "I am certain they are devoted to each other, only they can't see it. Want of brain, I suppose."

"They certainly are exceedingly foolish, both of them," says Georgie, emphatically.

The voices are drawing nearer; as their owners approach the corner that separates them from the Branscombes, Clarissa says, in a clear, audible tone,—

"I never in all my life knew two such silly people!"

"Good gracious!" says Branscombe, going up to her. "What people?"

"You two!" says Clarissa, telling the truth out of sheer fright.

"You will be so kind as to explain yourself, Clarissa," says Dorian, with dignity. "Georgie and I have long ago made up our minds that Solon when compared with us was a very poor creature indeed."

"A perfect fool!" says Mrs. Branscombe, with conviction.

The brightness of their tone, their whole manner, tell Clarissa that some good and wonderful change has taken place.

"Then why is Dorian going abroad, instead of staying at home like other people?" she says, uncertainly, feeling still puzzled.

"He isn't going anywhere: I have forbidden him!" says Mrs. Branscombe, with saucy shyness.

"Oh, Jim, they have made it up!" says Miss Peyton, making this vulgar remark with so much joy and feeling in her voice as robs it of all its commonplaceness. She turns to Scrope as she says this, her eyes large with delight.

"We have," says Georgie, sweetly. "Haven't we Dorian?" And then again slipping her hand into his, "He is going to stay at home always for the future: aren't you, Dorian?"

"I am going to stay just wherever you are for the rest of my life," says Dorian; and then Clarissa and James know that everything has come all right.

"Then you will be at home for our wedding," says Scrope, taking Clarissa's hand and turning to Branscombe.

Clarissa blushes very much, and Georgie, going up to her, kisses her heartily.

"It is altogether quite too nice," says Mrs. Branscombe, with tears in her eyes.

"If you don't look out, Scrope, she will kiss you too," says Dorian. "Look here, it is nearly six o'clock, and dinner will be at seven. Come back, you two, and dine with us."

"I should like to very much," says Clarissa, "as papa is in town."

"Well, then, come," says Georgie, tucking her arm comfortably into hers, "and we'll send you home at eleven."

"I hope you will send me home too," says Scrope, meekly.

"Yes, by the other road," says Mrs. Branscombe, with a small grimace. And then she presses Clarissa's arm against her side, and tells her, without the slightest provocation, that she is a "darling," and that everything is quite, quite, *quite* TOO delicious!

That evening, in the library, when Georgie and Dorian are once more alone, Branscombe, turning to her, takes her in his arms.

"You are quite happy?" he asks, questioningly. "You have no regrets now?"

"Not one," very earnestly. "But you, Dorian," —she slips an arm round his neck, and brings his face down closer to her own, as though to read the expression of his eyes more clearly,—"are you satisfied? Think how unkind I was to you; and, after all,"—naïvely,—"I am only pretty; there is really nothing in me. You have my whole heart, of course, you know that; I am yours, indeed, but then"—discontentedly—"what am I?"

"I know: you are my own darling," says Branscombe, very softly.